ISLAND OF GLASS

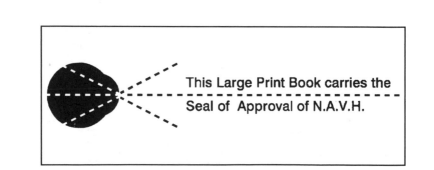

This Large Print Book carries the
Seal of Approval of N.A.V.H.

ISLAND OF GLASS

NORA ROBERTS

LARGE PRINT PRESS
A part of Gale, Cengage Learning

GALE
CENGAGE Learning·

Farmington Hills, Mich • San Francisco • New York • Waterville, Maine
Meriden, Conn • Mason, Ohio • Chicago

GALE
CENGAGE Learning®

LIBRARY OF CONGRESS CATALOGING-IN-PUBLICATION DATA

Names: Roberts, Nora, author.
Title: Island of glass / by Nora Roberts.
Description: Large print edition. | Waterville, Maine : Thorndike Press, 2016. |
  Series: The guardians trilogy ; #3 | Series: Thorndike Press large print core
Identifiers: LCCN 2016039871 | ISBN 9781410493309 (hardcover) | ISBN
  141049330X (hardcover)
Subjects: LCSH: Large type books. | GSAFD: Fantasy fiction.
Classification: LCC PS3568.O243 I853 2016b | DDC 813/.54--dc23
LC record available at https://lccn.loc.gov/2016039871

ISBN 13: 978-1-4328-3424-1 (pbk.)
ISBN 10: 1-4328-3424-X (pbk.)

Published in 2016 by arrangement with The Berkley Publishing Group, an imprint of Penguin Publishing Group, a division of Penguin Random House LLC

Printed in the United States of America
1 2 3 4 5 6 7 20 19 18 17 16

For my grandchildren.
They are the magic, and the future.

He lives, he wakes —
'tis Death is dead, not he.

PERCY BYSSHE SHELLEY

All for one; one for all.

ALEXANDRE DUMAS

PROLOGUE

They met on the high hill, far above the world, beneath a sky struck with the dazzle of stars and a white, waiting moon.

Together the goddesses looked out beyond the castle shining on its own fair hill, to the dark glass of the sea.

"Two stars found, and held safe." Luna lifted her face to the sky in joy, in thanks. "The fates that be chose well with the six. The guardians' own hearts are strong and true."

"Their test is not finished," Celene reminded her. "And what they come to face will need more than true hearts."

"They will fight. Have they not proven themselves warriors, sister?" Arianrhod demanded. "They have risked. They have bled."

"And will risk more. I see battles to come, blood to spill. Nerezza and the evil she created want more than the stars, more than the blood of the guardians. They want annihilation."

"It has always been so," Luna murmured. "In her heart, it has always been so."

"They have weakened her." Arianrhod put a hand on the jeweled hilt of the sword at her side. "All but destroyed her. Without the human she turned, they would have destroyed her."

"Did we not think the same," Celene reminded her sisters, "on the night of the queen's rise, on the night we created the stars?"

Celene stretched out her arms, and below, on the edge of the great sea, the images of what had been shimmered.

"A night of joy," she continued, "of hope and celebration. And we three conjured three stars. For wisdom, forged in fire."

"For compassion," Luna added, "fluid as water."

"For strength," Arianrhod finished, "cold as ice."

"Our powers, and our hopes, in a gift to the new queen. A gift Nerezza coveted."

On the beach, white under a white moon, the three goddesses faced the dark one. As they sent their stars flying toward the moon, Nerezza lashed out, black lightning, to strike them, to curse them.

"And so we cursed her," Celene continued, "cast her into a pit. But we did not, could not destroy her. It was not for us, this duty, this task, this war."

"We protected the stars," Luna reminded her. "They would fall, as Nerezza had cursed them, but we protected them. When they fell, they would fall in secret, and remain hidden."

"Until those who came from us bound together, joined in the quest to find them, to protect them." Now Arianrhod's hand tightened on the hilt of her knife. "To fight, each and all, against the dark. To risk all to save the worlds."

"Their time has come," Celene agreed. "They pulled the Fire Star from its stone, gathered the Water Star from the sea. But the final tests of the quest wait. As will Nerezza and her army profane."

"Whatever their powers, whatever their gifts, the six face a god." Luna pressed a hand to her heart. "And we can only watch."

"It is their fate," Celene said, "and in their fates live the fate of all the worlds."

"Their time has come." Arianrhod reached out, took her sisters' hands. "And with it, if they are strong and wise, if their hearts remain true, may ours."

"The moon runs full, and so the wolf

howls." Celene gestured up to the comet streak arching through the sky. "So they fly."

"And courage flies with them," Arianrhod said.

"And there!" Luna pointed across the wide, dark sea where light bloomed, then fired, then quieted. "They are safe."

"For now." With a wave of her hand, Celene dismissed the wavery images on the beach. "Now begins the future."

CHAPTER ONE

A man who couldn't die had little to fear. An immortal who'd lived most of his long life as a soldier, waging battle, didn't turn from a fight with a god. A soldier, though a loner by nature, understood the duty, and loyalty, to those who battled with him.

The man, the soldier, the loner who'd seen his young brother destroyed by black magick, who'd had his own life upended by it, who fought a god's crazed greed, knew the difference between the dark and the light.

Being propelled through space by a fellow soldier, a shifter, while they were all still bloody from the battle didn't frighten him — but he'd have preferred any other mode of transportation.

Through the whirl of wind, the blare of light, the breathless speed (and all right then, there was a bit of a thrill in the speed), he felt his companions. The sorcerer who held more power than any Doyle had known in all his years. The woman who was as much the glue who bound them together as a seer. The mermaid who was all charm and courage and heart — and a pure pleasure for the eyes. The shifter, loyal and brave, and a dead shot as well. And the female — well, wolf now, as the moon had risen just as they'd prepared to shift from the beauty and battles of Capri.

She howled — no other term for it — and in the sound of it he heard not fear, no, but the same atavistic thrill that beat in his own blood.

If a man had to align himself with others, had to throw his fate in with others, he could do a hell of a lot worse than these.

Then he smelled Ireland — the damp air, the green — and the thrill died in him. The fates, canny and cold, would drive him back here where his heart and his life had been broken.

Even as he geared himself up to deal with it, to do what must be done, they dropped like stones.

A man who couldn't die could still feel the jolt and insult of hitting the ground hard enough to rattle bones and steal the breath.

"Bloody hell, Sawyer."

"Sorry." Sawyer's voice came from his left,

and in a kind of gasping wheeze. "It's a lot to navigate. Anybody hurt? Annika?"

"I'm not hurt. But you." Her voice was a musical croon. "You're hurt. You're weak."

"Not too bad. You're bleeding."

Bright as sunlight, she smiled. "Not too bad."

"Maybe we should try parachutes next time." Sasha let out a quick moan.

"There now, I've got you."

As his eyes adjusted, Doyle saw Bran shift, gather Sasha close.

"You're hurt?"

"No, no." Sasha shook her head. "Cuts and bumps. And the landing knocked the wind out of me. I should be used to it. Riley? Where's Riley?"

Doyle rolled, started to push himself up — and pressed a hand into fur. It growled.

"She's here." He shifted his gaze, met those tawny eyes. Dr. Riley Gwin, renowned archaeologist — and lycan. "Don't so much as think of biting me," he muttered. "She's fine. Like she tells us, she heals fast in wolf form."

He got to his feet, noted that however rough the landing, Sawyer had come through. Weapons cases, luggage, sealed boxes of research books, maps, and other essentials lay in a somewhat orderly pile a few feet away on the cool, damp grass.

And of great personal importance to him, his motorcycle stood, upright and undamaged.

Satisfied, he stretched out a hand to Sawyer, pulled the man to his feet.

"Not altogether bad."

"Yeah." Sawyer combed his fingers through his mane of wind-swept, sun-streaked hair. Then grinned when Annika did a series of cartwheels. "Somebody enjoyed the ride anyway."

"You did well." Bran dropped a hand on Sawyer's shoulder. "It's a feat, isn't it, juggling six people and all the rest across the sea and sky in, well, a matter of minutes."

"Got one bitch of a headache out of it."

"And more."

Bran lifted Sawyer's hand — the one that had gripped Nerezza's flying hair while he'd shifted her away. "We'll fix that, and anything else needs fixing. We should get Sasha inside. She's a bit shaky."

"I'm all right." But she remained sitting on the ground. "Just a little dizzy. Please don't," she said quickly, and pushed to her knees toward Riley. "Not yet. Let's just get oriented first. She wants to run," she told the others.

"She'll be fine. There's no harm here."

Bran helped Sasha up. "The woods are mine," he said to Riley. "And now they're yours."

The wolf turned, bounded away, vanished into the thick trees.

"She could get lost," Sasha began.

"She's a wolf," Doyle pointed out. "And likely to find her way around better than the rest of us. She changed, but as we were leaving, and needs her moment. Wolf or woman, she can handle herself."

He turned his back on the woods where he'd run tame as a child, where he'd hunted, where he'd gone for solitude. This had been his land once, his home — and now it was Bran's.

Yes, the fates were canny and cold.

In the house Bran had built on the wild coast of Clare, Doyle could see the memory of his own. Where his family had lived for gencrations.

Gone, he reminded himself, centuries ago. The house and the family, gone to dust.

In its place was the grand, and he'd have expected no less from Bran Killian.

A fine manor, Doyle mused, with the fanciful touches one might expect from a wizard. Stone — perhaps some of it from the walls of that long-ago home — rising a full three stories, with those fanciful touches in two round towers on either side, and a kind of central parapet that would offer mad views of the cliffs, of the sea, of the land.

All softened, Doyle supposed would be the word, with gardens fit for the faeries, blooming wild and free, with the mixed perfumes blown about on the windy air.

Doyle indulged himself for one moment, allowed himself to think of his own mother and how she'd have loved every bit of it.

Then he put it away.

"It's a fine house."

"It's good land. And as I said to Riley, it's yours as much as mine. Well, that's my feeling on it," Bran added when Doyle shook his head.

"We've come together," Bran continued as the wind tossed his hair, black as the night, around his sharp-boned face. "Were thrown together for a purpose. We've fought and bled together, and no doubt will again. And here we are, standing on where you sprang from, and where I was compelled to build. There's purpose in that as well, and we'll use it."

In comfort, Annika ran her hand down Doyle's arm. Her long black hair was a sexy tangle from the shift. She had bruises on her remarkable face. "It's beautiful. I can smell the sea. I can hear it."

"It's a ways down." Bran smiled at her. "But you'll make your way to it easy enough, I wager. In the morning, you'll see more of what it offers. For now, we'd best haul all of our things inside, and settle in a bit."

"I hear that." Sawyer reached down, hefted some boxes. "And, God, I could eat."

"I'll make food!" Annika threw her arms around him, kissed him enthusiastically, then picked up her bag. "Is there food to make, Bran? Food I can make while you tend the wounds?"

"I had the kitchen well stocked." He flicked his fingers at the big, arched double doors. "The house is unlocked."

"As long as there's beer." Doyle grabbed two weapon cases — his own priority — and started in behind Annika and Sawyer.

"It hurts him," Sasha quietly told Bran. "I can feel the ache in him, the ache of memories and loss."

"And I'm sorry for it, truly. But we all know there's a reason for it, why it's here that we've been led to find the last star and end this."

"Because there's always a price." On a sigh, she leaned against him, closed eyes blue as summer and still hollow from the battle and the shift. "But Annika's right. It's

19

a beautiful house. It's stunning, Bran. I'll want to paint it a dozen times."

"You'll have time for dozens of dozens." He turned her to him. "I said it was Doyle's and Riley's as it's mine. It's Annika's and Sawyer's as well. But, *fáidh,* it's yours as my heart is yours. Will you live with me here, at least some of the time in our lives together?"

"I'll live with you here, and anywhere. But now? I should take a look inside and see if it's as wonderful as the outside."

"It's a true home now that you're here." To dazzle her, he waved a hand. All the windows illuminated. Glowing lights shimmered along garden paths.

"You take my breath." She sighed it, then picked up the case holding most of her art supplies — her priority.

They went inside, into a wide entryway with towering ceilings where wide-planked floors gleamed. A heavy table with curled dragons for its legs held crystal balls and a tall vase bursting with white roses.

It opened to a living area with jewel-tone sofas, more heavy tables, sparkling lamps. And with another wave of the hand, Bran had red-gold flames erupting in a stone fireplace so large the muscular Doyle could have stood upright, arms stretched to either side.

As he walked in from the back, Doyle raised an eyebrow, toasted with the beer in his hand. "You went for posh, brother."

"I suppose I did."

"I'll get more if you'll see to Sawyer. His headache's real enough. I can see it on him. And he's carrying some ugly burns. Annika's hurt more than she lets on."

"Help Sawyer and Annika," Sasha said. "I'll help Doyle."

"He's in the kitchen with Annika." Doyle glanced at Sasha. "I can handle bringing in the rest. You've got your own battle scars, Blondie."

"Nothing major. I'm fine," she told Bran. "The dizziness only lasted a couple minutes this time, and the rest can wait. I could use a glass of wine if you have it."

"I do, of course. Let me see to him, then I'll help you with the rest."

She walked outside with Doyle, started to pick up more bags, then just stared out into the woods.

"She'll be back once she's run it off." Doyle took a pull on his beer. "But you'd be happier with all your chicks in the roost."

Sasha lifted her shoulders, let them fall. "I would. It's been . . . a day."

"Finding the second star should put a smile in your eyes instead of sorrow."

21

"A year ago I was still denying what I was. I knew nothing of any of you, of gods — dark or bright. I'd never harmed anyone, much less . . ."

"What you fought and killed wasn't *anyone.* They were *things* created by Nerezza to destroy."

"There were people, too, Doyle. Humans."

"Mercenaries, paid by Malmon to kill us, or worse. Have you forgotten what they did to Sawyer and Annika in the cave?"

"No." Sasha hugged her arms tight against the quick chill. "I'll never forget. And I'll never understand how human beings could torture and try to kill for money. Why they'd kill or die for profit. But she does, Nerezza does. She knows that kind of greed, that blind lust for power. And I understand that's what we're fighting. Malmon, he traded everything for it. She took his soul, his humanity, and now he's a thing. Her creature. She'd do the same to all of us."

"But she won't. She won't because we won't give her anything. We hurt her today. She's the one wounded and bleeding tonight. I've searched for the stars, hunted her for more years than you can know. I got close, or thought I did. But close means nothing."

He took another long pull from his beer.

"I don't like using fate or destiny as reasons or excuses, but the hard fact is we six are together, are meant to be. Are meant to find the Stars of Fortune and end Nerezza. You feel more than others. That's your gift, and your curse, to see and to feel. And without that gift we wouldn't be standing here. It doesn't hurt that you can shoot a crossbow as if born with the bow in one hand and a bolt in the other."

"Who'd have thought?" She sighed, a pretty woman with long, sun-washed hair and deep blue eyes. One who'd gained muscle and strength, inside and out, over the last weeks. "I feel your heartache. I'm sorry."

"I'll deal with it."

"I know you were meant to be here, to walk this land again, to look out at this sea. And not just for the quest for the stars, not just for the fight against Nerezza. Maybe — I'm not sure — but maybe it's for solace."

Doyle shut down — that was survival. "What was here for me was long ago."

"And still," she murmured, "the coming here tonight is harder on you, and the getting here tonight was hardest on Riley."

"Considering we'd just fought off a god and her murderous minions, it wasn't a ride on a carousel for any of us. All right," he said at Sasha's quiet look, "rough on her."

He put the empty beer bottle in the pocket of his scarred leather coat, hauled up suitcases. "She'll run it off, and be back by morning. Grab what you can, and I'll get the rest. We both know you'd be more help to Bran with the injuries."

She didn't argue, and he noted that she limped a bit. To settle it, he set the bags down inside, plucked her up.

"Hey."

"Easier than arguing. Is the house big enough for you?"

They passed wide archways and the rooms beyond them. Deep, rich colors, simmering fires in hearths, glinting lights, gleaming wood.

"It's magnificent. It's huge."

"I'd say the two of you will have to make a lot of babies to fill it."

"I —"

"That got you thinking."

She'd yet to regain speech when he carried her into the kitchen. There, Sawyer, looking a little less pale, sat on a stool at a long slate-gray counter while Bran treated the burns on his hands.

Annika, who managed to look gorgeous despite the cuts, the bruises, earnestly sautéed chicken in an enormous frying pan at what Sasha recognized as a professional-grade six-burner range.

"Okay, now you want to —" Sawyer broke off, hissed as Bran hit a fresh point of pain.

"I take the chicken out, and put the vegetables in. I can do it," Annika insisted. "Let Bran work."

"I'll help." Sasha poked Doyle in the shoulder. "Put me down."

The order had Bran turning, and moving quickly toward her. "What is it? Where is she hurt?"

"I'm not —"

"She's limping some. Right leg."

"It's just —"

"Put her down there, beside Sawyer."

"It's just sore. Finish with Sawyer. I'll help Annika, and —"

"I can do it!" Clearly frustrated, Annika dumped chicken on a platter. "I like to learn. I learned. I cook the chicken in the garlic and the oil, with the herbs. I cook the vegetables. I make the rice."

"You're pissing off the mermaid," Doyle said, and dumped Sasha on a stool. "Smells good, Gorgeous."

"Thank you. Sasha, you could tend to Bran's wounds while he tends to yours and Sawyer's. Then he can tend to mine. And we can eat because Sawyer needs to eat.

He's hurt, and he's weak from . . ."

Her eyes filled, glistening green pools, before she turned quickly back to the range.

"Anni, don't. I'm okay."

When she only shook her head at Sawyer's words, he started to rise. Doyle simply shoved him back onto the stool.

"I've got this."

Doyle crossed the rugged wood floor, gave Annika's tumbled hair a tug.

She turned, went straight into his arms. "I believed. I believed, but I was so afraid. Afraid she'd take him."

"She didn't. Dead-Eye's smarter than that. He took her for a ride, and we're all here now."

"I have such love." Sighing now, she rested her head on Doyle's chest, looked into Sawyer's eyes. "I have such love."

"It's why we're here," Sawyer said. "I believe that, too."

"He'll need some time to heal," Bran said. "Some food, some sleep."

"And a beer," Sawyer added.

"That goes without saying. And now you." Bran turned to Sasha.

"I don't see that glass of wine."

"I'm on it." Doyle pressed a kiss to Annika's forehead, turned her back to the range. "Cook."

"I will. It will be very good."

While Doyle poured wine, Bran rolled up Sasha's pants leg. Let out a string of oaths at the raw-edged claw marks scoring down her calf. "Bumps and scrapes, is it?"

"I didn't realize, honestly." She took the wine Doyle offered, took a quick gulp. "And now that I do, it hurts a lot more."

Bran took the glass from her, added a few drops from a bottle from his medicine case.

"Drink slow, and breathe slow," Bran told her. "The cleaning of it's going to sting."

Sasha drank slowly, breathed slowly, and when the sting — a dozen angry wasps — struck, grabbed Doyle's hand.

"I'm sorry. *A ghrá.* I'm sorry. Only a minute more. There's infection."

"She's okay. You're okay." Doyle lured her gaze to his as Sawyer stroked her back. "Hell of a kitchen you've got now, Blondie. Somebody who can cook like you ought to do handsprings."

"Yes. I like it — oh, God, okay — I like the cabinets. Not only the fact that there's about an acre of them, but all those leaded-glass fronts. And the windows. It must get wonderful light."

"She needs to drink more," Bran said through gritted teeth. "Sawyer."

"Drink it down." Sawyer held the glass to

her lips. "We'll have a cook-off, you and me — and Anni," he added.

"Challenge accepted." Then she let out a long, shaky breath. "Thank God," she said when Bran coated the wound with cool, soothing balm.

"You held up." Doyle gave her a pat on the shoulder.

"Your turn," Sasha told Bran.

"Give yourself a minute — and me as well." Bran sat beside her. "And we'll deal with each other. And when we're done, and while we eat, I imagine Sawyer has a story to tell."

"Believe me," Sawyer replied. "It's a winner."

The kitchen held a long table, backed with benches, fronted with chairs in a wide curve of glass. They sat together, with Annika's meal, with a loaf of brown bread and fresh butter, with beer and wine. And Sawyer's tale.

"When I went up — hell of a boost, by the way," Sawyer said to Bran, "she was fighting to control that three-headed dog she was on."

"The one you shot in all three heads," Sasha pointed out.

"Three for three." Sawyer made a gun with his fingers, said, "Bang. And she was focused on Bran."

"Knock out the sorcerer, knock out our magicks." Doyle shoveled in chicken. "It's not good, Annika."

"Oh!"

"It's damn good."

She laughed, wiggled happily in her seat on the bench as Doyle scooped up more. Then she leaned her head to Sawyer's shoulder. "You were so brave."

"Didn't think about it — that's the trick. She's got the eyeball on y'all, trying to get that beast under control. She didn't see me coming."

Looking down, he flexed his hand, all but healed now. "I grabbed the bitch by the hair — it was flying around, and handy. And then she saw me coming, baby, and it scared her. I could see that — we need to know that. I took her by surprise, and I saw fear. Didn't last long, but it was there."

"We hurt her before, in Corfu." Bran nodded, dark eyes intense. "We beat her back, got the Fire Star, and hurt her. She should be afraid."

"She had armor this time, so she's no idiot. And she's got a hell of a punch. You've got your lightning," he said to Bran, "and she's got hers." He rubbed his chest, easily reliving the burning punch. "Nothing to do but hold on. She thought she had me, and I've got to say, maybe for a minute, I figured she was right. But she'd have me where we weren't because I'd already started the shift. It got wild, really wild, but it was my thing, right? Shifting's my thing. I know how to deal with the force of that, and she didn't. Not so fast, so hard. She started changing."

"Changing?" Sasha prompted.

"I had her by the hair, right? All that flying black hair. And during the shift, the color started leeching out of it. And her face did a Dorian Gray."

"She aged."

He nodded at Sasha. "Put on the years. For a second I thought it was my imagination, and the fact that the wind, the lights were burning the crap out of my eyes, but her face started to sag, and she's aging right in front of me. She's aging, and her lightning strikes barely buzz me. She's weakening, man, and I let go. She nearly pulled me with her — she had that much left. But I pulled away, and she fell. I don't know where the hell, but she dropped. I couldn't get a bead because I'd about used it up by then. And I really needed to get back."

He turned his head, kissed Annika. "I really needed to get back."

Sasha gripped his arm. "Could it have

destroyed her?"

"I don't know, but I put a hurting on her, and that fall's going to leave a mark."

"According to legend, it's a sword that brings her end." Still, Bran shrugged. "And legends have been known to be wrong. In either case, despite cuts and bruises" — he paused to give Sasha a telling look — "we hurt her more than she hurt us. If she exists, it will take time for her to recover, and that's advantage us."

"We know she fears," Doyle put in, "and her fear is another weapon against her. With all that, this doesn't end until we have the last star."

"So we'll look, and we'll find." Bran settled back, confident and at home. "As here's where the quest led us."

"I believe we'll find it — the Ice Star," Annika said. "We found the others. But now that we're so close, I don't understand what we do once we have them."

"Go where we're led." Bran looked at Sasha, who immediately poured more wine.

"But no pressure," she murmured.

"Faith," Bran corrected. "All faith. But for tonight, we're all here, we're safe, and we've had a lovely meal."

Pleased, Annika smiled. "I made enough for Riley if she's too hungry to wait for breakfast. I wish she'd come back."

"She will, and soon enough."

"I can feel her," Sasha announced. "I can feel her now. She's not far, but not ready to come in. She's not far though."

"Then we're all safe, as I said. And though Sawyer looks better, it's rest he needs now. I'll show you the bedrooms, and you can choose what suits you."

It didn't matter to Doyle where he slept, so he chose a room at random, one facing the sea rather than the woods. The bed might have been fit for a king with its tall turned posts, but he wasn't ready to use it.

He opened the doors leading to the wide stone terrace that wrapped the sea-front of the house, let the moist air whip through the room, let the rumble and crash of the sea drown out his thoughts.

Restless, anticipating the memories that might flood back in dreams, he strapped on his sword and went out into the night.

However safe they were — and he believed they were for now — it didn't pay to forgo patrol, to ignore the need for vigilance.

Bran had built his home on the same spot where Doyle's had stood — though Bran's was surely five times the size. Doyle couldn't ignore the fact — couldn't pretend there were no reasons for it.

The house stood on the cliff, with a seawall built dry-stone style rambling at its edge. Gardens here as well, Doyle noted, and the scents of rosemary, lavender, sage lifted into the air from their place near the kitchen wall.

He walked out toward the cliff, let the wind stream through his hair, cool his face while his eyes, sharp and green, scanned the turbulent sea, the misty sky, the full white moon that shifted and sailed behind gray fingers of cloud.

Nothing would come tonight, from sea or sky, he thought. But if Sasha's visions held true — and they had till now — they'd find the last star here, in the land of his blood. They'd find it, and they'd find the way to end Nerezza.

His quest, one of centuries, would be done.

Then what?

Then what? he thought again as the soldier in him began to patrol.

Join another army? Fight another war? No, no more wars, he mused as he walked. He was sick down to bone and balls of blood and death. However weary he might be of life after three centuries of it, he was more weary of witnessing death.

33

He could do whatever he wanted — if he had any idea what he wanted. Find a place to settle awhile? Build his own? He had money set aside for it. A man didn't live as long as he'd lived and not have money, if he had a brain in his head.

But settling? For what? He'd been on the move so long, he could barely conceive the notion of rooting anywhere. Travel, he supposed, though God knew he'd done more than any man's share of that already.

And why think of it now? His duty, his mission, his quest wasn't done. Better to think of the next step, and leave the rest.

He came around the front of the house, looked up. He could see the good, sturdy manor his blood had built. See how Bran had used it, respected it when adding to it, making it his own.

For a moment he heard the voices, long stilled. His mother, his father, his sisters, brothers. They'd worked this land, built their lives, given their hearts.

Grown old, grown ill, died. And he was all that was left of them.

That, just that, was beyond sorrow.

"Bollocks," he murmured, and turned away.

The wolf watched him, eyes gleaming in the filtered light of the moon.

She stood very still at the edge of the wood — beautiful and fierce.

He lowered the hand that had reached instinctively for the sword sheathed on his back. Stood, watching the watcher while the wind billowed his coat.

"So you're back. You worried Sasha and Annika. You understand me perfectly well," he added when the wolf made no move. "If you're interested, Sawyer's healing up, and resting. Sasha was hurt more seriously than we knew. Ah, that got your attention," he said, when the wolf trotted forward. "She's resting, too, and Bran took care of them. She's fine," he added. "One of the bastards gouged her leg, and some infection set in before Bran got to it. But she's fine now."

He watched the wolf angle up, scan the house with those canny golden-brown eyes. "The place is full of rooms, enough beds if we were twice as many. I suppose you want to go in now, see for yourself."

The wolf simply walked to the big front doors, waited.

"Fine then." Doyle strode over, opened the door.

Inside, Riley's things sat in a neat pile.

"We didn't take them up as no one wanted to choose for you. You've plenty to choose from."

The wolf walked — pausing to study the living area, the fire simmering — then moved to the stairs, looked back.

"I suppose you want me to haul your bloody things up the bloody stairs now?"

The wolf held Doyle's gaze, unblinking.

"Now I'm a porter," he muttered, and picked up her duffle. "You can get the rest tomorrow." He started up, and the wolf kept pace. "Bran and Sasha are down at the end there, in the round tower. Sawyer and Annika, first door there, facing the sea."

He gestured the other way on the landing. "I'm down here, again the sea."

The wolf went down, in the direction of Doyle's room, stood in a doorway, moved on, another, and another, then doubled back and walked into a room facing the forest with an open-canopy bed, a long desk, a fireplace framed in malachite.

Doyle dumped her duffle, prepared to step out again and leave her to it.

But she walked to the fire, looked at him, looked back.

"What? I'm supposed to light a fire for you now? Christ."

Muttering all the way, he took bricks of peat from a copper bucket, arranged them on the grate as he had as a boy.

It was simple enough, took only moments,

and if the scent squeezed his heart, he ignored it.

"Now, if there'll be nothing else —"

She walked to the door, one leading to a little balcony.

"You want out again? For Christ's sake. It doesn't have stairs." He walked over, wrenched it open. "So if you want down, you'll have to jump."

But she only scented the air, walked back in, sat by the fire.

"Doors open then." Since he'd done the same in his own room, he could hardly fault her. "Anything else, you'll need to wait till morning and deal with it yourself."

He started out, paused. "Annika made enough of a meal for you, if you want it in the morning."

Unsure, he left her door open, started toward his own room. He heard the sound of her door closing as he reached his own.

So for what it was worth, he thought, Sasha had all her chicks in the roost.

CHAPTER TWO

Gnawing hunger and shivering chill woke Riley at first light. The fire had burned to embers; rain pattered on the terrace outside the open door.

She lay on the floor in front of the dying fire, naked, disoriented. She rarely slept through the change — it was far too intense. In the rare times she had, it was due to utter exhaustion.

Obviously, a vicious battle followed by a shift via Sawyer's magic compass equaled exhaustion.

Stiff, shivering, she pushed to her feet, shoved at her short, shaggy brown hair, and looked around. Her mind, her reason, her instincts worked perfectly well in wolf form, so she'd selected the room the night before due to not only its big, excellent bed, but also the desk.

She'd need a good work space for research.

But that was for later. Now she needed clothes, and God, she needed to eat. It wasn't just the fasting from sundown to sunrise — a hard and fast rule of her pack — but the massive amount of energy the change burned. From woman to wolf, from wolf to woman.

Now she felt weak, shaky, and grateful Doyle had, however reluctantly, carried up her duffle. She pawed through it, grabbing the first pants that came to hand, and dragged on ancient brown cargoes, then a faded Oxford sweatshirt and warm, thick socks an aunt had knitted her for her birthday one year.

She wanted a shower, a hot, endless shower, but needed fuel more.

Moving quietly, she stepped out of the room, scanned the hallway, thought back. She'd yet to see the kitchen, didn't know exactly where to find it, but went down the stairs.

She thought Bran had done damn well for himself with the big house on the Irish coast. Not just the size — though *wowzer* — but the style, the craftsmanship. And the clever, mystical touches here and there as a testament to his heritage.

Celtic knots worked into the decor — and dragons, sexy faeries. Good, strong colors;

thick, rich woodwork. Compelling art — which reminded her she needed to see two pieces in particular.

Two of Sasha's paintings — two in which Bran had magickally hidden the stars. She trusted, absolutely, they were safe, but she wanted to see them for herself.

Meanwhile, with a hand pressed to her empty belly, she wandered. It seemed most likely the kitchen would be toward the rear of the house, so she headed that way in the gloomy half light of a rainy dawn.

She passed a manly sort of office — lots of leather in chocolate tones, dark green walls, big gorgeous desk. Another that surprised her with its old grand piano, a cello — she'd always wanted to learn how to play the cello — a collection of bodhran drums, flutes, and fiddles. A spacious sitting room that managed to look cozy, a gorgeous library that nearly had her putting aside hunger.

All with wide archways, with gleaming floors, with hearths ready to offer warmth and light.

How many rooms did the man need? she wondered. And finally found the kitchen.

Not just a kitchen, for all its spiffy style, but a big-ass lounge with more leather in big-ass sofas and chairs, a ridiculously sized wall screen. Flanking the kitchen's other side? A game area — snooker table, a full bar that had certainly come out of some wonderful old pub, a couple of old-style pinball tables that again nearly had hunger taking a backseat.

She could have lived in this one huge room for the rest of her life. Especially with the wide glass doors bringing in that bad-tempered sky and gloomy sea.

"You've got class, Irish," she murmured, and all but fell on the fruit piled artistically in a wide, polished wood bowl. Biting into a peach, nearly moaning at the first taste of food, she yanked open both doors of a refrigerator.

Pounced again.

Prying open the container of leftovers, she hunted up a fork, ate Annika's chicken and rice dish cold, washing it down with a Coke — nearly giddy as her system celebrated the protein and caffeine connection.

Steadier, she studied the coffeemaker on the counter, decided, yes, she could work that. As she did, she heard footsteps. She tried not to resent them, but God, she could have used another hour of silence and solitude.

But when Sasha came in, when Riley saw the relief in her friend's eyes, she felt small about that resentment.

"Need coffee," she said.

"Me, too. How are you?"

Riley shrugged, grabbed mugs out of the glass-fronted cabinet. "Good. I inhaled the leftovers Annika left, so I'm good."

And when Sasha's arms wrapped around her from behind, Riley felt even smaller. "I had to run it off."

"I know, I know. I felt you come back, so it's all good. Are you still hungry?"

"Topped off for right now, thanks. How are you? You took some hits."

"Bran took care of it. Sawyer got the brunt."

"Yeah. Yeah, I know. But he's okay?"

"We all are. I hope he sleeps a few hours more — I thought you would."

"Later, most likely. Had to fuel." And fueled, Riley leaned back on the counter, smiled. "Some house."

"It's amazing, isn't it?" With her coffee, Sasha wandered the kitchen. "I haven't seen half of it yet — and I want to get outside, even in the rain, and just *see*. But it's amazing. And I slept in a tower room with a magician. What could be more amazing than that?"

"Slept or had sex?"

Sasha's eyes gleamed at Riley over the rim

of her mug. "We did both."

"I just knew you'd end up bragging." Riley wandered over to the glass doors, looked out at the slow, thin rain and the gray sea. "It could be out there. In or under the water, like the other two. Another island, so there's a reason there. I'll have to see about getting us a boat."

Sasha stepped up, looked out with her. "I appreciate you not asking, but I'll answer anyway. I don't know. I haven't felt anything, not yet."

"We just got here. We should have a little time to set things up before she comes at us again."

"Sawyer said she kicked back at him hard during the shift — and you could see how hard. But he also said she weakened, and aged, before he let go."

Riley nodded, sipped coffee. "That follows. We put that gray streak in her hair, those lines on her face after we busted her ass in Corfu. Maybe we'll be dealing with an old crone who can barely work up a bitch slap this round. And no," she added, "I don't really believe that."

"We have two of the stars, and we beat her twice. We'll find the third."

"Optimistic's good."

Sasha looked over at Riley. "Aren't you?"

"I won't diss positive thinking. It's a good tool — as long as you're willing to back it up." Riley gestured. "We've got some room out there to train. More in the front, the forest side, but either way. We could set up a decent target range out there. Then there's the woods. Gotta be at least five, six acres of them from what I ran through last night. Quiet, private. It's Ireland, so we're probably going to do a good chunk of training in the rain."

When Sasha said nothing, Riley shot her a glance. "And we just got here. We all need to take a breath. I'm revved up," she admitted. "Big, bloody battle, the moon, the shift."

"Was it different, traveling in wolf form?"

"Exciting in its way, and weird, at least at first because I was healing as we flew, and I couldn't really focus. The landing was fast and hard, and knocked me back."

"I hear you."

"Then I had to run it off. Mostly I like knowing my ground before the moon, so I can judge where's safe for a run. But I had to work it off. Lucky, like I said, there are acres of private woods. You hooked a big magick fish, Sash."

"You helped."

"Me? I don't remember casting out any

lures for you."

"You were my friend. The first friend I ever had who knew what I was, what I had, and accepted me for me. You gave me advice, you listened, you cared. And all that helped me be smart and strong enough to, well, cast those lures myself."

"Boy, you owe me."

Sasha laughed, gave Riley a one-armed hug. "I do. I'll pay you back, in part, by making breakfast. Since we're in Ireland, I'll go with Bran's specialty of a full Irish."

"I'll take it. I want to shower first. Didn't have a chance after the war."

"No rush. I want to walk and wander around the house first. I barely took anything in last night."

"Does Bran play the piano?"

"I don't know. Why?"

"He's got a beaut. Viennese parlor grand, mid-nineteenth century."

"Do you know everything?"

"Pretty much. He's also got a cello, violins, violas, flutes, and an exceptional collection of bodhran drums. He must play some of it."

"It's never come up, so I'll have to ask. Do you play anything?"

"Piano, sure, though it's been a while. And he's got a game room area over there that kicks major ass. And one small cathedral of a library."

"I think you've seen more of the house than I have."

"I didn't have sex."

"There is that."

Sasha turned as Annika — flowing hair, flowy dress, bare feet — came in.

"Riley!" As if it had been years, Annika dashed over, threw her arms around Riley.

"Yeah, good morning to you, too."

"We were worried. Doyle said not to, because you'd come back. But we worried. Now you're here! Good morning."

"How can you look like that first thing? Without coffee?"

"I don't like the coffee. But I like the mornings. Sawyer will rest a little longer, but he feels much better. He felt rested enough to mate, and I was very gentle."

"Sex." Riley shook her head. "It's always about sex. Tell me more — no, tell me more after I get that shower."

"I like sometimes to be above — on top," she corrected. "On top when it should be gentle and slow. Then I can have many orgasms."

"Right." Riley let out a breath. "This may be a longer shower than initially planned."

When Sasha laughed and Riley hurried

out, Annika offered a puzzled smile. "I don't understand. Does she need to get more clean?"

"No, she meant . . . I'll explain, but I'm going to need more coffee."

The next best thing to a hot shower was a hot meal. By the time Sasha — with an assist from Annika — put the meal together, the team had gathered in the kitchen.

Riley caught the scent — bacon! — heard the mix of voices as she wound her way back down.

"I keep a car here," Bran said. "It'll take all of us, but not comfortably."

"I've got my bike," Doyle put in. "And I can take one pillion."

"True enough. I can arrange for a van, a kind of backup, in the event we want or need to go any distance in one vehicle. And there she is," Bran added when Riley stepped in. "Sasha tells us you've healed and rested. And you found a room that suits you?"

"Yeah, thanks. I took one with a good-sized desk, facing the woods. It's a lot of house, Irish," she said as she snagged more coffee.

"It is. I thought, why go small? And when I have my family here, it fills up quick enough. We should eat, then I'll show everyone around the place."

"I hear the eating part." Sawyer pulled a platter of eggs and fried potatoes out of the warming oven, left someone else to grab the platter of meat and stack of toasted bread.

The table snugged in the rainy window showed Annika's handiwork with napkins shaped into hearts, wooden skewers arranged in a tepee with tiny flowers draping down and a single white rosebud spearing out of the top. Tea lights formed another heart, its center filled with rose petals.

Bran lit them with a flick of a finger, and made her clap.

"Your gardens are so pretty in the rain," she told Bran. "I think if I lived in this castle by the sea, I would never want to leave."

"I like knowing I can come back to it."

"She likes the rain, too." Sawyer heaped food on his plate. "I've gotta say, I'm going to miss the island sunshine."

"I'm ready for the rain." Sasha passed a platter to Doyle. "It'll give us a day to regroup."

"It's Ireland," Riley reminded her. "We're likely to get more than a day of wet. But yeah, a little regrouping's earned, considering. Any clue where you dumped her, Sawyer?"

"Not one. But she was hurting when I did."

As he ate, he filled her in as he had the others.

"It fits. We hit her where it hurts, she loses ground, her grip gets slippery. It should give us some time. What about Malmon? Or the thing Malmon's become?"

"Slipped through," Doyle said. "He's stronger, faster than he was."

"Can he stay that way without her?" Riley wondered. "That's a question. I'm going to assume you've got this place locked down, Bran."

"You assume correctly."

"So the stars are here, and safe."

"They are. I'll show you, as you'll want to see for yourself. I'm thinking you chose your room for the work space, and will likely use it. But there's another area you might find useful as well."

"Oh, yeah?"

"The north tower. We'll have a look at it after breakfast."

"Can you dig we've got a north tower?" Grinning, Sawyer ate more bacon. "A south one, too. And check it." He jerked a thumb at the pinball machines in the lounge area.

"Caught that. I'll kick your ass on them later."

"You will try," Sawyer told Riley. "You will fail. We need a new assignment chart."

Sasha nodded. "I'll take care of that this morning, but since Annika and I handled breakfast, I hereby assign Riley and Doyle to KP. I've had a look at the food and cleaning supplies, and we're more than set there for now, so that puts off shopping for a while, on the domestic front."

"I would like to shop in Ireland."

Riley arched her eyebrows at Annika. "If shopping was an Olympic sport, you'd have all the medals. But at some point, she's going to need some rain gear."

"Some extras there in the mudroom," Bran said, "but we'll want to get out and about. I know the land here, and villages, but I've never looked at either with the quest in mind."

"We'll need more ammo," Doyle pointed out.

"Something else I haven't had in mind while here."

"I've got some contacts." Riley shrugged. "I'll make some calls."

"And that's as big a surprise as Annika shopping. We lost some bolts in the last battle," Doyle continued. "And plenty of bullets."

"I'll take care of it, and once I unpack my

books and maps, I'll start working on —"

"Can we take a moment?" Sasha interrupted. "I know we can't let up. I know we need to take advantage of the time we might have before Nerezza comes at us again. But can we take a moment to just be? We're all here, around this table, in this place, after facing what seemed like almost impossible odds against survival, much less success. But we're here, and so are two of the stars. That's a miracle, I think. It was hard won, but still a miracle."

"You're right." Bran met her eyes, then scanned the table. "We'll take our moment, and be stronger for it."

"Works for me." Doyle spoke casually, then glanced at Sasha. "When you're doing that assignment chart, just make time and room for daily training. Including calisthenics."

Sasha heaved a sigh. "That's cruel, Doyle."

"Hey, I need my moment, too. You've toughened up, Blondie, but that was in Sawyer's island sunshine. Let's see how you handle fifty squats and push-ups in the rain."

"I may have an alternative to that. If we're finished here," Bran continued, "I can show you all. And the stars as well. KP can wait a bit, I'd think."

"It can wait for eternity in my world."

"Your world *is* eternity," Sawyer reminded Doyle, but took Annika's hand and rose. "I vote for full house tour."

"Let's start at the top then." When Bran rose, he held out a hand for Sasha's. "I've a lot to show you."

They trooped up the back stairs, followed Bran's lead as he made a turn on the second-floor landing and veered up to the right.

"Access to the roof area," he explained. "The views are spectacular from there, even on a wet day."

He wasn't wrong, Riley thought once Bran opened a thick arched door, and she stepped out into the rain.

The wide, flat area of the roof afforded a three-sixty view.

The angry chop of the steel-gray sea and its violent slap on rock and cliff. The thunder of it boomed and crashed below dense layers of clouds, sluggishly sailing in a brooding wind.

As she turned, she could see the faint shadows of hills curtained behind the gray mist of sky, and around to the forest, deep and shadowed and green. Beyond where she'd run the night before, she saw now a cottage or two, and fields dotted with sheep, the thin plumes of smoke from chimneys where hearths burned on a wet summer day.

"It's a good situation." Doyle spoke from behind her. "Even on a day like this, we could spot an attack from a half mile or more. And it's high ground, with cover close."

He moved over, looked down from the crenelated wall. "It'll be useful."

"I can smell the sea," Annika murmured.

"And hear it," Sawyer put in. "Taking a boat out on that's going to be tricky."

"I'll score us a dive boat and the equipment," Riley said absently. "We'll handle it. Is that a graveyard? At about ten o'clock? How old do you figure . . ."

She remembered, belatedly. This had been Doyle's family's land. Cursing herself, she turned to him. "I'm sorry. I wasn't thinking."

"The first would have been my great-grandmother, who died in 1582, in childbirth with her sixth child. So old enough. Though archaeologists usually want to dig deeper than that, don't they?"

"Depends."

"In any case," he continued as if she hadn't spoken, "it's a good, strategic situation."

"And before we all drown in the rain, let

me show you what else should be useful."

As Bran led the way back in, Sasha rubbed a hand down Riley's arm. When Riley mimed pointing a gun at her head, firing, Sasha shook her head, gave that arm a squeeze.

Then they both moved more quickly when they heard Annika's shout of delight.

They followed the sound, made a turn, and came into a third-floor area spread under a half dozen skylights.

"Hot damn!" Riley didn't do handsprings — as Annika did in front of the wall of mirrors that obviously delighted her — but she did rub her hands together.

The excellent home gym had bamboo floors the color of raw honey, a full circuit of machines. Two treadmills and a pair of elliptical machines faced the rain-splattered wall of windows, as did a recumbent bike. A TRX dominated one corner; a full-sized, glass-fronted refrigerator — already stocked with water and energy drinks — another.

It boasted weight benches, free weights, a rolled stack of yoga mats, kettlebells, medicine balls, balance balls.

"Oh, how I've missed you," Riley said, and immediately plucked a ten-pound weight from the rack.

"Good enough, I'd think, for those calisthenics if the weather doesn't cooperate."

Doyle shrugged at Bran's comment. "Battles happen in foul weather as much as fair. But . . . It'll be useful. Hmm. Chin-up bar."

"Oh, hell," Sasha muttered, and made him smile.

"Why don't you try it out, Blondie? Show us what you've got."

"I'm still having my moment."

"Tomorrow then. First light. I can work some circuits into the training, and the weights are welcome. But we run outside, rain or shine. A machine doesn't give you the feel of the ground under your feet."

"The walls are so shiny!" Annika executed a graceful and perfect handstand in front of the mirror. "I like to see how it looks."

"So would I, if I looked like you." After a few biceps curls, Riley replaced the weight. "Free to use anytime, Irish?"

"It's yours as it's mine."

"Solid. I'm going to grab some gym time later. That'll be my moment," she told Sasha.

"It takes all kinds. I intend to set up my easel."

"Speaking of easels, and paintings . . ." Riley turned to Bran.

"That's next. I should tell you there's a wet area through those doors."

"Wet?" Annika said, coming neatly to her feet.

"A steam room, a Jacuzzi, a shower, and a changing area. I regret the lack of a pool."

"Oh, it's all right. The sea's so close."

Smiling, he gestured toward the door. "There's some storage on this level," he began as he led them out. "More bedrooms, a sitting area."

"How big is this family of yours?" Sawyer asked.

"Including cousins?" With a laugh, Bran paused at a door in a rounded wall — a door of dark wood that looked ancient and had no knob, no hinges. "Well over a hundred, I'd think."

"A . . . *hundred*?"

He laughed again at Sasha's reaction. "Too late for you to back out now, *mo chroí*."

Bran held his hand to the door, palm out. He spoke in Irish, had Doyle shooting him a look.

For me and mine only, open.

At the words, the gesture, a bolt of lightning scored down the wood, glowed and pulsed blue.

And the door opened.

"Better than a police lock, riot bar, and guard dog," Riley said.

"It will only open for one of us. As will the doors on the second and the first level to this tower. What's held inside is safe from any who try to take."

Bran gestured them in.

Riley didn't gasp, but it was close.

His workshop, she thought, or magick shop. Sorcerer's den. Whatever the term, like the rest of the house, it rang all the bells.

It towered inside the tower — which shouldn't have been physically or structurally possible.

Then again, magick.

Floating shelves held bottles, jars, boxes. She recognized some plants — under eerily glowing lights — the chalices, the ritual knives, the cauldrons and bowls.

Balls and spears of crystal. Books with leather covers, some probably centuries old. Mirrors, candles, charms, statues.

Brooms, she noted, and bones, runes, and tarot cards.

And above a stone hearth, Sasha's paintings.

Here, of course, Riley thought. Magicks within magicks within magicks. Safe from evil, within the light.

"I told you I bought the first of your paintings before I met you, before I knew you." Bran put an arm over Sasha's shoulders as they studied them. "I saw it in a gallery in New York and wanted it. Needed it," he corrected.

"My path through the woods, one I knew so well, leading here. Though only I knew it led here. I often walked that path, toward that light you painted so beautifully, and I thought to hang the painting at my flat in New York to remind me of this. But I brought it here, even then. I placed it here, in my most precious place."

"I dreamed it." Alone, and so long before she'd ever met him. "I dreamed the path and the trees and the light, but I couldn't see the end of the path. Not until now."

"And the second, its companion, you painted from visions as well, visions that guided us here. Not just to home, but to the third star. We'll find it here."

The end of the path, Riley thought, the magnificent house where they now stood, glowing under soft light, festooned with gardens, rising over a turbulent sea.

Things came in threes, she thought — not only the stars, but other things. Would Sasha paint a third?

"Inside your visions, inside your art, the stars shine safe."

Bran lifted both hands. The paintings shimmered, an overlay of color. Red on the path, blue on the house. And they slid out of that world into his hands, closed in clear glass, bright and bold as truth.

"Ours to guard," Bran said. "And the third, the Ice Star, to find."

"And when there are three — fire, water, ice — in the hands of the guardians, the battles will not end." As she spoke, Sasha's eyes went dark, went deep. "When there are three, as three were made, as three were given to the worlds, the dark will seek more blood, more death. Defeat her in unity. Fall to her in chaos. Choices to make, paths to take. Hold true, hold three, one by two, and then, only then, will the Island of Glass appear. Only then will it open to the valiant and the brave heart.

"Will you travel the storm?" With the vision on her like a thousand suns, she whirled to the others. "Will you leap into faith? Will you see what lives inside the stone and sorrow? Will you hear what calls your name? And find the last, and finding, hold strong, hold true?"

On a long breath, Sasha closed her eyes. "It's cold."

Immediately Bran shot a look at the hearth, had flames leaping to life.

"No, I meant — Sorry. Where it is, the star. Wherever it is, it's cold. I can't see it, but I can feel it. And I don't guess any of that was much help."

"Beg to differ." Riley gave her a rub on the shoulder. "You let us know part three's not the finish. No point looking at it as done when it won't be. We find it, we fight the bitch, and we find the Island of Glass. And get there, with the three stars. Piece of cake, right? If you like rock-hard cake with dirt icing."

"I'm up for it," Sawyer said. "Cake's cake."

"I like cake," Annika said.

"Wouldn't be the first dirt I've eaten." Doyle looked at the stars. "We find the star, we find the island. Whatever it takes."

"I'd say unity's been met, and we've already chosen the path." Bran lifted the stars toward the paintings. They rose to them, slid inside.

To wait for the third.

CHAPTER THREE

With the stars again secured by magick, Bran led them to the central spiral stairs.

The guy had class, start to finish, Riley thought while she scanned the second-floor lounge area. And with its addition of a big, burly desk, it could serve as yet another office or work area.

She approved its mix of old and new — the big flat-screen, an old burl wood bar, plenty of seating in those deep, rich colors he seemed to favor for hanging out, a fireplace framed in granite the color of the forest.

Niches in the rounded walls held statuary, alabaster, bronze, polished wood. Intrigued, Riley stepped over, ran a finger down the fluid lines of three goddesses, carved together in alabaster.

"Fódla, Banba, Ériu." She glanced back at Bran. "Eyeballing it, I'd say circa AD 800."

"So I'm told. It's a favorite of mine, as are

the goddesses, so it's come down to me through the family."

"Who are they?" Sasha asked.

"Daughters of Ermnas," Riley told her, "of the Tuatha Dé Danann. They asked the bard Amergin to name the land — this land — for them, and he did. A triumvirate — not our three goddesses, but a triumvirate all the same. Queens and goddesses of an island. It's interesting."

She turned, gestured. "And that bronze. The Morrígan, caught in the change from female form to crow form. Another of Ermnas's daughters, another great queen and goddess. War goddess."

Riley moved to another niche. "Here we have the Lady of the Lake, sometimes known as Niniane. Goddess of water. And here in her chariot, Fedelm, the prophet, who foretold great battles."

"Representing us?" Sasha moved closer to the polished wood carved into the prophet goddess.

"It's interesting, I think. Irish here has plenty of most exceptional art throughout, but it's interesting these particular pieces are in this particular tower."

"Together," Annika said. "As we are. I like it."

"I'm pretty fond of it myself. It's

strength," Riley decided. "And it feels like good luck. I wouldn't," she added as Sawyer reached for the statue of the goddess rising from the water. "That's probably worth five, six mil on the market."

"Say what?" Sawyer snatched his hand back.

"The legend of that piece goes that one of my ancestors was enamored of the lady, and conjured the statue." Bran smiled. "However it came to be, it's another that's come through the family for generations. But your sensibilities on the grouping's intriguing, Riley. I put these here with my own hands. I chose their places here before I knew any of you. Yet they fit well, don't they?"

"They're so pretty." But following Sawyer's lead, Annika kept her hands to herself.

"Interesting, too, is I've placed in the other tower a bronze of Merlin the sorcerer, and one of the Dagda."

"Merlin's obvious. The Dagda, again of the Tuatha Dé Danann," Riley put in, "who among other things is known as a god of time." She shot a finger at Sawyer.

"And with him I have Caturix."

"King of the battle," Riley murmured, arching eyebrows at Doyle. "Fits pretty well."

"I have the mate to the triumvirate of god-

desses in the first tower as well. The Morrígan, Badb, Macha."

"The second set of daughters of Ernmas.
I'd like a look sometime."

"Anytime at all," Bran told Riley.

"As interesting as it may be, they're just
symbols." Doyle stood, hands in his pockets.
"Statues don't fight. They don't bleed."

"Says the guy cursed by a witch three
centuries ago. I don't expect the statues to
leap up and join in," Riley continued. "But
symbolism matters, and right now it feels
like it's weighing on our side."

"I absolutely agree. And that doesn't
mean I won't groan my way through pull-
ups tomorrow."

Sasha got a half smile from Doyle. "Fair
enough."

"The main level may give us more, tangi-
bly, to work with."

"You wouldn't happen to have Excalibur
down there?" Sawyer asked Bran.

"Sorry, no. My cousin in Kerry has it. Jok-
ing," he said when Riley's eyes popped
under her shaggy fringe of bangs.

"Never joke about Excalibur to an archaeologist. What's downstairs?" Without waiting, she started down the spiral.

Doyle heard her reaction before she was
halfway down. In his experience the sound

she made was one usually made by a woman at the hard crest of an orgasm.

He heard Bran laugh and say, "I thought you'd approve," as he circled down at the rear of the group.

Books, Doyle noted. Hundreds of them. Old, old books on rounded, towering shelves. The air smelled of their leather bindings, and quietly of paper.

One massive book sat on a stand, its carved leather cover locked. But others circled the room with its wide stone hearth. Windows, narrow and tall, offered soft light and recessed seats between the shelves.

A long library table stood gleaming in the center of the room.

His own interest piqued when he noticed the maps.

"Books, collected over generations," Bran began. "On magicks, lore, legend, mythology, history. On healing, on spell casting, on herbs, crystals, alchemy. Journals, memoirs, family lore as well. Maps, as Doyle has discovered, some ancient. You'll find some duplicates to what you already have," he said to Riley.

She just shook her head. "It makes what I already have look like a toddler's bookcase. I could live here." She let out a long breath. "If I can't find answers here, there aren't answers. And there are always answers."

"I've looked, of course, but I don't have your comprehensions all the same. And at this point, the search is more narrow and focused." He crossed over, pulled a thin volume from a shelf. "This is said to have been written by one of my ancestors — on my mother's side. It tells of his visit to the Island of Glass to celebrate the rising of a new queen. It's written in old Irish."

Taking it, Riley opened it carefully. Reverently. "I can work on translating. Doyle's better there, being as he is old Irish."

"I can't speak to its veracity," Bran continued. "But the family lore generally holds it up."

"I can dig through lore and myth." Riley spoke absently as she scanned the book. "I'm assuming what's in here stays in here."

"This chamber is magickally controlled to preserve the books — paper, bindings. Some are so old they'd crumble outside this air, and with handling outside this spell."

"Got it. It's a kick-ass place to work anyway." She laid the book on the long table, gestured to the one on the stand. "What's that one?"

"The Book of Spells, again from my family, from the first set down to the latest. I've added what I created on Corfu, and on

Capri. Only one of my blood can open it."
As he spoke, Bran walked to it. "It came to
me when I reached my twenty-first birthday.
I will pass it to the one who comes after
me. It holds knowledge, and legacy, and
power."

He laid his hand on the book, spoke in
Irish. And as he spoke, the book began to
glow. It began to sing.

"Oh!" Annika grabbed Sawyer's hand.
"It's beautiful. Can you hear it?"

"Yeah. And feel it."

The air moved; the light changed.

"I am of the blood," Doyle translated
Bran's words for the others. "I am of the
craft. I am all who came before, all who
come after. This is my pledge, this is my
duty, this is my joy."

When Bran lifted his hand, the thick lock
was gone. He opened the carved cover — a
flash, a snap of sound. Then silence.

"Here, all who held the book mark their
name."

"So many," Sasha murmured as he turned
the page. "Yours is the last."

"So far."

"Would . . . our child?"

"If the child is willing. If the child ac-
cepts."

"A choice?"

"Always a choice. The spells are cata-logued. For healing, for knowing, for protec-tion, for deflection, for worship, and so on. If any of you have the need to find a spell, you've only to ask and I'll open it."

"The illustrations," Sasha said as he turned a few pages. "They're wonderful, so vibrant."

"The book creates them. You'll see each page bears a name. If a spell is found use-ful, we write it out, offer it. If the book ac-cepts, it's added."

"The book accepts?"

"It has power," he said again. "If you have need, ask."

He closed the book, held his hand over it. The lock materialized, snapped shut.

"One day, when we've got plenty of time to spare, I'd like to look through it. But for now . . ." Riley turned a circle. "I think I have enough to keep me occupied."

"For a couple of decades," Sawyer put in.

"It's okay if I dig in, get started?"

"Of course." As a welcome, Bran gestured toward the fire, so flames leaped into life. "I'll be on the third level later. There are drinks on the second level, and the makings for tea or coffee."

"Like I said, I could live in here. I'll get some things from my room, then start that digging. My cell phone will work in here, right?"

"Here and anywhere else."

"Can I help you with anything here?" Sasha asked.

"Maybe, but the fact is, Doyle would be more useful."

He didn't look very pleased about it, but shrugged. "I've got some things to see to, then I can give you some time."

"Good enough. I'll make some calls, haul some things down here, get going. Bran?" Hands on hips, Riley turned a circle. "This rocks it."

Before she started, Riley contacted family. She should actually call, actually speak to her family, but . . . email was quicker, simpler, and she could blast one out to everyone at once.

She'd call her parents after the moon, but she could give them and her pack details about where she was on the quest — and where she was literally — via email.

Then she scrolled through her contacts list. She needed to line up a dive boat, scuba equipment. Since both the other stars had required diving, she'd assume they'd need it.

She found an archaeologist she'd worked

with on a dig in County Cork years before, gave that a try.

It meant some conversation, some catching up — which was exactly why she'd chosen email for the family connection — but she scored a local name.

Within twenty minutes, a lot of phone flirting and negotiation, she had what she needed on tap.

She boxed up the books she wanted, along with her laptop and tablet, a couple of legal pads, and carted everything to the tower.

Wouldn't she have loved working in here alone? she thought as she walked back in. Just her and hundreds of old books — and her own electronics. A big fire, a big table. Rain spitting outside, a little music from her playlist.

But she needed Doyle.

The man spoke and read as many languages as she did — and some of them better than she did. Which was annoying, she admitted as she set up her laptop.

Then again, he'd had a few centuries to learn linguistics. And everything else.

He had a good mind for strategy and tactics — she didn't always agree, but he had a good mind for them. As a drill sergeant he was brutal — but she respected that. This was war, and war on an impossible level, so you trained brutally or you died.

And in battle, he was fierce, fast, and fearless. Of course, being immortal, why fear?

Not fair, she reminded herself. The man felt pain, just like anybody.

Anyway, it wasn't a competition. Which was bullshit, she admitted as she arranged her things. For her, most everything was some sort of competition. She knew how to work on a team — pack animal, after all. But she preferred being an alpha.

Considering the night she'd put in, and what she hoped to accomplish now, she went up the circling stairs, made a pot of strong coffee. After a brief hesitation, she grabbed two thick white mugs.

If Doyle showed, having the second would save time.

Then she settled down at the table, fire roaring, rain pattering, and began to read — as best she could — the book written by Bran's ancestor.

She made notes on the legal pad as she went, stopped when she needed to in order to check a word or phrasing with her laptop.

She barely glanced up when the door opened.

She wondered if the faded Grateful Dead T-shirt he wore was a snarky private joke about his immortality, or if he was — as any sensible rock lover should be — a fan.

Either way, it showed admirable pecs to advantage.

"Bran's many-times-great-grandfather was full of himself," she began. "Or maybe it just comes across that way. His writing's pretty florid, and he's pretty damn smug about getting invited to the rising. It's what he calls the birth of this new queen."

"Okay." Doyle dumped coffee in the second mug.

"You could read this faster."

"You seem to be getting through it. Besides, some guy's trip to the Island of Glass hundreds of years ago doesn't do much for us in the here and now. It's wherever it chooses to be — that's the legend, isn't it?"

" 'It comes and goes as it wills,' " Riley quoted, " 'sailing the mists of time and place. Many have sought its shores, but the glass parts rarely. Only those chosen by the fates, those whose feats and deeds and powers merit, are gifted to pass through.' " She tapped the book. "Or words to that effect. This guy — Bohannon — is pretty pumped up about his personal merit. He's taking the queen two jeweled birds — a lark and a nightingale — as his gift. One to sing her to sleep, one to sing her awake. There's a whole passage about how he conjured them."

"And that helps us how?"

"It's information, Sparky. He's definitely talking about an infant — so this verifies a birth. Most of the info we've dug up does, though there are theories about a young girl, à la Arthur, being chosen through a task or deed. But he writes about the infant queen, Aegle, and her guardians: Celene, Luna, Arianrhod."

"We've had that much before."

"More confirmation," Riley insisted. "And his invite came through Arianrhod — Celtic to Celtic, I'm thinking. And he traveled from Sligo, to the coast of Clare — that's here and now for us. He had to sail from here, which was rough on him — again thoroughly recounted. Dark sea under the full moon, blah, blah, but then it gets interesting."

Riley flipped back in the book, pushed it to him.

"Read that. Out loud," she said, impatient, when he started to skim the words. "It helps me to hear it."

"Bloody hell. Fine then. 'Though the sea rolled beneath me, and the moon danced behind clouds to blur the light, I did not fear. I drew my power around me like my

73

cloak, and sailed on my own enchantment as the mists swirled and thickened. For a moment, even the moon was lost, and the sea shuddered as if in fear. Some might have cried out, or turned the boat around, but I sailed on, blood cool as I —' For Christ's sake."

"Yeah, yeah, but keep going."

" 'As I stayed my course, though the water demon roared.' " Doyle paused, gave her a cool look. "Water demon."

Riley shrugged. "Could be a Wahwee, though that's Aborigine, maybe a Munuane — maybe a whale, a waterspout. Or just hyperbole. Keep going."

"Water demon," he muttered, but continued. " 'Through the mists, lights, torches burning bright, and the moon slipped her clouds to shine a beacon to light the way. For me the glass parted, and the sea calmed, and the Island of Glass shimmered like a jewel before me.

" 'Sand, white as the moon, with those tall torches blazing. Forests, thick and green, alight with drops of dancing colors. On a hill the palace shined in silver. The music of pipes and flutes and harps enchanted the air. I saw jugglers and dancers, and could smell meat on the fire, mead in the cup as young boys raced into the shallows to pull my boat to shore.' "

When Doyle paused again, Riley just circled her finger in the air.

He cursed under his breath, but continued.

" 'And while the night had been chill and damp when I left the shore of my world, here it was warm and dry. I stepped from the boat onto the white sand of the Island of Glass where Arianrhod waited with her sisters to greet me. As my foot touched the ground, I knew I had been granted what few had before, and few would after me. For here is the beating heart of the power of all worlds.' "

Doyle looked up. "You buy that one?"

"Not enough information, but it's interesting, isn't it? Magick is — we can't deny that one. What if there is a core to it, a heart, a world where it generates? It sure makes sense that Nerezza wants the stars — created there, by the three goddesses. It makes sense if she got them in her evil little hands she'd have all the power, and the ability to destroy, well, everything. So it's interesting."

She sat back. "Keep going."

"If I'd known I'd be reading you a story, I'd've gotten a beer."

"I'll get you a beer if it saves me from

translating."

"Deal."

She went up the stairs. "Something else to think about," she called down.

"I have plenty to think about. What's your something else?"

"I'd need to run tests to get a better estimate of the age of this journal, but I'm going with ninth century."

"Okay."

With a roll of her eyes, she looked down over the rail. "Have some intellectual curiosity, Doyle, and ask why."

"You're going to tell me anyway."

"I am." She started down with his beer. "They had a mathematical layout for manuscripts in the ninth century, and the scribes ruled the parchment in hardpoint by scoring it with a stylus on the back. Sometimes they cut too hard. You can see the scoring on the parchment in the book. Bo here's inflated, pretty pleased with his station in life. He'd have some lackey do the scoring. And if it was more like twelfth century — which, by the ink, I don't think so anyway — they started using a kind of pencil to rule the page."

"So it's old, which we knew. What's a couple hundred years matter?"

"Easy for you to say, old man. It matters,

in this case?" She handed him the beer, sat. "Because while I've found snippets of the legend of the island that appear to date further back, this is the oldest serious account, and a first-person account. An account of traveling there for the celebration of the rising. When the stars were created, Doyle. It tells us when the stars were born. It's what we call, in my circles, a discovery."

"Dating the stars isn't finding the third one."

"Sometimes knowledge is its own reward." She said it dryly, believed it absolutely. "But if I can date this, and somehow authenticate it, we'd know when the queen was born, the stars created. We know this enchanter dude sailed from the coast of Clare — alone. Odds are slim he had to sail far, as he left at night, arrived the same night. Putting magicks aside a minute, we assume the island was here, off the coast of Clare, which I like because so are we."

Frowning over that, Doyle picked up the beer. "That would make us pretty damn lucky."

"Considering the last couple months, luck be damned. We're where we're meant to be. I don't know if we're going to sail out one night and hit that portal, but using this account, putting it together with other sightings, doing the math, calculating currents, maybe we'd have ourselves a location, or an area anyway. There's always a pattern, Doyle."

He took a slug of beer. "Now you're interesting me."

"Good. This has to be more secondary after today. Logically, we can't take the star back until we find it. But it'd be to our advantage to have a direction, to give Sawyer some possible coordinates when we do find the third star.

"She's going to be even more pissed."

"She's hurt. Maybe we find it before she's back in action. And no," he said when Riley just raised her eyebrows. "I don't believe that for a minute."

"Okay then. To round it up. Find the star, find the island, get the job done. Hope getting the job done includes destroying Nerezza."

"A sword does her, according to our seer."

"And it would be extra nice if it was yours, but neither of us thinks it's going to be that clean and done."

"Bran enchants it with that in mind. It may be time to start working on that part of the deal."

"It couldn't hurt." She'd thought of it herself. "Could be with the spell Bran's already put on the weapons, we're already covered there. But . . . Let's lay it out while we're here and the others aren't."

She could talk straight to him, she thought. Say things to him she'd hesitate to say to the others. Things that weighed against hope.

"If we don't finish her before we get the stars back to the island, we've still saved the worlds. Yay, us. But she's going to come for us when we've done our job. She can afford to wait."

Her eyes held his, cool and steady as she continued. "Bran and Sasha go off and get married, have a couple kids. Annika and Sawyer are living on some island — on land for him, in the sea for her. They'll probably even make that work. Me, I'll find a dig or write a book. Likely both. You'll do what you do. And she'll come for us, one or two at a time, and pick us off like flies. She can't kill you, but she can probably come up with something worse."

The image didn't sit well, so she reached over, took his beer, had a sip. "We've been set on this course, every one of us. We've been brought together for one purpose, all of us. To find the stars, return them, save the worlds. We're getting there. I believe we can do it. I think we can complete the quest.

But after that, Doyle, nobody says we all live happily ever after. Nobody says we're fated to kill the dark god and do a victory dance."

"Then we'd better say it, and do it." He took the beer back, sipped. "Because no way I'm being the sex slave of some psycho god for eternity."

"I was thinking she'd more likely keep you slow roasting over an open fire pit for eternity."

"I like the heat, but the point remains. We'd better do it, Gwin. All the way. Or nobody rides off into the sunset until we do. We're stuck together until she's blown out of existence."

She'd thought of that, too, but . . . "Annika's only got a couple months before she's mermaid all the time."

"We do it before. We'll put Bran on the sword. We'll be ready for her when she comes back."

"Okay. One god-destroying sword goes on the list." Riley gestured. "Read."

In her chamber, in her cave, deep underground, Nerezza stirred. The pain! The pain scored like claws, bit like teeth under her skin, burned like jagged tongues of fire and ice over it.

80

In all of her existence, she had never known such pain.

Her scream of rage sounded as a gasping whimper.

The thing that had once been Andre Malmon — human, wealthy, savage in his way — held a chalice to her lips in his clawed hand. "Drink, my queen. It is life. It is strength."

The blood he fed her trickled down her scorched throat. But the pain, the pain. "How long? How long now?"

"Only a day."

No, no, surely it had been years, decades. She had suffered so much. What had they done to her?

She remembered whirling wind, a terrible fall, scorching heat, blazing cold. Fear. She remembered fear.

And the faces, yes, she remembered the faccs of those who'd struck out at her.

Tears burned down her cheeks as she drank, as Malmon's lizard eyes stared into hers with a mixture of adoration and madness.

This, this is what they'd brought her to.

"My mirror. Get my mirror."

"You must rest."

"I am your *god.* Do as I command."

When he scurried away, she fell back,

limp, each breath a torture. He came back, clawed feet clicking on stone, held the mirror up.

Her hair, her beautiful hair, now gray as fetid smoke. Her face yellowed and scored with lines and grooves, her dark eyes clouded with age. All her beauty gone, her youth destroyed.

She would get it back, all of it. And the six who'd caused this would pay beyond measure.

As rage fed her, she grabbed the chalice, drank deep. "Get me more. Get me more, then you will do what I tell you."

"I will make you well."

"Yes." She stared at his eyes, mad into mad. "You will make me well."

CHAPTER FOUR

As Doyle read, translating smoothly, Riley took notes. It helped her form a picture of the island — a sketch really, but something more tangible. And one of the three goddesses. Dressed in white robes, belts of silver or gold or jewels. And Arianrhod — Bo definitely had a crush going there — stood out in the description. The slender beauty with hair like a flaming sunset, eyes bright as a summer sky. Yadda, yadda, Riley thought as she wrote *blue eyes, redhead.* He praised her alabaster skin, her voice — like harp song.

Wants to bang her.

"What?"

"Huh?" She glanced up from her notes, met Doyle's eyes. "Didn't realize I said it out loud. I said — wrote down — he wants to bang her. Bo's hot for Arianrhod."

"And that's relevant how?"

"It's called an observation, Lord Oblivious. I also observe we're talking about a forested island, one with tall hills — and a castle, palace, fortress built on one of the tallest. That's strategy. You want high ground. We know there was a civil war, and the rebels lost, ended up being banished, stuck in the Bay of Sighs. Where we found the Water Star. Something else we pull out of this journal may be a step toward the Ice Star."

After considering it, Doyle summed it up. "I don't think Bo getting a woody over Arianrhod tells us anything more than he's got a dick and she's hot."

"Maybe not, but odds are the other two also rate hotness, and he's all about the one. Plus, he writes Arianrhod invited him. Maybe they've got something going. We come from them, that's the story. You gotta bang to beget. It might not make any difference which of us come from which of them, but it's relevant if Bran's ancestor and the goddess — the one with a Celtic name — did the tango, and Bran's a direct descendant."

After a moment, Doyle gave her an eyebrow jerk she took as acknowledgment of her point. And went back to reading.

He had a good voice, she thought. Not what you'd call harp song, but a good, strong voice. He read well, and not every-body read well out loud.

She wondered how many books he'd read. Thousands maybe — imagine that. Here was a man who'd gone from tallow candles to laser technology, from horse and cart to space travel.

She could spend a decade picking his brain on what he'd seen, how he'd lived, what he'd felt.

For the moment she continued to take notes, following Bohannon's observations and descriptions as he continued on horse-back from the beach, through groves of orange and lemon trees — the blossoms perfuming the sweet night air.

"We can surmise spring — orange blos-soms."

"That's considering the island runs on the same rules of seasons as this world," Doyle pointed out. "And on this side of the equa-tor."

"Point." And a damn good one, she had to admit. "But we stick with the physical location, at Bo's time and place, and we get spring. Surmising. A well-kept island, too. He talks of the groves, the wide, dry road — lit with torches. A full moon, which also helps estimating a time. The silver palace —

you have to wonder if that's literal or just prose."

She filled in details as he read. Expansive gardens, women in flowing gowns, music piping through open doors and windows, out onto wide terraces. The new queen's standard — a white dove soaring over a blue sea — flew atop every tower.

Doyle got as far as the entrance hall — brilliant tapestries, gilded trees flowering in silver urns — when he put the book down.

"If I have to read interior design, I'm going to need more than a beer."

"And when I can describe the island, the palace — in detail — to Sasha, she can draw it. And drawing it might trigger a vision. The vision might get us closer."

He finished off his beer, set it down. "That's a good idea."

"I have lots of them."

"You have lots of ideas. Some of them are good."

"If you want another beer, bring me down some water. I went up last time. And I need ten."

"Ten what?"

"Ten minutes." She pushed away from the table, went to the sofa by the fire, stretched out. And was asleep in a finger snap.

Doyle appreciated the skill, one a soldier

developed. Sleep on command, sleep anywhere.

He left her to it, wandered upstairs and
decided water was likely the better choice
for now. Opening a bottle, he drank while
walking to one of the windows.

A fist closed around his heart, twisted
viciously. From here he could see the well,
one he'd fetched water from countless times
in his youth. Bran had kept it, made it part
of a garden area. A garden Doyle knew his
mother would have found charming.

Flowers, shrubs, small trees, winding
paths ran over what had once been a plot
for crops, and the stables were long gone.
Likely gone to rubble before Bran had
bought the land.

He made himself look out, look over to
the gravestones, and felt a new jolt when he
saw Annika kneeling beside his mother's
grave, arranging . . . flowers and little
stones, he noted.

She had the sweetest heart, he thought,
the kindest he'd ever known. And he'd
known kindness in his time, as well as
brutality. She shifted, took more flowers
from her basket, arranged these on his
father's grave, along with her pebbles.

She would do this, show these people
she'd never known this respect.

And he'd yet to walk out to them.

Nothing there but dust, he told himself, but in his own heart he knew better. Riley had the right of it. Symbols did matter, and respect should be paid.

But for now, he turned away, went back down the stairs.

He took a good long look at Riley. She slept flat on her back, her head on one of the fancy pillows, her arms crossed over her belly at the wrist. A sheathed knife on her belt.

He imagined if she'd had her hat, she'd have tipped it over her face.

It wasn't bad as faces went. It was no Annika, but few were. But she had good bones that would likely serve her well into old age — if she lived that long. A strong jaw that could take a punch, a wide mouth that always had something to say.

He supposed the short hair suited the face, even though he suspected she hacked at it with her own knife when needed.

He'd been known to do the same.

He remembered the first time he'd seen her in wolf form — that night on Corfu, in the midst of battle. The shock of it, the absolute magnificence of her as she'd stared him down with those gilded eyes.

Eyes that had wept for him when she'd

thought him dead.

He'd forgotten what it was to have a woman weep for him.

He hadn't allowed himself to have a woman for anything other than the most basic release in a lifetime or two. Looking at Riley now, reminding himself she wasn't remotely the type of woman he'd ever been attracted to, he wondered why she should make him think of that release, and more.

Likely because they were the only two of the six who weren't getting that release. Probably just that simple.

Then she opened her eyes, looked directly into his, and he knew it was far from simple.

"Problem?" she demanded.

"Your ten minutes are up."

"Right."

She sat up, stretched, and he swore he saw the wolf in the gesture.

When she stood, he remained where he was, blocking her.

"Repeat. Problem?"

"No. I forget you're short."

"I'm not short. I'm average. You're taller than average."

"You're short," he said flatly, and moved aside. "I'll give this another hour, then I have to move, get some air."

"I hear that. I wonder who's in charge of lunch."

"You're hungry again?"

"It's the cycle. It keeps the metabolism on a slow burn. Anyway, another hour or so and we should be able to finish the journal. Did you read any more while I took ten?"

"No."

"So, I'll bet you twenty he bangs the goddess. Or she bangs him. I've got a feeling she'll take the lead there."

Doyle thought of the prissy purple prose. "I'll wager that. She can do better."

He picked up the book; she went back to taking notes.

At the end of the hour, Riley held out her hand, palm up. "Pay me."

"He could've been lying. I nailed the moon goddess in the castle on the hill."

"Pay up."

Resigned, Doyle dug twenty out of his pocket.

"If we had more journals, I'd go double or nothing the sister goddesses did their own bouncing during the celebration." Riley stuffed the bill in her pocket. "It follows. We started there, too, on the island. Our bloodlines. It all started there. And more than a millennium later — by my surmise — we're working our way back there. We're

90

able to do that because of that bloodline, because each of us has something more, a kind of gift."

"I was cursed. It wasn't a gift."

"I'm sorry." Sympathy and briskness mixed in her tone. "I'm sorry for what happened to your brother, and to you. But putting the emotion of it aside, that aspect of you, the curse of immortality is part of the whole. Every one of us brings something special to the table, and together it makes the meal."

His face, his eyes hardened and chilled. His voice flashed, iced fire. "You're saying that my brother was meant to die so I could be cursed?"

She might have answered temper with temper if she hadn't clearly heard the guilt and grief tangled in it. "I'm not, and there's no point getting pissed. I'm saying that even if you'd saved him, you'd have been cursed. If the witch had never lured him, there would have been some other connection, altercation. You said yourself you'd searched for Nerezza, for the stars, for hundreds of years. No luck. But you hook up with us, and in a couple months we have two of the stars, and we've kicked her ass twice. It was always going to be up to us."

"And what was he then, my brother, in

your surmising? No more than a pawn to lure the knight?"

"He was your brother." Her tone rolled over the keen edge of his. She didn't flinch from it. "Why something evil chose him is impossible to say. I'm saying something else chose you, and the rest of us. The journal, for me, adds more weight to that."

Though she kept her eyes level with the barely banked fury in his, she paused a moment. Now her tone gentled a little. "I'm the last one who'd ever devalue the bond of family. It's everything. I'm just trying to get a sense of the really big picture, and logic the crap out of it to try to move us forward."

"Logic's the least of it though, isn't it?" He rose again. "I need the air."

After he strode out, she hissed out a breath. "I'm a freaking scientist," she uttered in frustration, then picked up her notes and went out to find Sasha — and lunch.

Since everyone appeared to have scattered, she made her way to the kitchen, hunted up the makings for a sandwich.

As she layered turkey with ham, considered her choice of cheeses, Sasha came in with a new task chart.

"I figured lunch as a free-for-all today," Sasha began, "as everyone's settling in. I've got you down for it tomorrow, unless we head out somewhere."

"Works. You want one of these?"

Sasha glanced at the enormous sandwich in the making. "I think much less. Bran spent some time talking to his family in Sligo, and he's going to work in the tower. Annika wanted to help him, and Sawyer went out to start scouting the best place to set up target practice."

Sasha set the canvas chart, suitably artistic as well as practical, on a ledge.

"So you've got some time?" Riley asked her.

"I can, if you need something."

"Doyle and I worked our way through that journal. I've got notes. Bran's ancestor — kind of a pompous boor — did it with Arianrhod."

"Did what with — Oh. Oooh," Sasha repeated, lengthening the word.

"Exactly. You get the implication."

"That it's possible Bran's descended from her? That would make sense, wouldn't it?"

"Logic." Vindicated, Riley poked a finger in the air. "What I didn't add, logically speaking, to Doyle, as he was getting pissy, is we've got two Irishmen who live in the same place — a few hundred years apart, but the same place."

"Doyle could be from the same line." Nodding, Sasha put the kettle on for tea. "It follows, doesn't it?"

"Down the line for me. Let me give you some highlights from the journal."

While she did, Sasha sliced an apple, some cheese, added some crackers, and settled down with tea.

"It may have been right off this coast," Sasha stated. "It may be again."

"I've got some details on what it looks like — sketchy, ha-ha. And what the palace looks like, what the goddesses — Arianrhod in particular — look like. If you were to draw them from my notes . . ."

"Maybe I'd see more. I can try. And the queen was a baby, so the birth was literal."

"He presented his gift — the songbirds — to the goddesses, and was himself presented to the infant queen." Riley flipped through her notes. " 'A fair bairn with golden hair and eyes of blue, deep lakes, already wise. And on her shoulder, bared for all to see, the royal mark. The star of destiny.' "

"Another star. Did he write about her parents?"

"He was more about the food and wine, a lot more about the goddess, the clothes, the queen. He was a little bit of a jerk, at least in his own telling. And by his account the palace comes off as fairy-tale sparkle. Big and silver and full of art and elaborate rooms. But he also talks about the thick forests, and a stone circle on another hill where he walked to pay respects to the ancients. A waterfall and a troubling path, the Tree of All Life."

"And Nerezza?"

"Gossip. Pretty juicy." Riley took a swig of beer, wiggled closer in her chair. "First, no invite for her. She lives on the far side of the island, semi-banished to that area when she tried stirring up trouble for the former queen. Not much hard data there, but she's feared and disliked. Everybody gives her a wide berth. On the night of his arrival, our narrator hears what he thinks is a storm. He ignores it at first, but it sounds like a big one. He gets out of bed — lots of description of his chamber — and looks out. He sees this scorched gulf cutting across the beach. Deep and black, he says, and the three goddesses on one side of it. He claims he felt the power shake the world, and the white sand flows over the split. As things settle, he looks up, as the goddesses are, and sees three new stars under the moon. More brilliant and beautiful than any star in any heaven and so on. Before dawn, Arianrhod appears in his chamber, they get it on. He's there three days and nights, and she comes to him every night."

"To conceive a child, part god, part sorcerer," Sasha concluded as Riley took a huge bite of sandwich.

Riley nodded, circled a finger in the air. "I figure maybe he comes off smug and pompous in his journal, but he had to have some qualities she valued and wanted. When he left, she gave him a ring with a brilliant white stone. The Stone of Glass, she called it, and told him she would send into his world a greater gift, one that would one day return to her."

"The child. Its descendants."

"Same page, Sash."

"It's sort of lovely. I'll get my sketchbook. It's stopped raining, so I'd like a walk, I'd like to get a sense of where we are, where Bran's home is, then I'll see if I can use your notes to sketch anything."

"I need to unpack and organize a little more."

"I've got dinner tonight, with Bran assisting. I thought I'd try my hand at Guinness stew. I'll make sure it's done before moonrise so you can eat before the fast."

"Appreciate it. Take the path you painted," Riley advised. "In the moonlight it was pretty fantastic. Going out from here's a winner, but coming back? Absolute champ."

Sasha rose, then stopped. "Bran wants me to meet his family."

"Well, sure."

"There are so many of them. And I'm — I'm this American woman they've never met, and who's only known Bran for —"

"Cut it out." Still eating, Riley sliced a finger through the air. "Stop putting up problems. Meeting the parents, et cetera? You can be a little anxious, sure, but, Jesus, Sasha, you're a freaking warrior. You're fighting gods here. This'll be a snap."

"I know I have to meet them — want to meet them," she corrected. "Eventually. I just don't want to mess anything up."

"Look at the man. He's pretty great, right?"

"Beyond that."

"And it's a pretty sure bet his parents had something to do with that. They're probably great, too. Relax."

"It's silly to worry about something like this when there's so much else to worry about."

"It's human," Riley corrected. "Can't get around being human. Except for me, three nights a month."

Sasha smiled. "And even then. You're right. I'm putting this aside and away. Leave your notes there, and I'll see what I can do with them after I take a walk."

"Will do. And I'll be around if you have any questions."

Doyle walked to the cliffs, and as he had as a boy, climbed down the treacherous rocks, down the unstable hunks of turf. The boy had believed, absolutely, he'd never fall. The man knew he'd survive if he did.

He told himself he risked the fall — the pain of dying and resurrection — in order to survey the caves pocked in the cliff wall. However unlikely the star lay so close to hand, you didn't find until you looked.

But under the excuse, he knew full well he climbed, without rope or harness, simply because he'd done the same as a boy. He did so then, did so now, as the whip of the wind, the throaty roar of the sea, the slick and chilly face of the cliff exhilarated. To cling like a lizard high above the wave-tossed rock, defying death, gulping life like the salt-flavored air.

Oh, how he'd longed for adventure as a lad. To fight brigands, or to be one, to ride off to swing a sword against tyranny, to set sail on a journey to some undiscovered land.

Mind what you wish for, he thought as he paused on a narrow ledge to watch the lash and swirl of sea and rock below.

He'd had adventures, fought brigands — been one from time to time. Lived a soldier's life in war by war by war until he'd lost all stomach for it. He'd sailed, and he'd flown, to lands ordinary and exotic.

And Christ knew he'd grown weary of it all.

But he'd set himself on this quest, and set that course centuries before any of the other six had been born. He'd see it through.

And then . . . he had no notion whatsoever.

A quiet life for a time — but then he wasn't built for the quiet life. Traveling? But there wasn't a place in the world he had a burning desire to see again. He could entertain himself bedding women, as that desire always burned — though tedium could creep in when the spark guttered.

Whatever he did, however he did it, wherever he did it, he could never stay above a decade or so. Could never create bonds, even loose ones, as after a time people noticed a man who never aged a day.

And to those who wished for immortality, he'd again advise: Be careful what you wish for.

No point brooding over it, he reminded himself. His lot was his lot. But the trouble was once this quest was done, so was the companionship he'd, however reluctantly, come to prize.

Being part of an army equaled comrades, true enough. But being part of this? Part of six who lived and slept and ate and fought and bled together against such odds?

It made family.

Each of them, despite their talents and powers, would go through the natural cycle. They would age, they would die.

He would not.

And no point brooding over it, he thought again as he picked his way over the ledge to the narrow mouth of the cave he'd sought.

Once it had been his secret place — one where he could sit on this same ledge and dream his dreams with no one knowing where he was. He'd snuck tinder and tallow into it, honeycakes and mead. He'd dreamed, and he'd whittled, made wishes, had his sulks, watched the seabirds wing.

The mouth was smaller than he remembered, but wasn't everything? The boy had slipped easily inside, and the man had to work at it a bit.

It smelled the same — dank and delicious — and inside, the roar of the sea echoed so the air seemed to tremble with the sound. For a moment he crouched, shut his eyes, and smiled as in that moment he was transported back to simple, innocent boyhood, where the future lay ahead, all full of color and courage and chivalry.

Rather than the stub of a candle, he took out a flashlight, let the beam play.

Not so much smaller than memory, he noted as he crab-walked back until he could stand — just barely stand. And there, the little jut where he'd kept a candle. Bending, he rubbed his fingers over the hardened pool of wax. And there, the tattered remains of the old blanket he'd stolen from the stables. It had smelled of the horses, and that had been fine with him.

The cave curved into a little chamber, what he'd designated as his treasure room, as the wall nearer the mouth angled to hide it.

There still lay the bounty of his childhood, like artifacts. The broken cup he'd pretended into a grail — perhaps one of Arthur's. Pebbles and shells hoarded in a chipped bowl, some copper coins, an old arrowhead — ancient even then — bits of rope, the knife he'd used for whittling — and had used to carve his name in the rock.

Again he used his fingers, tracing the name the boy had so painstakingly carved.

Beneath it he'd done his best to carve a dragon, as he'd designated the dragon as his symbol.

"Ah, well," he murmured, and turned away.

The beam of his light struck the shallow depression in the facing wall, and the tiny bundle of oilcloth.

"After all this time?"

He stepped over, drew it out, unrolled it. Inside lay the pipe he'd carefully made from a small branch of a chestnut tree. He'd imagined it magic, made for him — and only him — to call up the dragon. The one he, naturally, saved from certain death. The one who became his friend and companion.

Oh, to be a boy again, he thought, with such faith and so many dreams.

He brought it to his lips, placed his fingers over the holes, tested it. To his pleasure and surprise it carried a tune true enough. Mournful perhaps in the echoing cave, but true.

He allowed himself the sentiment, rolled it back in the cloth, and slipped it into his pocket.

The rest could stay, he thought. One day another adventurous boy might find the treasures and wonder.

He climbed back up, leaving the cave, the memories, the sea.

When he swung over the wall, Sawyer hailed him.

"Hey! Did you climb down?"

"Having a look around."

Shoving up his cap, Sawyer leaned over, looked down. "Tricky. I've been having a look around myself — on more even ground. What do you think about setting up the targets over there?"

Doyle followed the direction. "In front of those gardens?"

"Yeah, well, you can't get away from the gardens, not really, unless we set up in the woods. We could do that, but this is more private. We've got a lot of land, but from what I gather, people can just sort of wander around, and some do. Back here, the noise from the water will mask gunshots."

"The private suits me, though I suspect Bran's well enough known around the area, and no one would make trouble."

Though he knew the ground well, Doyle considered it.

"More room to spread out on the other side of the house, and we can use that for other training. But this would do well enough for weapons training."

"Good enough. Word is Riley's scored us the boat and gear."

"Has she?"

"She's got some network. I want to take a look at the maps, but I've scouted out the general area, gotten the lay of it."

"So you can get us back here from wherever we might go."

Sawyer jerked a thumbs-up. "No sweat. More word is Sasha's sketching from the notes you and Riley put together out of the journal, hoping for . . ." He circled his fingers in the air. "Don't know how that's going. And apparently you and I are on weapons detail, so since we've got the target area picked, we can set that up.

"After a beer."

"Can't argue with it."

The fact was Doyle found it hard to argue with Sawyer about anything. The man was affable, canny as a fox, unbreakably loyal, and could shoot the eye out of a gnat at twenty yards.

They went in through the mudroom, into the kitchen that smelled temptingly of whatever Sasha stirred in the pot on the stove as Riley looked on.

"Wow." As he had an interest in cooking as well as eating, Sawyer went over to her. "What is it?"

"Guinness stew. I found a couple recipes online, and I've been playing with them. I think it's going to work."

"Looks awesome. We're after a beer. Want some wine?"

"I think it's just about that time, thanks. I've been dealing with this, sketching. I think the cooking's more successful than . . ."

She turned, saw Doyle had picked up her sketch pad.

"It's hard to be sure I'm even close, considering I'm going on more or less general descriptions."

When he said nothing, she moved to him, studied, as he did, one of her sketches of Arianrhod. "I can't know if I made her beautiful because the journalist found her beautiful. I don't know the shape of her face, or the length and style of her hair, shape of her eyes. I just went on instinct, I guess."

"This is your instinct?"

The rawness in his voice had her looking up at him in alarm. She saw that same rawness in his eyes.

"Yes. What is it? What's wrong?"

"Dude." Sawyer stepped over, put a hand on Doyle's arm. "You all right?"

"I read the way she was described myself.

It's from my reading Riley took the notes for you. And this is how you've drawn the goddess?"

"Arianrhod, yes. It's as close as I can imagine. It's — it's just how I saw her from the notes. Why?"

"Because . . . you've drawn my mother. This is my mother's face you've drawn in your book."

CHAPTER FIVE

Bittersweet. That was the term used, wasn't it? Doyle thought as he stared at the sketch. Those opposing sensations twisting and twining together until they merged into one shaky emotion.

He'd never understood it quite so well until now.

When he forced himself to look away, look up, he saw they'd surrounded him. Sawyer at his back, the women on both sides.

He had to fight the instinct to pull away.

"I won't ask if you're sure," Riley said carefully, "because it's clear you are. Sasha's sketched your mother from the description of Arianrhod."

Another internal battle — to hold Riley's gaze, to keep everything steady. "My mother might have sat for this."

"There are others." Reaching down, Sasha turned pages in her sketchbook. Profiles, full face, full body.

He made himself take the book, flip through as if it meant nothing . . . personal. But Jesus, even the half smile in this sketch here, the one that said: I know you've been up to something.

His mother to the life.

"She never dressed so . . . elaborately, and would usually have her hair braided back or put up, but these might have been drawn of her when she was young."

"Could Sasha have, you know, picked up on Doyle's memories? Not on purpose," Sawyer said quickly. "But just felt them?"

"I don't think so. I really don't. Doyle wasn't around when I worked on these, and I used Riley's notes."

"I've got a theory."

Doyle glanced over at Riley. "Naturally."

Before she could speak, Annika came in with Bran, leading with her laugh.

"I like helping make magick. I'd like to — Oh, hello." Her quick smile faded when she focused in on the faces of her friends. "Something's wrong. Do we have to fight?"

"No, not now, but it's good we're all here. We can go over all this at once." Sasha held out a hand to Bran. "Let's sit over in the lounge by the fire."

"If there's a pint involved, I'm ready for that." As he took her hand, Bran glanced down at her sketches. "What's this now? Did you dig out some old photos?"

"What? No, I —"

"This is my grandmother — my mother's mother — to the life. Well, when she was twenty or so." As he reached for the sketchbook, he caught Doyle's hard stare. "What is it?"

"It's the sound of my theory ringing the damn bell," Riley said. "Your grandmother, Doyle's mother." Riley slapped a finger on the sketch. "Arianrhod."

"I see." Nodding slowly, Bran looked back at the sketch. "I feel I've missed a great deal."

"She's so beautiful." Annika angled around for a better look. "Is Doyle's mother Bran's grandmother, and also a goddess? I don't understand how this could be."

"I don't think so." Sawyer slid an arm around Annika's waist. "Let's get you some wine, and catch everybody up."

When they settled in the lounge, the fire snapping, drinks at hand, Riley remained standing. She rarely taught, and more rarely lectured — formally in any case — but when she did, she knew how to punch her points.

"I'm going to sum up, but first, Bran, you've read your ancestor's journal, the one you gave me."

"Of course. While it may have been written in purple, it gives a good firsthand accounting of the rising of the new queen, his time on the island. Some salt may be doused over the purple."

"I don't understand."

"Expressions," Sawyer told Annika. "I'll explain later."

"So you know he claims to have slept with Arianrhod — on all three of the nights he stayed on the island."

"Well, even gods and sorcerers have needs, and it was quite the party. I don't . . . Ah, I see. Of course." Leaning back, lifting his beer, Bran nodded to Doyle. "She wanted a child — a magickal child."

"Bloodline," Riley said. "A child she could one day send to Ireland, to continue the bloodline. Descendants of that child settled right here, others migrated. Your family's in Sligo."

"They are, most of them," Bran agreed. "And my grandmother's grandmother was a Clare woman, a witch from Quilty. Not far from here, as the crow flies. So it fits, very well, wouldn't you say? Brother?"

Doyle brooded into his beer. "I don't know of any witches in my family history. And I wasn't born immortal."

As, to her, his grief bled through the iron

shield he'd erected, Riley might have felt for him. But she had to press. "No talk around the fire of a relation with the sight or the power to heal, to commune with animals?"

He shifted, shot her an annoyed look. "There's always talk. And it's Ireland, so . . ."

"Talk has roots somewhere. Regardless, you're not going to argue the facts. Sasha drew Arianrhod, and the resemblance to your mother, to Bran's grandmother is unarguable. We're connected, the six of us. Sasha connected us, every one, when she was still in the States, drawing and painting visions she didn't want to have. We all came to Corfu, at the same time. We all came together. You and Bran, you come from the same root, planted the night of the stars on the Island of Glass. And so do we all."

"We're all from her?" Annika asked.

"There are three goddesses. I doubt they'd have put all their eggs — pun intended — in one basket. Big celebration, lots of magickal people. Plenty, I imagine, of men who suited their needs. Shapeshifters, travelers, merpeople.

"Arianrhod came to Bran's ancestor on the night of the stars, the same night Nerezza cursed them," Riley continued. "The night the goddesses understood the seeds of

— let's say misfortune — had been sown. So they took steps to conceive and create guardians. The six. Us."

"Six who carry their blood," Bran stated.

"Plenty diluted," Sawyer observed, "but you have to call it cool. We've got the blood of gods, man."

"They used us even then?" Doyle demanded as insult — pure and hot — burned through the grief. "Sealed our fates? Determined my brother would die an agonizing death before he was really a man so I would be cursed with immortality?"

"I don't think so." To offset the rise of his anger, Riley spoke briskly. "I'm not claiming the gods can't be cruel, but I also don't believe they refine the details. You'd have had a run-in, somehow or other, with a force that turned you. Sasha might have embraced her gift all her life, but she'd still have ended up in Corfu. Me, too, even if I'd opted to write and teach rather than going for fieldwork.

"But yeah," she said after a moment, "they used us. They gave us some of themselves, and that part of the blood may have influenced us all to come together, to stay together, to risk what we're risking."

"And don't you think it's helped us beat Nerezza?" Sasha met Riley's eyes. "You think that, and so do I now. I'm so sorry, Doyle, and I wish I'd known or felt before you looked at the sketch. I wish there'd been a way to prepare you."

"It's not on you. I read the damn description, and didn't put it together." He could wonder now why it hadn't struck him, but there was no going back. "I don't like the idea that a trio of gods started my bloodline for their own purposes."

"You can take that up with them when we find the island." Riley shrugged. "Odds are they're still around, being gods. And I think odds are we're going to find the island from here, that it's going to be off this coast, just as it was for Bran and Doyle's mutual ancestor."

"I can swim out and look." Annika snuggled next to Sawyer. "Sawyer said he'd take me down tonight so I can swim. I can look, too."

"You can, but I don't think it'll be that easy."

"And it's not time," Sasha added. "No, not a vision, just logic. There's no reason for the island to reveal itself until we have the last star."

"Agreed." Now Riley dropped into a chair, slouched, and stretched. "We probably have some time before Nerezza comes

113

after us, so we shouldn't waste it."

"Training starts tomorrow, dawn," Doyle said.

"Check. And I've lined up the boat and equipment. Do you know these waters, Anni?"

"Not very well, but I'll swim, and look. For caves."

"You got it." Riley toasted her. "So Annika's scouting, I'm on equipment, Bran's already working on more magickal supplies."

"Doyle and I are going to set up the target area," Sawyer put in.

"And I'll finish making dinner, try more sketching."

"I'll grab a bowl of that soup early," Riley told her. "I'd rather not cut it so close to the change again. Bran, any way you can do something on one of the doors so I can get back in on my own?"

"I can, and should have thought of it. I'll charm the door leading into the kitchen so you've only to step up to it."

"Thanks. Unless anybody has more to say, or needs me, I'm going to go use the gym for a while."

"You did hear training at dawn?"

Riley grinned at Sasha. "Entirely different. Hey, come up with me. We'll do some lifting."

"I'm going to lift a wooden spoon to stir the soup."

"I would go with you." Annika popped up. "I like the gym with the mirrors."

"Yes, I know. Come on."

"What will we lift?" Annika asked as she followed Riley out.

"I bet she finds a way to make pumping iron a game." Sawyer smiled after her, started to sip some beer, caught Sasha's glance.

"I've got something," he decided. "Be back in a couple minutes to set up, Doyle."

"I want a fresh pad." Sasha stood, moved out of the room with him. And left Doyle and Bran alone.

"My grandmother lives," Bran began. "She walks five miles daily, rain or shine, has a cat named Morgana, pesters my grandfather over his cigars, and enjoys a whiskey every evening. It will be a hard day for me when her time comes."

He paused, considered. "My family comes here from time to time, and came during the time I was having this house built. My grandmother walked the bones of the house with me in the early stages. She said to me: *'Boy, you've chosen well. This place has*

115

known love and grief, laughter and tears, as most have. But this place more than most. You'll honor that even as you make it your own.' "

"She's a seer?"

"She's not, no. A witch, of course, but not a seer with it. She felt it, I think, felt what was here, as I felt it. Something that called to the blood. Yours calling to mine." Bran leaned forward toward friend, toward brother. "You lost your family, Doyle, some through cruelty, some through the natural order of things. I want to say you have family still."

"Whether I want it or not?"

Bran merely smiled. "Well now, we never can choose that, can we?"

He'd clicked with Bran, he had to admit it, quicker and easier than he'd clicked with anyone in recent, even distant memory. Something there, Doyle thought now, that had simply spoken to him.

In the blood.

"I'd stopped wanting it. Wanting family," Doyle said. "That's survival. For all your power, you don't know what it is to see centuries of sunrises, to know at each dawn there'll be no end for you, but there will for everyone who matters to you. If you let them matter."

"I can't know," Bran agreed. "But I know what's now matters, too. We're blood, and before we knew that, we were comrades and friends. I've trusted you with my life, and the life of the woman I love. I would trust you again. There's no closer bond than that."

The bitter in the bittersweet still sat hard in his belly. "They brought me back here, the gods, the fates."

"But not alone."

Nodding slowly, Doyle met Bran's dark eyes. "No, brother, not alone. So, here it started for me. It may be here we'll finish it."

As the day faded, Riley took a bowl of soup up to her room. She ate while doing more research. Over the years she'd been to Ireland, and this part of Ireland many times on digs. With her parents as a child on studies.

There would be caves — on land, under the sea — and ruins and stone circles. Until she'd read the journal she'd leaned toward the star being in or around Clare — but had opened to the possibility it fell in another part of Ireland.

But now she was certain Clare held the star.

The Fire Star had been in a cave under the water. Part of a rock in an underground cavern. It had called to Sasha.

The Water Star, again in the water, but this time part of the water, waiting for Annika to find the statue of the goddess and form it back into its brilliant blue.

Pattern would suggest the water again. A cave or cavern in the cold Atlantic waters off the coast. Ice, cold. That fit, too.

Would it sing or call as the other stars had? Who would hear it? Her money, for now, was on Doyle. Possibly Bran, but Doyle had the deepest roots here.

She'd be keeping an eye on him, just in case.

Annika would scout — as only a mermaid could — in the sea itself. And while she did, Riley determined she would dig in her own way, through books, the Internet, maps.

If nothing else, they could start eliminating. If Sasha had a vision or two to give them some direction, some bread crumbs, so much the better, but to Riley's mind nothing replaced research and action based on it.

She lost herself in it, but this time — considering the race to strip down before the change — she'd set the alarm on her phone to go off ten minutes before sunset.

At its warning, she turned off her laptop, closed her books, opened the balcony doors.

No one and nothing stirred in her view. Under the best of circumstances, she much preferred to go through the change in private. Not just for modesty — though, hey, that counted — but because it was personal.

Her birthright, her gift. One she now believed had a connection to the three goddesses. Maybe she'd write a paper on it, she thought as she undressed, send it to the council. It could be someone had more information there. Information that might add to the whole.

Naked, she sat down on the floor in front of the fire as the sun sank in the west, over that cold Atlantic sea.

She felt it building, that rush, the breathless inevitability. Snaps of power, the first hints of pain. Alone, secure, she flowed into it, absorbed it, accepted.

Bones shifted, stretched. Pain, pressure, and a kind of joy.

Her spine arched as she rolled to all fours, as the dark pelt sprang up along her flesh.

She smelled the night, the fire, the smoke, her own sweat.

And with the night came the fierce triumph.

I am.

The wolf became, and inside it the woman rejoiced.

Fierce and free, she raced through the open doors, leaped over the rail into the cool night air, into the shimmering dark.

And landed on the ground, body quivering with impossible energy. Throwing her head back, she howled at the sky, then all but flew into the thick shadows of the woods.

She could run for miles, and often did in the first hour. She smelled deer, rabbit, squirrel, each scent as distinct and vivid as a photograph.

Even had she been starved, she would neither hunt nor feed. The wolf fasted.

She kept to the trees, instinctively veering away whenever she caught the scent of man or exhaust, heard the rumble of a car on a road. Though they would see only a wolf — what many would take for a large dog.

Lycans weren't the stuff of horror movies, shambling around on furry legs with nightmare faces and crazed eyes, desperate to rip the throats out of wayward humans.

As much as she loved popular culture, most werewolf movies and books bugged the crap out of her.

Whatever the roots of that lore, they'd

been dug up long ago, when lycans had civilized, when rules were set. And any who broke those sacred rules were hunted in turn and punished.

At last she slowed, the manic energy burned off by speed so she could walk and enjoy the night. She explored as she went. Perhaps the forest held secrets or clues.

An owl called, low and long, a nocturnal companion. As she looked up, she saw its eyes gleam back at her. Above the trees, the moon sailed full and white. She let go her own call, just once, honoring it, then turned to take the journey back to Bran's house on the cliff.

She could have run and explored for hours yet, but dawn came early, and she'd need rest before it did. She thought of her family, her pack, so far away, and missed them like a chamber of her heart. Their scents, their sounds, that elemental bond.

Through the trees she saw the glimmer of lights, caught the scent of peat smoke, of roses. Everyone would be asleep by now, she thought, but they'd left lights on for her. Unnecessary, of course, but considerate.

She cast a glance back, tempted to get in one more run, watched the owl swoop over the path, its wings spread wide in the moonlight. It pulled at her, as did the night. She nearly turned, raced back, but she caught another scent.

It, too, pulled.

So she moved to the edge of the woods, looked through the shadows to where Doyle stood in his family's graveyard.

The wind kicked just enough to billow his long coat while he stood, still as a statue in the drenching blue moonlight. His hair, dark as the night, tumbled around a face roughened by a few days' growth of beard.

In wolf form, where everything was heightened, she felt the lust she managed to tamp down otherwise. She could imagine his hands on her, hers on him, a tangle of hot bodies giving in to the animal and taking, just taking in a frenzy until needs were met.

And imagining, those needs clawed and bit inside her.

She quivered with it, shocked, angry at the intensity, at her inability to shove it down again.

She'd run after all, she thought, but before she could move, he whirled, the sword on his back out of the sheath and into his hand with a bright shiver of metal.

His eyes met hers. Hers, keen, caught the embarrassment, then the annoyance in his before he controlled it.

"You're lucky I didn't have the bow. I might've shot a bolt." He lowered the sword but didn't sheathe it. "I thought you'd be inside by now. It's past one in the morning."

As if she had a curfew.

"Bran dealt with the door, so you can get in on your own. And as you didn't think of it yourself, Sasha opened your bedroom door, shut the ones to your balcony."

He wanted her to go — she could plainly see — and her preference was to give him what he wanted, as she wanted the same. But he looked unbearably lonely standing there, the sword shining in his hand, with his family buried under his feet.

She moved toward him, through the headstones, over the uneven grass.

"I'm not after company," he began, but she simply stood, as he did, looking down at the grave. Lichen had grown on the headstone, pretty as the flowers beneath it.

Aoife Mac Cleirich

"My mother," Doyle said when she sat beside him. "I came back and stayed until she died. My father, there beside her, died two years before her. I wasn't here for her when she lost him."

123

He fell into silence again, finally slid his sword back in its scabbard. "At least you can't talk me blind or argue." Doyle lifted his brows when she turned her head, stared coolly. "You do just that, at every possible opportunity. You see there she was sixty-three when she died. A good long age for the times she lived in, for a woman who'd birthed seven children. She outlived three of them, and each who left the world before she did left a hole in her heart. But she was strong, my mother. A strong woman.

"Beautiful," he added. "You saw that yourself from Sasha's drawing. But that wasn't the image of her I've been carrying with me all this time. That one was of age and illness, of a woman ready to move on. I don't know if it's good or not to have the image replace that of her young and vibrant and beautiful. Does it matter at all?"

She leaned against him a little, a kind of comfort. Without thinking, he laid a hand on her head. And she let him.

"I believe there's an after. With all I've seen there's no choice but to believe it. And that's a hell for me knowing I can't reach it. But it's helpful to know they have. Or sometimes it's helpful. It's easier not to think of it at all. But today . . ."

He broke off a moment, took a breath.

"You see there, how Annika laid the flowers and the stones on every grave here. On my mother's she put them down in the shape of a heart. Christ but Sawyer's a lucky man. He'll have a lifetime of sweetness. So Annika came out and gave them this respect, this sweetness, this remembrance. How could I not come and stand here, even knowing they're not here?"

He looked down, stared at his own hand a moment, then quickly lifted it off her head, stuck it in his pocket. "We need sleep. I'm going to work your asses off come morning." At her snort he gave her a thin smile. "I'll take that as a challenge."

He turned with her, walked back to the house and inside, switching off the kitchen light as they walked through.

Up the back steps, he as quiet as the wolf.

She veered off to her room, gave him one last look before nudging the door closed.

He walked to his own, wondering why he'd said so much, why he'd felt compelled to say so much. And why now he felt lighter of heart for having done so.

In his room he opened his doors to the night, lit the fire more for the pleasure of having one than for warmth. As a matter of habit, he propped his sword beside the bed, within reach, with his crossbow and a quiver of bolts beside it.

He expected no trouble that night, but believed, absolutely, in always being prepared for the unexpected.

He stripped down, switched off the lights. By moon and firelight he lay in bed, let his thoughts circle for a moment. But since they circled to the wolf, and the woman inside it, he shut them off as routinely as he had the lights. With a soldier's skill, he willed himself to sleep.

He often dreamed. Sometimes his dreams took him back to childhood, sometimes back to wars, sometimes more pleasantly back to women. But the dreams that chased through sleep flashed and burned. The witch's lair, his brother's blood, the shocking pain of the curse hurled at him that for one agonizing moment had seemed to boil him from the inside out.

Battlefields littered with the dead, more than a few by his own hand. The stench of war, so much the same whatever the century, the weaponry, the field. That was blood, death, fear.

The first woman he'd allowed himself to love, a little, dying in his arms, and the child she'd died for stillborn. The second woman he'd risked, a century later, growing old and bitter with it.

Dying, the pain of it. Resurrection, the pain of it.

Nerezza, the hunt, around the world, across time. Battling with five he'd come to trust. More blood, more fear. Such courage.

The slice of sword, the death song of a bolt, the snap of bullets. The scream of creatures unearthed from a dark god's hell.

The wolf, impossibly beautiful, with eyes like hot whiskey.

The woman, brilliant and bold, sharp and quick.

Those eyes — they compelled him to wonder.

Beside him the wolf curled, a companion in the night. Warm, soft, and bringing him an odd sort of peace. Dawn broke in bleeding reds and golds, striking the moon away with color and light. The wolf howled once.

Bittersweet.

And changed. Flesh and limbs, breasts and lips. A woman now, the tight, disciplined body naked against his. The scent of the forest on her skin, a beckoning in her eyes.

When he rolled to cover her, she laughed. When he crushed his mouth to hers, she growled, nails biting into his back. He took her breasts, firm and perfect in his hands, smooth as silk against his rough palms. Tasting of the green and the wild under his mouth.

Strong legs wrapped around him as she arched in demand. So he plundered, thrusting, thrusting, hard, fast, deep into the tight, the wet, while those eyes — wolf, woman — watched him.

He drove her, himself, next to madness. Drove mercilessly until . . .

He woke in the dark, hard as iron and alone.

He cursed, as for an instant the dream scent of her, forest wild, followed him.

The last thing he needed were sex dreams starring a woman who deviled him half the time. Until this quest was done, he needed to keep his mind, his body, his focus on the stars, on defeating Nerezza, on making sure the five who fought with him survived.

When that was done, he'd find a willing woman for a night of uncomplicated, impersonal sex. And then . . .

That was as far forward as he needed to think.

Restless, annoyed — he wouldn't have dreamed of her if she hadn't come to stand with him in the graveyard — he rolled out of bed.

He could smell dawn, see its approach in the slight lessening of the dark. Naked, he strode to the open doors and through for air, for the fresh and the damp of it.

The faintest sound had him whirling, braced and ready to spring back for his sword. Down the terrace, facing the sea, Sasha stood at her easel, one of Bran's shirts over her own thin nightshirt. Bran, wearing only jeans, stood behind her while the light from their suite washed out and over them.

In it, Doyle could see the intensity on Sasha's face as she swept charcoal over the sketchbook.

Bran glanced down, angled his head. "You'll want some pants," he called out. "It appears we'll start the day with visions."

"I'll wake the others."

He dressed quickly and, considering the start of the day, grabbed his sword before going on. He knocked briskly on Riley's door, remembered the sun had yet to rise — any moment now — and just shoved the door open.

The wolf stood in front of a fire gone to embers, quivering. And let out a low, warning growl.

"Save it," Doyle snapped. "It's Sasha. No, she's fine," he added as the wolf poised to spring out of the room. "She's painting. Bran's with her. She —"

He broke off as the wolf threw back her

head, let out a long moan. The eyes stayed fierce, locked on his, anger striking out. But under it was a helplessness that had him stepping back. Though he considered witnessing the transformation fascinating, he closed the door, gave her privacy.

He heard the howl, pain and triumph, as he hurried away to wake the others.

CHAPTER SIX

As he saw no point in waiting for the others, Doyle went straight into the master suite in the tower. It opened into a gracious sitting room where the doors stood open to the sea terrace.

Bran glanced back at him.

"She woke — or came out of sleep — only a few minutes before you stepped outside. She said she needed her easel. I barely managed to get the shirt on her — it's so cool — before she was coming down here and starting."

He gestured Doyle closer, then to a table on the terrace. "She's done those already."

Doyle studied the charcoal sketches in the backwash of light. Another of Arianrhod, this in warrior garb, a sword at her side. The others would be Celene and Luna. One a dark beauty, also dressed for battle, holding a bow, the other lovely as sunrise, a dove on her shoulder, a sword in her hand.

He saw something of his sisters — the oldest and the baby — in the dark one, felt that old, hard twist. And his lost brother in the other, so sweet of face, kind of eye.

Projecting, he told himself. Projecting as his family's stones projected from the ground. He stepped back as he heard Sawyer and Annika come in.

"Has she said anything?" Sawyer, his hair still tousled from sleep, moved in to look over Sasha's shoulder.

"She's deep in the drawing," Bran told him, "as you can see."

With Annika, Sawyer turned to the table.

"Oh!" Annika clasped her hands together. "It's my mother. I mean, it's my mother as this is Doyle's. This is how my mother looks."

"Some mother," Sawyer noted. "You look like the other one."

"I do?"

"The eyes. You have the same eyes as the blond one. And, I've got to say, the blonde looks a lot like my grandmother — or photos I've seen of her when she was young. She was hot."

"Then your granny and my mother are twins," Riley said from behind Sawyer. "I'd say my theory's been as confirmed as it can be. Each one of us — because when Sasha's finished, one of these will ring for her — came from one of them."

"I think it's more."

Riley glanced at Doyle. "More what?"

"This could be a drawing of two of my sisters — not as exact as the Arianrhod to my mother, to Bran's grandmother, but it's striking. And this? The one who rings, as you call it, for you and Sawyer? My brother Feilim."

"Interesting. I say we take a close look, in better light, when Sasha's done." So saying, Riley picked up one of the sketches. "And see if there's more crossover."

"What?" Sawyer scratched his head. "We're all cousins?"

"Considering it's been maybe a millennium since this family tree took root? Yeah, I'm going with the crossover."

"This is so nice." Annika hugged Riley, then Doyle. "We're even more family now."

"We are of the blood." Sasha spoke as in the east the sky bloomed with light. "Conceived and born on the Island of Glass, suckled and nurtured by the mothers, by the gods, and sent from one world to another. Conceived with the stars, born with the moon, gifted and given. Wherever taken by the winds of fate, brought together, blood of the blood, a millennium plus two since the fall.

"The star waits, the Ice Star, frozen in time and place. Its day comes when the worlds still for five beats of a heart. Fire to see, water to feel, ice to fight, to take their place when the Tree of All Life blooms once more."

Drenched in visions, Sasha lifted her hand to the eastern sky. "And she waits, weak and cold, tended by her creature. She waits and gathers powers dark to strike at the heart, the mind, the body. This world will quake from her wrath. Seek the past, open the heart."

Now she lowered that hand, pressed it to her own heart. "Follow its path. Its light is your light. It waits. Worlds wait. She waits. Reach into yesterday, and bring them home."

Sasha lowered her arms, swayed. "I'm okay," she said when Bran put his arms around her. "But I could sit down for a minute."

"You're cold. Damn it. Inside with you. Annika, there's water in the wet bar over there."

"Wet bar?"

"I've got it." Riley dashed inside, pulled open the small cooler in back of the angled bar while Bran half carried Sasha to a chair in front of the fire he set blazing.

Annika pulled a deep green throw off a sofa, tucked it around Sasha's legs.

"Thanks. I'm really okay. It just kept going, stronger and stronger, then dropped away so fast." She took the water with another thanks, sipped. "Honestly, I'd kill for coffee. Why don't we go — Oh." When a thick mug appeared in Bran's hand, she smiled, her voice melting with love as she touched his cheek. "Bran. Don't look so worried. I'm fine."

"Your hands are cold," he told her, and wrapped them around the mug.

"It all felt so urgent. I *had* to get the images down. I swear I heard their voices in my head, telling me to show them to you, to all of you. I saw them as clearly as I see all of you. And . . . I felt, I almost felt I could reach out and touch them."

She sipped coffee, sighed deep. "Your mother, you said, Anni, the brunette with the bow."

"It's so like her. She's very beautiful."

"And my grandmother — like Bran and Doyle's connection. I didn't know her — my mother's mother — when she was young. I barely know her at all, really. But I know it. The goddess is Celene, the seer, who created the Fire Star, to gift the new queen with sight and wisdom. Riley and Sawyer's closest connection is Luna — dove and sword — the Water Star, who gifted the queen with heart and compassion. And the last is Arianrhod, the warrior, for courage."

"And we six have some of all of them," Riley said.

"Yes. They chose a mate, conceived a child, guided, loved, nurtured, and sent the child, on their sixteenth birthday, from their world to ours. I felt their grief."

Annika knelt down, laid her head in Sasha's lap. "My mother wept when I left to come to you. She was proud, but she cried. It would be hard to send a son or daughter away."

"It was, and from that time, they could only watch. And to this time, they can only watch, and hope. It's hard to explain, but we're their children. They feel we are. We're their hope, what they began that night."

"The last drawing?"

Sasha looked up at Doyle. "A nightmare."

Riley stepped out, lifted the sketch pad, brought it back. "Looks like things are going to get hot."

With a weak laugh, Sasha looked at the sketch. They stood between house and cliff, armed in the dark night while Nerezza rode the firestorm. Flames rained from the sky, singeing the ground, the trees, opening fissures in the earth that yawned wide, vomited up more fire. It burned even her winged creatures that dived and slashed at the six.

On her beast, Nerezza hurled down spears of flame while her hair, black-streaked white, flew behind her. Her beauty calcified, like a sharp gem crusted with mold.

And the mold was madness.

"I can't say when she'll come like this, but she'll come. She wants the stars, craves them, but she'd destroy us even if that destroys her chances of getting them. When she comes, as she comes here, it's only to burn us to ash."

"I can work with that."

All eyes shifted to Bran, who stroked a hand over Sasha's hair. "I can certainly begin to. The firestorm here is more powerful, more vicious than what we dealt with in Capri. But foretold is forewarned, after all. And we'll be forearmed."

"I appreciate your optimism," Riley said. "But, you know, even witches burn. Historically anyway."

"That simple fact means we like to conjure protections and shields and spells against just that. And as this will be no ordinary fire, it'll take an extraordinary spell. I'll work on it."

He leaned down, kissed the top of Sasha's head. "For now, I believe it's Sawyer's round in the kitchen."

"After training," Doyle said flatly. "Train, then eat. With the exception," he said before Riley could speak. "As Riley needs fuel. Grab it quick," he told her, and looked down at the sketch again. "We've a lot of work to do."

To make it quick, Riley blended an energy smoothie — added in a couple of raw eggs. Not the tastiest, and certainly not what her appetite yearned for — but it would do the job.

He'd already started them on warm-ups — stretching, light jogging — by the time she stepped outside. Standing back for a moment gave her a different perspective of her team. Sasha looked a little washed out — small wonder — but game. Annika — well, Annika was Annika, laughing her way through squats and lunges. Bran and Sawyer? They'd both been in excellent shape when this whole deal started, but now? Ripped City. You had to admire it.

Doyle? The man had started out the sheriff of Ripped City. Though he looked a little rough around the edges to her eye, as promised, he began to work everybody's ass off.

She joined in, determined to work her own ass off. Fiery fissures in the ground, flames raining from the sky, and a very pissed-off god with psychotic tendencies served as one hell of a motivation.

Calisthenics followed by a five-mile run, and Riley broke a good sweat. She didn't complain when Doyle ordered them up to the gym. Hell, she was just getting started.

He split them into groups. Free weights, bench presses, pull-ups, switched them off, switched them again.

"How much can you handle?" he asked Riley when she lay on the bench.

"One thirty-five."

He gave her a dubious stare. "That's more than you weigh."

"I can press one-three-five. Five sets of ten."

He set the weights. "Show me."

She set, regulated her breathing, began. By the last set her muscles burned like acid, and the sweat ran like a river. But she did her fifty.

"Not bad. Towel off, hydrate. You're up, Blondie."

"You're actually going to make me do that?"

"You're stronger than you think." But he adjusted the weights, dropped them down to ninety pounds. "Try that. Three reps to start. Rest, three more."

Guzzling water, Riley watched Sasha struggle through — grit and guts, and yeah, more muscle than she'd had a couple months before.

"Three more."

"You're a bastard, Doyle."

"You've got three more."

She had three more, then let her arms fall. "Can it be over?"

"Good work. Stretch it out. Hit the showers."

"Thank God." Sasha crawled off the bench, sat on the floor.

Riley took her a bottle of water, sat beside her. "You couldn't have done one rep of ninety the day you walked out on the terrace of the hotel in Corfu."

"I never dreamed of doing one rep of ninety. Ever. I like yoga, maybe some Pilates."

"Both excellent, in most circumstances. We're going to need to get in some tumbling practice with Annika later."

"Yeah, yeah. Let me wallow in this pool of my own sweat for a minute."

Riley poked a finger at Sasha's biceps.

"You got guns."

Lips pursed, Sasha flexed. "I kind of do."

"Not kind of do. Girl, you are cut."

Sasha tipped her head to Riley's shoulder. "Thanks. I'd trade all of it for a two-hour nap followed by a gallon of coffee. But thanks."

"Come up." Rising, Riley held out a hand. "We'll hit those showers, get that coffee. I could chew the beans by this time."

By the time she'd showered off the night, the workout, dug out a sweatshirt, cargoes, pulled on her beloved Chucks, the smoothie was a distant memory. She needed food, and plenty of it. Coffee — enough to swim in.

She smelled the coffee as she jogged down the back stairs, followed that siren's song. Sawyer stirred something in an enormous bowl while Annika stirred something else in a smaller one.

Riley scowled at Sawyer. "I figured you'd have it fried up by now."

"Needed to shower."

"Sex in the shower is so nice," Annika said with an easy smile. "But it takes a little time."

"Great. A woman could starve to death while you're doing the slippery slide."

She dumped coffee in a mug.

"Pancakes, bacon, sausage, yogurt-and-berry parfait." Sawyer turned to the stove. "Set the table and you'll eat faster."

Riley grabbed plates, knowing if Annika could manage it, she'd add plenty of flourishes to the traditional setting. For herself, she was a lot more interested in bacon.

The minute Sawyer transferred some from pan to platter, she grabbed a slice, tossed it from hand to hand to cool it. The first bite burned her tongue, but it was worth it.

And when he flipped a pancake off the griddle, she rolled it like a burrito, chomped in. By the time the others wandered in, her pre-breakfast had cut her hunger down to tolerable.

Bran studied the table and the three bud vases Annika had added to it. She'd put a rose in each one — white, red, yellow, draped the vases in white napkins, tied at the "waist" with ribbon, added a wooden skewer for a sword.

"The three goddesses."

"I thought they should join us."

Bran gave Annika a grin. "The food looks fit for gods."

As she considered it more than fit for her, Riley sat, loaded her plate. "I'm going to dig back into the tower library. Anything specific in there on the stars, or the island?"

"The fact is I haven't read a fraction of what's in there, but I do know of a few. Various languages," Bran added. "I'll show you after breakfast."

"Weapons training at noon." Sawyer sampled his pancakes, approved.

"I'll be ready for the break. I'm on lunch today. It's going to be sandwiches."

"Hand-to-hand follows that." Doyle studied the pretty parfait suspiciously.

"It's good," Annika told him, scooping out a spoonful. "Sawyer says healthy, too. I made it."

His soft spot for her left him no choice but to try it. "It's good," he told her, though personally he could live his immortal life without ever consuming yogurt.

"I'll be working on defense and offense — magickally — in the tower, so I'm close if needed."

"I'm on maps," Sawyer said, "so me and my handy compass can get us wherever we need to go."

"Annika and I can help Bran, or Riley, or Sawyer — depending on what's needed." Sasha glanced over at her chart. "Annika's in charge of laundry."

"I like laundry. It's fun to fold, and it smells good."

"It's all yours," Sasha told her. "Since the place is so big, I assigned everyone to different sections for basic cleaning." She lifted her eyebrows at Doyle. "Team morale stays higher if we live and work in a clean house."

"I didn't say anything."

"Out loud," she qualified. "And you're on dinner tonight."

He grunted, glanced at Bran. "Where do I get pizza around here these days?"

"Well now, I'm thinking you'd likely have to go clear into Ennis for it, unless you're meaning frozen. It may be there's closer, but none I know of offhand."

"Ennis then. I'm past ready to get the bike on the road anyway."

"It's a village? With shopping?" Annika all but bounced in her chair. "I can go with you. I like the bike."

Riley didn't trouble to hide her smirk, and inspired Doyle for his out. "I'll take you out for a ride after breakfast." He liked her company, and enjoyed her pure delight in riding pillion. "But if I'm heading all the way to Ennis, Sawyer should go along. We need ammo."

"Then you need Riley." Reaching for the coffeepot, Sawyer missed the looks of annoyance from both Doyle and Riley. "She's the one with the connections. I did inventory there," he continued. "Got a list for you. I don't know if your connections go this far, but I was thinking. The way this place is set up, we've got some excellent vantage points from inside. If we had a couple of long guns with scopes."

"The towers." Thinking it through, Riley nodded. A good long-range weapon, a good shooter — yeah, it could be an advantage. "You any good with a rifle, Dead-Eye?"

"I hold my own. You?"

"Yeah, I hold my own, too. I'll make some calls."

After breakfast, she flipped through a couple of the books Bran pulled for her. She decided she'd work through the ones written in English first, then tackle the one handwritten in Latin — could be fun. And finish with the two in Gaelic, as she wasn't as fluent there.

She set up her laptop, her tablets, pulled out her phone. Started making calls.

Forty minutes in, Doyle surprised her. She'd figured he'd find almost anything to do but join her in the library venture. With the phone at her ear, she pulled one of the books out of her stack, shoved it across the table, circled her finger.

"No problem at all," she said into the phone. "But I'd want to look them over, test them out." She rose, wandered to the window and back as she listened. "Fair enough. I've got a list of ammo. If you can supply us there, it may be we can work out what you'd call a volume discount." Now she laughed. "Don't ask, don't tell, Liam. Sure, hang on."

She dug Sawyer's list out of her pocket, began to read it off. She rolled her eyes to the ceiling, picked up her water, drank. "Like I said, we're a kind of club, having what you could call a tournament of sorts. Reach out to Sean. He'll vouch for me. No question about that, but he's no more full of shit than the next guy. Like I said, I worked with him in Meath on the Black Friary, and again about three years ago on Caherconnell in the Burren. Check with him and let me know. Yeah, this number. Later."

She hung up, blew out a breath. "We're going to score there, but it's going to take another hour or two to confirm."

"Another gunrunner connection?"

"Not exactly, but this Liam's got connections to certain people who'd supply certain products."

"But he doesn't know you."

"Not directly. He's the cousin of the ex-girlfriend of an associate of mine. My associate, the ex, and the cousin remain

146

friendly, seeing as my associate introduced the ex to her husband, with whom she has two kids, and the cousin is godfather to the oldest. My associate and the cousin hunt together once or twice a year. The cousin also runs a kind of side business, cash only, out of his barn, which is, handily, only about twenty kilometers east of Ennis. This works out, we get pizza, guns, and ammo in one trip."

Not on his bike, Doyle thought with disappointment. So it would mean taking Bran's car. "I'm driving."

"Why is that? I know the roads better."

"And how is that?"

"Because I've been here in the past decade and, in fact, consulted for a time on the Craggaunowen Project, which we'll pass on the way to this barn."

"Then you can navigate, but I'm driving."

"We'll flip for the wheel."

"No."

"You prefer rock, paper, scissors?"

He didn't dignify that with an answer, and just continued to read. "This accounting is worthless. It talks of four sisters — in Ireland — charged with guarding an infant queen. Three were pure, and one was lured by a dark faerie, who with promises of power and eternal beauty, turned her against the other three."

"Not worthless," Riley disagreed. "Just the Telephone Game of Time. The root's there."

"Well tangled. It says the three good sisters hid the infant in a castle of glass on an invisible island, and flew to the moon, becoming stars. And in her rage, the fourth sister struck them down from the heavens, blah, blah. One fell as lightning, striking the earth with fire, another into the sea in a swirling tempest, the last into the north where it covered the land with ice."

"Not that far off."

He spared her a single look that mixed equal parts annoyance and frustration. "Far enough when you've got the queen — apparently growing up fast — flying from the invisible island on a winged horse to do battle with the evil sister, vanquishing her and turning her to stone."

"Shake out the probable hyperbole, and you find roots. Nerezza materialized out of a stone column in a cave on Corfu."

Doyle put the book aside. "I've lived a long time without seeing a winged horse."

"I'll bet you lived a long time without seeing a Cerberus until recently."

He couldn't argue that. And still. "It's a Brothers Grimm version, and bastardized at that."

148

"Retellings get bastardized and elaborated," Riley pointed out. "That's why you dig out the root. Four sisters." She held up four fingers. "Four goddesses. It's not the first time I've heard or read of them being sisters. It may be they are. Invisible island, Island of Glass, appears and vanishes as it wills. Three stars — fire, water, ice."

"It doesn't add anything."

Civilians, she thought, with some pity. "Not yet. Being thorough may be tedious, Doyle, but being thorough's how you find what's been overlooked or discounted. There are worse things than sitting in a comfortable chair in a library reading a book."

"A little sex and violence in it would keep it from being so tedious."

"Read on. You could get lucky." Her phone signaled, and she smiled at the readout. "I'm betting we just did. Hello, Liam," she said, and wandered back to the window as she brokered the deal.

Since she clearly had it handled, Doyle went back to the book. He could be grateful, at least, that the particular story in it was fairly short. Though the queen defeated the evil sister, the loss of the others, the stars, grieved her. She returned to her island, exiling herself until prophet, siren, and warrior lifted the stars from their graves so they shined again.

He pulled over Riley's pad, scribbled a note.

He started to flip through, see if another story in the book of folklore addressed the stars, then set the book down when Sawyer came in.

"Okay if I use the other half of the table? I want to try out the maps in here."

"No problem. In fact, I'll work with you, leave the books to Gwin."

"That's not all you can leave to Gwin." Riley smiled, smug, as she pocketed her phone. "I just scored us all the ammo on your list, Dead-Eye."

"The underwater rounds, too?"

"Yeah, them, too. And I got us a pair of Ruger AR-556, along with two dozen thirty-round mags."

"Never shot that model," Sawyer said.

"Me either. The deal's contingent on me looking them over, testing them out. But I googled it while he was talking, and they should be more than fine. Doyle and I can pick them up, along with the ammo, swing back, get the pizza, and we're set."

"Unless you want to go along," Doyle put in. Send the two of them, he thought, and spare him the drive with Riley.

"Wouldn't mind, but no way I'd talk Anni out of coming if I did." Sawyer's eyes, gray as fog, showed both fear and humor. "Then she's loose in Ennis. Shopping."

"Forget it. There and back. Good thing I hit an ATM in Capri or I'd be light on my share." Riley checked the time. "I'm going to dive in here until noon."

"I'll be working with Sawyer on the maps," Doyle told her.

"Fine." She sat, frowned at his scribbled note. "What's this about prophet, siren, and warrior?"

"According to the fairy tale you had me slog through, the queen's exiled herself on her island until they find the stars and let them shine again."

"Always a root," Riley muttered, picked up the book herself.

And happily gave herself over to digging.

CHAPTER SEVEN

Sporting a few bruises from hand-to-hand — Sasha was becoming fierce — Riley tossed a small pack over her shoulder, headed out to Bran's car.

She preferred to drive rather than ride, honestly didn't understand anyone who didn't. But Doyle had called it first, and as one who respected dibs, she climbed in the shotgun seat, prepared to relax.

Ireland had excellent scenery, and when you drove — at least the way she did — you didn't have a chance to enjoy it.

When Doyle got behind the wheel, she decided she'd be friendly.

"Too bad we can't take the bike. How was the ride with Anni?"

He backed up, swung around, headed down the bumpy drive toward the road. "There's a village about eight kilometers off the route I took. It has a couple shops. I'm still wondering how she talked me into turning off and stopping."

"She has breasts."

"She's another man's woman."

"Who still has breasts. And a whole truck-load of charm." She shifted to take the weight off her left hip.

"You took a good spill toward the end of hand-to-hand."

"Sasha's craftier than she used to be. My mistake for holding back."

"Bran could have taken care of any bruises."

"You don't have a few bruises, it wasn't a good fight."

The world was beautiful here, she thought. Untamed and rugged even with the rolls of green, the bundles of cropping sheep. It had a wild, timeless feel that had always spoken to her.

The farmer in the field with his tractor — hadn't his ancestors cultivated that same field with plow and horse? And the simple art of those stone walls. Hadn't those stones been dug and pulled out of those same fields by hands now buried in graveyards?

Take away the paved road, the cars, the scatter of modern houses, and it wouldn't look so very different from when Doyle had lived here. Which was something, she thought, he was bound to feel.

Above, the sky had gone from soft blue to sulky with clouds. They drove into rain, then out again.

"Biggest invention or discovery."

He spared her a frown. "What?"

"What's your pick for most important invention or discovery — since you've seen a bunch of them in three centuries — to date."

"I'm not looking to take a quiz."

"It's not a quiz, it's a question. I'm interested in your opinion on it."

He might have preferred silence, but knew her well enough now to know she'd keep at him. "Electricity, as it opened the door to other advances that needed it."

"Yeah, a big leap. I go with fire — the discovery. But for technology, can't argue with electricity."

"If you're going back to the dawn of time — which is well before mine — you'd have the invention of common tools, the wheel."

"Discovering salt and its uses," she added. "Herbal medicines, learning how to make brick, cut stone, build wells and aqueducts. Did you go to school? You're going to want to take a left on the road coming up."

He made the turn, said nothing.

"It's tough for someone in my line of work not to have some curiosity about a man who's lived through eras I've studied. That's all."

"I had schooling."

"I wondered if, given the amount of time and opportunities, you'd gone for more education."

"I learned when something interested me."

"Uh-huh." The road narrowed, wound, and snaked. She loved these kinds of roads, the quick turns, the hedgerows, the blurry flash of a dooryard garden. "Languages. You've got a good head for languages."

"I've been looking for the stars longer than you've been alive. Longer than your grandmother's been alive. So I've traveled. Traveling's more productive if you speak the language."

"No argument. Next road, right. Why a sword? You're a solid shot with a gun."

"If I'm going to kill a man, I'd rather look him in the eye. And," he said after a long beat of silence, "it helps me remember who I am. It's easy to forget."

"I don't think so. I don't think you ever forget."

He didn't want to ask, had deliberately *not* asked. But now couldn't stop himself. "Why did you come to the graves last night?"

"I was heading back and I saw you. I respect the dead, who and what they were, what they did, how they lived, what they left behind. You said they weren't there. You're right, and you're wrong."

"How can I be both?"

"They've moved on, recycled, which is how I think of reincarnation. That's how the system works for me. But they're still there, because you are. Because the land they lived on, they worked on, where they built a home and a life, it's there."

Riley kept her eyes on the scenery as she spoke because she felt it would be easier for him. "There are trees in the forest that lived when they lived, and they're still there.

"The Craggaunowen Project, where I consulted? It's not far from here. Neither is Dysert O'Dea, both amazing places. There are countless places absolutely amazing in Ireland, because it respects its history — its long and layered history — and those who came before, what they did, how they lived and died. That's why you can feel them here, if you let yourself, and other places in the world are voids because in those places everything's about what's next, and nobody much cares about what was."

She gestured. "That's the place. Big white barn, old yellow house — and okay, really big brown dog."

"You should be able to handle a dog."

"Never met one I couldn't. And I'll handle Liam and the deal."

Doyle pulled into the long gravel drive where the house was set well back, and the barn farther back still. The dog let out a series of deep, throaty warning barks, but Riley climbed out, gave the dog a long look as it stiff-legged toward her.

"Knock it off, big boy."

"Sure he only takes small bites." The man who stepped out of the barn wore a tweed cap over tufts of steel-gray hair, and a baggy cardigan and jeans over a bone-thin frame. He grinned, hands on his narrow hips, obviously amused.

Riley opted to set the tone, grinned back, then gestured to the dog. "Come on and have a sniff, pal."

The dog's tail wagged, two slow tick-tocks. He stepped to her, sniffed her legs, her orange Chucks, then licked the hand she held at her side.

"Well now." Liam strolled forward. "That's a new one altogether. While it's true enough he won't take those bites unless I tell him, he isn't one to make friends with strangers."

"Dogs like me." Now that they'd settled

the matter, Riley leaned over, gave the dog a quick, rough stroking. "What's his name?"

"He's our Rory. And who's your guard dog this fine afternoon?"

"This is Doyle, part of my team." She offered Liam a hand.

"It's good to meet you, Dr. Riley Gwin, who our friend Sean says is as smart and quick as they come. And you, Doyle . . ." He let it hang as he offered Doyle his hand.

"McCleary."

"McCleary, is it? My mother, she married a James McCleary, and lost him in the Second Great War. He left her a widow and a babe in her belly — and that would be me brother Jimmy. She married my own father some three years later, but we've McCleary relations. Do you have people here, Doyle McCleary?"

"Possibly."

He pointed a long, bony finger. "I can hear some of the Clare under the Yank. And you, the famous Dr. Gwin."

"A mongrel, like Rory, but with some of the roots in Galway and Kerry."

"Mongrels, I find, are the smartest and most adaptable. And how long do you plan to be staying in Ireland?"

As she knew the country need for conversation, Riley stood hipshot and relaxed with the dog leaning companionably against her leg. "Hard to say, but we're enjoying the time. We're on the coast, staying with a friend. Bran Killian."

Liam's eyebrows shot up. "Friends with the Killian, are you? An interesting lad — a magician, it seems. Rumors abound."

"I'm sure he enjoys that."

"Quite the place he has on the cliff, I'm told, and built on what was, long ago, Mc-Cleary land. Are you connected there, Doyle?"

"Possibly."

"Doyle's not as keen on digging up the origins as I am," Riley said easily. "You're an O'Dea, an old name, and a prominent one. It's likely your father's people lived in Clare, maybe in the villages that carried your name. Dysert O'Dea, Tully O'Dea. The old name was O'Deaghaidh, and means searcher, likely a nod to your clan's holy men. You lost a lot of land in the rebellions of the seventeenth century."

"Sure Sean said you were quite the scholar." Liam's faded blue eyes danced with amusement. "My mother was born Agnes Kennedy."

Okay, she thought, I'll play. "Kennedy's Anglicized from the nickname Cinnéide or Cinneidigh. *Cinn,* meaning head, *eide* translates to grim or to helmeted. Cinnéide was nephew to the High-King Brian Boru. There's a record of O Cinnéide, Lord of Tipperary, in the *Annals of the Four Masters,* twelfth century."

She smiled. "You come from prominent stock, Liam."

He laughed. "And you've an impressive brain in your head, Dr. Riley Gwin. Well now, I expect you want to do some business, so we'll go into the barn and see what we have for you."

The barn smelled of hay, as a barn should. It held tools and equipment, a skinny, ancient tractor, a couple of stalls. A refrigerator that had surely been plugged in the first time in the 1950s — and, Riley imagined, held beer and snacks.

In the back, the sloping concrete floor led to a small, orderly arsenal. Rifles, shotguns, handguns stood in two large gun safes. Ammunition, and plenty of it, stacked on metal shelves. A long workbench held the tools for making shotgun shells.

"Make your own?"

Liam smiled at Riley. "A hobby of mine. This would be your interest today." He took a Ruger out of the safe, started to pass it to Doyle. Riley intercepted.

She checked its load — empty — tested

its weight, aimed it toward the side wall.

"Not to speak out of turn," Liam said, "but that's a lot of gun there for a woman of your size."

"There was a drunk in a bar in Mozambique who thought I was too small to object when he put his hands where I didn't want them." She lowered the gun, offered it to Doyle. "He and his broken arm found out differently. Can I see the other?"

"Mozambique," Liam said, chuckling, then passed her the second rifle.

"I haven't shot this model before. I'd like to test it."

"You'd be a fool if you didn't." Liam took two mags from the shelf. "Out the back, if you don't mind." He offered ear protectors. "The wife's doing some baking in the kitchen. Just let me give her a text so she knows what we're about."

They went out the rear of the barn where the land gave way to fields and stone fences, and a pair of chestnut horses grazing on the green.

"They're beauties," Riley said.

"My pride and my joy. Not to worry, as they're used to the noise, as is our Rory here. I like to shoot some skeet out here, and kill some paper targets as well."

He gestured to fresh circle targets pinned

to wooden planks, backed by thick stacks of hay.

"These have a good long range as you know, but as you're not familiar with the gun itself, you may want to move closer."

"This is close enough." About fifty yards, she judged, and when it came to the real purpose, she'd want to shoot true a great deal farther. But this would do.

She slapped the mag in place, lifted the weapon, took her stance, sighted. She'd expected the kick, and the rifle didn't disappoint.

She missed the bull's-eye, but by no more than an inch.

"Well done," Liam said, pleased surprise in the tone.

Riley adjusted, fired again, hit the center. "Better," she murmured, and shot a more than respectable grouping of five.

"It's quick," she decided. "I like the hand grip, the trigger pressure. It's got good balance, and doesn't weigh me down." She glanced at Doyle. "Your turn."

He did as Riley did, loaded the second rifle, set, fired. Caught the outside of the first white ring, plugged one inside it, managed a decent grouping if not as tight or accurate as hers.

"It'll do." Doyle ejected the mag.

"Well now, since you're making it so easy, I'll throw in cases for them. Anything else I can show you for your . . . tournament?"

"These do the trick — along with the ammo we discussed."

"Some tournament you're having." But Liam left it at that, and the deal was struck.

They loaded the guns in their canvas cases, the ammo, in the back of Bran's car, covered it all with a blanket before saying their good-byes to Liam and the dog.

Riley kicked back in her seat. "You're a decent shot with a long gun, but you pull a hair to the left."

Since he knew she was right, he didn't respond. "Did you pull that data about his name, his mother's name out of your ass?"

"Out of my brain," she corrected. "You can look it up. I did refresh myself with his surname before we headed out — in case. Kennedy? That's an easy one. Mostly, if I read something, study something, I remember it. Or enough of it. It's interesting, isn't it, he has McCleary relations, and given the location, it's more than likely they cross with yours."

"Just a coincidence."

"You may want to believe that, but you've lived too long to believe it. Too many crosses with you here, McCleary. The land, the site of the house, the most direct connection with Arianrhod. Our prophet finds the Fire Star, our siren the Water Star. You're a sword-wielding warrior, pal. My money's on you for the ice. And if Nerezza makes the same connections, she'll come at you the hardest."

"Let her."

"We'll take her down. I damn well finish what I start, and I swear I'd like to go all Black Widow on her ass. But I'm reading the signs, heeding, we'll say, the seer, so it's most likely going to be you. A sword ends her — so says the prophet."

"If I do, it'll be the biggest pleasure of my life. And I've had more than a few."

"Really?" Since he'd opened the door, she shifted to face him. "So it's not all dour and dark in immortal land?"

"You're a pain in the ass, Gwin."

"I have a medal. Truth," she said when he flicked her a glance. "It's a silver disk with PITA engraved on it. A professor I had as an undergrad gave it to me. I wore it when I gave the valedictorian address. I worked with him on a dig about five, six years after, and we ended up sleeping together one night."

"Just one?"

She only shrugged. "Nothing there, on

either side. We decided we'd been attracted to each other's brain, and the rest didn't work. It was just weird." She pointed at him. "Weirdest sexual encounter."

"No."

"Come on!" she said with an easy, appealing laugh. "I slept with my anthropology prof's brain in a tent in Mazatlán. Balance it out."

He wanted to laugh, barely restrained it. "All right, at random. I slept with a woman who performed in a traveling circus. Tightrope walker, aerialist."

"What was weird about it?"

"She was crazy as a rabid cat, claimed she was really a snake who'd taken human form in order to procreate."

"Huh. What century?"

"Ah . . ." That took a little thinking. "The nineteenth, early nineteenth, if it matters."

"Just curious. What part of her did you sleep with? Yeah, yeah, all of her, but I mean like my professor's brain."

"She was fearless."

"That may have been the crazy, but fearless appeals. Pull over."

"Why?"

"Pull over," she repeated.

Though he muttered, he swung over to the excuse for a shoulder. "If you need to

165

piss, we'll be in Ennis —"

"See that bird?" she interrupted. "On the signpost."

"I see the bloody raven."

"It's not a raven, and it's the seventh I've spotted since we left the barn."

"It looks like a damn raven." But he felt a prickle along the back of his neck as the bird sat, the bird stared. "And there are more than seven ravens in the county of Clare."

"It's not a raven," she said again, and shoved out of the car.

When Doyle saw her pull her gun from under her shirt, he pushed out quickly. "You're not going to shoot a goddamn bird just for —"

As he spoke, the bird screamed, flew straight for them. Riley shot it in midair, turned it to ash.

"Not a raven," she said yet again, spun around, shot two others who came at them from the rear.

"I stand corrected."

"Damn right." She waited, watching, but no others came. "Scouts. She must be feeling better." After holstering the gun, Riley turned back to the car.

Doyle took her arm. "How did you know what it was? I've got eyes, same as you."

"Moon or not, the wolf's always in me. The wolf knows when a raven's not a raven." She took a moment, leaned back against the car, looked out over the near field where sheep cropped among gravestones and the ruin of what she judged had been a small chapel.

And the quiet was glorious, like a deserted cathedral.

"Don't you wonder who built that, and why there? Who worshipped there, what they worshipped?"

"Not really." But the pettiness of the lie stuck between his shoulder blades. "Yes," he corrected, "now and then, if I walk through a place. You're right when you say you can feel what and who were there before. In some places, at some times."

"Battlefields, I find, especially. Ever been to Culloden?"

"Yes, in 1746."

She pushed off the car, eyes alight, and now she gripped his arm. "April 16? You were *there*? Actually there, in it? Oh, you've got to tell me about that."

"It was bloody and brutal and men died screaming. That's any battle."

"No, but —" She stopped herself. He didn't tell war stories, but avoided them. "You could at least tell me which side you were on."

"We lost."

"You were in the Jacobite army, in the rising." Completely fascinated, she stared up at him. "Captured or killed?"

"Captured and hanged, and it's an unpleasant experience."

"I just bet. Did you —"

When he drew away, skirted the hood, she decided to detour from wars before he just shut down. "Most important societal advance," she said when she got in the car.

"I don't think about it."

"You have to live in society."

"I try not to."

"Sociopolitical movements, whether or not they spark and result from revolution, form past, present, future. The Magna Carta, the Elizabethan Religious Settlement, the Bill of Rights, the Emancipation Proclamation, the New Deal. And you can go back to —"

He gripped her shirt at the shoulders, lifted her out of her seat. The movement, completely unexpected, had her falling into him. He had his mouth on hers before she could react.

Then her reaction was elemental, as his mouth was hot, a little frenzied, and stirred needs barely buried. His mouth was rough;

so were his hands.

And that was just fine.

He'd snapped, no question, but at least now he had something he wanted. A taste, a release, however they incited more hunger. He'd known, just known, she'd grab on rather than pull away. Known she'd cover him in that wild and earthy scent.

He gripped her hair now, the carelessly sexy chop of it, and took his fill.

Then released her, plopping her back in her seat as abruptly as he'd yanked her out of it.

She'd have sworn her insides sizzled, but kept her voice steady. "Well, that was interesting."

"I had an itch, and you make it worse because you won't shut the hell up."

"Intellectual curiosity isn't a flaw in my world." Mildly insulted, she gave his shoulder a sharp poke. "I defy anyone sitting next to a three-hundred-year-old man not to have questions."

"The others don't badger me with them."

"If Annika badgered you, you'd find it charming. And who can blame you? Sawyer, he's got a way of figuring out what he wants and needs to know with the subtle. If Bran hasn't asked you some direct questions in a one-to-one, I'm a dancing girl from Tupelo.

And Sasha doesn't have to ask, but when she does, it comes off — I don't know — next thing to maternal."

He waited a beat. "Tupelo?"

"They have dancing girls. Hold on." This time she just opened the window, hitched up, and shot the black, staring bird off the signpost where it perched.

Satisfied, she put her gun away, closed the window, sat back. "Now what?"

Was it any wonder he had this damn itch?

"Now we go pick up some pizza."

"Sounds right."

Better to pretend it never happened. That's what Doyle told himself. They drove into the village in blissful silence — since Riley took out her phone, began scrolling something or other.

It took some doing to maneuver the narrow streets thronged with traffic, with pedestrians swimming over the sidewalks.

He supposed tourists found it charming — the pubs, the shops, the painted walls, the flowers spilling out of baskets.

For himself, he preferred the open.

Still, unlike Annika, Riley didn't exclaim over every shop window they passed — from the car or on foot once they parked.

She moved briskly, a woman on a mission,

a trait he appreciated.

"Should be ready," she said as they weaved through the pedestrians taking advantage of a pretty day. "I texted our order from the road."

Something else to appreciate, he admitted. She thought ahead, didn't waste time.

She'd ordered four large, a variety, and since it was his turn to provide dinner, waited for him to pay. She carried half as they navigated back to the car.

They loaded pizza boxes with the weapons.

"I've had a lot of time to acquire funds and what I need."

She angled her head, tipped down her sunglasses, stared at him.

"I can all but hear the questions rolling around in your head. Where do you get your money, McCleary? What do you do with it? What do you think about the evolution of the tax system?"

"Didn't ask." She poked a finger in his chest. "Sir Broody."

"You will. I may have scared you off for the moment, but you'll start up again."

Now she grabbed his shirt, a fast fistful, rose up as she jerked him down. Caught him in a hard, challenging kiss.

"Do I look scared?" Flicking him away,

she opened her door, got in.

He'd baited her, Doyle admitted. Deliberately baited her because he'd wanted another taste, another rush of her.

Now let that be enough, he warned himself.

He got in, pushed the start button.

"I don't badger."

He maneuvered out of the crowded lot, onto the crowded street. "It's the word that pisses you off."

"The insinuation of the term, yeah. I'm wired to learn, and you've got centuries of knowledge and experience stored up. But I get there's knowledge and experience you don't particularly want to revisit. So it's a pisser to have what's natural to me termed as something rude and heartless."

"You can be rude, I don't mind that. I've never thought heartless."

He could breathe clear again when they drove out of the crowds, into the hills and fields.

"I admire the Declaration of Independence," he said, "as a document created from human intellect, courage, and compassion."

"I agree. Thanks." Again she tipped down her glasses, gave him a smile with her eyes. "Best era for music."

"You're daring me to say the time of Mozart or Beethoven, and it was a time of brilliance and innovation."

"No argument."

"But I'm going to say the mid-twentieth century and the birth of rock and roll, because it's tribal, and it comes from the loins. It's seeded in rebellion."

She pushed her glasses back up, sat back. "You have potential, McCleary. You have potential."

CHAPTER EIGHT

Since Sawyer stepped out of the house when Doyle pulled up, Riley called him over.

"Mission accomplished," Sawyer said while Riley pulled out the pizza boxes. "Bran and I kicked around where to store all this — other than the pizza. We figured the sitting room, second floor, north side."

"Attack comes at night, better on the bedroom level." Riley nodded. "I've got dinner. You guys get the rest."

She carried the boxes straight back to the kitchen, saw Annika and Sasha sitting out on the cliff wall drinking wine. Deciding she'd earned herself a glass of same, she poured one, stepped out.

"You're back." In invitation, Sasha patted the stones beside her. "Have a seat."

"Sounds good, but you may want to come in, see what we bought."

"I like pizza." Annika jumped nimbly from the wall. "But I don't think you bought something fun like a new dress. The rest is guns."

"Yeah, and I know you don't like them, but you should know what they are and where they are." Riley looked at Sasha. "And you're totally Katniss with the crossbow, but you need to be familiarized with the Rugers."

"You're right." Sasha slid down, gave Annika's hand a squeeze. "It was a nice break, to just sit for a while."

"See any ravens?" Riley asked.

Sasha frowned. "Ravens?"

"I'll explain. We actually picked up more than pizza and guns, in the information department." She led the way in, considered, then grabbed the bottle of wine to take upstairs.

"While you were gone," Annika began, "Sasha and I helped Bran. He's making a fire shield."

"Cool. Is that a shield against fire, or a shield *of* fire?"

"Both! You're so clever."

"If he pulls that one off, I'd say Bran wins the clever award." She headed for the sound of male voices, and into the sitting room — handy between her room and Doyle's — where the three men loaded boxes of ammo into an antique display cabinet.

"Edwardian," Riley noted. "Circa 1900. Nice."

"You do know everything," Sasha commented.

"You gotta try. Not its original intent, but it works, and it'll make it easy to keep track of inventory. Still, maybe we should take a share of it to the main level."

"Doyle said the same." Bran stepped back. "Kitchen panty, I'm thinking."

"And that works, too." Riley looked over as Sawyer unzipped one of the rifle cases. "It's got a kick," she told him.

"It looks very mean."

Understanding, Riley gave Annika's back a pat. "It is mean. We're going to need mean."

"You stick with your Wonder Woman cuffs." At Sawyer's comment, Annika rubbed the copper bracelets Bran had conjured for her. "You don't have to touch these."

For himself, Sawyer opened the terrace door, took the rifle out, tested its weight, dry fired a few times.

"We tested it at about fifty yards. We need to practice more distance." Riley unloaded the second rifle herself, offered it to Sasha. "Get a feel."

Long resigned to weaponry, Sasha took it.

176

"It's heavy."

"Compared to your bow or a handgun, sure. But not for what it is. We'll work in some practice tomorrow, after the dive."

"We dive tomorrow." The tension in Annika's face dissolved. "This is much better. I can show you some caves, but the water will be much colder for you than the waters in Capri or Corfu."

"We'll manage." Riley topped off Annika's glass, Sasha's, then her own. "What do you say, a box of each caliber, a quiver of bolts, down in the pantry? Rotate them from here as we go."

Because he felt he'd earned a drink himself, and hers was handy, Doyle took Riley's glass, downed half of it. "It'll do. But I think now we should have bought a third rifle — he had a Remington in stock. We could keep that in the pantry, have another on the main level if needed."

"Hindsight." Riley snatched her glass back. "We can go back if we decide we need another."

"You said you'd picked up more," Sasha reminded her. "Information."

"Yeah, we did. I vote we go down, get into the pizza. I had to smell it all the way home, and I'm ready to eat."

"Don't have to ask me twice. I'm going to

take this down now," Sawyer said, rifle in hand. "I'd like to try it out after we eat."

When they started down with the main floor supplies, Sasha held Bran back.

"Something happened between them — Riley and Doyle."

"They argued? Not surprising."

"I don't mean arguing."

"Ah." Now he smiled. "I don't suppose that's something that should come as a surprise either, should it? Two healthy, attractive people in a close and intense situation. More inevitable than surprising. Why would it worry you?" He tapped a finger between her eyebrows. "I can see the worry."

"If it's just sex, that's one thing. Despite assignment charts, family meals, Annika's shopping sprees — all we do to establish a kind of order and normality, we've been risking our lives every day since we met. So sex, well, that's another kind of normality. But . . . he's closed his heart off, Bran. It's his only defense against living decade after decade while everyone he knows dies. Even the trust, the connection, the affection he feels for all of us is troubling and difficult for him."

"I know it. And Riley knows it as well."

"But Riley is, well, she's a pack animal. It's her nature. She needs and values her

178

solitude, her studies, but at the core she's team and family oriented. And wolves, they mate for life, don't they?"

"I have a strong suspicion Riley mated before this."

"He's her counterpart."

Now Bran frowned. "What do you mean?"

"I've felt it all along. From her, not him. He's so closed off, it's rare for him to send out any feelings or emotions — and I don't push in."

"You don't, no."

"It's more what I feel when I look at them together, or think of them together. He's what she wants, whether she knows it or admits it, he's what she wants for the long haul. I think she could fall in love with him, and it could hurt her."

Bran laid his hands on Sasha's shoulders. "She's the first true friend you've ever had."

"Yes. And she's the one who offered the friendship, the first who did knowing what I am."

"So it's natural you'd worry for her, worry about her. And still, Riley's a woman grown, and as smart and tough as they come. She'll have to walk her own path on this. You'll be there for her wherever it takes her."

With a nod, Sasha moved in for a hug, held on, and wished with all she had, her first true friend could be as happy as she was.

"Hey!" Snapping with impatience, Riley's voice boomed up the stairs. "Jump each other later, or we eat without you."

"We're coming now." Sasha eased back, took Bran's hand.

They'd opened another bottle of wine, and even for such a casual meal, Annika had shaped napkins into swans, draped the necks with collars of tiny flowers, set them to swimming on a pale blue plate.

"We've got your plain cheese for the boring," Riley began, "your pepperoni, your meat, meat, and more meat, and your veggie extravaganza."

"I think I'll start out boring and work my way up." Sasha sat, laughed when Bran flicked a hand over the offered pies to send the cheese bubbling again.

"Riley and Doyle have reports." Because it was so pretty, Annika chose a slice of the vegetable. "So do we. Who should go first?"

"I've more work to do on my part," Bran began, "so I'll cede the first slot to Riley and Doyle."

"Since the Lord of Few Words here will skim over it, I'll take the lead." Riley opted for meat. "It turns out my guns and ammo contact here in Clare has a half brother —

the oldest. A McCleary."

"Just like Doyle," Annika said.

"Just like. Sir Cynic wants to call it co-incidence."

"It wouldn't be." Sasha looked at Doyle with some sympathy. "It just wouldn't."

"Not to say you wouldn't come across plenty of McClearys in Clare or Galway or anywhere in the country," Bran added. "But no, it wouldn't be. You knew this man from before?"

"Nope." Riley washed down pizza with wine, considered it the best of the best. "He's the cousin of a friend's ex. Interesting guy. He knew your name, Bran. And I got respect and curiosity from him there. Short version, Liam — that's the guy — Liam's mother married a James McCleary, he went off to World War II, leaving his pregnant wife, was killed in the war. She had his son, and a few years later remarried. I'm going to say I could've gone in a couple directions to get what we wanted here, but I went straight for this one. Liam made us a fair deal, didn't ask too many questions, and has a direct connection to the clan McCleary."

"Going to make a point," Sawyer said over a mouthful of pizza. "We didn't find the blood connections — the confirmations —

before we got here, to this point. So I'm saying it wasn't the time and place for them before. This is."

"We were already family."

He leaned over, kissed Annika. "Damn right. And maybe we had to get there before we got here."

"Not just a team now," Bran stated. "A *clann.*"

"In Irish, children or progeny. So from that clan or tribe," Riley continued, "people united by kinship, actual or perceived. It fits."

"We started separately." Sasha laid a hand over Bran's. "Formed an alliance, because we weren't a team, not at first."

"You made us one." Sawyer lifted his glass to her. "More than anyone."

"We made us one, but thanks. And Annika's right, from there we became family. And family remains even as a clan."

"We should get us a coat of arms."

Annika gave Sawyer a puzzled look. "But a coat has arms already."

"No, it's a symbol, like an emblem."

"A heraldic design," Riley supplied. "And you know, I like it. Sasha should draw us one."

"That would be a first, but I can try."

"Symbols matter." Doyle shrugged when

all eyes turned to him. "It's been said often enough around this group. Clan. So it would matter."

"I'll work on it."

"We can order up matching T-shirts, but in the meantime." Riley paused to grab another slice. "Pretty sure Nerezza's feeling a little better."

"She came at you." Sasha jerked in her chair. "I didn't feel —"

"Not directly," Riley interrupted. "She sent scouts. Ravens. I took out a few of them."

"You killed birds?" Annika, clearly distressed, laid a hand on her heart.

"Birds don't turn to ash when you put a bullet in them. These did."

"Weregirl recognized them for other." When Riley sneered at him, Doyle just smiled. "Apparently the wolf knows a raven from a minion."

"Scout," Riley corrected. "Not that they wouldn't have clawed our eyes out given the chance, but they were weak — which hopefully translates to her still being weak."

"But she knows where we are," Sawyer put in.

"I'd say she does. Not ready to do much about it, but she knows we're here."

"And when she's ready," Bran said, "so

will we be. A clan, a coat of arms, and for my part, a shield. When the time comes, we'll fight fire with fire."

"And firepower. Did some scouting of my own," Sawyer told them. "My take is rather than in the towers, outside on the — let's have fun and call them battlements — makes a better position for the long-range rifles. You don't have the cover, but you'd have a three-sixty, and when whatever she sends gets within, say, twenty yards, you'd get cover. Plenty of time for it."

"That's good thinking. I'd like to check it out, too."

"I already have," Doyle said to Riley. "Sawyer's right. It's a better position to target on land, sky, sea."

Riley considered. "Bran, you know how to do those flying balls for Anni and her Wonder Woman deal?"

"I do, and yes, that's also good thinking. I can give you targets — land, sea, air."

"Very cool. We can try it out tonight, after we finish here."

"I would clean up." Annika sent an imploring look around the table. "I don't like the sound the guns make. I would stay here, clean up."

"That's okay." Sawyer gave her hand a squeeze under the table.

"We dive tomorrow." Wanting to make Annika smile again, Riley changed the subject to something her friend liked. "We should be ready to drive out by eight thirty, so we can pick up the boat, the equipment. Or a couple of us go to get the boat, pilot it back here, and Sawyer travels the rest of you down to it. We'll keep the boat here for the duration, just have to deal with getting the tanks refilled as we need them."

"More efficient." Sawyer circled a finger as he ate. "Riley and Doyle — best at piloting — go for the boat. When we spot you coming back, I'll get the rest of us on board."

"Can do. Eight thirty," Riley said to Doyle, who just nodded.

They went up, leaving Annika to deal with the debris, and outside to look over the crenelated wall into the coming twilight.

"Days are longer — calendar and geography," Riley said. "She likes the dark, but she may hit more often in daylight. It's the last round, and she lost the first two."

"Day or night, we'll knock them back." Ready, Sawyer loaded a rifle. "Give me a target, at least fifty yards out."

"Where would you like it?" Bran asked.

"Surprise me."

Obliging, Bran sent a globe into the air, out above the sea. Sawyer shifted his stance, fired, struck it dead center.

"Figures." Riley lifted the second rifle. "Give me one."

This one Bran sent high into the north. Riley took it down.

"Okay, let's make it a hundred yards, multiple targets. You game?" Sawyer asked Riley.

"I invented the game. Go."

After the barrage of fire, Riley lowered her weapon. "You don't miss, cowboy."

"You didn't either."

"I only nicked a couple of them. You hit dead-on, every one. More practice for me. You need to try it." Riley offered the gun to Sasha.

"I don't know how I can shoot what I can barely see."

"Bran's going to bring it in for you. Start at twenty yards, Bran, straight ahead over the water."

Doyle stepped behind Sasha. "It'll recoil, so you need to go with that." He adjusted her stance, put his hands over hers. "Use the sight, hold it steady. Do you have it?"

"Well, I can see it, in the cross — the crosshairs."

"Steady," he said again. "Don't jerk when

you pull the trigger. You want it smooth, building the pressure, like drawing a line. Keep drawing it even after you fire. A slow pull, all the way. Take a breath, hold it, fire."

She did as he told her, let out an embarrassing squeal when the kick shoved her back against him. "Sorry. And I completely missed."

"You pulled up and to the right," Riley told her.

"Steady," Doyle repeated. "Try again."

She didn't squeal this time, but hissed. And by the third time she just dinged the bottom of the globe.

"It won't be your primary weapon," Doyle began.

"Thank God." Happy to relinquish it, she passed it to Doyle.

"But you'll learn how to handle it, clean it, load it, and use it with accuracy."

"All right." She rolled her aggravated shoulder. "I'll learn."

"And you." Doyle gestured to Bran. "Not even close to your primary weapon."

"And still," Bran agreed.

They spent twenty minutes destroying target globes before stowing the weapons.

"I'm going to take Anni down, so she can swim. It'll smooth her out after all the gunfire."

"Dawn, as usual," Doyle reminded Sawyer.

"Not likely to forget."

"I've got another hour's work in me," Bran decided.

"And I'll start working on that coat of arms."

Riley closed the outside door as the others filed out. Doyle stowed the rifles.

"We'll take my bike tomorrow."

"Fine with me. With Sawyer bringing everybody to us, we should be able to start diving around nine thirty. Annika's right about the water temp, so we'll have to limit underwater time. Maybe do a couple of thirty-minute dives tomorrow, get acclimated."

Since he made no move to leave, she studied him. "Have you ever dived in the North Atlantic?"

"A few times."

"You're not going to tell me you were a Navy SEAL, are you?"

"It seemed like a good idea at the time."

"Seriously?" A dozen questions popped into her mind, but she shook her head.

"Five years. Any longer than that with one group is risky."

"I can see that. But right now, we're not just a group, and we already know who you are. It should make things easier for you."

"It doesn't."

When he walked out on that, Riley let out a sigh. "It should," she murmured.

In the morning, after a sweaty hour under Doyle's training whip, a hot breakfast where they refined and confirmed the diving plan, Riley pulled on a battered leather jacket. As a hopeful sun had broken through the earlier gloom and drizzle, she pushed on her sunglasses.

She had her tank suit for diving under her sweatshirt and cargoes, her gun on her hip under the jacket, and her cell phone secured in the inside pocket.

And considered herself good to go.

She'd been quick, and walked outside at eight twenty-seven. She couldn't say, exactly, why it irritated her that Doyle waited beside his bike.

He held out a black helmet with a small emblem of the dragon that flew over the side of the bike.

"Why do you even have this?" she wondered. "A fractured skull wouldn't hold you back for long."

"It's the law in a lot of places, and you make fewer ripples if you follow local laws. And a fractured skull wouldn't kill me, but it fucking hurts."

She strapped on the helmet. "Haven't had the experience, but I bet."

He swung on the bike. "Navigate."

"You could just let me drive."

"No. Lay out the route."

"South on the coast road toward Spanish Point. Should be a sign about a half kilometer this side for Donahue's Diving. Follow that down to the beach. I'm licensed," she added, swinging on behind him.

"Nobody drives my bike."

He kicked it to life. The dragon roar of bikes had always appealed to her, as had the sensation of speed and the freedom of blasting down the road open to the wind.

It all appealed less when riding pillion.

Still, his bike, his rules.

She set her hands on his hips, and *imagined* she was driving.

Down the bumpy lane, around the curves where Bran had let the hedgerows of fuchsia rise to form borders, and sassy wildflowers poked up to edge the dirt track. Around and beyond the forest where the track turned onto pavement.

While she enjoyed the speed and power, the smell of green still damp from the morning shower, she kept a sharp eye out for any ravens — for anything that struck her as *off*.

No need for conversation with the roar and buffeting wind, and no need to direct as Doyle wound them to the coast road. She imagined he'd made the journey on horseback or cart more than once.

Had he played on the beach as a boy, splashed in the waves, shouted out laughing as the chilly water rolled over him? Sailed out in a currach, fished the seas?

She could imagine it, she could see him — a tall boy with long dark hair, eyes green like the hills, running over shale and sand, through the shallows with his siblings as boys had and would.

A good life, she thought as she leaned with him into a turn.

She shifted a little, looked out over the water, a rough and ready blue with tinges of green. Gulls swooped, white or gray, and farther out she saw the roll of a white fishing boat.

He slowed through villages decked with flowers, slapped the gas again once they moved beyond.

She tapped his shoulder, pointed when she spotted the little sign up ahead. He only nodded, then slowed into the turn.

The wind kicked harder now, and brisker as they took the narrow ribbon of road down. She smelled the sea, cool and briny, and the roses from the garden of a cottage, the smoke from a chimney of another.

Chickens, she thought. Though she couldn't see or hear them, the scent of their feathers tickled her nose. She smelled the dog before it ran out and along a tumbling stone wall to watch them.

She tapped Doyle's shoulder again when she saw the blue building with the long pier. She spotted the dive boat, a fishing boat, and a sweet little cabin cruiser with a man on deck patiently polishing its brightwork.

Doyle pulled up beside a pair of trucks and a compact, cut the engine.

"I've got this," she said, slid off the bike, and strolled toward the boat where the man stopped, put his hands on his hips.

Her deal, Doyle thought, and walked over the shale to the thin strip of dark gold sand.

It would be here, wouldn't it? he thought. Fate's quick poke in the ribs. Here, where he'd come as a boy — of nine or ten, if memory served. A cousin had lived nearby. Christ, what was the name? Ronan, yes, Ronan had been the boy about his age, son of his father's sister. And they'd come to visit, barely a hard stone's throw from this spot.

His two sisters nearest his age chasing birds. The brother who came after them splashing in the shallows while a younger sister clung shyly to his mother's skirts. His young, doomed brother barely toddling. Another babe — though he hadn't known it then — in his mother's belly.

All there, his mother and father, his grand-parents, aunt, uncle, cousins.

They'd stayed three days, fishing, feasting, playing music, and dancing late into the night. And he and Ronan had plied through the water like seals.

The following winter his aunt whose name escaped him died in childbirth. His father had wept.

Death unmans us all, Doyle thought.

Riley stepped over to him. "You've been here before."

"Yes."

"With your family?"

"Yes. Did you make the deal?"

She studied him a moment longer, then nodded. "Done. We can load the equip-ment."

They didn't speak again, or only of practi-calities as along with Donahue they carted tanks, wet suits, equipment.

Riley addressed her conversation to Don-ahue, some talk, Doyle realized, of the dives a mutual acquaintance had taken a few years earlier.

When Donahue asked about the motorcycle, Riley just smiled and told him someone would pick it up later. And they'd be back to refill the tanks when needed.

Since she'd made the deal, she took the wheelhouse, eased the boat away from the dock with a wave to Donahue, already heading back to his brightwork.

"Making some small talk also causes fewer ripples," she pointed out.

"You were doing enough for both of us. It's a good boat."

"The friend we small talked about is a marine biologist, and he's partnered with a marine anthropologist. So Donahue came highly recommended. The anthro's also a lycan. The daughter of a friend of my mother's."

"Small world."

"Situationally."

It was a good boat, and she knew how to handle it. She headed north, kept within sight of the coast until she spotted a cove.

"A good spot," she called out, "for dropping four people out of the air."

She navigated in, using the shelter of the cliff face for cover, then pulled out her phone.

"Latitude and longitude for Sawyer. I've got an app for that. You'd better come up here so somebody doesn't splat on top of you."

He moved up with her while she found the coordinates.

She still smelled of the forest, he noted, if the forest grew out of the sea.

"Hey, Sawyer, we're about halfway between here and there." She read off the coordinates. "Same type of RIB we've been using. Yeah, you got that. We're in the wheelhouse, nosed into a cove, bow toward the cliff, so you've got the rest of the boat. Don't miss," she added, then pocketed the phone.

"They'll be a minute. You know, given my bloodline and line of work, I've always been open to, we'll say, the unusual. But up until recently I wouldn't have seen myself hanging out waiting for four pals to pop out of thin air."

"A small and fluid world."

"Fluid works."

Water lapped and rocked against the boat, and Doyle — who could go weeks happily speaking to no one — found himself restless with the silence.

"Do lycans tend to go into science?"

"I wouldn't say so. I know teachers, artists, business types, chefs, lazy asses, politicians —"

"Politicians."

"Yeah." Now she smiled. "We've had a few in Congress, Parliament. There was this guy about twenty, twenty-five years ago I heard about who had higher ambitions. Leader of the Free World ambitions, but the council strongly discouraged him. You go for that, people start digging pretty deep. Better not to risk it. A shame really."

"A lycan president."

"We could do a hell of a lot worse."

"And likely have."

"Definitely have," she said with a grin. "But hey, three nights a month, a lycan couldn't answer that three a.m. phone call, so no-go there."

"And a Secret Service code name 'Furry' lacks dignity."

Very deliberately, she tipped down her sunglasses, peered at him over them. "You made a joke."

"I considered a career in comedy."

"And two for two. I have to circle this day on my calendar."

The way her eyes danced with humor, so gold in the sunlight, made him want to touch her. Just touch her hair, her skin.

He started to lift his hand to do just that when with a shimmer and a shudder of air the others appeared on the boat, and saved him from what he realized would have been a grave mistake.

"Dead-Eye strikes again," Riley said. "Perfect landing."

"Practice makes perfect." Sawyer glanced around. "You picked a good spot."

"I thought so. Settle in, friends and neighbors." Riley turned back to the wheel. "Where to, Anni?"

"Oh." Annika managed to look sexy even in one of the macs borrowed from Bran's mudroom. "If you sail as if we were going back to Bran's, I'll tell you when to stop."

"Good enough. Enjoy the balmy breezes while you can."

"You call this balmy?" As Riley steered the boat out of the cove, Sasha huddled beside Bran.

"Compared to what it's going to be like under the water? This is damn near tropical."

CHAPTER NINE

Even with wetsuits, the Atlantic shivered in, and it swallowed the sun. Riley, armed as Sawyer was with an underwater pistol, switched on the headlamp on her balaclava so its beam cut through the dank gloom of the water.

They swam in pairs, Annika and Sawyer in the lead — with Annika turning somersaults before she swam ahead. Sasha and Bran followed, and Riley couldn't complain when Bran circled a hand in the water, added light with a swirl. She took flank with Doyle.

They all knew what could streak out of the sea, if Nerezza had the strength for it. Mutant sharks and toothy fish thirsting for blood. Both Doyle and Sasha carried harpoons.

And look at her go, Riley thought, watching Sasha cut through the water, remembering how nervous the novice diver had been on their first dive off the coast of Corfu.

She learned fast. They'd all had to shore up personal weaknesses on this quest. Maybe that was part of the whole, she mused, turning weakness into strength, and for all, learning to trust enough to become that clan.

She watched a school of mackerel — just ordinary fish — head away from them, followed Bran's silvery light toward the mouth of a cave. In front of it, Annika executed a graceful turn, waved, then slid inside.

Singly now through the narrows, and again two by two when the channel widened. Then spreading out to search for . . . something, Riley thought. A glow, a sparkle, a *feeling,* anything that would lead the way to the last star, the Ice Star.

Cold enough for it — that thought crossed her mind. With the patience of her calling, she searched the underwater cave inch by inch, using her eyes, her gloved fingers, doing all she could to keep her mind and instincts wide open.

But she nodded when Sawyer tapped his wrist, once again took flank with Doyle for the return trip to the boat.

When Riley hauled herself out of the water, she saw Bran holding Sasha close, laying a serious kiss on her.

"Oh, God, that's *wonderful.* I'm warm again."

"Magick mouth?"

Bran laughed over at Riley as she dripped frigid water onto the deck. "Just a personal benefit." He took Riley's arms, squeezed lightly. And warmth flooded her.

"Excellent, even without the lip-lock."

He moved to Annika.

"I like kissing," she told him, and brushed her lips to his. "And I like warm."

Bran slapped both Sawyer and Doyle on the shoulder. "No point in any of us shivering our way through this. Anything, *fáidh*?"

"No, sorry. It's so different from where we've been before. All so shadowy and stark in a way. But I didn't feel anything. Anyone?"

"I felt good," Annika told her. "But there's no singing, like there was for me with the Water Star."

"Up for round two?" Riley asked.

Sasha turned her back to Bran so he could help her change tanks. "It's what we're here for."

The second dive of the day gave them no more than the first. In Riley's book that meant two locations checked off.

Routine, Riley told herself when they secured the boat below the cliffs of Bran's house. Part, an important part, of discovery was routine.

They took the easy way — Sawyer's way — back to the house. And she folded herself into routine by scarfing down leftover pizza, closing herself in with her books.

The rain came back in the night, lashing rain with grumbling thunder that echoed off the sea. The storm woke her from a dream she couldn't quite pull back. And with the crashing waves, whirl of wind, she doubted she'd pull back sleep either.

She dragged on a sweatshirt, flannel pants. She wanted to see the storm boil over the sea and cliffs so slipped out of her room, walked quietly down to the sitting room that faced the Atlantic.

Glorious, she thought as she opened the doors. It flashed and burned, whipped and snapped so the wind screamed with it. Like a banshee, she decided, since it was Ireland.

The wild had always, would always call to her blood, and a wicked storm whirling over the night-dark sea, the rough and rugged land heated that blood, had her stepping out just enough to let the rain pelt her upturned face.

Then she looked down, saw movement, saw a figure near the cliff wall, and instinctively reached for the gun she hadn't thought to bring.

In a flash of lightning the figure became Doyle, and her instincts took a hard turn into lust.

Dark and brooding in the storm, coat swirling, sword in hand as if prepared to strike against the elements. Gorgeous, she thought again, and primal and violently sexy.

Yeah, she'd always been drawn to the wild.

As she thought it, he turned, lightning sizzling above him, and in its fire, his eyes met hers. He tightened those thoughts into a noose that clutched at her throat.

Pride and sheer will made her stand there another moment, meeting those eyes, holding them even when the dark fell again, turned him into a shadow.

Then she stepped back, shut the doors against the storm, against the man, and went back to her room alone.

Routine, Riley reminded herself when they went through it, step-by-step, the next day.

A dawn run through the wet forest, jumping over a few limbs brought down in the storm. Polishing it off with a sweat-popping session in the gym as watery sunlight struggled through the clouds.

A shower, breakfast, two more dives,

weapons training.

She opted for a fire in the library, the books while Bran worked at the top of the tower, while Sasha used the other tower's sitting room to paint. Sawyer and Doyle drove out to refill the tanks, do a food supply run. And Annika charmed her way into going with them, as a trip to the village meant shopping.

Now and again as she worked, she'd hear something rumble up above and assumed Bran made progress. But two hours into it, she found herself restless. Fresh air, she decided. She needed to move, to think. At some point in the gathering of data, you needed to stop, let it roll while you did something else.

Since the day had turned — that watery sunlight strengthened by late afternoon — she'd take a walk in the forest. Armed, of course, she thought as she patted the gun on her hip. Aware, always, but a good walk in the woods.

Odds were long she'd stumble across the star there, but thinking time was never wasted time. She slipped on a ragged hoodie, zipped it, went out by way of the main steps, nearly turned back when she saw both the car and the bike outside.

They'd gotten back while she'd been

working, she supposed, and since the back of the car remained open, supplies inside, they were still unloading.

Could probably use some help. She headed toward the car when Sasha called her name.

"Hey!" She looked over, shot Sasha a salute as her friend stood just outside the trees at the head of a path. "Looks like you had the same idea as I did. I was going for a walk, but —"

"Good. There's something — come with me."

"Just let me haul some of this in first."

"I need to show you something. I'm not sure . . . I need you to see."

"What?" Intrigued, Riley detoured from the car.

"It's hard to explain. I went off the path, nearly got lost. But I found these marks on a tree. Carvings. I don't know what they are."

"Carvings?" The single word had Riley quickening her steps. "Recent?"

"I don't think so." As she spoke, Sasha looked back into the woods. "I should have taken a picture with my phone. I didn't think of it, just started back to tell everyone. Let me show you, and we'll take some pictures to show the others."

"Sash, you don't even have your knife."

"Oh. I don't know what I was thinking, but well, I'll be with you now." Sasha took Riley's hand, tugged. "I really want you to see this. It must mean something."

"Okay. Lead the way."

Doyle came out, saw Sasha and Riley move into the woods. He shook his head, grabbed two bags of groceries. "Thanks for the help," he muttered, and headed in.

In the dappled sunlight Riley breathed deep. "I just wanted a break from the books, and some air. Didn't figure on finding something cool. Did you get a vibe from it?"

"What? Vibe?"

"You know, a feeling?"

"I felt it was old — older than made sense. If that makes sense." Sasha moved quickly, gestured as she cut off the track. "I just — I guess I felt pulled to go this way."

"Must be a reason. So is it letters, symbols?"

"Both. I've never seen anything like it."

"I was all over these woods, two nights running, and didn't see it. I should have," Riley added as they skirted around brambles and brush. "I've got good night vision. That makes me think you were meant to find it. But you didn't get a strong sense, any sort of vision, so —"

She turned her head. The backhand exploded pain in her cheekbone, lifted her off her feet, propelling her into the air. She crashed hard into a tree, saw stars, felt something *crunch* in her right arm.

She screamed as her instinctive reach for her gun shot agony through her. Sasha leaped over the brush, sprang off the moss-coated trunk of a fallen tree.

Her eyes glowed.

In defense, Riley tried to roll, to reach cross body for her gun. The savage kicks to her ribs, to her back, her belly stole all breath.

Sasha laughed.

A nightmare, dreaming. Not real. Engulfed in pain, swimming in shock, Riley struggled to unsheathe her knife with her left hand.

The sound she made when Sasha's boot stomped on her hand was a high-pitched shriek. Her vision wavered; her stomach pitched.

Then her friend's artist's hands closed around her throat.

Doyle strode into the kitchen where Annika happily put groceries away, and Sawyer sniffed a fat tomato.

"Still more, right?" Sawyer set the tomato aside. "I'll bring it in."

"You going to make that salsa?"

"As advertised."

"Do that." Doyle grabbed a cold beer from the fridge, took a long pull. "I'll get the rest."

"There's a deal."

After one more swig of beer, Doyle set the bottle down, started back through the house. A beer, he thought, some chips with Sawyer's salsa would be a solid way to offset Annika's shopping enthusiasm.

In any case, they'd gotten everything they should need for a good week. And next time, somebody else would deal with the mermaid.

He glanced up, momentarily baffled when Sasha jogged down the steps.

"I didn't hear you get back. I was painting on the other side of the house. How —"

"You've been upstairs?"

"Yes, I went by the tower library just now to see if I could help Riley, but —"

"Jesus Christ. Get Bran, get the others. Riley's in trouble."

"What? How?"

"Get them." He drew his sword from the sheath on his back, was already running. "She's in the woods."

He'd barely reached the verge when he heard her scream.

He didn't think, just moved. The sound had been agonized, and he already might be too late.

He caught the sound of laughter — horrible, gleeful — and sprinted toward it off the track. No time for stealth, and his instincts demanded he make more noise. The sound of someone coming, and fast, might stop whatever was being done to Riley.

He didn't pause when he saw Riley crumpled on the ground, bleeding, unmoving, and Sasha — or what had taken Sasha's form — standing over her with a wide, wide grin.

"She's dying," the thing said with Sasha's voice, then long teeth shimmered between Sasha's lips, claws sprang from her hands. "You'll all be dying soon."

Even as Doyle charged, it delivered a vicious kick to Riley's head. When Doyle's sword cleaved down, it struck empty air as the thing coiled down into itself and ran through the trees with preternatural speed.

Doyle dropped to the ground, pressed his fingers to the pulse on Riley's raw throat. Found a pulse, thready, but beating.

Bearing down on fear, on rage, on a kind

of grief he'd sworn never to feel again, he ran his hands over her, checking her injuries. Her face, sickly gray under the bruising, bleeding, abrasions, was the least of it.

He heard running, shouting, tightened his grip on his sword, prepared to defend Riley should foe join his friends.

They burst through the trees, armed for battle. But Doyle knew the battle was done for the moment.

"She's breathing, but she's been choked, and her hand's broken, ribs, too. I think her right elbow's shattered. And —"

On a keening sound of distress, Sasha all but fell on the ground beside Riley. "No, no, no, no."

"Let me see." Bran dropped down beside her.

"We need to get her inside, heal her." Tears shimmering, Annika knelt by Riley's other side, stroked her bloodied hair.

"I don't think we move her until we know . . ." Sawyer's knuckles showed white on the grip of his gun. "You're not supposed to move her, right, because it can make it worse?"

"Sawyer's right. That's sensible." Calm as a lake, Bran cupped his hands on Riley's head. "Neck and spine. We should see if they're injured."

"I can do it."

Bran looked into Sasha's eyes, eyes glazed with shock. "Calmly, *fáidh*. Slowly. Just the surface now."

"All right." Closing her eyes, Sasha took in air, let it out until her breath was nearly steady. She used her hands, her heart, and with Bran's hands on her shoulders to aid her, she let herself feel.

"Oh, God, oh, God, so much broken, so much damaged."

"Neck and spine, Sasha," Bran said quietly. "Start there."

"Bruised, jolted. Not broken."

"Then we can take her inside." Those tears streamed down Annika's cheeks. "She shouldn't lie on the ground. It's cold. She's cold."

"Yes, we can move her." When Bran started to lift her, Doyle nudged him aside.

"I've got her." She moaned when he gathered her up, and her eyelids fluttered — both of which he took as good signs. For an instant, her eyes opened — blind with pain, with shock, met his. "I've got you, *ma faol*."

Her eyes rolled up white, closed again as he carried her out of the forest.

"Straight to her room," Bran ordered. "I'll get my medical kit. Anni, towels and hot water. Sawyer, a pitcher of cool water. Not cold, cool, and a clear glass. Sasha, strip her bed down to the sheets for now."

They scattered as Sasha ran up the stairs behind Bran. Though he wanted to run himself — and could have, as she weighed nothing much to his mind — Doyle moved carefully, doing what he could not to jar her.

When he turned into Riley's room, Sasha had tossed the bedding and pillows aside.

"I can help her."

"Wait for Bran." As if she were made of thin, fragile glass, Doyle laid her on the bed.

"I can help. If she comes to before . . . I don't know how she could stand it."

"She's tough. She'll hold up." With great care, Doyle unzipped her hoodie, ignored the blood, removed her holster, her knife sheath. "Wait for Bran."

Fighting tears, Sasha sat on the side of the bed, took Riley's good hand. "How did you know?"

"I saw her go into the forest when I was taking in supplies. Saw her going in with you minutes before I went out for more, and you came down."

"With me? With *me*?"

"Hold it together." He issued the order with a snap. "You can't help her if you don't

211

hold it together."

"You're right. I will. And if Bran's not here in thirty seconds, I'm —"

"I'm here." He came in with his kit and a satchel. "I needed to get some more things. Pour a half glass of that," he told Sawyer when Sawyer came in. "I need to bring her around enough for her to swallow."

"Not like this. Bran, not like this. Let me try to help first."

He looked at Sasha. "She's gravely injured. Understand that and go lightly. Just enough, do you understand, to ease the worst."

"I'll be careful."

She laid a hand on Riley's bruised and swollen cheek, held back a hiss as she felt the pain.

"Just enough," Bran repeated.

She tried, tried to go lightly, to ease only, to skim over what she understood were critical injuries, internal as well as shattered and broken bones.

But love, and an ability she'd only just learned to use, overwhelmed.

She laid a hand over Riley's crushed one, felt the vicious bootstrike, the agony as bones snapped and shattered. And, horrified, saw her own face looming over Riley's prone body. Her own face filled with jubilant hate.

The pain, the overwhelming pain, struck her.

Bran cursed when Sasha melted to the floor.

"I've got her, I've got her." Sawyer rushed to Sasha as Annika hurried in, towels under her arm, a kitchen pot of water in her hands.

"You can make it hot quicker than the stove. I remembered."

"Of course I can. I wasn't thinking. Set it down there," Bran told Annika.

"I'm sorry." Sasha rubbed hands over her face. "I went too deep. Let me try again."

"You'll wait. Doyle, Sawyer, I need you to hold Riley down."

"No." Sasha rocked herself. "Oh, no."

"I'll be quick, but she needs this in her now. Lift her head so she takes it in," Bran told Doyle, "and hold her still."

Sasha knelt beside the bed, took Riley's good hand again. "Just to let her know we're here. I can let her know we're all here. It will help."

"It will." Bran shoved up his sleeves. "Annika. Eight drops from the blue bottle. Two from the red. Blue, then red."

With Sawyer holding Riley's legs, Doyle on the bed behind her propping her head up, holding her shoulders, Bran straddled her, gripped her purpling jaw in one hand.

His eyes, black as onyx, went deeper, went darker. Riley stirred, struggled. Howled.

"Damn it," Sawyer muttered, forced to add weight to his grip. "Goddamn it."

"Get it in her," Doyle demanded, and lost control enough to lower his face in Riley's hair. "Take your bloody medicine, Gwin, and don't be a baby about it."

And suffering, he murmured to her.

Bran took the glass from Annika, poured the contents ruthlessly down Riley's throat.

Her eyes shot open, wheeled in her head. Her body arched, limbs trembling as they tried to drum. Then she collapsed, shuddering, shuddering, until she lay pale and still as death.

As he eased off the bed, Bran swiped sweat off his brow. "Now we can start."

She woke in agony, she floated in dreams. She struggled in nightmares, she searched for peace.

She found peace now and then, hearing the voices of her friends. Sawyer . . . reading? Yes, reading Terry Pratchett, an old one, with the female cop — who happened to be a werewolf.

Just like her.

Annika singing — opera and Adele. Curled on the bed with her, softly crooning and smelling of spring rain.

The nightmares would close in, and the pain spike. And then Sasha would be there with her, telling her she wasn't alone, and the pain would subside, a little.

Bran running his hands over her, sometimes chanting in Irish or Latin, sometimes talking to her or to someone else who talked back to him with an accent as Irish as his own.

And Doyle, so often Doyle. He read Shakespeare. Who knew he had a voice so suited to Shakespeare? And when the demons chased her, demons with the faces of friends, he held her close.

"Beat them back, *ma faol*," he told her — demanded of her. "You know how. Fight!"

So she fought, and she drifted, and agony turned to grinding aches.

Doyle was there when the woman came, and urged the contents of some vial between her lips.

"No. I don't want —"

"It's what you need that counts. Swallow it down, there's a good girl."

She had red hair and eyes fiercely green, and a beauty that had survived decades. "Arianrhod."

"No, indeed. But one of her daughters, it seems. As you are. Sleep awhile more, and this fine young man will watch over you."

"I'm older than you are, by far."

The woman laughed at Doyle's comment, stroked a hand over Riley's cheek. "Sleep," she said.

And Riley slept.

When she woke minutes later — hours, days? — Doyle was beside her, propped up on pillows, reading *Much Ado* out loud by lamplight.

"I wrote a paper on Beatrice as a feminist."

Doyle lowered the book, shifted to study her face with eyes that looked exhausted. "You would."

"Why are you in bed with me?"

"Doctor's orders. Witch doctors. You look like hell, Gwin."

"Matches how I feel. What happened? What the hell happened? I don't —" Then she did, tried to bolt up, but Doyle held her down one-handed. "Sasha. She's possessed. You have to —"

"No, that wasn't it. It wasn't Sasha."

"She knocked the crap out of me, so I ought to know . . . No." Riley closed her eyes, forced herself to try to remember what came in fragments. "No, not Sasha. Malmon."

"That's been our theory."

"I'm sure of it. It looked and sounded like

216

Sasha, until it clocked me. It felt like being hit with a brick." Cautiously, she lifted her hand to her cheek, pressed. "Feels okay now. I couldn't get my gun. I couldn't . . . My hand." She lifted her left hand, stared at the bandage wrapped around it. "Uh-oh."

"Nearly healed. They don't want you moving your fingers much as yet."

"She — he — it — stomped on it. I think I passed out."

"A lot of bones in the hand. Passing out would be the wise course when having them all broken or crushed."

She braced herself. "How bad am I?"

"You're not dead, and would've been without Bran and Sasha, and even then. Internal injuries — kidneys, spleen, liver — severe enough we nearly hauled you to the hospital, but Bran had another solution. His grandmother."

"She looks like Arianrhod. I talked to her. I think."

"You did, more than once, I'm told. She's a healer, an empath. Bran swore by her skill, and he didn't exaggerate. I'm not sure you'd have full use of that hand again without her."

"Then I'm grateful. How long have I been down? A day? Two?" she asked when he only shook his head.

"You walked into the forest five days ago."

"Five?"

When she shoved up, gritted her teeth against a gasp of pain, he rolled out of the bed, poured something into a glass. "Drink it."

"I don't want to sleep again. Five days?"

"Fine."

"Where are you going?" she demanded, close to panic as he turned to the door.

"To get the others."

"Don't. Just wait. I want to get up."

"I want to dance with a naked Charlize Theron. We all have to face limitations."

"I'm serious. What time is it? Where is everybody?"

"Even though you talk in your sleep, it was more peaceful when you were unconscious. It's nearly ten thirty — that's p.m. — and I imagine the rest are downstairs."

"Then I want to go down. If you could just help me up, just give me a hand."

He huffed out a breath, walked back, plucked her out of bed.

"I didn't say carry me down." Mortifying. "I don't want to be carried."

"I go down and bring them to you, or I carry you down. Choose."

"I'll take the ride. Wait — mirror."

He stepped around, turned so she could

get a look in the cheval glass in the corner of the room.

She saw a big man all in black holding her as if she weighed as much as a puppy. And she looked pale, fragile — too thin.

"I do look like hell. I should appreciate the honesty."

"No point in lying about it. You looked worse even yesterday. He all but choked the life out of you."

In the mirror, their eyes met, and on the meeting his went blank. "I don't remember that. Why did he stop?"

"Best guess is he heard me coming."

"You? How did you know to come?"

"I saw you head into the woods with what I thought was Sasha," he began as he carried her from the room. "And then I saw Sasha come down the stairs in the house. Easy enough to put it together. I wasn't quick enough to stop him from giving you a kick in the head. You were seeing double every time you came out of it for the first two days. Sicked up even the broth they tried to get into you until yesterday afternoon."

"Glad I don't remember that. I hate puking. You read to me. You and Sawyer and —"

"Brigid said reading, talking, being close

219

enough you could feel us would help the healing. We took shifts, like we did when Sawyer was hurt."

"He was tortured and knifed and beaten and burned, and he wasn't down and out this long."

"Men did to him — that's what Bran and Brigid say about it. A creature of Nerezza's did to you. There was poison in you. Be glad Bran won the argument about a hospital. They'd never have addressed the poison."

"More gratitude." When she heard voices, she tensed.

"It wasn't Sasha."

"I know."

Doyle stopped. "She's suffered. You need to know. Whatever worry, even fear, others knew over the last days, she felt it more keenly."

"It wasn't her fault."

"Convince her," Doyle said simply, then carried her toward the voices.

CHAPTER TEN

When Doyle stepped in, Riley in his arms, everything stopped.

Sawyer, on the point of demonstrating to Annika the proper way to hold a pool cue, jerked upright and grinned like a maniac. Annika let out a joyous laugh, and somehow managed to execute a backflip in the relatively confined space.

At the bar pouring a whiskey into a short glass, Bran set the bottle down, stepped over to lay a hand on Sasha's shoulder. She sat on a sofa with Bran's grandmother, who crisply laid out a tarot card spread.

"She'll be fine now," Brigid said as Sasha jolted to her feet, even as Sasha's breath caught and her eyes filled.

"There she is!" Sawyer laid the cue down, used one hand on the back of a chair to hurtle over it. He grabbed Riley's face in his hands, kissed her hard and noisily. "Yeah, there you are."

"Put me down somewhere." Riley punched Doyle lightly on the shoulder. "You're making it a thing."

"It *is* a thing. Here, give her to me." Sawyer pulled Riley away from Doyle, spun in a circle. "Ladies and gentlemen, she's back!"

"Cut it out." As Riley laughed, Sasha burst into tears. "Oh, seriously, cut it out. Down," she muttered to Sawyer. "Down, down."

He carried her around the sofa, set her — gently — down.

"Sash—"

"Sorry. I'm sorry." Even as she swiped at her eyes, Sasha dropped down to kneel in front of Riley, grip her hands. "I'm so sorry."

"You didn't *do* anything. So stop. No, that's wrong. You did. You all did. So gratitude — extreme gratitude. Can I get something to eat? Pretty much anything."

"There's soup on the simmer." Brigid continued to lay the cards on the coffee table in front of her. "Sasha had a yearning to make chicken soup, and it's just the thing."

"I'll get it. Riley, I'm so happy," Annika said as she danced to the stove.

"I'm feeling pretty cheerful myself." Still holding Sasha's hands, Riley studied Brigid.

"You look just like her."

"I've seen our Sasha's sketches, and I do. But for a few decades."

"I think you saved my life. It's appreciated."

"You're more than welcome. Bran, are you going to give me that whiskey or let the glass sit half empty until the years pass?"

He poured a healthy four fingers, brought it to her. Kissed her on both cheeks. "My endless thanks, Móraí."

"My gracious welcome. You're pale yet," Brigid observed, studying Riley over her glass. "But clear of eye. Sasha?"

"Oh, I don't —"

"You do." Brigid dismissed the protest. "You know how to look, how to see. So see to your sister, and no whining about it."

Sasha took a breath — shaky — closed her brimming eyes. "There's still pain, but it's tolerable. There's still healing to be done, but it's progressing. She's hungry, and that's a good sign. She needs to eat, carefully for now, and rest another day or two."

"And the hand?" Brigid probed.

"Ah . . . Will hurt when the bandages come off — Bran treated them," she told Riley, "numbed the pain. But it's all healing well. The bandages should come off tomorrow." Sasha looked over at Brigid. "Is that right?"

"It is. You've so much more than you think. She knows better in the head," Brigid said to Riley, "but she blames herself in her heart."

"Then she's stupid. That's bullshit."

"Sure it is." Brigid stroked a hand down Sasha's hair. "But love is so often full of bullshit, isn't it?"

"Here's food!" Bright as the sun, Annika brought over a tray. "Sasha made soup with chicken and noodles and vegetables, and Móraí made brown bread."

"You sang to me," Riley said as Annika set down the tray.

"You heard me? Móraí said you would hear in your heart if we talked or sang, and we should lie with you, stay close."

"I heard." She turned to Sawyer. "Terry Pratchett."

"I found *Night Watch* in your stash. It looked like you'd read it a million times."

"Close enough." Riley spooned up some soup. It slid into her like glory. "Oh, my God."

"Slowly," Brigid warned. "Else you'll sick it up."

"Give me a minute here, then we can do a roundup, but I feel like I haven't eaten in weeks." Riley spooned up more, tried to go slow. "You sent for reinforcements," she said to Bran.

"I didn't know enough. We were losing you."

"I've seen dead men on the battlefield with more life than you had." At the bar, Doyle poured himself a whiskey.

"Way to ease into it," Sawyer muttered.

"Straight up's better." Riley ate another spoonful, sat back. "You're right. Slower's better. It was Malmon."

"You're sure?" Bran demanded.

"Pretty damn sure. I went outside — it's a little scattered yet — but I went outside. I needed a break, was going to take a walk. I saw the car. I hadn't heard Doyle and the others come back, but I saw the car. I saw the supplies, so I started to go over, grab some. Help out. And Sasha —"

She broke off when Sasha sat back on her heels, wrapped her arms around herself.

"Not you, okay? He made himself look like you. Or Nerezza made him look like you."

"If I'd come out again, it might have been Bran, or Sasha, or you," Doyle said with a nod to Riley as he leaned against the bar. "The illusion tailored for circumstance."

"Yes." Grateful for the clarification, Riley

took a careful nibble of bread. "I think . . . I think if I'd just headed into the forest as I'd meant to, he'd have been waiting for me inside. As Sasha, or any of you. But I detoured, started for the car, so he had to lure me in. He said he'd found something I needed to see. I didn't hesitate, why would I? I went right in. Carvings, something about carvings. On a tree?"

The memories wavered, caused her head to ache.

"Something like that. We walked, and went off the track. Oblivious, I was just oblivious, and he sucker-punched me. I fucking flew. Hit something. A rock, a tree. I felt things cracking and breaking inside me. My arm . . . wouldn't work. Couldn't get to my gun, or my knife. I couldn't fight back, just couldn't, and he was basically kicking the crap out of me. I thought I was finished. Done."

"Sasha called us." Annika brought Riley a mug of tea. "She ran in, said to hurry. Doyle said you needed us, so we all ran out, as fast as we could. But . . ."

"He was gone when we got there," Sawyer finished. "Doyle was there first. Doyle found you. Saw him. Malmon."

"He couldn't hold the illusion, or didn't want to." Doyle shrugged. "The illusion of

Sasha wavered, just for an instant. He wouldn't stand and fight. He ran."

"Doyle carried you home, and Bran got his magicks, and Sasha tried to heal you, to start, but it was so much she — what is it called?" Annika asked Sawyer.

"She passed out."

"I didn't — I didn't have enough," Sasha managed.

"Nor did I," Bran reminded her. "The extent of the injuries, how they were inflicted, and the poison that had already moved into you. Healing is not my specialty."

"It might have been." Brigid tapped a finger in the air. "But you had a bent for flashier. You're loved, *sí-mac tíre.*"

Irish for she-wolf, Riley translated, amused.

"Well loved, and valued. My boy here sent for me. And none too soon. You've a strong heart, spirit, body. It served you well. And so did I." Brigid lifted her glass, toasted, drank.

"Thank you, *máthair,* for my life."

Brigid nodded in approval. "You have respect. Eat. Bran, pour our girl here a half glass of wine."

"They wouldn't even let me have a beer when I got my ass kicked," Sawyer complained, and Brigid laughed.

"Sure, you should've called for me. A beer never hurt a fine, strapping man such as you."

"Next time. We shot a couple dozen ravens while you were out," Sawyer added.

"Ravens."

"Nerezza wanted to gloat, I'm thinking. But we gave her little to gloat about." Bran brought the wine. "Your color's better. I'm glad to see you, darling."

"Yeats," Riley remembered. "You read Yeats."

"It seemed apt. You need more sleep."

"I feel better."

"And sleep will be better yet."

"I'm not —"

"Sleep now." Brigid merely tapped Riley's shoulder. Riley dropped off. "Carry her back up, Doyle, there's a good lad." Brigid stroked a hand over Riley's hair, smiled and nodded. "She'll do. She'll do well enough now."

The sun streamed when Riley woke again, and a sweet breeze scented of flowers and forest wafted in the open doors of her balcony.

For a moment all the rest seemed like some ugly dream until she shifted to sit up, felt that wave of weakness that came from a hard illness or injury.

And Sasha stepped in from the balcony.

"Wait." Immediately Sasha hurried over to pile pillows behind Riley's back. "Take it slow. God, you look better. You look so much better."

"If you tell me I slept another five days, I'm going to belt you."

"Not even one. A little more than half of one." Voice cheerful, Sasha mixed something from a vial with something from a bottle into a glass.

Riley's eyes narrowed in suspicion. "What is that?"

"A restorative. Brigid said you were clear for it when you woke naturally."

Now Riley eyed the glass with more interest. "Like the one Bran made for Sawyer?"

"Brigid tamed it down."

"Spoilsport." But Riley took it, drank it. "How long does it take to — Okay." The dragging hangover from long sleep faded off, and at last — at last — her head felt clear. "I'd like a few samples of that for the next time I go on a tequila binge."

"Riley."

"Don't start again, Sash. I may have been half off last night, but I remember enough. This isn't on you."

"I need to get it out." Sasha eased onto the side of the bed. "Do me a favor, okay? Let me."

"Okay, but if you wander off into stupid-ville, I'm cutting you off."

"I know it could have been anyone who walked out of the house alone — that it was random and opportunistic."

"So far, you're in the right lane."

"But it was you. I know any one of us could have been used as a false face to draw you away from the house, into the woods. But it was me. It horrifies me, and it enrages me to know you have an image of me attacking you, hurting you, almost killing you. Switch places for a minute, and tell me it wouldn't do the same to you."

Grateful her mind was clear, Riley took a moment to organize her thoughts — and feelings with them. "I thought it *was* you. When you called me, when I went with you. I thought it was you when you knocked me like a sledgehammer into what felt like a concrete wall. I thought it was you," she repeated even as Sasha's lips trembled. "And you'd been possessed, taken over by Nerezza. My bell had been rung, and hard, and right then, lying there, looking at you, I thought she'd gotten into you somehow. I tried for my gun — I remember that — I remember if my arm hadn't been useless and I could have, I'd have shot you. I'd have tried to hit you in the leg, but I'd have shot you, thinking it was you."

"Defending yourself against —"

"It horrifies me, and it enrages me to know I'd have shot you. We're both going to have to get over the horror and the rage, Sash. That's it. Move it away, or they've won this round."

"I want the rage." And it burned in the blue of Sasha's eyes. "I want to give her pain, and misery, and horror for making you think, even for an instant, I'd hurt you. For making you have to choose, even for an instant, to hurt me."

"Okay." Riley nodded. "Rage is good. We'll keep it. But we're square, you and me."

"We're square."

"Excellent. I have to get up."

"You still need rest."

"I really have to pee. I mean seriously pee."

"I'll help you."

"Let me just try to get up on my own. I feel reasonably okay."

She managed it. A little wobbly maybe, Riley considered, but the room stayed steady and her vision didn't waver. "So far, so good. It's not about modesty — I don't have that much at the best of times — but I'm going to try to empty my now desperate bladder by myself. Stand by."

She didn't bolt to the adjoining bathroom, but moved briskly, and felt grateful she could. But no amount of gratitude could match what she felt when that desperate bladder emptied.

"Success! Could a hot shower be next?" She stepped out first, held out her bandaged hand. "How about taking this off first?"

"Let me get Bran or Brigid."

"Why?"

"They're so much more experienced."

Riley just lifted her eyebrows. "I'm on my feet. I'm lucid. I pick my own healer. Take it off for me, check it out."

Understanding — the creature with her face had mangled the hand; the woman, the friend, would judge its health — Sasha unwound the treated bandage.

"Hold it still," Sasha soothed as she cupped Riley's hand between hers. "It feels . . . clean. Sore, stiff, but clean. You can wiggle your fingers."

Feeling them, watching them move brought Riley such intense relief she nearly couldn't speak. When she did, her voice shook. "I was afraid I'd lose use of it, or at least some use of it."

She made a fist, opened it, closed it. "Sore, yeah. Maybe one and a half on a scale of ten." Emboldened, she rolled her right shoulder, flexed her biceps, tested range of motion. "Maybe two on the scale, but that'll ease up with use."

For the major test, she walked to the cheval glass. Hollow-eyed, gaunt, she thought. Weak. "Jesus, I look puny."

"Other than the soup last night, you haven't had a solid meal in nearly a week."

"I'll make up for that. Any of it left? The soup?"

"Yes."

"I want that — after a shower, real clothes."

"I'll stand by."

The shower ranked as miraculous, as did being able to use her hands, her arms with minimal discomfort. As she dressed, she noticed Sasha's easel on the balcony, and the painting in progress of the forest.

"I was angry with the forest, too," Sasha told her. "Ridiculous really, but that's how I felt. I thought painting it would exorcise that, and it's helped. Seeing you on your feet finishes it."

"Wait until you see me eat. While I do maybe you can fill me in on what's been happening while I was out of it."

"Bran's made real progress on the shield he's creating. Doyle's been cracking the whip when he hasn't been at the books."

The idea of Doyle researching without prodding had Riley stopping short. "At the books?"

"Translating mostly. Some passages in Greek, others in Irish or Latin on the stars, and the island. No definitive answers yet there."

As they came down the back steps, Sawyer walked in from the mudroom. "Hey! I was just going to head up to check. Look at you!"

"Don't look too close," Riley advised, but he wrapped his arms around her in a hug. "Aw, you missed me."

"Did. Nobody around here wants to discuss the details, small and large, of the cinematic pastiche that is *A New Hope.*"

"You've really suffered."

"Tell me." Though he was subtle about it, he kept an arm around Riley's waist to walk her to the table. "But you're looking for food."

"Damn skippy."

"I've got this," he told Sasha. "Bran's still out with Doyle at target practice. Annika's out there with Brigid — Brigid's teaching her to knit," he told Riley as he took the container of soup out of the fridge.

"Knit?"

"Yeah, they've bonded over yarns. Anyway, they'd like to know the prodigal's returned."

"I'll go out." Sasha took a last glance at Riley, went out.

Curious, Riley sat back. "Okay, you got rid of her."

"Just wanted you to know she's worried you'll look at her different."

"Don't, won't, and we settled all that."

"Knew you would." While the soup heated, he cut her a generous slab of bread, deftly sliced up an apple, cubed some cheese. "Appetizer."

"Thanks. Missed you, too. I guess the search for the star's been on hold."

"Not altogether. We talked about maybe diving, since Brigid was here for you, but it didn't make sense — and didn't feel right. It needs to be all six of us, so we tabled that. Unanimously. Doyle and I mapped out some areas on land. Annika says he's a little bit stuck on you."

"What sort of areas . . . What? *What?*"

Obviously amused by her reaction, Sawyer smirked. "Could be because Sasha gave her *Pride and Prejudice* to read to you. Annika thinks Doyle's like Mr. Darcy."

"Oh, please."

"What I said." He jabbed a finger in the air. "She's romantic. Bonus for me. Still, Doyle's been pretty messed up about what happened to you. We all have been, but . . ."

He glanced at the door — just in case — as he ladled soup into a bowl. "I guess I noticed some myself. We had to hold you down." Blowing out a breath, Sawyer set the soup in front of Riley. "Don't like going back there. Seriously horrible, every level. But we had to hold you down while Bran and Sasha worked on you, when we got you back upstairs. I was pretty focused on you — had your legs. Doyle's behind you on the bed, propping you up so Bran could get some potion into you, holding your shoulders."

"I don't remember . . . exactly. It's all jumbled."

"That's probably a good thing. Leave it jumbled. Anyway, he looked rough. He doesn't let a lot show, you know? But he looked rough. I guess we all did. I didn't think much of it until Annika started with Darcy and all that, but Doyle, he kept talking to you — mostly in Irish and low, so I don't know what he said, but it was the *way*. Just speculation, take it for what it's worth. I just figured you'd want to know."

"Anni's rubbing off on you."

"Every chance I get."

Laughing, Riley dismissed it, applied herself to the soup. "You know what I said to you when you were brooding and sulking about being weak and hurt?"

"I wasn't sulking." And Sawyer sulked a little at the idea. "Maybe brooding, marginally."

"Just throw it back in my face if I do the same."

"Consider it done."

"How close was I to buying it? Don't hold back."

He gave her a long study first, gray eyes assessing. "You were pocketing the receipt, telling dead relatives calling to you from the light to keep the change."

Nodding, she ate. "Then I won't brood and sulk much, because hey, alive."

"A fine attitude," Brigid said as she came in with Annika. "It will serve you well. Let's have a look." Stepping around the table, Brigid took Riley's chin in one hand, laid the other on top of her head. "Clear-minded, a bit weak, a bit sore. You'll tire more quickly than you'd like for another day or so. Rest and the restorative will help there. The soreness will pass, as will the weakness. Red meat for you tonight, girl."

"And my gratitude knows no bounds."

"Can she have the biscuits? Móraí showed me how to make them. They're very good."

"A couple of sugar biscuits never hurt a soul, and some tea with it, my angel," Brigid added. "With two drops only from the vial. You're a sweet boy, Sawyer King, and a brave one. You nearly deserve her."

"I'm working on it."

As the others came in, Riley tried to block out Sawyer's speculations, return Doyle's gaze casually. It helped when Bran walked to her, repeated his grandmother's gesture. "Nearly back altogether. I'd say rare steak for you tonight."

"Already got that bulletin."

"We're having tea and biscuits," Annika announced.

"And I'm all about both. Sasha caught me up a little on what's been going on the last few days. She said you'd made progress."

Bran sat, stretched out his legs. "We'll be ready for her should she come at us as Sasha foretold. We may have lost diving time, but it's given me more time for my own work. And Doyle and Sawyer made use of that time scouting out the land hereabouts."

"A few possibilities we should check out," Sawyer added. "Annika found a couple more caves farther up the coast, so there's that."

Riley picked up one of the cookies from the tray Annika put on the table. "I hear you've been librarian," she said to Doyle.

"I haven't found more than bits and pieces, and nothing that adds to the whole. You're welcome to the position now that you're back on your feet."

Riley sampled the cookie, found it excellent. "Doesn't anyone think it's odd we haven't been attacked while we were a man down?"

"The ravens came," Annika said, still busy with the tea.

"More ravens — you said something last night. I'm vague on it."

"They hit two days after you were attacked." Doyle remained standing. "Shortly after dawn. The day after, we didn't go out."

"Bran sent for Mórai." Annika set the pot on the table. "You were hurt so much, and we needed to help you, so we didn't have calisthenics or training."

"But when you did, she sent ravens?"

"A couple dozen." Doyle glanced out the window, as if checking for more. "More nuisance than attack."

"She's weak."

Attention turned to Sasha.

"Don't be afraid of it," Brigid murmured.

"I'm not. Only that she'll find a way to use me. But I can feel . . . she's weak. Growing stronger, but . . . Ah. Transforming Malmon, the illusion to disguise the creature, it took all she had. He failed. Even with all she gave him, he failed. She wants to bleed him. But she needs him. He feeds her; he serves her. He loves beyond reason. He has no reason. She is all. And the Globe of All . . . Wait, wait."

Sasha held out both hands, palms out. "She drinks a bloody brew. It sustains her. And the Globe of All is murky, clears only for moments, and at such a cost. She sees the house on the cliff, and what was before. Oh, if she had destroyed what came before, there would be no now. There would be no guardians. Why did he not *finish* the woman, the wolf? Take one, take all. Why did he not finish before the immortal came? Bring me her dying body, bring me her blood. The blood of the wolf, the blood of a guardian. Their blood, my blood. I will gorge on it, and take the stars into the dark."

Letting out air, Sasha sat.

"A drop in Sasha's tea as well, darling," Brigid told Annika.

"I'm all right. She felt me, and she pushed back, but she's still too weak. He —

240

Malmon — wasn't meant to kill you, just nearly, and bring you back to her. You or whoever he was able to get to. To drain you, to bring her back to full strength — to restore her youth as well as her power. To keep you alive, draining you slowly. Blood of the living is more powerful than blood of the dead."

"So it has always been in such matters." Brigid picked up her tea. "Nasty business."

"Almost enough to put me off this cookie." Deliberately Riley bit into it.

"It's the first I've been able to get past her defenses since you were hurt. I don't know if that means I've been too distracted or if we just needed you back. Either way." As deliberately as Riley, Sasha chose a cookie, bit in. "We're back now."

"We're back," Riley agreed. "Now let's fuck her up. Sorry," she said to Brigid.

"It's a sentiment I'm behind altogether. I'll be on my way in the morning and leave you to it."

"Oh, don't go, Móraí." Annika wrapped her arms around Brigid from behind.

"I'll come back when you're done with this, and I expect you all to find a way to visit me and mine. But I want my own bed, and my man. More?" She patted Annika's hand as she looked into her grandson's eyes.

241

"This is for you. For the six of you. All I am will be with you. Drink your tea," she told Riley. "And have one of this lot go out with you for a bit of a walk. It'll do you good."

"Yes, ma'am."

"Móraí," Brigid corrected. "For I'm yours as well."

"Móraí." *Grandmother,* Riley thought, and drank her tea.

CHAPTER ELEVEN

As was his habit, Doyle took a last patrol after midnight. A soft rain fell, obscuring the waning moon, turning the world into a dark, quiet mist. It cushioned the slap of the sea so that its steady beat became the pulse of the world.

At his back, the house stood behind the thin curtain of rain with lights shimmering through here and there to give it life.

Though his route around the house had become routine, he remained alert and ready. And when he saw the hooded figure standing among the gravestones, his sword leaped into his hand.

Not Nerezza, he thought as he moved closer, silent as a cat. Too slight for that. For a moment, he thought: Riley, and his temper spiked at the idea of her standing in the rain when she'd barely gained her feet.

But the figure turned. His first jolting thought was: Ma.

The spirit of his mother rising out of the mist. To comfort? To torment? At times one felt the same as the other.

Then she spoke, and he knew her for flesh and blood.

"You move like the air," Brigid commented. "But your thoughts are a shout."

"I took you for Riley, and more than my thoughts would have shouted. You shouldn't be out here either, in the rain and the dark."

Rain beaded on her hood, forming a dark, wet frame for a face of strength and enduring beauty.

"I'm an Irishwoman, so rain doesn't trouble me. And what witch is worried about the dark? The sweet girl leaves tributes for your dead."

Doyle glanced down. Annika had added shells to the stones, brought fresh flowers. "I know."

"They live on in you, and in the others as well. In me and in mine. You favor my uncle — my father's brother, Ned. A rebel he was, and died fighting. I've seen pictures of him when he was your age."

"I'm more than three hundred years old."

Brigid let out a hooting laugh. "You hold up well, don't you? From what I know of Ned, he lacked your discipline, though he believed in his cause, gave his life for it. I've tried to see if your lives will be given, and I can't. I don't have the power that Sasha holds."

Seeing his surprise, she smiled. "Myself? I'm for the science of magicks. I like to think Bran took that from me. And I'm for healing. The cards can guide me to some answers, but Sasha is the most powerful seer I've known in my long life, and she's yet to tap the whole of her powers. And you, my boy, I know only that you won't reach the whole of your own until you break down the borders you've put up yourself."

"I don't have powers."

Brigid ticked her finger in the misty air. "There you are, that's one of your borders. Each of you has what you were given, willing or not. I've loved a man more than a half century. That may not be such a thing for one of your great age, but it's no small business. I've borne children, known the joys and sorrows, the frustrations and delights, the pride and the disappointments children bring with them into a mother's world. I can tell you, standing here on this holy ground, you gave your mother all of that, and it's all a woman asks from a son."

"I wasn't her only son."

"And evil took him, your young brother. She took that grief to her grave. But not for

245

you, boy. Not for you." She lifted her chin toward the house, smiled. "Your wolf is restless."

He glanced back, saw the light had come on in Riley's room. "She's not my wolf."

Brigid only sighed. "One who's lived as long as you shouldn't be so boneheaded. But that's a man, I suppose, be he twenty or two hundred and twenty. I wish you a good journey, Doyle, son of Cleary, and happiness along your way. Good night."

"Good night." He watched her go, saw her safely into the house.

Then continued his rounds. Before he went inside for the night, he saw Riley's room was dark again, and hoped she slept.

Riley rose at dawn, determined to get back to routine, to push herself through training. When she stepped outside, she aimed I-dare-you looks at the others.

Maybe basic stretching brought on some pings and twinges, but she assured herself her muscles thanked her. And maybe shuffles, squats, lunges had her heart laboring, and those muscles quivering, but she gritted her way through them.

And through nearly a dozen push-ups before those quivering muscles simply gave up and sent her face-first into the damp grass.

"Take a break," Sasha began.

"Don't baby me." Hissing out a breath, Riley struggled back to plank position. She lowered halfway down, and sloppily, when she felt her arms giving up again.

She cursed when Doyle shot a hand under her hoodie, grabbed her belt and pumped her up and down. When he dropped her — not too gently — she shoved up to her hands and knees, ready to snarl and bite.

Sawyer crouched in front of her, poked a finger between her sulky eyebrows. "Do I have to give you The Talk?"

For one soaring moment, she wanted to punch him. Then her anger deflated as completely as her biceps. "No. Tantrum avoided."

"You did more than anyone in your point of recovery has a right to," Sasha pointed out. "It sort of pisses me off."

"Okay, that's something."

"Three-mile run," Doyle announced.

"We do five," Riley countered.

"Today it's three."

"I can do five."

"Bollocks. And pushing it to five only means you'll be in worse shape tomorrow. Three, and we pace you."

She started to bitch, caught Sawyer's arch look, decided she really didn't want her own words shoved in her face. She got to her feet.

"How about this? The five of you run the usual. I'll use the machine in the gym, keep it to three miles. I'll only slow you down."

"I can stay with Riley," Annika said.

"No need for that. I'll be in the house, in the gym. Treadmill, three miles." Riley crossed a finger over her heart.

"Done. Let's move," Doyle ordered.

She hated that he was right, already knew she could only manage five miles if she'd limped or crawled through it. Better to keep it to three, moderate pace, and try for more next time.

She barely made the three, even with music to distract her.

Dripping sweat, she sat on a bench, guzzled water. She made herself stretch, consoled herself she already had her breath back.

And eyed the weight rack.

She hadn't promised not to lift.

She picked up a pair of twenty-pound weights, set, began a set of curls.

"Take it down to ten," Doyle said from the doorway.

"I can do twenty."

"And you'll strain muscles instead of building them back up."

Sheer stubbornness had her doing another rep before she racked them, picked up the tens. "You're right." She reset her position for triceps kickbacks. "I don't need a spotter."

"A keeper's more like it. You're too smart for this, Gwin. You know you'll set recovery back by overdoing."

"I won't overdo, but I need to work it some. I've never really been sick, not seriously. A couple of days, stomach bug, a cold, whatever. Hungover, sure. But I bounce back. I need to bounce back."

Saying nothing, he walked to the rack, took a fifty. He sat, smoothly curled.

"Show-off."

She switched to shoulder raises, moved to chest curls, onto flies, found a simpatico rhythm with him working nearby.

"That covers it," Doyle announced when she finished a second set.

She'd have argued, for form, but a third set was beyond her. "I just want to do one set of bench presses. One set. I'm a little sore, but it's a good sore. You know what I mean."

He walked to the bench. "One set."

She replaced the free weights, swiped her

face with a towel, then crossed over to lie down. "I won't say I don't need a spotter, because I'm not an idiot."

He set the weights, nodded. "I've got you."

Something tapped at her memory at his words, stirred something, then slipped away. Riley focused, fixed her grip. "Okay, I felt that," she muttered as she pressed one. "One set of three. That's all I've got."

And the third rep was shaky, but gave her a lift of satisfaction.

"Okay. Okay, that's it. That's good enough." It wasn't until she sat up she noticed the weights. "You cut it down to ninety."

"I'm impressed you could manage that. Day after tomorrow you can try for a hundred. Stretch it out."

She decided ninety wasn't mortifying given the circumstances. And besides, she felt good, accomplished, healthily fatigued rather than exhausted.

"I'm bouncing."

"According to Bran's grandmother, the wolf accelerates your recovery time."

"Probably. Like I said, I've never been down like that before."

She stretched, and so did he. When he did, she noted, everything rippled and bulged and sleeked out in exactly the right way.

She had to give it to him, the man was shredded.

What if he did have a kind of a little thing going for her? She had her own lusty — perfectly normal — thoughts in his direction.

They'd even managed a gym session without busting each other's balls. It followed, logically, another form of healthy exercise — mutual — might just cap it all off.

"We could have sex."

He had his left arm across his chest, cradled in the crook of his right for the stretch. And moved only his head in her direction. "What?"

"It's not like it hasn't occurred to you." She went for another bottle of water, then studied him as she would a potential bootie buddy.

Sweaty, as she was, the mass of dark hair curling a little from the damp. Green eyes watched her suspiciously out of a face with hard planes and angles.

And the body? Well, Jesus, what woman wouldn't want to play with that?

"I'm single, you're single. I'm here, you're here." As she spoke, she wagged a finger toward him, toward herself. "We've already had a lip-lock that wasn't half bad."

"Half bad."

"I'm good at it. I'm just saying." She swigged water. "Or so I'm told. I'm betting you're pretty good at it, too. Straight sex, Doyle, which I haven't had for eight months and five days."

"That's very specific."

"I was on a project in Brittany, ran into an old friend, scratched an itch. My record for a dry spell is eight months, twenty-three days. I'd hate to set a new one, frankly."

"You want me to help you keep your current record intact?"

She shrugged. It didn't trouble her he'd continued to stretch, continued to watch her. If you couldn't be straightforward about sex, what was the point in being an adult?

"Unless I'm reading you wrong — doubtful but possible — you could use a roll the same as me. It also occurred to me we're going to be right back in the bloody thick of it anytime. I don't want to go down without getting laid if I can help it. So I'm saying you could scratch my itch, I could scratch yours. No frills, no worries."

She capped the bottle. "Think about it. If it doesn't work for you, no problem."

She got halfway to the door when he gripped her arm, spun her around. "People spend too much time thinking about sex."

"Well, it's an endlessly fascinating and diverse activity."

He fisted a hand in her shirt, hauled her to her toes. "Thinking and talking about sex means you're not having it."

"There's a point of agreement."

Both amused and aroused, she sprang off her toes, jumping lightly to hook her legs around his waist. "So? Want to think and talk some more?"

"No."

He took her mouth, that clever mouth that talked entirely too much. She tasted of cool water and hot salt, and the sound she made wasn't words — thank Christ — but transmitted pure pleasure.

Her body, warm, limber, damp, pressed against him as he gripped her hips, as she gripped his hair.

Not enough, he thought. Not close to enough. They'd finish this, start and finish what had been wound tight inside him for far too long.

He turned with the single idea of carting her to his room.

And Sasha stepped in. "Oh. Oh, I'm *sorry!* I'm — Oh, God."

Before a vibrating Riley could react, Doyle dropped her to her feet. "I'd say breakfast is ready. You need to eat," he said to Riley, and walked out.

"Riley. God, Riley, could I have timed that any worse?"

"Well, we could've been naked." She waved a hand in the air. "It's okay. Shouldn't have started that in a public area, so to speak. You know, I think I'm just going to sit down for a second."

Which she did, right on the floor.

"I didn't know — I mean I knew." Babbling, Sasha came to sit beside her. "But I didn't know. I just came in to tell you we're about to eat, and . . . I should've *known*. I felt — I thought you were working out, like . . . pumped up."

Now Riley lowered her head into her hands and laughed. "We did, we were. We will again, absolutely. No way we're leaving this undone. I am officially both shaken and stirred, and by God, I'm gulping down that martini."

"What?"

"Popular culture reference. Don't worry about it." She patted Sasha's shoulder. "I definitely need to eat. I'm going to need to be in top form for the next rounds."

She stood, offered a hand to Sasha. "What's for breakfast?"

■ ■ ■ ■

She ate like a wolf. Along with the others, she said her good-byes to Brigid, then took herself off for some time in the library before weapons training.

Doyle didn't join her, which she didn't find surprising. He'd know as well as she did with the unfinished business between them they'd be rolling around naked on the floor inside ten minutes once they were alone behind closed doors.

She'd wait, he'd wait. They'd wait. If he didn't come to her room that night, she'd go to his.

Situation settled.

Anticipation gave her an edge, one she used as she selected books, opened her own notebook.

In it she puzzled over Doyle's notes. Apparently a few centuries of practice hadn't given him clear and legible handwriting.

Look to the past to find the future.
It waits in the dark, cold and still.
Blood of the blood frees it. And so the ice
    will burn bright
as a sun.

She read his notes again, read others. At

least he'd marked down the books and the pages so she could verify.

As she worked, she frowned over some of his translations, wrote down questions and her own interpretations.

When she needed it, she bolstered herself with a ten-minute nap, made more coffee, dug deeper.

"See the name, read the name," she muttered as she read. "Speak the name. What name?"

As she read on, Annika burst into the room. "Sasha says something is coming. To hurry."

Riley leaped up, left the question unanswered.

By the time she got downstairs, ran out, the others were armed and waiting.

"From the sea." Sasha gestured. "It's not her — she's not ready — but she's sending plenty. A dark cloud. I see a dark sweep of cloud, blocking the sun."

"We can take the towers. Me and Sawyer."

"Not this time." Doyle searched the pale blue sky, the stacks of white and gray clouds. "We save that tactic for when she comes full force. This is a test run." He gestured with the sword in his hands. "There, due west."

They came, swirling into a funnel that

spun the clouds, darkened them. Until they became the clouds, black and alive. They spun, a kind of whip and wave inking the pale blue to midnight.

"Impressive." Sawyer drew both his side-arms. "But what's the point?"

At his words that whip cracked, a sonic boom that shook the ground, and smothered the sun.

"That's the point," he said when the world fell into dark, absolute. "Can't hit what we can't see. Bran?"

Then came the thunder of wings, the cyclone of wind. Bran struck against the dark, turned the black into a murky, green-tinged gray.

"That'll do." Riley fired with her right, gripped her combat knife in her left. Red-eyed ravens, long-toothed bats with over-sized heads and twisted bodies.

Their wings, she knew, would slice like razors if they met flesh.

But the bullets Bran had enchanted hit home. Nerezza's winged army flashed in fire, fell in a rain of bloody ash. To her left, Annika shot light from her bracelets, pounded into a handspring, and shot again. Sasha's bolts flew, accurate and deadly, while Bran burned a swath with twin lances of blue lightning.

And all the while, even over the scream of wind, she heard Doyle's sword sing and strike, the brutal music of the battlefield.

Were they slower than before? she wondered. A multitude, no question, and even with skill, they'd be overcome without Bran's powers. And still, she'd nearly misjudged a couple of targets, moving more sluggishly than others.

She dived and rolled to avoid an attack, reloading as she moved, firing from the ground. She sprang up, punching out with her knife as one veered close. Then the wind gripped her like a hand, tossed her up and back. Her body, not quite healed, knew fresh pain.

Winded, she fired again, fought her way to a crouch. Her blood froze when a swarm within the swarm peeled off, arrowed toward her. Not enough bullets, she thought, but made what she had count.

She rolled, slowed to a crawl by the force of the wind. She felt the bite of a wing graze her calf, another bite into her shoulder as she kicked and slashed.

Dozens fell around her as her comrades destroyed them, and still they came.

She fired again, stabbed one before it could slice wing and talon over her face. Three coalesced, eyes bright and mad, lancing toward her as she struggled to reload.

Doyle's sword sliced through them, cleaved and struck as he shoved through that crazed wind. With one hand he reached down, gripped her by the neck of her sweatshirt, and dragged her behind him.

"Stay down!"

She didn't believe in staying down. Using his body as a windbreak, she pushed up, reloaded. She stood with him, back-to-back, half mad herself as she peppered the air with bullets.

Annika leaped through, bracelets flashing, then Sawyer, then Sasha.

"Bran?" Riley shouted.

"He said to get here, stay here," Sasha shouted back, sent a bolt through one creature that continued through another. "And he'd —"

For an instant, the light blinded. It carried a flood of heat, a burn of power that scorched the air. What died didn't have the chance to scream.

Overhead the sky bloomed blue again.

Shaken more than she liked, Riley bent over, braced her hands on her thighs as she caught her breath.

"You're hurt." Annika hugged arms around her.

"No. Just a couple of nicks."

Though it did no good, she protested when Doyle yanked her sweatshirt off her shoulder, studied the wound. "A graze."

"Like I said." She jerked the shirt back in place.

"They swarmed you." Sasha lowered her bow, looked back as Bran strode toward them. "I didn't realize it until it was nearly too late."

"Quantity over quality, that's what I was thinking." Sawyer swiped a splatter of blood from his cheek. "Enough to keep us busy, but on the weak side."

"Yeah." Riley nodded. "I thought the same. Then the wind picked me up, tossed me — like getting slapped by a tornado. A couple hundred of them banked toward me." She snarled out a breath. "She knew I'd been hurt, figured I was the weak sister. Well, fuck that."

"We were too far away to help." Annika rubbed Riley's arm. "If Doyle hadn't been closer, if he hadn't . . ."

Realizing she still held her gun in an iron grip, Riley made herself holster it, look at him. "Yeah. Thanks for the assist."

"All in a day's."

His eyes said something different, she thought, something not so cool and dismissive. She kept hers locked with his as Bran checked her shoulder.

She heard him speak, didn't register the words. He and the others might have stepped into another world. Hers raced, pumped with adrenaline and lust.

Doyle gripped her arm, said, "Now."

She sheathed her knife. "Now."

She moved with him toward the house. Apparently she didn't move fast enough to suit him, as he plucked her off the ground. Since that was fine with her, she wrapped her legs around his waist, dragged his head down to hers.

"Oh." Delighted, Annika hugged her arms. "They're going to have very good sex."

Sasha watched Doyle carry Riley up the terrace steps. "Shouldn't we treat her wounds before . . ."

Bran simply took her hand. "She'll be fine for now. Let's get cleaned up, have a beer, and let them . . . tend each other for the moment."

"Clean up. Good idea." Sawyer grabbed Annika's hand.

"Oh, we're going to have sex, too."

Laughing, Bran wrapped his arms around Sasha. "Sounds brilliant," he said, and winked her straight up to bed.

Doyle ignored the bed. The minute he

kicked the terrace door closed, he spun around, slapped Riley's back to the wall.

"No frills, you said."

"Not necessary." She took his mouth again, added a testing bite as she fought to remove his sword and sheath.

She wanted flesh, the scent, the taste, the *feel* of it, and let the sheath fall with a thud so she could drag off his shirt and find it.

He'd already found her, his hands streaking under her sweatshirt to close around her breasts. Big, rough hands — exactly what she was after.

But more, more, she wanted *penetration.* Wanted invasion, hot and hard. The unspeakable thrill of life after near death.

He had grazes and nicks of his own. Together they smelled of war — of blood and sweat and battle.

Impatient, he didn't pull her shirt off, but hooked his fingers where it was torn and ripped it — or most of it — away. The violence of the act, the rending, pumped through her blood, had her fighting with his belt as he dragged at hers.

Need growled in her throat, tied quivering knots in her belly.

He yanked her jeans over her hips, and then — thank God then — drove ferociously into her.

A pause, a beat, a breath. Absorbing the shock, the *glory,* and once again her eyes met his.

Held his while her breath tore through her lungs, while he plundered. She came in a torrent, release, blessed release, then fisted her hands in that thick hair, let him whip her up again while she pumped against him to take him in turn.

When it struck her again, the hot lash of a whip, she felt his body shudder as he fell with her.

CHAPTER TWELVE

She didn't have to hold on. She was trapped between his body and the wall, still suspended off the floor. But she held on anyway. After a flight like that, she wasn't at all sure she wouldn't just spin off like a dust mote.

The fast and the furious, she thought, more than pleased. And a job damn well done. The fact that he was winded added an extra layer of satisfaction.

She took pride in her work, after all.

Since she was holding on for a bit longer, she explored the muscles of his back. Speed had eliminated some of the finer details. And he had a really exceptional back. A really fine chest, too, which was currently pressed hard — a rippling steel door — against hers.

In fact, on a strictly physical level, she'd never seen a finer specimen, much less had one. Bonus points, she decided, and at last opened her eyes to find his on hers.

"Nice work, Sir Studly. Let me know when you want to put me down."

He managed to hold her in place and hitch his pants back up. Turning, still carrying her, he walked to the bed, dropped them both.

She let out an *oof.* The exceptional physical specimen had some weight to him.

"Sorry." He rolled off, lay flat on his back a moment. "No frills," he said again.

"Do I strike you as the frilly sort?"

"You don't, but there are certain details . . . I didn't think, wasn't thinking, about protection."

"Right. I've recently broken an over-eight-month fast. I'm clean. I assume the same goes."

"I'm immune to any sort of disease or disorder. There are other reasons for protection."

"I use LARC — long-acting reversible contraception. Not to worry."

"Good."

She looked down at herself, and the tattered remains of her shirt. "I liked this sweatshirt."

"It was ruined anyway. And you didn't complain at the time."

"At the time I was a little wound up, and

ripping clothes adds to it. Just saying, I liked it."

Gone now, she thought, and pulled away what was left. "I'm going to want to borrow something until I can change. Not that everybody doesn't know what we just did, but I hold the line at flashing Sawyer or Bran."

"Borrow what you need." He rolled up to pull off his boots, glanced back over his shoulder. Turned the glance into a long study as she lay bare, with her jeans still caught around her knees.

"You lost some weight."

"I'll get it back."

"You will. You have a strong, agile body. Compact, efficient."

Amused, she fluttered her lashes. "Girls love to hear how efficient their bodies are."

"It's a compliment when it comes to war and warriors. I've wanted it. Wanted you."

"Same goes — except for the compact part. You're just ripped."

"I'm going to want you again."

"That works for me. In fact." She sat up to untie her high-tops. "Why don't we go another round after you have a little recovery time."

"I heal, and recover, quickly."

"Even better, so . . ." Her eyebrows shot

up as he stood to remove his pants. "Oh, well. Hello." Laughing, she tossed her shoes to the floor. "I bet that's a benefit to immortality you don't brood about."

"We'll see if you can handle it."

"Oh, I can handle it," she told him when he straddled her.

She handled it, and handled it again when they showered off sex and war. Not sure if she could handle a fourth bout, she grabbed one of his shirts, dashed over to her own room.

She changed, tossed his shirt over a chair to return later, then turned to the mirror to take stock.

To her own eye she looked about as relaxed as a woman could outside of a coma. And more than a little used up. In fact, she thought she could flop on the bed and sleep for hours — except she was starving.

Add to that, they all needed to talk about the battle before the bouts.

She tugged her fresh shirt away, studied her shoulder. Doyle had treated it and her leg with Bran's balm — and she'd done the same for his minor wounds. Since it already looked better, she gave it a little poke, felt no twinge.

Barely a scratch, she thought. A sky filled

with death, and barely a scratch.

They'd been weak. A test run, just as Doyle had said.

But the run had been focused on her, and that burned. Twice now she'd been a target. She intended to reap some payback before she was done.

She put on her belt — gun on one hip, knife on the other — and went down to find food, drink, and friends.

She found them all in the kitchen, hit the post-battle snack platter first, grabbed a deviled egg.

"Sasha made Bellinis!" Annika immediately poured one for Riley, who made approving noises over a cracker topped with salami and cheese. "Did you have good sex?"

"Yes, thanks." Riley sent Doyle — already sipping a beer — a wide, exaggerated smile.

"Sawyer and I had good sex, and so did Bran and Sasha. I think it's nice we're all having good sex now. Móraí said it's good for the body, the mind, and the spirit, especially on a quest."

Bran choked. "What? My grandmother?"

"She's very wise. I miss her. She taught me to knit. I'm making everyone scarves. When we're not together like this, they'll be like a hug."

Riley gave her a one-armed one. "Wherever you go, I'm coming to see you. Where's Sasha?"

"She wanted to finish something," Bran said. "She won't be long. Do you have pain?"

"Absolutely none. The couple of nicks are already healing. Let me just say, I know I'd have been in it deep if it wasn't for all of you. Not just because I wasn't a hundred percent — because I'd say I was closing in on ninety — but because she turned it on me, specifically. Even at a hundred, I couldn't have defended myself."

"She doesn't understand us, the unity of us." Bran gestured with his beer to encompass the room. "That we don't just fight together, don't just search together. We defend and protect each other, no matter the threat."

"We do." Carrying a canvas, Sasha walked in. "And we will. I wanted to finish this because, as we've said, symbols matter. This, I think, is a symbol of that unity. Of what we are, each of us, and what we are together."

She moved to the table, turned the canvas around, propped it against a vase of flowers cut that morning from the garden.

"A coat of arms," Sawyer said.

269

"Actually, it's an achievement, as it displays all the components, not just the armorials on the escutcheon, and . . ." Riley trailed off when she noted the puzzled looks — or in Doyle's case the cool stare.

"We'll just go with coat of arms." Riley lowered her glass, walked closer. "An amazing coat of arms."

"This is me, the mermaid." Annika linked her hand with Sasha's, squeezed, gestured to the painted woman with iridescent tail, with copper cuffs on both wrists, perched on a rock in a lapping sea. "And this stands for Sawyer."

The man had a gun on each hip, and the compass he held in an outstretched palm seemed to glow against a shimmering sky.

"And you, Riley!"

"Yeah, so I see."

Sasha had painted the image of a woman with her face thrown up to a full moon, her body a wolf.

"I told you I wanted to paint you transforming," Sasha reminded her. "This called for it."

"You captured it. I mean, I've never actually seen myself change — a little busy — but there's a joy to it you've captured. Got you, too, Doyle. All broody look, billowy coat, and the sword in your hand."

"It's not brooding. It's thoughtful. And there's herself," he added with a rare Irish idiom, "with crossbow and paintbrush, and eyes full of visions."

"And you." Sasha turned to Bran. "The sorcerer on the cliffside, riding the lightning."

"Each of us as individuals in the panels," Bran observed, "and here, under the crest, six together, standing together, as one."

"Dragons for the supporters," Doyle added.

"I liked the look of them." Sasha studied her work. "Wanted something strong and mystical."

"The three stars and the moon make the crest," Sawyer noted. "Bull's-eye, Sasha. What's it say? The, you know, motto. Is that Latin?"

"It says: *To seek the stars. To serve the light. To guard the worlds.*"

Sasha looked at Riley with relief. "I got the Latin right? I was afraid I'd bungle it — then I couldn't decide at first. Gaelic, Latin, Greek. But I kept coming back to the Latin, so I went with it."

"It's perfect."

"And beautiful," Annika added. "The colors are strong, because we are. And it has six sides, because we are six. Even the . . ." When she couldn't find the word, she traced the edge of the coat of arms.

"Border," Sawyer told her.

"Yes, the border. It's three strands of two — yes — braided together. Because we are. Can you make drawings — like the sketches — for us all?"

"I think I can do something else," Bran put in. "Leave it to me. This, *fáidh,* is magnificent, and it's powerful. Will you let me use it?"

"Of course."

"You took strangers and brought them together, for purpose, for family."

"I didn't —"

"Your vision," he interrupted. "And your courage. I think we'd have come together, we were meant to. But without you, not when and where we did. Or, I believe, how."

He turned to her and kissed her gently. "I had intended to do this when we were alone. Tonight, with candles and wine under a quiet moon. But I think now, here, together."

He reached in his pocket, took out a small white box with the symbol for eternity etched in silver on the top.

"Bran."

"Móraí gave this to me before she left this morning. I had thought to create one for you myself, but this was her grandmother's, created by her grandfather in love, in magick, in pledge. Will you take it, wear it, this symbol of always?"

"Yes. Of course, yes." She took his hand. "I love you."

When he opened the box, she gasped. The ring caught the light, showered the room with every color, before it shimmered into quiet, steady shine.

"It's beautiful. It's —"

Magnificent, elegant, the center stone a heart of pure white framed in tiny round diamonds that glistened like a rainbow.

"I give you this heart because you're mine."

"I'll wear it because you're mine. Oh, it fits. It fits."

"Magick," he said, drew her close, kissed her long.

"Okay, break it up. Let's get a good look." Riley snatched Sasha's left hand. "That's some rock. Nice," she told Bran.

"How's a guy supposed to follow that one?" Sawyer wondered, and gave Bran a light punch in the shoulder.

"I would like a ring from you. I'm so happy." Tearfully, Annika embraced Bran and Sasha in turn. "I have so much happy."

"It looks right on you."

Sasha smiled at Doyle. "Feels even better." Then she turned into Bran's arms. "I have so much happy, too. And it makes me feel strong." She drew away. "It makes me feel valiant. It makes me believe, more than ever, we'll do what it says on our crest. We'll seek the stars."

"And serve the light," Bran said.

"And guard the worlds," the others said together.

Riley stepped back, picked up her drink. "To do those three things means fighting, surviving, and destroying Nerezza. Not just her minions and whatever the hell Malmon's become."

"Agreed. Since we're all here now," Bran began, "why don't we sit down and talk about this last fight."

"Do that, but give me five." Sawyer pulled open a drawer for kitchen scissors. "I need some stuff out of the herb garden for this marinade. Didn't realize when I decided on rack of lamb we'd be celebrating an official engagement. We're going fancy tonight, boys and girls."

As he went out, Riley moved into the lounge area to sit. Propped her feet on the coffee table.

"I'm always up for a celebratory meal," she said, "but it seems particularly timely tonight."

Sasha sat beside her. "Really?"

Catching the subtext, Riley laughed. "Yeah, we're all having sex. Drop the confetti. What I mean was Sasha's got a ring, we've got a coat of arms and a kick-ass motto. Best, we're all alive."

"Barely scratched," Bran pointed out.

"They were slow and weak. Sawyer said —" Pausing, Annika glanced toward the door. "Should we wait to say — but he knows because he said. They were slow and weak."

"I wouldn't have thought so if it had been the first attack." As she drank, Sasha curled up her legs. "There were so many this time, more than we've had before. But without the — without the same ferocity. Except toward Riley."

"We should — Here he is," Annika said as Sawyer came in with a basket of herbs.

"Keep it going. I'm multitasking."

"All right. I want to say first, I didn't sense, not initially, their focus on Riley. And when I did . . ." Sasha laid a hand on Riley's outstretched leg, rubbed. "It was nearly too late."

"They — or Nerezza — figured I was off my game."

"You were," Doyle responded, mercilessly.

She wanted to bristle, made herself shrug. "Marginally. I'd like to see you take on a few hundred mutant birds from hell all determined to slice and peck you to death."

"He pretty much did." As he spoke, Sawyer continued to chop herbs. "The rest of us were too spread out."

"Okay, point, and again, thanks for the save."

"I'm not looking for thanks. You were off your game," Doyle repeated. "A soldier still fights. It's more to the point we *were* spread out. Nerezza may be off her game as well, but she had the tactics here. She pulled us away from each other, or more accurately, pulled us away from Riley, in hopes of eliminating the one she believed was most vulnerable."

"It came too close to working." In his chair, Bran studied his beer. "We can't forget to protect each other."

"We did. Not arguing about how close she came to turning this around," Sawyer continued. "But we did protect each other. And we won. She went for the shock and awe, right? Blocked out the freaking sun. And it worked — temporarily. Each one of us was so busy cutting them down we didn't have each other's backs. But then we did."

"I saw you fly," Annika murmured. "The

wind, it was alive. It wrapped around you, and threw you."

"Felt that way," Riley admitted. "It was like — not that I've had the experience — being sucked into a tornado."

"It threw you," Annika said again, "even more away from us. I saw you fall, and I was afraid. But I was even more very, very angry."

"I was a little pissed off myself. You came running. All of you. She doesn't have that in her bag of tactics. That all-for-one deal. And I'm feeling a hell of a lot better."

"She'll be feeling better, too," Sasha pointed out. "Whatever she sends next won't be as slow or weak."

"We work on positions." Doyle nodded when Sawyer pulled another beer out of the refrigerator, waggled it. "No one gets cut off, separated, or pulled away. They may have been slower, weaker, but we weren't sharp. Not sharp enough."

"If I'd sensed the intent, even five seconds sooner —"

"It's not all on you, Blondie," Doyle said. "We got flanked."

Since one of Sasha's sketch pads sat on the table, he picked it up, took one of her pencils. He drew quickly.

The structure, to Riley's eye, looked more

like a barn than Bran's house, but it made the point. So did the curved lines, the squiggles to represent garden paths, shrubs, trees, the cliff wall.

And as far as she could tell, he had everything in its place, and nearly to scale.

"We started here." He used first initials — and an SK for Sawyer — to note positions. "Annika shifted here, Bran here." Now he used dotted lines to note the change in positions, for each. And again until he laid them out when Riley had been tossed.

"How do you know where everyone moved, during the thick of it?" Sasha demanded.

"I know where my people are."

Studying the diagram, Riley leaned closer. "Impressive. And assuming this is accurate — and I do," she added before Doyle could snap at her — "it illustrates how easily she drew us apart. Bran — magick man — is the full length of the field from my position when I hit my ass. Whatever she thinks of the rest of us, she respects power, his power. Sawyer's closer, but again, pulled way back. Lowers the chances of him pulling out the compass, getting me out of there."

"Sasha is back against the wall above the sea."

"And facing away. I was facing away. That

was probably deliberate, too."

"I was closer, but . . ." Annika looked at Doyle. "She would think me stronger in the sea than on the land. Yes?"

"She'd be wrong, but yes."

"And you, here, closer than all but me. But still far. It helps to see it like this, like a picture. Can you draw what we should have done? The positions?"

Doyle smiled at her. "Yeah. The thing is, those positions have to be flexible. You have to react in the moment. You could take a hit, or need to move to help someone else. But."

As Doyle sketched out, explained battlefield strategy, Riley rose to get another drink, watched Sawyer finish rubbing his herbs and garlic — and she thought maybe mustard — over the big rack of lamb.

"That smells really good."

"A couple of hours in this?" He slid the rack into a huge plastic bag, poured olive oil over it. "It'll taste even better," he promised as he turned the bag to coat the meat.

"She conned us." He said it to Riley, then repeated it for the others. "Nerezza conned us, and so we underestimated her. Lesson learned."

"This has value." Bran gestured to the

sketches. "And so will the drills I believe Doyle will exhaust us with."

"Starting now."

"Now?" Riley nearly choked on the olive she'd popped in her mouth. "Been drinking," she pointed out.

"And if an attack came now, you'd have been drinking. We need to know how to break off into teams. We've been over that, but it went to hell today. So we drill."

"How long before you have to deal with the rest of that meal you're making?" Bran asked Sawyer.

"I've got an hour."

"An hour then." He pushed to his feet, pulled Sasha to hers. "Then I need an hour of my own with the painting."

They drilled. Riley hated to admit Doyle was right, but they needed to. Maybe it was weird to think — and feel — battles with evil forces had become a kind of routine, but as she'd nearly had her ass handed to her, she had to admit that as part of the issue.

She'd gotten sloppy, and she hadn't been alone.

When he called it, she slipped off. Not to hit the books, but to give in to recovery. She stretched out on the sofa in the tower library, fire snapping, and took a much-needed nap.

Refreshed, she wandered back into the kitchen, and into the marvelous scents of roasted meat and potatoes.

"Good timing," Sawyer told her. "Lamb's resting. We eat in ten."

Glancing over, she noted Annika had already set the table. She'd fashioned a bride and groom out of salt and pepper mills, draping a train of white linen for Sasha, creating a bow tie out of a black ribbon for Bran. She'd even created an arbor of flowers over them.

"Sweet," Riley declared.

"She is that. I thought aquamarine."

"Huh?"

"For a ring. For Anni."

"Oh. Because it represents the sea. Nice, Sawyer."

"I don't suppose you know where I can get one — the stone. Just the stone. I'm thinking Sasha could help me design a ring, and maybe Bran could . . ." He wiggled his fingers.

Sweet, she thought again. "I'll make some calls."

They had their celebratory meal, with the bridal tablescape and champagne. Doyle might've preferred beer, but he figured

281

some moments deserved the sparkle.

They didn't talk of war but of wedding, and as a man who'd lived lifetimes as a soldier, he knew there were moments as well to put the blood and the battles aside and give over to love and life.

He might not have had much to say about either, but his companions didn't appear to need him, as conversation never lagged.

"Would you marry me here?" Bran asked. "When the stars are returned, and our lives are our own again?"

"Here? I can't think of a more perfect or beautiful place. My mother —"

"We'll bring her over, and my family will come in droves, believe me."

"Móraí." The idea delighted Annika. "I can show her the scarves I've made. But . . ."

"You're worried you won't be able to come, that you'll be back in the sea," Sasha said. "Bran?"

"I'll make you a pool," he promised. "If your time on land is up, you'll have a pool, and be part of the day."

"You'd do that for me?"

Bran reached over to take her hand, to kiss her knuckles. "You're my sister."

"And mine. Both you and Riley. So you'll be my maids of honor. You'll do that, won't you?"

"Couldn't stop us, right, Anni?"

"Oh, we will be so happy to be maids of honor. What is it?"

As Sasha laughed, Riley reached for more potatoes. "Like attendants. It's a tradition with a long history — which I'll refrain from recounting."

She ignored the applause that rounded the table.

"But to bring it current, we stand up for Sasha, help make the day perfect for her. Then we party."

"I would like that very much."

"And I have my best men here, with Doyle and Sawyer. It's very like what you and Riley will be for Sasha."

"You can count on us, bro. You can count on us to throw you the mother of all stag parties, right, Doyle?"

"You will have deer?" Annika wondered.

"Stag parties arc an excuse for the groom and his pals to drink themselves stupid and hire a stripper," Riley told her.

"They have too much class for strippers," Sasha objected.

"No, we don't." And Doyle reached for more champagne.

"We'll have our own version," Riley assured her.

"You'll make some calls," Doyle assumed.

"I've got some contacts."

Bran waited until the meal wound down.

"I'd like everyone to join me outside in an hour. For a kind of ceremony, you could say. You'll need your weapons."

"If it's another drill after that meal . . ." Riley groaned as she pushed back from the table.

"Something else. In an hour," Bran said again, "by the seawall."

Riley spent the bulk of the hour making those calls, then pocketed her phone to go gather weapons. Since Bran hadn't been specific, she decided to haul out all of them.

When Sawyer walked into the sitting room turned armory, she realized he'd had the same idea.

"I was going to hunt you up after I took down the first load."

"No hunting required, and with two of us, we should be able to handle it in one trip."

"Speaking of trips," she said as she slung the long-distance rifle over her shoulder. "I've got a source for your aquamarine."

"You — Already?"

"We deliver. Bran didn't say ammo, but . . ." She shoved extra mags in her pockets.

"Wait. Where? How?"

"How is I know a guy who knows a girl whose family owns a jewelry store in Dublin. They make and design as well as sell, so they have loose stones."

"In Dublin."

"Yeah, the other side of the country, but I don't see that as a big for a shifter like you. The uncle of the girl the guy knows can have some stones to show you in a couple of days. If that's the way you want to go, we zip over there, take a look, zip back."

"Yeah, I . . . I didn't expect it to be like now."

"Your move, Cowboy."

"Right. My move. I'm in. Wow."

"Good. Load 'em up. Let's see what Bran's got cooking."

Cooking wasn't far off, Riley noted, as Bran had a cauldron hovering over the ground. Sasha's painting of the coat of arms floated over it.

"You started the show without us," Riley said.

"You ain't seen nothing yet." Bran looked over as the others crossed the lawn. "We've talked of unity. We've shown our unity. Sasha's given us a symbol of unity. We take another step here, if all are willing."

"We're with you," Sawyer said simply.

"Every one."

Riley nodded. "So say we all."

"Then here I cast the circle." Taking an athame from his belt, Bran pointed it north, south, east, west. "On this land, at this hour, we cast our light, we lift our power. Spark the fire, stir the air."

Under the cauldron, fire burned. The wind rose to shimmer the circle of light around the six.

"Against evil conspire, to stand in times foul or fair. Earth bloom, water spill. Both sun and moon defeat the gloom, so against the dark we test our will."

Flowers tumbled out of the grass within the circle. Pure blue water fountained out of the air and into the cauldron.

"We are kinsmen, of blood and heart. As one together or apart. This symbol we create, our unity to celebrate."

The air thrummed. Riley felt it beat in her own blood, felt the wolf inside her open to the power, to the sheer beauty as Bran held his hands over the cauldron. As he turned them up to the sky. In them now were two vials, gleaming white.

What poured to them to her eyes was liquid light.

Mists rose, and what stirred inside the cauldron hummed.

"This was passed to me, hand to hand, magick to magick, son to daughter, daughter to son." Bran held up the athame, then slid it into the cauldron. "Your bow, *fáidh.*"

Sasha held it out to him. In her eyes Riley saw not only the love, the absolute faith, but a great deal of the wonder she felt herself.

When he'd put the bow in the cauldron, he turned to Annika, who wordlessly held out her arms. He took the cuffs, added them.

In full trust, Riley gave Bran her guns, even the knife at her hip. Sawyer did the same, then pulled out his compass.

"You should take this, too."

"Are you certain?" Bran asked him.

"Yeah. Passed to me, hand to hand."

Adding it, Bran turned to Doyle, took his bow. "Will you, again, trust me with your sword?"

"You, and all within this circle, as I've trusted no others in three hundred years."

Bran lowered the sword, impossibly, into the cauldron.

"We fight for light, our might for right. All we are in body, in spirit, in mind bound beyond the stars we find. On this night, by this mark, we are *clann,* and under this symbol united stand."

The mist above the cauldron stirred and formed the symbol of the coat of arms.

"Do you will this to be?"

Rather than speak, Riley took Sawyer's hand, then Doyle's. And all six joined around the circle.

"Then by our wills, so mote it be."

In the smoke, the replica of the coat of arms burned bright, flashed into flame, then lowered into the cauldron.

And all went still.

"Wow. Can I hear an amen?" Sawyer asked.

Riley blew out a breath. "Amen, brother. You got some major chops, Irish."

"Well, we do what we can." Bran drew out Doyle's sword, held it to the moonlight. Just below the hilt, the coat of arms was etched into the steel.

"It's ours," Annika murmured. "Our family."

Bran lifted out her cuffs, slipped them back on her wrists. She traced her fingers over the new symbols. "They're only more beautiful now."

"And potentially more powerful." Bran handed Riley the guns. "Unity is strength, and I believe that will translate."

Sawyer took his sidearms, studied the symbol on the grips, like Riley's. "It's a good thing." And took his compass, now bearing the coat of arms. "A real good thing."

Let her come, Riley thought, and searched the sky. Let her come and test the Clan of the Guardians.

CHAPTER THIRTEEN

Nerezza didn't come that night, or the next. She sent no vicious creatures to attack when they dived the cold waters of the Atlantic to search.

Nothing lurked in the forest, hovered in the sky.

Sasha had no visions.

Riley used the time to her advantage. She drilled, she practiced, she worked out until her body began to feel like itself again. She spent hours with books, computers, notes.

And hours more with Doyle in bed. Or on the floor.

She went with Sawyer to Dublin, using a trip for supplies as cover. Leaving a sulking Annika behind. Since they were there, she replaced the ruined sweatshirt.

And since they were there, she dragged a somewhat shell-shocked Sawyer into a pub for a pint.

"Maybe I should've just bought a ready-made."

"This way means more."

"Yeah, but . . . then it would just be done."

Riley settled back to enjoy her Guinness, as to her mind there was nothing quite like a well-built Guinness, savored slowly in a dimly lit Irish pub.

Add a plate of chips still hot from the fryer and drizzled with salt and vinegar? Perfection.

"Getting cold feet?"

"No. No, it's just . . ." Sawyer took a fast, nonsavoring pull from his own pint. "I'm going to get engaged — ring and everything. It's a moment."

Happy to drink to that, Riley hefted her pint. "Here's to the moment."

"Yeah." He clinked glasses with her, glanced around as if he'd forgotten where they were. "It seems weird to be here — all these people — just sitting here having a beer. Nobody knows what the fuck, Riley, except you and me."

Biting into a chip, Riley looked around herself — the buzz of conversation, the energy and color.

Low lights on a day when the sun couldn't make up its mind, air smelling of beer and fried potatoes and pureed vegetable soup.

Voices — German, Japanese, Italian. American, Canadian, Brit, Irish accents.

She'd always considered a good European bar a kind of mini UN.

"I missed people," she realized, "and that's not usually true for me. But I've missed the noise and the vibe. The faces and voices of strangers. It's good they don't know what the fuck. They can't do a damn thing about it. So it's another moment, just sitting here like normal people, having a normal beer in a normal pub."

"You're right. You're right. At the bottom it's what we're fighting for."

"A world where anybody can have a beer at four o'clock on a Tuesday afternoon."

"Or get engaged to a mermaid."

"That might be stretching it for most anyone but you in this pub, or in Dublin. But yeah, I can drink to that." She glanced over at the waitress, a young, fresh-faced girl with deep purple hair. "We're good, thanks."

"When I'm done, and this world is dark, I'll drink your blood."

The girl had a quick smile, a pretty lilt in her voice. And her eyes were blind and mad. Riley slid a hand under her jacket, snapped open her holster.

"Don't," Sawyer whispered, gaze fixed on

the waitress's face. "She's innocent."

"You're weak. Did you think what you hold could destroy me? I grow stronger."

As they watched, the purple hair grew, went smoke gray streaked with black. Blue eyes went black as they shifted to Riley. "I may keep you as a pet, and let Malmon have you."

Though she kept one hand on her gun, Riley picked up her glass. "Yawn," she said, and drank.

The table shook; the chairs rattled. And the other patrons drank on, talked on, feeling nothing.

Deliberately, Sawyer twirled a finger in the air. "Hey, if you're playing waitress — nice look for you — maybe you could get us some beer nuts to go with the pints and chips."

Rage stained the creamy Irish skin florid pink. "I'll peel the flesh from your bones, feed it to my dogs."

"Yeah, yeah. Beer nuts?"

"The storm comes."

The waitress blinked, pushed dazedly at her purple hair. "Beg pardon, my mind went somewhere. Can I get you something more?"

"No, thanks." Riley took a deep drink, waited until the girl wandered off. "That was fun."

"No beer nuts."

On a laugh, Riley offered her fist to bump. "You've got stones, Sawyer. And I'd say we'd better get our asses home, spread the word. Nerezza's on the mend, and on the prowl."

Sawyer sighed as they slid out of the booth. "Now we've got to tell them we've been in Dublin."

"No way around it," Riley agreed. "Let me take the lead there."

"Happy to follow."

Given the situation, Sawyer had no problem letting Riley take point. When they got back, wound their way back to the kitchen, he just slid his hands into his pockets — and over the jewelry pouches he'd stuck there — and kept his mouth shut.

Sasha worked alone, forming dough into baguettes. "Hey, you're back."

"Yeah, something smells really good."

"I've got the sauce going for lasagna, and trying my hand at making Italian bread. It's fun. I hope you found the ricotta and mozzarella."

"Oh." Shit. Now Riley's hands found their way into her pockets. "About that —"

"Need some help bringing in the supplies?

Annika's up with Bran, and — I don't know where Doyle is." Choosing a knife, Sasha made diagonal slices on the loaves. "Just let me cover these to rise, and I'll help."

"We didn't actually get supplies."

"What? Why? Where have you been?"

"Annika's in the tower, right? Sawyer wanted to bag some stones for an engagement ring, so —"

"Sawyer!" Tossing the dishcloth aside for the moment, Sasha raced over, hugged him hard. "This is so . . . Stones? Not an actual ring?"

"See, I was thinking you could help me design one, then maybe Bran —"

"Oh! That is the best idea!" She hugged him again. "She'll love it. I can't wait to start. Tell me what you have in mind."

"Actually, we need to wait a minute on that. Right?" He appealed to Riley.

"Right. When we were in Dublin, we —"

"Dublin?" Sasha gaped, actually gave Sawyer a little shove as she stepped back from him. "You went to *Dublin.*"

"Long story short. I had a contact, so we zipped there, got the stones, and we were having a drink when . . ."

When Sasha held up a finger, Riley trailed off. "The two of you went all the way to Dublin — it doesn't matter how quickly you

295

got there and back —" Sasha said, effectively cutting off Riley's main argument. "You didn't tell anyone you were going. Then you stopped for a *drink*?"

"Maybe you had to be there. And okay, I bought a sweatshirt. I needed a sweatshirt. It wasn't like we were trolling Grafton Street."

"Anyone who leaves the property needs to make it clear where they are. Obviously something happened while you were gone. I'll get the others, and you can explain yourselves."

As Sasha carefully covered the loaves with the towel, Sawyer shifted his feet. "Can we leave out the why we went? At least when Anni's around?"

Sasha sent him a cool stare. "All you had to do was tell me, or Bran or Doyle. We know how to keep a secret. I'll get them."

Alone with Sawyer, Riley let out a long breath. "Mom's very disappointed in us."

"I feel like an idiot. How did she make me feel like an idiot without raising her voice?"

"Skills. I'm opening wine. We never finished that pint, and I have a feeling we're going to need some adult beverages."

"We didn't get the supplies either. How did we forget the supplies?"

"We were in a little bit of a hurry to get back," Riley reminded him. She opened a bottle of red, set out glasses. And prepared to face the music.

Annika danced down the back steps — sulks long forgotten — as Doyle came in from the outside.

"Are we having wine? Bran and I have been working very hard. Wine is good." Annika wrapped arms around Sawyer, snuggled in. "So are you."

Stroking her hair, he shot Riley a wan smile over Annika's head.

"Show some solidarity," Riley said to Doyle before he could go for a beer. She poured six glasses.

Before he took one, he studied her face. "What's the deal?"

"All at once, everybody at once." And she noted from the look on Bran's face as he came in with Sasha he'd already been partially briefed.

"Okay, here's the deal." To fortify herself, Riley took a glass, took a gulp. "Sawyer and I shifted to Dublin."

"What is Dublin?" Annika asked.

"The capital of Ireland." Doyle's gaze hardened. "On the east coast of the country."

"That's very far for food supplies. It's a

city?" Annika continued, drawing back from Sawyer. "But you didn't take me?"

"No, I . . . Well, we —"

"He needed to go there to do something for you. A surprise for you."

Far from mollified, Annika frowned at Riley. "A surprise for me? What is it?"

"Anni, a surprise means you don't get to know yet. I went to help him with it."

"Regardless," Bran interrupted, his tone as dismissive as Sasha's had been. "Traveling that far, for any reason, without telling the rest of us, is directly in opposition to everything we've done and become."

"It's my fault —" Sawyer began, but Riley cut him off.

"No, we're in it together. And you're right. I'm going to say we got caught up and leave it at that. Sawyer can grovel later."

"Hey."

"I just think you'd be better at groveling than me. We can keep talking about how stupid or irresponsible or whatever we were. Or we can tell you what happened that's a hell of a lot more important."

"You suck at groveling," Sawyer muttered.

"Told ya."

"Nerezza. It was Nerezza." Sasha stepped forward. "I can feel it now."

"Alive and in person. Or in the person of

a waitress at this pub off Grafton."

"You went for a pint?" Doyle demanded.

"Oh, like you wouldn't have done the same. We finished our . . . business, went for a beer before heading back. And I've barely gotten a good start on my Guinness when the waitress comes over. At first, it was her own face and body, her own voice. But the words?"

Riley closed her eyes a moment to bring it back. "She said: 'When I'm done, and this world is dark, I'll drink your blood.' " Riley glanced down at the red wine in her hand, considered, then drank it almost for spite. "And if you don't think it's a jolt to hear some pretty young waitress say that in an Irish accent, let me tell you, it is."

"People are just going about their business," Sawyer added. "We can't go at her. She's just a girl. Nerezza's using her, so it's not like we could knock her on her ass."

"Or shoot her, as Sawyer pointed out to me. She said we were weak, and she was growing stronger."

"To prove that, she showed us. The girl changed, and there she was, standing in this crowded pub. Her hair's not all gray now. It's got black streaks through it, and she's got some age on her, but not like she did when I had a grip on her over Capri."

"She's healing," Sasha murmured. "Regaining her strength and powers."

"Riley dissed her. Pulled the 'bored now' bit."

"Bad Willow. Buffy reference."

Doyle gave Riley a light shove. "Do you mind?"

"Look, seeing as it was, in reality, some innocent girl, dissing was all I could do. All we could do."

"She said maybe she'd make Riley a pet, give her to Malmon."

"As if."

"Don't toss that off," Sawyer argued. "For whatever reason she's gunning for you right now. When she got pissed at Riley, the pub shook. Bottles, glasses rattling around. Nobody noticed."

"Then Sawyer took a solid dig at her, said maybe she could get us some beer nuts. Pissed her off more, so then it was all peeling our skin off, feeding it to dogs. Since we couldn't go at her, we shrugged it off. The last thing she said was: 'The storm comes.' Then the waitress was back, looking dazed and confused."

"She didn't try to harm you." With a nod, Bran finally picked up the wine, passed one glass to Sasha. "She had you down to two, in an enclosed, public space where you'd

300

have hesitated to use force or violence, but she didn't strike at you."

"Because she couldn't," Sasha concluded. "She's not strong enough for that yet. For illusions, for using other means. But not striking out herself."

"She wasn't actually there. Do I have that right?" Doyle turned to Bran. "The illusion of her only."

"That would be my take on it, yes."

"If she had been stronger, we wouldn't have been with you." Annika stepped over to Sasha — away from Sawyer. "We wouldn't have known you were far away. And if you were taken or hurt, we wouldn't know."

"We weren't." Sawyer felt it vital to point that out. "I'm sorry, bad judgment, but we weren't taken or hurt. And all of us are alone or with only part of the team all the time."

"Not alone or in part in bloody Dublin," Doyle snapped.

"Hence the bad judgment. It was the wrong way to go about it, but we pulled in some information. You can keep slapping us back for the bad judgment, or we can use what we brought back."

"You suck at groveling, too," Riley commented.

"Apparently. Look, what I went to do was really important to me. I went about it wrong, and I'm sorry. Mea culpa squared, sincerely. That's it."

"Maybe we should all just cool off a little, then we can talk about this more reasonably." Sasha moved over to stir the sauce. "And we still need those supplies."

"You didn't get the buggering supplies."

"We got a little distracted," Riley snapped back at Doyle. "We'll go get the buggering supplies now."

"No, Annika and I'll go get them."

"Yes." Annika linked her arm through Doyle's. "We will go, and I will get cool so we can talk again."

She held her hand, palm up, to Sawyer. "You have the list of what we need to buy."

He pulled it out of his back pocket, handed it to her. Said, "Balls," when she sailed out beside Doyle.

"She'll get over it. You're all going to have to get over it," Riley said. "We did what we did, copped to it. If you're going to scold us some more, I want more wine."

Sasha glanced back from the stove. "It was unnecessarily risky."

"It didn't feel like it." Riley shrugged.

"Until you were waiting for the dark god to bring you beer nuts?" Bran suggested.

"Even then. It was clear intimidation, Irish. Did it give us a jolt? Sure. But what was she going to do? She doesn't, or hasn't, come to fight on her own. We should have told you guys — sans Anni. Not doing that was stupid, just stupid. I can only say I guess we were so into the secret mission we didn't think of it."

"Shortsighted, impulsive. And under-standable."

"Under—" Shocked nearly speechless, Sasha swung around, gaped at Bran.

"*A ghrá.* A man in love often thinks with heart instead of head."

Sawyer tried a winning smile in Sasha's direction, patted his hand over his heart.

She sniffed. "Riley's not a man in love and should've known better."

"For friendship one also does the foolish."

"Foolish isn't — I'll shut up," Riley decided. "Come on, Sash, all's well that ends with everybody breathing. And you know you want to see the rocks. You really want to see the shinies Sawyer bought for the ring."

"I really don't — Damn it, of course I want to see them."

Grasping the reprieve, Sawyer pulled the pouches from his pocket. "This one's the big kahuna."

He poured the stone into his hand. Perfectly round, beautifully blue, it gleamed there like a small pool.

"Aquamarine." Smiling, Bran rubbed a hand on Sasha's shoulder. "As legends say the mermaids once prized the stones."

"Blue sea — the name means blue sea, so it fits," Riley added.

"It's lovely, Sawyer. Can I?" Sasha lifted it, held it up. "Oh, look how many shades of blue in the light. You couldn't have chosen anything more right for her."

"You think? I've got these little stones." From the second pouch he poured a stream of tiny diamonds, pink sapphires, more aquamarines. "I was thinking you could come up with something, and I got these." From a third pouch he took two bands of platinum. "And then maybe Bran could put it all together."

"I'd be happy to."

"And I've already got a couple of ideas." Sasha took another study of the stone, handed it back. "That doesn't mean I'm not still annoyed."

"Down to annoyed's progress." Sawyer repouched the stones, the bands.

"In the name of progress, I'd like to add one thing. When the bitch said a storm's coming, the hair on the back of my neck stood up."

Sawyer looked at Riley. "You, too?"

"Oh, yeah. Something there, something big. That wasn't just bluster. For me, it was slipped in out of pique, but it had weight. Maybe it'll springboard something for you."

"Not right now," Sasha told her.

"Something to think on. I'm going to think on it while I hit the books. That's my penance."

"Researching isn't penance for you. Making a salad, however —"

"I'm better at that; she's better at the books." Sawyer tried that winning smile again. "Let's play to our strengths."

"Good plan. I'm in my room, digging in if needed." Riley escaped while she had the chance.

Maybe she didn't like having Doyle and Annika still pissed, but she figured Annika wasn't wired to stay mad for long. And she had a plan where Doyle was concerned.

As she had her balcony doors open, she heard them come back. Biding her time, she continued to work, take notes. It didn't take him long.

When he walked in, she sat at her desk. Wearing nothing but his shirt.

He closed the door with a decisive snap. "That's your research outfit?"

"This?" She swiveled in the chair. Yeah, still pissed, but . . . interested. "I figured you'd get around to wanting your shirt back. Just wanted to have it handy."

"You think you can distract me with sex?"

"Sure." She rose. "I get wanting your shirt back, but it seems a little redundant when you're already wearing one."

While he stood, she took off his sheath, stood the sword beside the bed. Came back and began unbuttoning his shirt.

"You're that sure of your allure?"

"Allure? Please. I've got all the necessary girl parts. That's allure enough, especially with a man who's already cruised them."

She tossed the shirt aside, gave him a little nudge toward the bed. "Sit down, big guy, and I'll get you naked."

"It didn't trouble you that Sawyer or Bran might have walked in rather than me?"

Another nudge. "First, I'm covered. Second, you're the only one who'd walk in without knocking. Sit," she repeated.

"I didn't come in here to have sex." But he sat on the side of the bed.

"Life's full of surprises." She pulled off his boots, smiled as she unhooked his belt. "Surprise."

"I can have sex and still be pissed at you."

"Handy for both of us." She gave him a

shove to push him onto his back. Moving quickly, she tugged his jeans down, kicked them across the room.

Then climbed on to straddle him.

"What do you say we talk later?"

He gripped her hair, none too gently, to haul her down. As her mouth met his, he flipped her onto her back.

She expected him to simply take her, just pound away — and wouldn't have objected. Instead he changed his grip from her hair to her wrists, yanked her arms over her head.

Instinct had her trying to tug free. "Hey."

"Shut up."

He ravaged her mouth, spinning her system into overdrive. She struggled — not in protest, but in the desire to get her hands on him.

She'd have to say no, tell him outright to stop, or she'd take what he gave her. Temper still burned in him, and burning with it was a scorching lust. She thought she could play him — and by God she had — but she'd know the full force of what he wanted from her before he was done.

He liked her helpless, for once, pinned under him, her hands cuffed by his. Her body quivering and bucking when he closed his mouth over her breast. When he used his teeth to hint at pain.

She could tie him into knots with those eyes. Now she'd know what it was to feel choice dissolve in outrageous desire.

He yanked her arms down, kept her wrists clamped in his hand. And moved ruthlessly down her body. She cried out when he used his tongue. Arched and writhed and cried out again when he didn't relent.

But the word she cried wasn't no.

It was yes.

She knew what it was to burn. Knew what it was to give in to needs, however feral. But this, now, spurred her beyond the known. He shoved her over the edge only to whip her onto another. And again until her lungs seared and her heart beat to bursting.

When he released her hands so he could use his own on her, to press and grip and plunder, hers could only grip the sheets and let what he did rage through her.

Everywhere, everywhere those rough hands moved shuddered, as if her nerves lived over her skin now.

When he jerked her up, her head fell back. Her body quivered, every inch, at the threat of more. At the welcoming of it.

"No, no, you'll look. You'll open your eyes and look at the one who takes you as you're meant to be taken. Look at me, damn you, look at the one who knows what lives in you."

She opened her eyes, looked into his, so fiercely green they were nearly blinding. But in them she saw that need and that knowledge. For her, of her.

She gripped his hips. "I see you."

Half mad, he thrust into her. He plundered her as his blood burned and his heart leaped where it had no business falling. Because he saw her, he knew her, and she him.

And so he feared both of them were damned.

Taken over, she thought when they'd both gone limp as wax. That one step she'd never allowed with another, she'd allowed him. To take her over — body, mind, and all she was.

Once that step was taken, how did she go back?

How could she go back?

When he rolled away, to lie on his back beside her, her instinct was to curl in. But she quashed it, stayed as she was.

Keep it light, she warned herself. She knew how to address facts and keep it light.

"Maybe I'll keep that shirt. It obviously works on me."

"You can have what's left of it."

Puzzled, she looked down, noted the torn

remains of it at the foot of the bed. "We keep this up, we'll both be walking around mostly naked."

He rolled, grabbed the bottle of water from her nightstand, drank half of it down. Almost as an afterthought, he offered her the rest. "I've marked you."

She took stock. Bruises on her wrists, a couple more here and there. "Nothing much."

But he got up and brought her jar of balm back to the bed.

"You pissed me off," he said, even as he stroked the balm onto the bruises.

"Bitch at me all you want because nothing's going to reach the level of Sasha's stern disapproval." Now Riley hissed out a breath. "It flattened me. We should've told somebody what we were doing, where we were going. Sawyer wanted to get the makings of an engagement ring for Anni, and —"

"I figured that out on my own, though I figured you'd gone for a ring altogether. Doesn't excuse it."

"Message received, loud and clear. It was a slap to the whole unity thing, and thoughtless. Even with that, all of this . . . old habits. I'm sorry. Best I can do is I'm sorry."

Because she still felt just a little fragile,

she got out of bed, pulled on his torn shirt. "I'm going to — Wait. You said you figured out why we went. Has Anni?"

"She might have, as she's no idiot, but I steered her in another direction. I suggested the two of you'd gone so he could find her a new dress, maybe some earrings. A present."

"Good thinking."

"It mollified her, as did the half a torturous hour she spent in the little shop that sells various trinkets."

"I'd say I owe you for that, but considering recent activities, I claim paid in full. I'm going to grab a shower, then head down to finish the amends by helping with something domestic."

When he made no move to join her, she went into the bathroom, closed the door.

Closed her eyes.

He'd shaken everything inside her, she realized. Shaken it, tossed it in the air so it fell back in an order she didn't understand.

She'd figure it out, she assured herself. Whatever the puzzle, the problem, the code, she figured it out eventually.

She took off the shirt, realized it smelled of both of them, a mix of them. A blend.

And folding it onto the counter, she felt

ridiculous because she knew she had no intention of tossing it away.

CHAPTER FOURTEEN

After days of quiet, the routine of training and diving, Doyle calculated it was time, past time, to mix things up. He tracked Bran down in the tower, stood a moment watching as his friend wrote in the thick spell book.

It wasn't all whirlwinds and calling the lightning, he thought. Some of magick was — well — toil and trouble, and more was, apparently, as pedestrian as pen and paper.

Bran set the pen down, studied what he'd written. Then he laid his hand on the page. Light flashed, held. Dissolved.

And a great deal, Doyle considered, was sheer and stunning power.

"Got a minute?" he asked when Bran glanced over.

"I do now. Things must be written down and the magicks sealed. For ourselves, and for those who come after."

Curious, Doyle walked over to see what

Bran had written.

"In the old tongue."

"The language of my blood — and yours. Of the old gods, of the old powers."

"A kind of locator spell," Doyle said, translating. "Using the coat of arms as . . . a homing device."

"More or less. Let's have some tea." He rose, leaving the book open, and walked over to plug in an electric kettle.

"You don't need electricity and teapots."

"Well now, the gods help those who help themselves, we could say. No point in being lazy about basic practicalities."

"Others would."

"And have. It's not how I was taught. The spell," Bran said, winding back to it as he measured tea leaves. "I thought of what happened to Riley, and again what she and Sawyer did. So this will find any of us who might become separated. I've given it some work since Annika and Sawyer were taken in Capri, but other matters bumped ahead of it until now."

"Because we've had a little more time on our hands in the last few days."

"For as long as it lasts. Impatient?"

"Brother, I may have all the time in the world, but if this is the time — and we all believe it is — we shouldn't waste it."

"I'll agree, though I'll tell you it's been pleasant having Sasha settle in here, have that time to paint without being plagued day and night with visions."

He made the tea, offered Doyle a mug. Setting his own aside, he locked the spell book. "Let's sit so you can tell me what you have in mind."

"Sawyer's huddled up with Sasha in the other tower."

"Working on the design for the ring, yes." Bran smiled and sat back. And reading the smile, Doyle shrugged.

"I respect the women without qualifications. I'm more used to talking war with men."

"There are none of us, put together, who has the experience in battle you do."

Though he'd have said the same once, Doyle shook his head. "That doesn't fly, not now. But putting that and gender equality aside —"

"Sometimes a man must talk to a man. And a woman to her own."

"It's no great change. The exploration of underwater caves has given us nothing but locations to cross off."

"Agreed. We found the same in Corfu and Capri."

"It feels different here." Restless, Doyle

glanced toward the window. "I don't know if it's my own feelings about being here, or if it *is* different."

"Would you go back?" Bran asked. "It's something I've wondered. Would you, knowing you couldn't save your brother then, do differently if you could go back to that day?"

"Not try? Sure I'd have a normal life span, but what measure of life would it be, knowing I'd done nothing for him, and all for myself? I've had more than enough time to resolve I did all I could. I failed, and that will never leave me, but I did all I could do, and would do it again."

Doyle studied his tea, dark and strong. "You wonder why I haven't asked Sawyer to take me back so I could kill the witch before she harmed him — or try. Sawyer would, as there's little he wouldn't do for a friend. I'll ask you, wizard, could I change the fates?"

"I don't know, but I know this. You might save one brother and lose another. Or start a war that takes the lives of thousands. The past, to my mind, isn't to be meddled with. The gods themselves let it lie."

"Change a moment, change an eon." Doyle stared into the fire, the shadow and light. "I've thought the same. I failed, and the man he might have been was lost. The man I might have been was lost with him."

"The man you are is enough. We're here, you and I, and four others, blown by the winds of fate to some extent. But more, I believe, through every step we've taken, every choice we've made along our way. So we're here."

Bran waited a beat, arched his scarred eyebrow. "What do you want to do?"

"I've thought of the words spoken, Sasha's visions. Of coming here of all the places in the world. The gods make us pay, for all those steps, all those choices."

And this, Doyle knew, would be one of the most painful he'd ever made. "I know the cave where my brother died. It's time I went back. Time we looked there."

Doyle's eyes narrowed on Bran's face. "You've thought the same."

"Whatever I thought, it had to come from you. If you're ready for it, we'll go together."

"Tomorrow."

"Tomorrow," Bran agreed. "I've thought of other words, ones spoken to you, you told me, by a redheaded witch. How love would pierce your heart with fang and claw."

Doyle nearly laughed. "Riley? She's not looking to pierce my heart. We understand each other."

Bran might have spoken again, but Sasha rushed in.

"Oh, sorry. I'm interrupting."

"No, we've finished." Doyle started to rise.

"Just sit a minute, and you can add your opinion. After considerable attempts, I've got a design Sawyer's about ninety-eight percent sold on. Have a look. He's gone to make sure Annika's occupied. And to think about it."

She flipped through pages in her sketchbook, each holding several designs that all looked more than good enough to Doyle's eye. Then stopped on a page holding a single design in the center.

She'd used colored pencils to enhance it, the deep-water blue of the center stone, surrounded by a halo of white diamond chips, and those flanked by two pink sapphires. The band held the sparkle — pink, white, blue — repeated in the wedding band.

"It's lovely, and very like her. Unique," Bran added. "As she is."

"It's hard not to push him on it, because I think it's right. I want to show it to Riley. What do you think?" she asked Doyle.

"Not my area. It looks fine to me. Plenty of sparkle, which she'd appreciate."

"I hear something." Sasha pointed at him. "I hear a but."

"Not my area," he repeated. "I was just thinking how she liked the design around the coat of arms, the braids. If the bands were braided —"

"Oh!" Sasha gave him an enthusiastic punch on the shoulder. "Oh, that's perfect. That's inspired. I'm going to fix it right now. And if Sawyer doesn't say go, something is *wrong* with him."

She rushed out as she'd rushed in.

"Well then, that's settled." Bran eased back with his tea, smiled at Doyle. "And it seems each of us has a hand in it. Things are meant as they're meant."

Contemplatively, Doyle rubbed his shoulder. "Your woman's got a firmer punch than she once had."

"In all things."

It didn't take her long, and Sasha decided she'd hit the mark when she found Sawyer working with Riley in the tower library.

"Annika?"

"Doing laundry. I've never seen anybody as happy with laundry." Sawyer set his compass on a map, shook his head. "And she's having better luck with it than I am with this."

"I've had tremendous luck. I've added another touch to the design."

"I was pretty well sold on the other."

"But not a hundred percent. I think

Doyle's idea will change that."

Riley looked up from her book. "Doyle?"

"He had a suggestion. Look here, Sawyer. The bands, we can braid the bands with the same design I used on the coat of arms."

"I don't know if that's . . ." Then he looked. "Oh, yeah. Score. It's like — *it*. It's it. Why didn't we think of that?"

"Don't know. Riley?"

"If she doesn't do handsprings over this, it's because she's doing backflips. You rang the bell, Sash. You going for it, Dead-Eye?"

"I'm so going for it."

"You ought to take it to Bran, get him started on the mojo."

"Right. You're right." He pocketed the compass, took the sketch when Sasha tore it from her book. "Thanks."

Sasha watched him go. "You wanted to move him along."

"We're not getting anywhere here. Everything feels stalled. I need to move. Maybe we drag Anni away from laundry, work on those handsprings and backflips."

"I still suck at both."

"Exactly."

"There's something more."

Riley pushed back from the table, rolled her shoulders. "Maybe we'll talk about it after I move."

■ ■ ■ ■

She'd been twitchy, Riley admitted as she dragged her friends outside. She hadn't been able to shake it — not with work, with diving, with sex, with sleep. The minute her mind wandered from the task at hand, the twitchiness started.

So maybe some time away from men altogether, and some solid sport that required a mind-body connection.

The sky held blue and nearly cloudless, and the sun beamed. Pleased, Riley tossed aside the hoodie she'd grabbed on the way out, stood with her hands on her hips, wearing a faded red T-shirt that said DIG IT!

It wasn't Capri or Corfu, but this taste of Irish summer — that might actually last an entire day — just shined.

She took a running start, executed triple handsprings, stuck the landing.

Oh, yeah, she was coming back.

And Sasha didn't suck as much as she had. Sure her landings were still shaky, but she was getting more height. Then there was Annika — nobody could come close. She might as well have wings instead of a tail.

Following Annika's orders, Riley hit a back handspring, pivoted into a side kick.

God, she wished she had someone to *fight.*

Annika's next order had Sasha looking a little sick, but she charged Riley, who basketed her hands. When Sasha's foot slapped the basket, Riley pushed up hard.

The soaring backflip was more than decent, the landing rough to Riley's eye, but Sasha steadied quickly, punched a fist in the air.

"I did it! I'm going to do it again. Better."

This time as she flew up, Sasha mimed shooting her bow. Riley found herself grinning, even as Sasha lost the landing, fell back on her ass.

"One more time," Riley shouted.

On one more time, Sasha stuck it, then did a little Rocky-at-the-top-of-the-steps victory dance.

After an hour, Riley had worked up a nice sweat, her muscles felt well used, her brain clear. And the twitchiness snuck back in.

"Okay, we moved. Boy, did we move." Sasha sat on the ground to stretch. "Now, what's the more?"

"I don't know exactly." Riley rolled her shoulders as if trying to get to an itch.

"Do you still hurt?"

"No." Shaking her head at Annika, Riley stretched her calves, her hamstrings. "I'm good, and back to fighting weight. I guess ready for a fight. The waiting's getting to me. We're so close. I want to finish it."

As she stretched her quads, she glanced up. Doyle stood on the terrace, the breeze in his hair, his eyes on her. After a long moment, he slipped back inside.

"Crap."

"Did you fight with Doyle?" Already sympathetic, Annika rubbed Riley's arm. "You like to fight with Doyle. It's like the foreplay."

"Yeah. No. I mean we're not fighting. We probably will, and that's okay. It's . . ." She looked at Sasha. "You've already got an inkling."

"I'm sorry. It's hard not to. You have feelings. Why wouldn't you?"

"I'm all right with feelings. But I have more than I want or know what to do with. I wasn't after this kind of a thing, and now it's kind of got a hook in me."

"Oh! You're in love. This is wonderful!" Annika threw her arms around Riley.

"It's not wonderful for everybody."

"It should be."

"And I don't know if it's like that. I'm just . . . Why can't it just be sex? There's nothing complicated there. I know what to do about that. I don't know what to do about this."

"You suit so well."

Riley gaped at Sasha. "What?"

"You do, so well. Just fit. I'll admit I've worried about it because you're both combative, and hardheaded."

"I'm not hardheaded. I'm rational."

"And feelings aren't. You helped me resolve mine for Bran, to see my own potential, alone and with him. So I'm telling you, if Doyle's who you want, go get what you want."

"I've sort of got him."

"I like sex," Annika said, and flipped her long braid behind her back.

"We've heard." Riley rolled her eyes. "Literally."

"It's joyful, and exciting. But with Sawyer, I learned it's more. With love it brings more, means more. When I no longer have the legs, we can still mate. I'm glad. But I'm sad to know I won't be able to walk with him, or make food with him, or lie in bed and sleep together."

"Oh, Anni." Sasha moved in to hold her. "It's so unfair."

"But we'll be together. I mean to say that. We've found a way to be as much together as we can, and will be happy. If Doyle would make you happy, you should listen to Sasha."

"How am I supposed to know if he'll make me happy?"

"Find out," Sasha said. "You're too smart — and yes, you are hardheaded — to do otherwise. He needs you."

"He — *What?*"

"He may not know it, may not be able to accept it yet, but he needs you. And when the man meets the boy, when the boy sees the man, the dark echoes, old blood spills fresh."

"Anni," Riley ordered, "go get the others. Quick. What do you see, Sasha?"

"Memories and grief, faced anew. Old scabs, old scars torn open. She feeds on the pain, stirs the old to rise and strike. She lies. Hold strong, hold true, pass this test. For the star waits in the dark, in the innocent. Bring back the light to the man, to the boy. See the name, read the name, say the name. And find the bright and white."

Sasha closed her eyes, held up a hand. "Need a second. That was intense." When she felt Bran's arm around her, she leaned into him.

"Do you remember what you said?" Riley prompted.

"Yes, and what I saw. A cave, but it's not clear. It changed. Maybe it was the light. Your light, at first, so clean, so white," she

325

said as she reached down for Bran's hand. "But then the shadows. Not shadows. And she came. Nerezza. But not her. Not exactly. I'm not making any sense."

"Let's go inside," Sawyer suggested. "You can sit down, take a minute."

"No, actually, the air feels good. It got so cold. A cave, but not underwater. I'm sure of that. It seemed big at first — then small. But big enough for us all to stand. It's a bad place. A very bad place." Her fingers whitened on Bran's. "Terrible things there, old and terrible. Just what she wants and needs. But . . . God, then it's just the opposite. It's happy and quiet."

"Maybe we take out what's old and terrible, and that changes things."

Sasha nodded at Riley. "Maybe. I just don't know. I only know we have to go there." Now she turned to Doyle. "I'm so sorry. We have to go there. To where you lost your brother."

"I know it. I spoke to Bran about it."

"Making plans without the whole class?" Riley snapped.

"To start. I know the cave, and how to find it. It's less than fifty kilometers from here."

"You can show me on the map," Sawyer said, "so I've got it logged. In case."

"We'll map it out." Bran rubbed Sasha's shoulder. "Steady now?"

"Yes."

"I'd say some food would be in order. And wine."

"Won't argue with either."

"Soup's on. Anni, why don't you check on that? I'll get the map." Sawyer gave her hand a tug, and left Doyle alone with Riley.

"I don't like explaining myself," he began.

"Then don't." She started to walk away; he gripped her arm.

"I wanted to talk to a brother, and a witch, because I'd be talking about going back where I lost a brother, and killed the witch who cursed me."

"Okay."

"That's it?"

"Jesus, Doyle, buy a clue. We all know it sucks, we all know it's brutal. So you needed to lay it out to Bran first. Fine. I — We're with you."

"I'd have spoken to Sawyer before you."

"Now you're pissing me off again."

"Why did you come out here with the other women?"

"I wanted some practice. Sasha needs the practice." Then she mumbled a curse. "And okay, I wanted the female for a while. I get it."

He hesitated, then gentled his hold on her arm. "If I had a life to lose, I'd put it in your hands. That's trust and respect."

"I could be an asshole, claim that's easy for you to say. But I'm not an asshole, and I know it's not. We're cool." She held out a hand to shake on it.

He gripped her elbows, hauled her up, kissed her. "You're not a sister to me."

"Good thing."

"But you are . . . essential. Going where we're going tomorrow, I want you with me."

Struck, touched, she laid a hand on his cheek. "I will be."

He dropped her to her feet, considered a moment, then took her hand. Rather than shake it, he held it as they walked back to the house.

Well armed, they set out early in the morning. Riley rode with Doyle on his bike as they traveled away from the coast, wound through land where the hills rolled green and serene into a sky that held in a sweet summer blue.

She imagined Doyle taking a similar route on that very hard day, on horseback. Hooves striking the ground, Doyle's cloak flying as he pressed for speed. A faster trip now, she thought as they whizzed around curves where wild lilies sprang yellow as the sunlight they danced in. But a harder one for him. Before he'd believed he'd save his brother, bring him home to family.

Now he knew he never would.

But if they found the star . . .

Did that place that had once held such evil now serve as the resting place for the Ice Star?

Either way, they rode toward a fight. And she was more than ready for one.

Essential. He'd said that to her. She tried not to think too much of it, just as she tried not to probe too deeply into her own feelings. Far from the priority right now, she reminded herself. Whatever she felt, whatever he felt, didn't rise up to the fate of worlds.

He slowed, veered off onto a narrow, bumpy track.

"We walk from here," he told her. "Bran's car can't handle this."

She swung off. "How far?"

"A little more than a kilometer."

He paused, looked left over a stone wall to a small farm where a spotted dog napped in the sun and cows grazed in a field beyond.

As he stood, the farmhouse with its blue trim, the outbuildings, an old tractor, even the spotted dog faded away.

There on the field and up the rising hill sheep cropped. A shepherd boy sat dozing, propped against a rock. He opened his eyes, pale blue, and looked back at Doyle.

"Do you see him there?"

"The dog?"

"The boy. He watched me that day. He watches me now."

"There's no boy." Riley kept a hand on his arm, looked back as Bran walked up with the others.

"His hair's almost white under his cap. He's half asleep, with his crook over his lap."

"There's a smear over the air." Bran lifted a hand, pushed. Narrowed his eyes against the resistance, pushed again.

The pretty farm sat quiet, and the dog slept on.

"She's working on you, man."

Doyle nodded at Sawyer's words. "Up this track, about a kilometer. The cave's in a hillock of rock and sod. There's a small pond outside it. It swam black that day."

And what lived in it, he remembered as they began to walk, had slithered under the oily surface like snakes.

Now along the narrow track were the yellow lilies and overgrown hedgerows dripping with fuchsia. A magpie winged by.

One is for sorrow.

As they neared he saw the signs and talismans — carved in wood or stone, fashioned from stick and straws. Warnings and protections against evil.

As the others said nothing, he knew they saw only the rambling stone wall, the wildflowers, the scatter of cows in the field.

A raven swooped down, perched on the wall. As Riley reached for her gun, Doyle stayed her hand. "You see that, at least." He pulled his sword, cleaved the bird in two.

Trees sprang up, and birds called from them. The cheerful, country birds that did no harm. Through the trees, he caught the glint of water from the pond. He angled right, strode through the sheltering grove.

Dark blue water amid wild grasses and choked with lily pads.

Then black and oily, rippling with what lived beneath.

"What do you see?" he asked Riley.

"A lily pond that needs some clearing out."

"Another smear." Once again Bran held up a hand. "And through it, the water's thick and black."

"The cave." Sasha gestured to the high, dark mouth. "Blood and bones. A cauldron bubbling with both. It's not clean, not clean.

She lies, and everything inside is a lie." Sasha let out a breath, steadied herself. "She's waiting."

"I should go in alone. Alone," Doyle repeated before anyone could protest. "There's nothing she can do to me."

"What bullshit."

"I'm with Riley on that," Sawyer said. "All or nothing. I vote all."

Riley drew her gun. "Maybe you could hit the lights, Bran. It'd be nice to see where we're going."

The mouth of the cave flooded with it, bright and white. Together they moved toward it, into it.

High and wide as he remembered. Leaves, pine needles had blown in to litter the floor. Animals who'd used it for shelter left droppings behind. Bumpy skins of moss, bony fingers of weeds grew over the rock walls.

"I guess we spread out," Riley said. "Look around."

"Stay close," Sasha warned. "It's not . . . right."

"Two by two for now, we'll say. As Sasha's on the mark." Bran peered through his own light. "It's not right."

They searched. Riley crouched down to study the cave walls inch by meticulous inch. No more than two feet away, Doyle ran his hands over it, crumbling moss.

Tension gripped the back of his neck like clawed fingers. The muscles of his belly coiled as they might before a leap into battle.

He could hear Annika talking quietly to Sawyer, hear Riley's boots scraping the ground as she moved along the wall.

The light changed, going to a dirty gray, and the air chilled with it. He turned.

Bones littered the floor, and he smelled the blood that seeped into the dirt. In the cave center, a black cauldron smoked over a fire red as a fresh wound.

The witch he'd killed stood stirring with a ladle fashioned from a human arm. Her hair was mad coils of black, her face blinding beauty as she smiled.

"You can save him. Take back the time here and now. He calls for you."

She gestured.

There, sprawled on the floor of the cave, pale as ice, bleeding from a dozen wounds, was his brother.

He held out a hand that trembled. "Doyle. Save me, brother."

With sword in hand, Doyle swung back to strike the witch, but she vanished in laughter. He ran to his brother, dropped down beside him as he had so long before. Felt the blood run on his hands.

"I'm dying."

"No. I'm here. Feilim, I'm here."

"You can save me. She said only you could save me. Take me home." As a trickle of blood slid between his lips, Feilim shivered. "I'm so cold."

"I need to stop the bleeding."

"There's only one way to stop it, to save me. Strike them down. It must be their blood for mine. Strike them down, and I live. We go home together." His brother's hand clutched at his. "Don't fail me again, *dearthàir.* Don't let me die here. Kill them. Kill them all. For my life."

Holding his brother in his arms, Doyle looked back.

The others battled, gun and bow, light and cuff, knife and fist as winged death flew through the smoky air of the cave.

He couldn't hear them. But he heard his brother's pleas.

"I'm your brother, one you swore to protect. I'm your blood. Take the witch first. The rest will be easy."

Gently, Doyle laid a hand on his brother's cheek. And rising, lifted his sword.

CHAPTER FIFTEEN

In him the rage held cold, an iced fury as the hot licks of blood and madness swirled around him. His brother. Young, innocent, suffering. The life draining out of him, out of a body wracked with pain.

The war screaming around him.

Always another war.

Through the fetid air he saw Riley slash through an attacker with her knife, then another as she shouted something at him that he couldn't hear.

Didn't she know, couldn't she see he wasn't part of them now? He was removed, for that moment removed and separate. Away.

Bran's lightning couldn't penetrate the distance, nor Sasha's bolts.

His brother, he thought. His blood. His failure.

"Save me."

Once again Doyle looked down at the face

that had haunted him through the centuries. So young, so innocent. So full of pain and fear.

Images flashed through his mind, etched in joy and grief. Feilim toddling on unsteady legs on a seaswept beach. Struggling not to cry when Doyle sucked a splinter out of his thumb. How he'd laughed when he'd ridden a chubby brown pony. How he'd grown so slim and straight, and still would sit with avid eyes around the fire when their grandfather told one of his tales.

And now this image overlaying all, Feilim, face bone white, eyes mad with pain, bleeding at his feet.

And the boy lifted a trembling hand to the man. "This one thing, only this one thing, and I live. Only you can save me."

"I would have given my life to save my brother. You're not my brother."

And cased in that ice, Doyle rammed the keen point of his sword into the heart of the lie. It screamed, piercing, inhuman. Its blood boiled black, went to ash.

Now the sword was vengeance, cold and slashing as Doyle cleaved all and any that came. If they clawed or bit, he felt nothing. Inside him was another scream, a war cry, ringing in his ears, pumping in his heart.

A thousand battles whirled in his head as

his sword slashed and thrust. A thousand battlefields. Ten thousand enemies as faceless as the mad creatures created by a vengeful god.

No retreat. Kill them all.

He saw one of the black, murderous beasts hook claws into Sawyer's back. With one bare hand, he tore it away, stomped its vicious head to dust with his boot.

He spun away to destroy more and saw nothing was left of them but blood and gore and ash. He saw Sasha lower to her knees, waving a hand when Bran rushed to her side. Annika embracing Sawyer as much to hold him up as hold on.

And Riley, her gun lowered, her bloody knife still gripped, watching him.

His breath was short, Doyle realized, and his head filled with tribal drums. And he who'd fought those countless wars wanted to tremble at victory.

He made himself turn to Bran. "Purify it."

"Sawyer is hurt."

"I'm okay." Sawyer closed a hand over Annika's arm, squeezed as he studied Doyle. "I'm okay."

"Purify it," Doyle repeated. "It's not enough to strike them down."

"Yes." Bran helped Sasha to her feet.

"Your hand, *fáidh*. And yours. And all. Flesh to flesh, blood to blood."

He cupped the blood from their wounds in his palm, reached up with another. Pure white salt filled it.

"With bloodshed we rebuke the dark." He walked a circle around the others, spilling their joined blood on the ground. "With salt now blessed we make our mark," he said as he retraced his steps, letting it sift through his fingers. "With light to spark." He held his hands over the ground. "Now fire burns the unholy lie, rise up the flames to purify."

The fire snapped, sparked, spread around the circle he'd created. It burned hot red, cold white, then at last, pure, calming blue.

"So evil is banished from this place, defeated by valor and light and grace. We six stand witness willingly. As I will, so mote it be."

The circle of fire flamed up, turned the air a soft blue, then shimmered away.

"It's done."

Doyle nodded, sheathed his sword. "If the star's here, it'll wait. We have wounded to tend."

"Just like that?" Riley asked as he stalked out. Bran stayed her when she would have stalked out after him.

"That's for later. We're all more than a bit

battered. I've a small kit in the car, but . . . Sawyer, are you able to shift us there? I'd rather not even attempt that short walk."

"He's hurt. His back, his arm."

"Not that bad," he assured Annika. "I can handle the shift."

Sasha limped out with Bran's help. Riley ignored her own wounds, though the back of her shoulder burned like a bitch, and stepped out.

Doyle stood, his face a mask under spatters of blood.

"We're shifting to where we left the car, the bike," Bran told him. "We do have wounds to tend."

"Move in," Sawyer requested. "Easier that way."

With a hand not altogether steady, he took out his compass. Breathed in and out a moment, nodded.

Riley felt a quick bump, then found herself standing beside Doyle's bike. She noted Sawyer didn't object when both Annika and Sasha helped him into the car.

"I'm driving," she told Doyle.

"Nobody drives my bike."

"Today I do. Look at your goddamn hands." She pulled a faded bandanna out of her back pocket, shoved it at him. "Wrap that around the worst one, and don't be a complete fuckhead."

She got on the bike, kicked it into a roar.

"It'll be healed before we're back."

"I don't give a rat's ass. Get on or walk."

Because he knew he wasn't as calm as he wanted to be — needed to be — he swung on behind her.

She drove the bike as she drove everything else. Recklessly fast. But he was in the mood for reckless. She knew how to handle it, which didn't surprise him, and took them snaking around curves and turns, sweeping by stone walls, skimming by hedgerows.

The blur was fine with him, as was the sting and burn of his healing wounds. It masked, for now, his own ugly and intimate nightmare.

By the time she roared up to the house, cut the engine, he judged himself healed and calm. It took seconds to understand she was neither.

"Did you forget there were five other people in that cave?" she demanded. "Or did you just decide you were the only one capable of getting the job done?"

"I did what needed doing." He walked away from her as his own words brought back his brother's face, the killing edge of the sword on his back.

"Bullshit, bullshit, bullshit." When she

would have torn after him, Sasha called her name.

"Riley. He's in pain."

"He stopped bleeding before we were halfway here."

"Not that kind of pain."

"Help with Sawyer, will you?" Bran scooped Sasha off her feet. "Let's heal the flesh, then deal with the spirit."

"I'm okay. Just a little . . ." Sawyer swayed in Annika's hold. "Rocky."

Since he was pasty white, and his pupils wide as saucers, Riley realized he was far from all right. "Gotcha, dude."

Grateful for the support, he swung an arm around her shoulders, felt the wet. "That's not my blood, Doc. It's yours."

"I took some hits. Anni?"

"I have some hurts, but it would be worse. Sawyer blocked them from me, and one dug into his back. Then Doyle . . ."

"Yeah, saw that part."

They dragged themselves in, and back to the kitchen where Bran already tended wounds on Sasha's leg, her arms with Doyle's help.

"Want a beer," Sawyer managed as he slid onto a chair.

"Who doesn't? Get his shirt off, Anni. I bet you know how."

Annika sent Riley a wan smile as she gently drew off Sawyer's torn and bloody T-shirt. "Will you help me . . . Oh! Oh, Bran, it's very deep."

Riley took a look, hissed. "Looks like a raging infection already."

"One moment. Drink this, *a ghrá.*"

"It's already easing." She drank. "Honestly, it's better. Deal with Sawyer."

"Annika, work with Doyle — and, Doyle, help Annika treat herself as well. She just needs the balm now, Anni," Bran told her. "Even the small cuts. There's poison."

He stepped to Sawyer, sent Riley a grim look over his head. From his kit he took a knife, a vial, three candles. He lit the candles with a thought, then reached for a small bowl.

"I have to drain the poison first."

"He's shocky," Riley said as Sawyer's teeth began to chatter.

"Hold on to him, as this is going to hurt like a thousand hells. You brace yourself, Sawyer."

"Right. Yeah."

"Look at me." Riley gripped both his hands. "I've got a question. Iron Man versus Hulk. Who wins?"

"Iron Man."

Riley shook her head. "Hulk smash."

"Yeah, sure. Stronger, but no strategy. Iron Man's got the smarts, the intellect."

"Hulk's got the instincts. Primal."

"That doesn't — *B'lyad.* Holy fuck. *Fuck!*"

"Hold on." Bran spoke between his teeth as he used the treated knife to drain poisoned blood into the bowl.

On a sob, Annika broke away from Sasha, threw herself down beside Sawyer.

His hands clamped so fierce on hers Riley imagined bones crushing, but she kept talking. "Intellect versus instinct. It's a hard call."

"So says the — *fuck me, fuck me* — the werewolf."

"Yeah, so I ought to know. Think about it. You put Mr. Spock against the Hulk."

Breath labored, body shaking, Sawyer set his teeth. "You're crossing the streams. Motherfucker!"

"Nearly done," Bran promised. "It's washing clean now."

"Okay. Okay."

Riley watched Sawyer's color come back, felt his crushing grip ease.

"Just the balm now."

As Bran applied it, Sawyer closed his eyes, breathed out. "Oh, yeah, that works. Don't cry, Anni." He drew a hand from Riley, stroked it over Annika's hair. "I'm okay. You let Sasha finish fixing you up now."

"It's all right." Annika raised her head, lifted drenched eyes to Bran.

"It is, I promise you. You'll use the balm on the wounds every two or three hours for now, and I'll check again before bed. But it's clean and already healing. I can tell you it would have been worse, a great deal worse, if that bastard, buggering thing had gone any deeper or dug in any longer."

"Thanks."

Doyle jerked a shoulder at Sawyer. "No problem. Beer?"

Sawyer just gave a thumbs-up.

"You're my heart." Annika stood, bent down to kiss Sawyer softly. "And you are all my heroes. I have only little hurts now, Sasha. Riley has more."

"Shit. She's got a bad one on her shoulder." Sawyer got, a little shakily, to his feet. "Switch it, pal."

Resigned, Riley took his seat, yanked off another sweatshirt that would never be the same, and sat in her black tank and jeans while Bran studied the wound.

"I'm happy to tell you it's not nearly so serious as Sawyer's, and I won't need to use the knife to drain it."

"Yay."

"Beer?" Sawyer asked her.

"Tequila. Double shot."

"You got it."

It hurt, and hurt enough that once she'd knocked back the first shot, she held up the glass. "And again."

As it eased, she downed the second, sat while Bran treated her lesser cuts and gashes.

"All right now, your turn." Sasha pointed at Bran. "Now you sit. Anni, let's heal the healer."

"Wouldn't mind a beer myself."

Doyle pulled out one for Bran. His curse healed him, he thought. The others? They healed each other. He stood there, as separate as he'd been during that horror in the cave. Turning, he headed for the door.

"Nobody leaves," Riley snapped.

"I want some air."

"It'll have to wait."

"You don't give me orders, Gwin."

"Then I will." Her voice cool as she treated Bran's wounds, Sasha glanced toward Doyle. "Nobody leaves until we talk about what happened."

"What happened?" He wanted to peel it off as he peeled off the bloody cloth around his hand. "We walked into a fight, not unexpected, and we walked out again."

"That's hardly all. She blocked you from

us," Bran continued. "She used that place, and your memories of it against you."

"Mind-fucked you, dude. Or tried," Sawyer qualified. "And we couldn't get through. Like a wall, or a freaking force field. Us on one side, you on the other with . . ."

"You saw him?"

Riley decided on one more shot. "A man — boy really. Young, bleeding. We couldn't hear, but you were talking. It's like you were in a trance. The minions, they swarmed, but they left you alone. You were . . ."

"Trapped," Sasha said. "I think the whole reason we were drawn there was to separate you, to pull you away from the rest of us. To take you back to before."

"If you could go back, I asked you, and save him, would you?"

Doyle shook his head at Bran. "It wasn't him." Doyle gave up, sat. "It looked like him, sounded like him. And at first . . . It was being back, it was having another chance. I couldn't hear you, and even when I saw you fighting, it seemed vague and unimportant. To save my brother, to take him home, it's what mattered."

"Then why didn't you?" Riley demanded.

"He said to save him I needed to strike you down. Your blood for his, and he'd be spared. I'd failed him before, but I could save him now. Just do this one thing. I've killed more than my share. What's five more for the life of a brother I'd sworn to protect?"

"He asked you to do an evil thing," Annika stated.

"That's right. And I knew what I already knew. It wasn't Feilim. He'd never have asked it. Never. He was full of heart and sweetness. His name, it means ever good, and he was. He . . . He was like you," Doyle realized. "So I did what I had to do."

"What?" Riley slapped down the shot glass. "One minute you were standing there in a trance, the next you were wading into the fight like a madman."

"I put my sword through his heart."

"Its heart," Sasha said gently. "Its heart, Doyle."

"Yes. Its. And its heart had my brother's face." He shoved up. "And I need some goddamn air."

Sasha set the balm aside, kissed the top of Bran's head. "If you don't go after him, Riley, you'll disappoint me."

"He wants to be alone."

"What he wants and needs are different things."

"I don't know what to —"

"Then figure it out, but go after him."

"Hell." Riley grabbed her ruined shirt, dragged it on as she went out.

"You're wise and kind, *fáidh*." Bran drew her hand to his lips.

"I know what it is to feel apart. And I know what it is to love when love seemed impossible."

Riley didn't feel particularly loving. In Doyle's place, she'd have kicked and punched at anyone who got in the way. She reminded herself she could take a punch, shoved her hands in her pockets, and crossed the lawn to where he stood at the cliff wall.

"I've said all I have to say. I don't want to talk to you, or anyone."

Fair enough, she thought, and said nothing.

"Go the hell away."

Going the hell away would be the easy route, and preferable, she admitted. She took the hard one, sat on the wall, looked at him in silence.

"I've nothing to say to you." His fury lashed out, stung him more than her. "I don't have to justify anything to you, to anyone."

When she said nothing, her silence only enraged him. He gripped her by the shirt, dragged her off the wall. "I did what I had to do. That's all there is to it. I don't need anything from you."

He'd yet to wash off the blood — but then neither had she. His face was rough and shadowed beneath a couple days' growth of scruff. And his eyes were shattered.

Instinct, she considered, versus intellect. She went with instinct. He shoved at her when she wrapped her arms around him, so she just held on. When it jarred her healing shoulder, she set her teeth, gripped tighter.

And instinct proved the right course when he went still, then dropped his head on the top of hers.

"I don't want your sympathy."

"You're going to have to take it. And the respect that goes with it."

"Respect, my ass." He broke her hold, stepped back.

"I've got something to say, and you're going to have to listen."

"Not if I gag you."

She planted her feet, lifted her chin. "Try it and you'll bleed. She exploited your grief, she pulled you back to the moment when that grief was the sharpest, and she offered you a lie. The lie was changing what was, and it came from the image of someone you loved, you lost. She hooked you, Doyle, the way she did me in the woods, the way she went at Sasha in that first cave on Corfu, but not with violence, not for you. With cruelty."

"I know what she did. I was there."

"Don't be a dick. Especially when I'm going to point out something essential you seem to be too pissed off to latch on to. You were stronger than she was. You did what you had to do, yeah, but you did it because you were stronger."

"It wasn't my brother," he began, and she moved in, short-jabbed a fist to his chest.

"Bullshit. It looked like him, sounded like him, bleeding and dying in the same cave where you lost him. You had a choice, and don't tell me, don't fucking tell me, that for one fraction of an instant you didn't wonder if you'd done what she wanted, you'd have had him back. You'd have broken the curse. Don't tell me that in all the years you've lived the choice you made today wasn't the hardest."

"To save him, I'd have cut my own throat when cutting it would've mattered. Today? Even if it had been a real choice, even if it had been my brother, I wouldn't have sacrificed you, or anyone in that house."

"I know it."

It mattered that she did, more than he could say.

"She separated me, and made me feel that distance so I could stand back, watch you fight, and think, what's the point of it all? They'll live, they'll die, and I'll just go on. That's the difference."

"Three nights a month I'm pretty different myself."

"Not the same."

"Oh, boo-hoo. I've got to live forever, feel my pain." Deliberately dramatic, Riley clutched at her heart. "I've got to live forever, young and hot and strong, feel my torment. Get over yourself, old man."

"You have no idea what —"

"Blah, blah, blah. Blah, blah, blah. Why don't you take a rest from the I'm cursed for a century or so. You've got the time."

"Christ, you're a pain in the ass."

"Want some there-theres, some cheek pats? Let me go get Sasha or Annika."

She started to turn, smiled to herself when he grabbed her arm, swung her around. She met his furious look with a sneer, and enjoyed — very much — how he wiped the sneer off her face.

The way his mouth crushed down on hers, hard and hot. The way his hands pressed, molded, possessed.

Just as it shook something inside her when that mouth, those hands gentled. When for one trembling moment there was real tenderness.

She squeezed her eyes tight when he held her, when his hands glided light and easy over her back.

"I loved him more than I can tell you."

"I know that. Anyone could see that."

"When he'd barely learned to walk, he'd follow me around like a puppy. So full of light, and . . . delight. If I shook him off, I'd feel like a bully. He was like Annika. It occurs to me that's why she struck a chord with me right off."

"It wouldn't have anything to do with being blow-your-pants-off gorgeous?"

"Bonus. I couldn't hear you, and in that fog, through that wall, you seemed very far away. But I knew you." He eased back, studied her face. "She couldn't reach that."

"She doesn't *get* that. That's how we'll win. Plus, we're just smarter. Or I am anyway. A lot smarter."

"Now who's being a dick?"

"Truth's truth. Had enough air?"

"I could use another beer."

"I could use food. It's my round for lunch, so it's sandwiches. You can help me with that."

"I'm on dinner tonight."

"So I'll help you get the pizza."

He looked back at the house, down at her, and felt something just let go. "Deal."

In her chamber beneath the earth, Nerezza raged. The creatures she'd created skittered and scattered. Only Malmon stood, prepared — even happy — to take her abuse.

"He should have slayed them like pigs. He should have done as I bid! Where is this human love? Where is this human grief? It's weak, weak and false."

She tore the head off a bat, hurled its still fluttering body against the wall.

"You'll tire yourself, my queen."

She flew at him, fingers curled into claws to gouge. An inch before his sickly yellow eyes, she stopped. Her hand gentled, stroked the cold, rough cheek.

"I'm strong again. You tended me well."

"You are my queen. You are my love."

"Yes, yes." She flicked that aside, paced the chamber. In the faceted mirrors of the walls she could see herself reflected, again and again.

Her hair was more black than white now, and nearly as silky as before. Yes, Malmon had tended her well. She'd skimmed the glass so the lines in her face softened, even vanished to her eye.

She'd have her full youth and beauty back,

and more. She would have all.

"Wine," she ordered Malmon. "Just wine. For soothing rather than strengthening."

Sitting on her jeweled throne, she toyed with changing her skirts from black to red, to black again. A child's trick, but after her fall, she'd been unable to do even that.

Now, she thought as she sipped the wine. She was strong enough.

"I've allowed my thirst for revenge to cloud purpose. I will kill them, of course. Kill them all and feast on them. The immortal? Nothing but a toy to torment for eternity. But first, the stars. I lost sight of the stars."

"You were so ill."

"But no more. I will reward you one day, my pet. We will go to them. I am stronger, but it costs too much to send power over distance. We need to be closer to be on them when they find the Ice Star."

"Travel will tire you."

"Their deaths, when the stars are in my hands, will rejuvenate me. I have plans, my pet. Such lovely plans. Soon, soon now, the worlds will scream in the dark. Soon, the stars will shine only for me. And I will return to the Island of Glass, drink the blood of the gods, the false sisters who banished me. I will rule all from there."

She picked up the Globe of All, smiled into it.

"See how the mists clear for me, how the dark swirls in? We'll dig our fortress deep, and we'll strike with a force of power that will rend the ground and crack the sky."

She turned that fierce smile on Malmon. "Prepare."

"My queen? Will I go with you to the Island of Glass, and sit beside you?"

"Of course, my pet." She waved him away.

Until I have no need for you, she thought, or worse, until you bore me. But on that day she would reward his loyalty by giving him a quick, clean death.

CHAPTER SIXTEEN

A couple days of drenching rain boosted color and bloom in the gardens, and made for wet, muddy training. It didn't stop six determined guardians from exploring caves and historical sites. In the plethora of books, Riley found references to stones, a name — never specified — carved into them that "marked the bed of the star." Following that lead, they scoured ruins, cemeteries, cave walls while the incessant rain pelted them and turned the hills to shining emerald.

With rain dripping off the brim of her hat, Riley stood on the bumpy grass of a graveyard, boot-deep in ground mist. Behind her, the ruins of an old abbey stood stark gray above a winding curve of the river, tea colored under sulky clouds.

Atmosphere-wise, in her opinion, it hit every glorious gothic note. She hoped, as she'd hoped on every rain-washed stop of the last two days, that atmosphere would nudge Sasha into a vision.

"Early twelfth century," Riley said. "Fertile ground for crops and animals, fish in the river. Not a bad spot. So, naturally, the Cromwellians had to sack it."

"Nice, spooky feel. And could it *get* any wetter?" Sawyer looked up at the sky.

"I like the rain." Annika gestured toward the purple spears arching out of crevices. "It makes the flowers grow in the stone."

"It keeps up you'll be able to swim on land. In or out," Sawyer added. "Though in, in this case, is out."

"Name in the stone," Riley reminded him. "I'd say headstones first."

"It might help if we knew the name we're looking for," Doyle pointed out.

"Blame the cryptic gods and their messengers." Since complaining about the weather wouldn't get them anywhere, Riley began to walk, to read headstones, to wonder.

It didn't seem egocentric at this point to wonder if the name they searched for would be one of theirs. An ancestor's. That connection. Certainly on a headstone or grave marker that made the most logical sense.

Barring that, she wondered if they would — at some point — find the names of the three goddesses, or the young queen — on some carving.

Or . . .

"Maybe it's the name of the star." Crouching, she ran her fingers over the faded name in a lichen-covered stone. "Most likely in Irish — *réalta de orghor* — since it's from Arianrhod. But possibly in Greek or Latin."

"It seems unlikely we're going to find it somewhere so open," Doyle began. "And as wet as it is, we might as well have dived."

"Stones, names, water — this place has all three. It's worth a look. And it's not what I'd call overrun by tourists."

"Any self-respecting tourist would be spending a day like this in a pub."

Hard to argue, Riley thought, and wound her way toward the ruin.

She understood the old, had always been drawn to it and the foundation it laid for the next to come. She could imagine the life here, inside the stone walls. One of prayer and intellect, of husbandry and service.

And superstition.

Some had been laid to rest inside, under slabs of stone where the names and dates were faint fingerprints, eroded with time and weather. But for her, it echoed of life and death, of fires burning, pots simmering, voices hushed in prayer.

Smells of incense and smoke and earth.

She started up a narrow curve of stone stairs, noting where the joists — long gone — had once held up the second floor, and the third.

She stepped through an opening, onto a wide ledge overlooking the lazily flowing river. She spotted the bird huddled in a tree, reached under her jacket for her gun.

Then relaxed.

Just a rook, idling on a rainy afternoon.

Below, she saw Annika turning a circle, hands held up as if to catch the rain.

"She makes her own fun."

"Wherever she goes," Doyle agreed from behind her.

Riley turned her head. "Boots ought to make more noise on stone steps."

"Not if you know how to walk. There's nothing here, Gwin."

"There's history and tradition, there's architecture and longevity. We're standing here where some buried below once stood. That's not nothing. But no, I don't think this is the place."

She watched Sasha walk into the ruins with Bran.

"She's feeling the pressure — from all of us. We've been here nearly three weeks now."

Riley followed his gaze, back to Annika.

"She's got time. She has more than another month. We haven't gotten this far together to stall, to just tread water so she'll have to go back before we finish."

"In Nerezza's place, from a tactical standpoint, I'd hold off until that time was up — until one of us, by nature, is separated from the rest." Resigned to the rain, Doyle scanned the mists and stones. "Even if we find the star first, we have to find the island, get there. And the clock's ticking."

"Screw tactics."

"That could've been Custer's motto."

"Yeah? Were you in the Montana Territory in 1876?"

"Missed that one."

"Then I'll point out Custer was an arrogant egomaniac, and part of an invading force that didn't quibble at genocide. Got his ass handed to him. I think Nerezza's got a lot more in common with him."

"The Lakota won the battle, but they sure as hell didn't win the war."

Tipping back her hat, she angled her head to study that hard, handsome face. "You know, maybe it's not the pressure of our combined thoughts blocking Sasha. Maybe it's your consistent pessimism."

"Realism."

"Realism? Seriously? I'm a lycan standing

here with a three-hundred-year-old man. There's a mermaid down there skipping around a graveyard. Where does that fit in with realism? We're a fucking mystic force, McCleary, and don't forget it."

"Three hundred and fifty-nine, technically."

"Funny. Now why don't you — Wait, wait." Eyes narrowed, she turned to him. "In what year were you cursed? In 1683, right?"

"Yes. Why?"

Struck, she thumped a fist on his chest. "Do the math! Three hundred and thirty-three years ago. Three-three-three. Three's a number of power."

"I don't see how that —"

"Three." Snapping out the number, Riley circled her hands in the air. "How the hell did I miss that?" She grabbed his arm, pulled him toward the stairs. Stopped halfway as Bran and Sasha had started up. "Doyle's three hundred and fifty-nine."

"He holds up so well," Sasha began.

"And he was cursed in 1683. Three hundred and thirty-three years ago."

Now Bran angled his head, laid a hand on Sasha's shoulder. "Now how did we miss that?"

"See!" Riley jabbed a finger at Doyle. "We

didn't think about the exact number because, hey, immortal to round things off. But it has to apply."

"You've lost me." Sasha glanced back as Annika and Sawyer stepped up.

"Three," Bran repeated. "A magickal number, one of power. As we are. Three men, three women, in search of three stars."

"Created by three goddesses," Riley finished.

"Next year it'll be three hundred and thirty-four."

"*Now* is what matters. Don't be a blockhead." Dismissing him, Riley waved the others back so she could come down. "This time, this year. Three, three, three. And this place — Ireland, Clare, where the house sits. You were born there, right? In the house?"

"The birthing center at the local hospital was full up at the time."

On a roll, Riley just slapped the back of her hand on his chest. "Maybe it ends where it began. Or Doyle began, and the clock started on the day he was cursed." Riley demanded. "What month? When in 1683?"

"January."

"Do you hear that click? Sasha, when did you first start dreaming of us, of the stars, of this?"

"You already know, because I told you. In January, right after the first of the year."

"Exactly. Click, click. You started being pulled into this when Doyle hit his triple threes as an immortal. And you pulled us all together." She looked at Bran now. "It's not nothing."

"It's not, no. Signs are meant to be heeded."

"There's a graveyard — stones — back at the house. Sorry, man," Sawyer added.

"Where we've been living," Doyle pointed out, "training, walking for weeks now."

"But not looking, or digging." Riley held up a hand at the flare in Doyle's eyes. "I don't mean digging literally."

"We would never disrespect your family," Annika added. "Is it possible your family helps protect the star? Is that the possible Riley means?"

"That's exactly the possible. Look." Now she turned to Doyle. "What I do, even the literal digging, is because I respect and value who and what came before. I don't desecrate, ever, or support anyone who does, even in the name of science and discovery. We need to check this out. We just go back and check it out for now. Okay?"

"Fine. We'll get out of this filthy weather. And tomorrow, as the chances of the last star popping out of my mother's headstone are thin, we dive, whatever the weather."

Since she figured everyone was entitled to mood, and she wanted to think, Riley said nothing as they trooped back to the car, squeezed in.

She spent the drive back using her phone to gather more data on the number three.

"Three divisions of time," she mused aloud. "Past, present, future. From the first three numbers, all the others synthesize. What makes up a man — or woman — mind, body, spirit. Three. Most cultures use three as a symbol of power or philosophies. The Celts, the Druids, the Greeks, Christianity. Art and literature."

"You had to say Beetlejuice three times," Sawyer commented.

"There you go. Third time's the charm. Actually — didn't think of it — the Pythagoreans believed three was the first true number."

"They were wrong, weren't they?" Doyle replied.

She lowered her phone, met his eyes. "Plato divided his Utopian city into three groups. Laborers, Philosophers, Guardians — who were, essentially, warriors."

"And in his Utopia, laborers equaled

slaves, philosophers rulers. Only Utopia for some."

"The point is three," Riley insisted.

The minute Bran parked, she shoved out. "We have to look. We know it's personal for you, we all do. But that may be part of it. So we have to look."

"So we look."

When Doyle started back, Bran signaled to Riley, then lengthened his own stride to catch up.

"Most of my family rest in Sligo," he began. "But those here are family all the same. For all of us."

"You didn't know them."

"I know you, as we all do. Tell us about them."

"What?"

"One thing," Bran said. "Tell us one thing that strikes your memory about each. And we'll know them."

"How will that help find the star?"

"We can't know. Feilim. This is the brother you lost. You've told us he was kind and pure-hearted. So we know him. What of this brother?"

"Brian? He was clever and good with his hands. Beside him is his wife, Fionnoula. She was pretty as a sunbeam, and he fell for her when he was no more than ten. Loved her all his life. Steadfast, that was Brian."

"And their children here with them?" Bran prompted.

"Three more than the two here. I barely knew them."

Doyle moved to his last brother. "Cillian, he liked to dream, to make music. He had a voice like an angel that drew the girls like bees to honey. My sister Maire's not here, but buried with her husband and children in a churchyard near Kilshanny. Bossy, opinionated. Always a scrapper."

He found a kind of solace, finding something about each of his brothers, his sisters. His grandparents. Paused at his father.

"He was a good man," Doyle said after a moment. "He loved his wife, his children, the land. He taught me to fight, to build with stone and wood. He didn't mind a lie, if it was entertaining, but he'd tolerate no cheating.

"My mother. She ran the house, and all in it. She'd sing when she baked. She liked to dance, and when Maire had her first child . . . I still remember her holding the baby, looking at its face. She said whoever you were, now you're Aiden."

Annika laid her head against his arm. "We believe when one of us dies they go to another place. One of peace and beauty.

After a time, there's a choice to stay there or to come back again. It's harder to come back again, but most do."

Solace, Doyle thought again. "I never thanked you for the flowers, the shells and stones you put on the graves."

"It's to honor who they were. Even if they choose to come back, we might not know them."

"That's who they were, or a part of it. I've said their names. There's no star here."

"We just need to figure out how to pick the lock. I'll work on it," Riley promised. "Maybe not here. Maybe in or around the house, or the old well. Somewhere in the woods. There's too much weight not to think it's right here."

"Let's go in, take a break. It's been a dreary couple of days," Sasha added. "We could all use a break."

"We can have wine, with cheese and bread. Sawyer said I could be chief cook tonight, and I could make . . . What am I making?"

"Baked potato soup — in bread bowls. Good for a wet day."

"Bread bowls? How am I supposed to think about research when I'm going to eat bowls of bread?"

Sasha took Riley's arm. "By having wine first."

"That could work."

Wine usually worked, in Riley's opinion. And she didn't mind having some in front of the fire, her feet up while she worked on her tablet. Especially when the air began to smell of whatever Sawyer taught Annika to chop, stir, or mix.

It seemed to her Sasha felt the same as she sat in the kitchen lounge sketching. Doyle had said something about a hot shower and disappeared. Since she thought he wanted space, she provided it.

She noted idly that Bran was absent for at least an hour, came back in, left again. Shortly after helping Annika form balls of bread dough, Sawyer told her to cover them with a cloth, time it for an hour.

He slipped out.

Riley lowered her tablet. "What if we tried something like a scavenger hunt?"

"Why would you hunt scavengers?" Annika wondered.

"No, it's like a game."

"I like games. Sawyer taught me one with cards, and when you lose, you take off a piece of clothes. Oh, but he said we only play it for two."

"Yeah, that's better as a duet. It's when

you have a list of things to find, and you hunt for them."

"Like the stars. So it's a quest."

"In a way."

Sasha glanced up from her sketch. "How does a scavenger hunt help us find the star?"

"It's a way to get us to comb through the house, to look for the unexpected. I don't know. Reaching," Riley admitted. "Doyle's family built on this spot. He was born here. Bran built, three hundred years later, on this spot. We've been driving and hiking around Clare, diving in the Atlantic. But it's making more sense, it's just more logical, the answer's right here."

"Don't you think Bran, being Bran, would have sensed it?"

Because Riley had rolled that around, she had a theory. "I think, somehow, it didn't really begin for us until January — and Doyle's unwilling rebirth. Yes, everyone but you already knew about the Stars of Fortune before we hooked up on Corfu — and that's another in the mix. We all knew; you didn't. The clock started when Doyle hit the magic number."

She pushed up, poured more wine. "It's a solid theory. January starts the clock, you start having visions about us, about the stars. It takes you a while, but you go to

Corfu — and so do the rest of us. Same time, same place."

"Riley is very smart." Annika poured more wine, too.

"You bet I am." She clicked her glass to Annika's, and feeling generous, took the bottle to where Sasha sat, topped off her glass. "You're drawing the house."

"I love the house. I don't think it's any more than that. But I do follow the theory. And . . . Bran brought the other two stars here, into *this* house. So maybe this is why."

"Good point. So we could go through it, top to bottom. Your visions, so far, say it's somewhere cold, talk about a name on a stone. First on the hunt list is a name, a stone. You talked about the boy seeing the man, the man the boy."

"We have three men," Annika pointed out.

"Right you are. One of them was born here, was a boy here. That could be it. Or . . ." Riley sipped. "It could be symbolic again. Something in the house from Doyle's time, or that represents —"

She broke off when Doyle came in.

"Who knew it was that easy to shut you up."

"She doesn't want to poke at a sore," Sasha told him.

"Nothing sore." He looked at the wine,

and since it was handy, got a glass. "You had a point before. The whole whims-of-fate deal pisses me off. It wasn't you, but like this wine, you were handy."

"Riley wants to hunt scavengers to find the star." Annika peeked under the cloth, pleased to see the balls were bigger.

"A scavenger hunt?"

"A form thereof," Riley said to Doyle. "We compile a list of things, symbols, possibilities that may apply, and we start looking. Hell, what else have we got to do on a rainy night?"

He shifted, caged her back against the counter. "Seriously?"

"You can have sex now," Annika suggested amiably. "There's time before dinner."

Doyle smiled at her. "Gorgeous, are you sure I can't talk you into tossing Sawyer over for me?"

"Nice." Not too subtly, Riley lifted her knee, pressed it firmly against Doyle's crotch.

"He's making a joke because he knows Sawyer is my only true love."

"Good thing," Sawyer said as he came in with Bran behind him.

"Sawyer, the balls are bigger!"

"Not mine." Doyle eased Riley's knee down.

"No, yours, too — Oh." Tossing her hair, Annika laughed. "You made another joke."

"He's a laugh riot." Riley shoved Doyle's chest, didn't budge him. "You're blocking me."

"I'm thinking of time before dinner."

"I'm using the time before dinner," Sawyer announced. "Anni —"

"But we can't have sex now because I have to make the dinner. It's my turn."

"Anni," he said again, and went to her, cupped her face, kissed her.

"Sasha could watch the balls of dough," Annika murmured, and circled his neck with her arms.

"I love you. Everything about you. Everything you are."

"Is this happening now?" Doyle muttered at Riley.

"Shut up."

"Do you remember when Riley and I went to Dublin?"

"It hurt my feelings you didn't take me with you, and the others were angry because —"

"Yeah, let's skip over that," Sawyer said quickly. "I went to get something for you, and Riley helped me."

"The surprise, but you never gave me the surprise."

"I'm going to give it to you now, because you like the rain, and we're making soup, and this is family. You're my family. Stay my family, Annika."

He took a pair of polished shells out of his pocket.

"It's beautiful."

But when she reached for it, Sawyer lifted the top shell.

Gasping, she pressed her hands to her lips. "A ring. Is it mine?"

"Made for you. We designed it — we all had a hand in that. Riley helped me find the stones, and Bran, well, made the magicks. The blue stone —"

"I know this stone. It's precious. It holds the heart of the sea."

"You hold mine. Always. Marry me."

"Sawyer." She laid a hand on her heart, her other on his. "Will you put it on, the way Bran put Sasha's on?"

"I take that as a yes." He slipped it on her finger.

"It's more beautiful, more precious than anything I have. Except you. I will be your mate, always."

She slid into his arms to seal it with a kiss, held tight, tight. "I thought I already had the biggest happy, but this is bigger."

"And that's our Anni." This time Riley

elbowed Doyle aside. "Show it off."

"It's so beautiful. It holds the sea, and the pink is for joy, and the bands are for all, for family. Thank you for helping." She kissed Riley's cheek. "Thank you." Then Sasha's, then Doyle's. "And you, for the magick." She hugged Bran, swayed.

Then swung away, holding her ring hand high. "Look! It's so, so pretty. It's the best of any surprise."

She leaped into Sawyer's arms, laughing as she took his mouth.

"Mmm. Sasha will finish the —" She jumped back when the timer buzzed. "The balls!"

"Brother." With a shake of his head, Doyle lifted his glass. "You'll never have a dull moment in the rest of your life."

Sawyer watched Annika whip the cloth off the dough, like a magician completing a trick. "I'm counting on just that."

They ate soup, drank wine, talked theories.

"Interesting," Bran considered. "The idea the star might be in, or even of, the house."

"Your builders might have mentioned it," Doyle commented.

"He's had three centuries to hone his skeptic creds." Deciding to ignore Doyle, Riley tore a chunk off her bread bowl, enjoyed it. "The hypothesis, like this quest, like everyone here at this table, is founded on the unarguable fact that alternate realities, para-realities, exist. Accepting that, we move to other facts. Doyle was changed in January three hundred and thirty-three years ago. In January, Sasha began to have visions about the Stars of Fortune, and about us. Conclusion, that's the kickoff."

"We were all drawn to Corfu," Bran continued. "Three of us met on the day we arrived, at the same hotel. Within days the six of us fought together, for the first time, against Nerezza. In our time there, a bond was formed." He lifted Sasha's hand to kiss. "Of varying degrees."

"A bond," Sasha repeated. "And each one of us came to the point where we were able to share our own heritage. I think, I really do, we're where we are now because of that bond. It didn't exist in January. It didn't exist when Bran built this house, or when Doyle was cursed. But . . . the potential of it did."

"Yes." Delighted, Riley slapped a finger on the table. "That potential began the minute the stars were created, and evolved. The stars fell, and the research on when's sketchy, but indicates they fell before Doyle was born. His birth — and the mystical rebirth from the curse? Another step in the evolution. The rest of us fill in. And don't you have to wonder at the mix? Witch, mermaid, immortal, lycan, seer, shifter. Why not six witches, six immortals?"

"The diversity brings strength," Bran surmised. "And challenges to overcome."

"You've got to admit — you said it yourself," Sawyer added as he looked at Doyle. "The closest you came to finding Nerezza was in that cave on Corfu, with us."

"I'll buy the timing mattered, the six of us mattered. It's the idea the Ice Star is behind the baseboard that doesn't ring for me."

"If we follow the dots." Lifting her wine, Riley spoke to the table at large rather than Doyle specifically. "What holds the most weight is the stars can only be found by the six of us — and couldn't be found until the six of us came together. Ergo, the Ice Star might have been hidden in the house where Doyle was born, and might be hidden in or around this one now. The house is stone, and the data and the visions speak of stone. And the sea, which is right out there."

"The man sees the boy, the boy sees the man. No, not a vision," Sasha said quickly. "Just remembering. A mirror, a glass?"

"Now you're thinking. And the bit about the name. Maybe something written down, something in a book."

"A painting. The signature of the artist," Sasha explained, "or the person in the painting."

"Memorabilia," Sawyer suggested. "A keepsake. Something engraved."

"I'm going to write this down." Riley rose to grab her tablet from the lounge. "Mirror, glass, book . . ."

"You make the words so fast." Annika angled over to watch them come on screen. "Can you teach me? I like to learn."

"Sure." But Riley said it absently as she finally looked at Doyle. "Why did you choose the bedroom upstairs?"

"It had a bed."

"Stop the smart-ass. Why that particular room?"

"And no particular reason except . . ."

"Except what?"

"It faced the sea. My room as a boy here did the same."

"Okay. That could matter. Talk among yourselves. I want to play with this." Riley took her tablet back to the lounge.

Doyle rose, followed her over. "You pissed about something?"

"No. Clearly, I'm working something out, whether or not you support the theory."

"You're pissed because I don't buy in?"

"No." She looked up now, held a level gaze. "Theories are meant to be debated and challenged. It's why they're theories. I'm a scientist. I worship ideas, even when they're contrary to mine."

"Then what's the attitude?"

"I'm working something out," she repeated. "This, and something personal. If I were pissed, I'd say so."

"Okay." He went back to the table, sat with the others.

Riley went back to ignoring him. It seemed the best course while holding an internal debate on whether or not to tell him she was in love with him. And if she told him, when. And if and when, how.

A lot of questions, and no clear answer.

She had a lot to work out, so let those questions circle in her mind while she added items to the hunt list, and let the conversation across the room wash over her.

CHAPTER SEVENTEEN

At the table Annika admired her ring, wiggled her fingers to make it sparkle. She thought she would most like to marry Sawyer on the island where he'd taken her — where one of her people had given his ancestor the compass. Where he'd told her he loved her the first time.

Everyone could come, the land people who were family, the merpeople. She hoped, so much, she could marry Sawyer while she still had the legs. Then she could wear a beautiful dress, and dance with him.

She caught Sasha smiling at her while the men talked of battle plans and hard things.

"I like to look at it, and to feel how it feels on my finger. Do you with yours?"

"All the time."

"You will come to the wedding, and stand for me, you and Riley, the way we will for you?"

"I thought you'd never ask." Sasha

laughed.

"I think, would like so much, if we could marry on the island. Our island."

Sawyer slid an arm around her. "I was thinking the same."

"Really? Oh, then everyone could come. Our family, your family, my family. We would have flowers, on the land and on the sea, and music. And wine. It's more than I can imagine. More than I ever did, and I used to dream of the rite, the promise when I was a girl. I had a place for dreaming special dreams, and that was the most special."

"What kind of place?"

"In the warm waters of the south where the water is so clear the sun strikes through it, I had a secret place just for me. A garden of coral and sea plants. I would curl there and dream my best dreams."

Now she had the dream, she thought, and snuggled against him. "Did you have a secret place?"

"A tree house."

Her eyes widened. "You had a tree for a house?"

"No, it's a little house built in a tree. Up in a tree. My dad and my grandfather built it, for the kids. We all hung out there, but I'd climb up, especially on summer nights, by myself. I guess I dreamed some pretty good dreams there."

"Especially after pawing through porn mags," Riley said from across the room.

"Different kind of dreaming."

"What are porn mags?" Annika wondered.

"I'll explain later. How about you, big-mouth?"

"Me?" Riley glanced over again. "We traveled a lot, so I found places wherever. Books were my place, not so secret, but my place. Plenty of dreams inside books. But now that I think about it, there's this old storm cellar back home. I guess that was my version of a tree house or sea garden."

"Sasha." Enjoying the conversation, Annika turned to her. "Where was your secret place?"

"I was going to say I didn't have one, but that's knee-jerk. Something you say without thinking first," she explained. "The attic. It was very secret for me, somewhere I'd go to be alone, when I had to get away from everything, everyone. I'd draw, and imagine being like everyone else. I wasn't happy the way I am now."

"I wish I could have been your friend when you were a girl."

"We're making up for that now. Let's keep it going. You're up, Bran."

"There's a stream a fair walk from our home in Sligo. I'd set off for it when I was a boy and had deep thoughts to think. I'd sit with my back against an old, gnarled rowan tree, watch the fish in the stream, practice magicks, and dream of being a great sorcerer."

"And you are!" Annika pressed her hands together. "Doyle, where was your place?"

"Days were full of work when I was a boy. Firewood to gather, peat to dig, stock to tend."

"Walking barefoot through snow ten miles to school. Uphill," Riley added, and earned his bland stare.

"You had no shoes?"

"She's talking in smart-ass clichés," Doyle told Annika. "I was the oldest, and so had more responsibilities . . . Knee-jerk," he said with a glance at Sasha. "Old habits. We were forbidden to climb on the cliff, so of course, nothing appealed more. If I could slip away from my siblings, from the chores, that's just what I'd do. I liked the danger of it, the sea crashing below, the wind whipping at me. And when I found the —"

He stopped, shocked, stunned. All along? he wondered as his mind struggled to grasp it. Had it been there all along?

"Not in the house. Not in the graveyard.

The star's not here, not there."

Riley had already gotten to her feet. Now she set the tablet aside, walked over to the table. "But you know where."

"I don't —" The fact that he had to settle himself infuriated. "I may," he said, calmly now. "A theory, following your dots. I climbed the cliffs, a bit, then a bit more, and when I didn't get caught and hided, more still. Even at night, by moonlight, and Christ knows if I'd lost my footing . . . But that was part of it all. That thrill, that risk. I was the oldest, after all, and Feilim, he'd just been born, and my mother distracted, my father besotted. He was beautiful, even a boy of nine could see how beautiful he was. He was days old when I found the cave.

"I could use a whiskey."

"I'll get it." As he rose, Bran glanced at the sketch Sasha worked on, quickly, skill-fully, in her lap.

"A cave in the cliff wall," Riley prompted.

"Aye. It was like a treasure. I went right in, as a boy with no sense would. The sea echoed in it. Here was something no one knew of but me, no one would have but me. I was a pirate, claiming my prize. Over the next weeks and months and years, it was my place. I took an old horse blanket, tinder, tallow, a small boy's treasures. I could sit on the ledge outside it, look out to the sea and imagine the adventures I'd have. I whittled a pipe to play, to call my dragon. I'd settled on a dragon for my spirit guide long before. Thanks."

Doyle lifted the glass Bran set in front of him. "I carved the symbol of one into the cave wall, and above it my name."

"Doyle Mac Cleirich, writ the boy in the stone, and dreamed of the man to be. Warrior, adventurer." Sasha set the sketch pad on the table.

On it she'd drawn a cave lit by a single candle held on a rock by its own wax, and a boy — dark, shaggy hair, dirt-smeared shirt — his face intent as he carved letters into the stone wall.

"Dreaming of what would be, he doesn't see the fire and the ice. Nor feel the heat and cold. That is for the man, one who knows war is blood and death and will still fight. The star waits for the boy, for the man. See the name, read the name, say the name and its ice burns through the fire. One for the seer, two for the siren, three for the soldier. Dare the storm, children of the gods, and take them home."

Sasha shuddered out a breath, reached across the table for Doyle's whiskey. "Mind?" she said and downed it. Shuddered again. "Wow. That was probably a mistake."

"You did well." Bran laid his hands on her shoulders. "You did brilliantly."

"You saw it?" Doyle tapped the sketch pad. "You saw this?"

"As soon as you started talking about the cliffs. It's been like a film over my mind — hard to explain. And when you started to talk, it just lifted. And I saw you — I saw you as a boy in this cave. I felt . . ."

Doyle picked up the bottle of whiskey Bran had brought to the table, tipped more in his glass. "Go ahead."

"Determination, excitement, innocence. Power all around you. You nicked your finger with the knife, and when you traced the letters you carved, your blood sealed them."

Doyle nodded, drank. "Here, all along. Just as you said." He looked at Riley. "I never thought of the cave. I even went there after we came here. Climbed down, went to see it again. I thought nothing of it. I felt nothing."

"You were alone. Next time you won't be."

"It isn't the easiest of climbs."

Riley arched her eyebrows. "Getting to the other two wasn't a stroll in the park either."

"I'd say give me the coordinates, but if

you're off by a foot or two." Sawyer scratched his head. "It's a long way down."

"We'll use rope." Bran looked toward the window. "But not tonight. Not in the dark, in the rain. In the morning then — please the gods we get a break in the weather — and together."

"Say we find it, and I say we will. What do we do with it?" Sawyer asked. "Where do we put it until we figure out how to take it home?"

"Well, according to the established pattern . . ." Riley looked toward Sasha.

"A painting. I've been painting when I've had the chance, but nothing's *compelled* me like the other two. Maybe, now that the film's gone, I'll be compelled. Otherwise, maybe a more ordinary painting will work as well."

"And question after that, where the hell is the Island of Glass? I'll keep hitting the books on it," Riley promised. "But I'm starting to think I'm not going to find that answer in the library or the 'net. Still, I'll keep digging. Starting now."

"If we climb, we climb at first light," Doyle told her.

"I'll be ready," she said and walked out.

She worked until after midnight, played

with a couple of theories. Discarded them.

She wrote a long email to her parents, catching them up with where she was, how she was, asking them if they knew of any lines to tug she'd missed.

Time to shut it down for the night, she told herself. Time to get some sleep — or try to. If tomorrow was the big next step, they all needed to be ready.

Not just ready to find the star, to protect it, but to fight. The minute Nerezza got wind they had the last star, she'd come calling.

Thinking just that, she left the library, made her way to the sitting room where they stored weapons. Doyle sat quietly by a low fire, polishing his sword.

"You should get some sleep," he told her.

"Heading that way. Same goes."

"Soon as I'm done here. I didn't think of the cave. I should have. I didn't."

"I didn't think to ask if anywhere around here had particular meaning for you. I was hung up on the graveyard because I knew it did."

"I thought you were right at first. I hated it."

She sat across from him. "You're entitled to want your family to rest in peace. I think . . . Do you want to know what I think?"

"When has that ever stopped you? Yes," he admitted when she said nothing. "I want to hear what you think."

"I think this is a gift. I think this is something given to you hundreds of years ago to help you resolve the rest. Every boy wants to be a hero, right? And now you are. You are," she insisted when he shook his head. "They just gave you the choice to be one or to walk away. You didn't walk away. You went back to the — gotta say evil — place where your brother was killed, and when Nerezza tried to use your grief against you, all of us, you kicked her ass. You didn't want to stand in the graveyard today, and talk about your family. But you did. That's not battle heroics, Doyle, but it's stepping up. So —"

She got to her feet. "Like I said earlier, I've been working some things out."

"On finding the island."

"Goose egg there. I mean the personal business. We made sort of a deal, and I'm sort of reneging."

He frowned at her. "What deal?"

"Just sex, just good, healthy sex. No sticky stuff. But things got a little turned around on me. In me."

He set the sword aside, very carefully. "Are you pregnant?"

"No. Jesus. You're irritating a lot of the time, and you're moody. And pushy," she decided.

"What does that have to do with sex?"

"It doesn't. It has to do with the sticky part that wasn't supposed to happen. I don't know why it happened. I like to know why, so that's irritating, too. I can hang some of that on you, too, as getting anything out of you is pulling teeth. Like I didn't know until today you were twenty-six when you were cursed."

"How do you know that?"

"I did the math, for God's sake. How old you were when Feilim was born — nine — how old you'd said he was when he died. Seventeen. Which makes you — excluding the immortality — a couple years younger than me. That hit strange."

Saying nothing, Doyle reached for his sword again.

"No, just hold off on that, and listen. I'm going to say that despite all that — and I could say you have qualities that balance out the bullshit, but this is already taking too long. Despite it, or maybe I'm twisted up because of it — I haven't worked out which — I'm in love with you."

"No, you're not."

Of all the responses she'd imagined, she'd never imagined a cool, calm dismissal. She'd prepared herself for hurt feelings, even a solid punch to the heart. She hadn't prepared for insult and anger.

"Don't tell me what I feel. Don't tell me what I have in here." She thumped a fist on her heart. "I'm telling *you* even though I'd rather not. Do I look happy about it? Am I doing the happy dance? Am I doing the cartwheel of joy?"

"You're caught up, that's all. We're sleeping together, and everyone else is talking weddings and flowers. You've conflated them."

"Bullshit. Insulting bullshit. Did I say anything about weddings and flowers? Do I *look* like somebody who can't wait to run out and buy some big white dress and grab a bouquet?"

He felt the first trickle of alarm. "No, you really don't."

"I don't like this any more than you, but it is what it is. I'm giving you the respect of telling you. You give me the respect of not accusing me of being some sentimental *girl.*"

He thought he should stand. "I'm saying I think we're in a strange and intense situation. We added sex to that. We . . . respect each other, trust each other. Obviously we're attracted to each other. You're a smart woman, a logical woman, a rational woman. A woman who has to know —"

"I'm smart enough to know that logic and rational thinking mean dick-all when it comes to who you fall for." Beyond pissed, she slapped her hands on her hips. "What do you think I've been telling myself? But I feel what I feel. God knows why."

"I can't give you what love asks for."

She shook her head as the temper in her eyes dimmed to pity. "Moron, love doesn't ask. It just is. Deal with it."

"Riley," he said when she started out, and she turned back.

"Don't tell me you care about me. That's cheap. That's beneath us both."

"There are reasons I can't —"

"Did I ask you for anything back?"

She'd asked for nothing, he thought. And what was he supposed to do with that? "No."

"Then leave it. Just leave it. I told you because whatever else I weighed in, I don't like regrets. I'm not going to regret telling you what I feel. Don't make me feel less for feeling it."

He let her go — that was best for both of them. But he knew in three centuries, with all he'd done, all he'd experienced, she was the only woman who'd managed to turn him inside out.

She slept well. She'd said her piece, Riley thought, solved the internal issue nagging at her by saying it. So she'd thrown off that weight and worry.

He hadn't hurt her, and she'd expected him to. After all, she'd never been in love before. In lust, in fairly serious like, but she'd never slipped over that very essential line.

No, he hadn't hurt her, Riley considered as she dressed for a rugged cliff climb. She was a smart, educated woman, reasonably attractive, healthy, well traveled. If Doyle couldn't see and accept love from her, that was absolutely his loss.

She'd never dreamed of weddings and marriage and happy-ever-after. Not that she stood against any of that. But she led a full and interesting life — even before waging war against a god. If she survived that war, she fully intended to continue leading a full and interesting life.

Doyle could be a part of it, or not. Choice entirely his.

But the priority of now outweighed the priority of maybe later. She strapped on her guns — don't leave home without them — clipped on her knife sheath, and took the back stairs to the kitchen.

Coffee — number one priority — scented the air, along with grilling meat, toasted bread.

"Omelettes," Sasha told Riley as she skillfully folded one in the pan. "Loaded. Annika set the table before I got down so Sawyer could take her down for a quick swim."

She'd built a cave out of napkins, Riley noted, set it on a stand above a flowing blue napkin obviously representing the sea. Inside the cave she'd placed six figures made out of pipe cleaners. They circled a dragon made of the same that held a small white stone.

"Let's consider that a prophecy." Riley poured coffee, and decided to take advantage of the moment. "I told Doyle I'm in love with him."

"Oh!" Quickly, Sasha slid the omelette onto a platter. Her smile faded. "Oh."

"Listen, I didn't expect him to sweep me up like the studly hero in a novel. I just needed to say it so thinking about saying it — or not — wasn't clogging up my brain. I did, so it's clear."

"What did he say?"

"Not much, but one of the standouts was

how I must be conflating — *conflating* — sex and all the wedding talk. That was insulting."

"Yes, it really is. To your emotions and your intellect."

"Boom." Riley tapped a finger on Sasha's shoulder. "Mostly he was stunned and annoyed — more heavy on the stunned. I'm not going to hold the stunned against him. We had a deal."

"Oh, for —"

"We did," Riley insisted. "I reneged."

Sasha made a *ppfft* sound. "As if you can make a deal about love."

"I get that. But I didn't get that when I made the deal. It's my first time in the arena." With a shrug, she hooked her thumb in her front pocket. "Anyway, by the time we'd finished up I felt sorry for him because of what he doesn't get. Love's precious, isn't it? It's not something you can find by digging, searching, reading. It just is, or it just isn't."

"Sorry for him, my ass."

On a laugh, Riley drank coffee. "No, really. And I didn't tell you so you'd be pissed at him."

"You're my friend. You're the first real friend I've ever had. What kind of friend would I be if I wasn't pissed at him? Of *course* I'm pissed at him. The jerk."

"Appreciate it. But if you can't make a deal not to fall in love, you can't make one to, can you? It just is, or it just isn't," Riley repeated. "I'm okay. More, a lot more important, we've got to hang together. No internal conflicts, especially today."

"I can be pissed at him and hang together with him." Scowling, Sasha poured beaten egg into the pan.

"Reverse the order. Hang together first."

"For you." Sasha added grilled bacon and peppers, shredded cheese. "I'll do that for you."

"I love you. I don't think about saying it very often. Today's a good day to say it."

"I love you, too."

Riley heard feet on the stairs. "You're going to tell Bran — no problem. Maybe just wait on that until after we get back. With the star."

"I can do that."

It wasn't Bran, but Doyle, and Riley gauged her reaction. She concluded she hit borderline amusement to see the big, sword-wielding immortal looking awkward and braced for female ire.

Maybe the reaction was small of her, but she didn't mind being small.

"We're fueling up on loaded omelettes

before the climb." Riley spoke *very* casually, topped off her coffee. "According to Annika" — she gestured toward the table with her mug — "we make it just fine."

"Good."

He glanced back, his relief just visible enough to tip Riley over the borderline into full amusement when Bran came down.

"Ah, just the man I wanted to see. I want to get the rope from the garage. We've time for that, Sasha?"

"You've got ten minutes."

"Time enough. Give me a hand, will you, Doyle?"

Riley held her snicker until they'd gone out.

In the garage, Bran lifted a coil of sturdy rope from its hook on the wall. "Well, now I know why I felt I had to have all this." He passed it to Doyle, lifted off a second coil.

"It's more than enough for this. The cave's about fifteen feet down."

"I could get us there without the rope," Bran considered. "Though I'd feel better about it if I'd been there first myself. It's orienting, really. Sawyer could do the same, once he logged it, but . . ."

"You have the rope," Doyle finished. "And think there's a reason for that."

"Tied together, rather than me taking us

down one or two at a time. I think it has to be tied together, yes." Bran angled his head. "Are you worried then?"

"No. No, it's a tricky climb, but nothing this lot can't handle."

"What then?"

"It's nothing. It's other. It isn't relevant." Bollocks. "Riley says she's in love with me."

Bran merely nodded. "Then you're a fortunate man."

"That might be, if I were just a man. And even then, we've got more pressing matters. If she's pissed off at me because I didn't — couldn't —" He broke off with a curse. "If she's distracted by what she thinks she feels . . ."

"I'd say Riley knows herself very well. That's one. And to add, she didn't seem pissed or distracted just now to me."

"She's canny," Doyle contested, and made Bran smile.

"That she is. And still from where I'm standing it's yourself who seems distracted and pissed. You have feelings for her."

"Of course I do. We're sleeping together."

"To borrow from Sawyer, just let me say: Dude."

That surprised a laugh out of Doyle. "All right, no, I haven't had feelings for every woman I've slept with. But we're part of a unit, we're connected." He studied the rope. "Tied together."

"I'm a man in love, and that love increases every day. It's amazing to me. So I've seen your struggle. We're connected — tied together — so I'd wish you happy, as I've seen, clear enough, she adds to you, and you to her. But it's for you to know, you to decide."

"There's nothing more to know, and no decision to make. And more pressing matters to deal with." Doyle took the last coil of rope off the wall.

Once they'd eaten, they stood at the seawall.

Sasha looked over and down, paled. "It's a long drop."

"Mister Wizard isn't going to let you fall." Expertly, Riley looped rope around Sasha's waist. "Plus, as discussed, Sawyer, Doyle, and I all have rock-climbing experience. All you have to do is watch your step, follow our lead."

"And don't look down," Sasha said.

"If the bow feels awkward, leave it here. You can take one of my guns. You're a better than decent shot."

"I'm better with the bow. I can handle it."

Riley secured a knot. She might have wished for some sturdy carabiners, a couple of belay devices, and some good harnesses, but you couldn't have everything. And the rope was first-rate.

She measured a length, moved to secure Bran.

"She'll be fine," Riley said quietly, "but if she gets jiggly, talk to her. That'll calm her down."

She shifted her gaze, noted Doyle looped Sawyer in beside Annika. Satisfied, she began securing herself.

"Let me check that." Doyle moved to her.

She took a mental survey as his hands brushed here, there. Yeah, she could handle it.

"The first real climb for me was in Arizona, studying the Ancestral Puebloans. Hot and dry," she added, glancing up to the soft blue of the morning sky. "Windless." She looked back at him, met his eyes. "Sasha's jittery, but she'll handle it."

"Okay. Secure the end."

He waited while Riley wound the rope around a tree trunk, tied it off.

"Want to check it?"

Doyle shook his head. As in most things, she knew what she was doing.

Though he didn't need the rope, he used it. And took the lead by vaulting over the wall. With her usual enthusiasm, Annika leaped over with him.

"Easy," Sawyer warned, and landed on the narrow edge of soft sod. "Not everybody has your balance."

"He means me." Sasha swung over. "I've got it. Don't worry."

Riley waited, let Doyle start the climb down, then rolled over the wall.

She considered the first five feet the kiddie slope, and would have enjoyed the challenge to come — along with the crash and spume of waves, the light swirl of wind, the feel of the cliff face — if she wasn't worried about Sasha.

"Doing great!" she called out as Sasha carefully lowered a few more inches, with Sawyer advising her to ease right, plant this foot.

It surprised everyone when ten feet down it was Annika who lost her handhold as a rock gave way under her fingers. She teetered, nearly overbalanced. Riley braced, dragged up slack, then breathed again when Sawyer pulled Annika back.

"I'm apology!" she shouted. "I mean sorry."

"Climb now," Riley called back. "Swim later."

With her own heart drumming still, Riley continued down.

She looked up once, saw the ravens perched on the wall above.

"Fire in the hole." She let go with one hand, toes digging in hard, pulled her gun. She managed to hit two before the others took wing.

Below, Sasha lowered to the ledge. "She's watching. I can feel it."

"Nearly there." Doyle gestured. "Just watch your footing."

Even as Riley reached the ledge, she saw him ease into the cave. Getting back up again was bound to be more complicated. So she'd think about it later.

She moved carefully over the ledge, followed the others into the cave.

"Tight fit." She squeezed in between Sasha and Annika.

"It's pure, like the boy. Can you feel it?" Sasha wondered.

It echoed with the sea, smelled of sea and earth, and when Bran held his hand over a rock, Riley saw the old wax pooled there liquefy and glow so the cave washed with soft gold light.

"I'd've made a fort in here," Sawyer commented as he looked around. "Irish cave version of a tree house. What kid could resist it?"

"It was for him, the boy, the boy who

dreamed of being a man. It is for him, the man who remembers the boy." Sasha reached out, laid a hand on Doyle's back. "It waits, and its time is now. The time of the six. Of the guardians. See the name, read the name, speak the name."

He saw the name he'd carved into stone so long ago, above the dragon symbol. He read the name, his own name, so it etched in his mind as it did on the wall.

And he spoke the name.

"Doyle Mac Cleirich."

The light changed, burned from warm gold to ice white, and with it the air went cold as winter.

The name, his name, blazed in the rock, each letter spilling fire. The dragon roared with it.

Heart at a gallop, blood all but singing, Doyle dropped to his knees, reached into the flame. And from the mouth of the dragon took the star.

It blazed like the fire — but pure and white, blinding bright. Cupped in his palm, its power sprang free.

"It's not cold." Doyle stared at the beauty in his hand. "Not now. It's warm."

And so was the air.

"We have it." He pushed to his feet,

turned, held it for the others to see. "We have the last star."

Chapter Eighteen

As he spoke, the ground shook. Loose rocks tumbled in front of the mouth of the cave, fell into the sea.

"I'd say she knows." Riley tried to angle around, face the mouth of the cave. A beam from Annika's bracelet struck the first bat that swooped in.

"I'd say that's our cue to get the hell out of here."

"But not the way we came in." Sawyer pulled out his compass. "Hold on."

The shift shot them into the light, the wind. Riley heard a hammerblow of thunder, saw something streak and flash. Then she felt herself falling helplessly, tumbling.

Not thunder now, she realized, but the waves crashing on rock. And she fell straight toward them.

The cold, the wet slashed across her face. Her hand groped for her knife. Cut the rope, cut the rope before she dragged the others with her.

Then her body jerked as that rope snapped taut. She flew up again, fighting to breathe, and landed in a wet, boneless heap on the lawn.

"Anni, everybody. Is everybody all right?" Sawyer's hoarse voice clawed through her stunned mind. "Sash— Jesus, Riley."

She waved away the hands that tugged at her. "Okay, not hurt. What the hell, Sawyer?"

"Inside! We can't risk the star in a fight." Doyle scooped Riley up. "Run," he ordered, and charged for the house as what had poured into the cave poured over the seawall.

Ignoring, for the moment, the indignity of being tossed over Doyle's shoulder, Riley reached back for her gun. "We're secured to the damn tree."

"Not anymore."

She got off a few rounds before Doyle shoved into the house.

He swung her off his shoulder, dumped her onto the kitchen island so they were eye to eye. "Are you hurt?"

"No. I'm wet." She shoved him back. "Again, what the hell, Sawyer?"

"She walloped us. Best I can say." He shoved his gun back in his holster.

"Knocked me off balance. I lost my grip, so to speak, for a couple seconds."

"I was falling, toward the rocks." Riley pushed at her dripping hair. "I think I almost hit."

"Would have," Doyle told her. "Without the rope to haul you back."

"I don't know what she threw at me," Sawyer added, "but I bet she's been waiting to do just that. I'm sorry. I lost it."

"Not your fault, and you got it back." Steadier, Riley looked to the window into the deep gloom, the lash of rain. "The storm."

"No." With a shove at her wind-ravaged hair, Sasha shook her head. "That's just anger. She's gathering more. Right now, Riley needs dry clothes, and as grateful as I am for the ropes, they have to go."

Bran merely waved a hand, whisked them away.

"Dry clothes can wait. I want another look at the star."

Once again, Bran waved a hand. Riley let out a sigh as her clothes, her hair, even her boots went warm and dry. "Gratitude."

"My pleasure. We'll take the star upstairs, with the others. Secure it."

"We've got no place to put it yet," Sawyer reminded him.

"We do." Bran slid an arm around Sasha. "Our *fáidh* painted until nearly half two this morning."

"You didn't tell us," Annika said.

"Bran and I talked about it, after I'd finished. We both thought we should focus on getting the star. Until we did . . ."

"What did you paint?" Riley hopped down from the counter. "Let's go see. And . . ." She wiggled her hand at Doyle.

He drew the star from his pocket, offered it.

"Weight and heat without mass. It's just amazing. And the light. Clear and pure as Arctic ice. It pulses," she murmured as they walked upstairs. "Like a heartbeat."

She looked at Doyle, grinned. "We did it."

He pushed her back against the wall, and with the star pumping between them, kissed her like a man possessed.

"I saw you fall. You were no more than a foot away from the rocks when I — we — managed to drag you back. You were going to cut the rope. You were going for your knife."

"Of course I was going to cut the rope. I thought I'd gotten knocked loose, and I'd drag everybody down with me. You'd have done exactly the same."

"I don't die," he reminded her, and walked away.

She looked down at the star, hissed out a breath, and stalked after him. "Is this really the time for attitude? We've just found the last star. We have in our possession something no one ever has but the gods. We —"

"Looking to put them in a museum with a plaque?"

She flinched — something he'd never once seen her do no matter the threat. Hurt looked out of her eyes at him, and that, too, was new. "That's not right."

"No, it's not. It's not. I apologize. I'm sorry." He paced two steps away, paced back. "Very sorry. That was stupid and undeserved."

She nodded slowly. "Bygones."

"Riley." He took her arm before she could walk away. "I saw you die in my head, saw you crushed on the rocks. In my head. It . . . screwed with my mood," he decided.

"Still here. So adjust. The others are waiting for us, and the star."

"Right." He walked with her, in silence, into the tower.

Riley rolled her eyes as conversation stopped, everyone turned. "Excuse the delay. We were just . . . Holy shit."

The painting glowed. Riley would have

sworn it pulsed almost as visibly as the miracle of the star still in her hand.

"That's . . . breathtaking. Sasha."

"I don't know how much I can actually take credit for."

"All," Bran told her. "All."

She touched a hand to his cheek. "I was explaining, it came on around midnight. I'd prepped a canvas, just in case, and that was a damn good thing, as the need to paint this just blew through me. I didn't just see it. I was *in* it. I could smell it, touch it, hear it. Every other vision or image I've had of it was pale, indistinct compared to this."

"I just have to say it, okay?" Sawyer gestured elaborately toward the canvas. "Behold, the Island of Glass."

On a gleaming indigo sea beneath a starstruck sky that held a wild white moon, it floated. Floated as if free to go and come on the wind. Its beaches shimmered white, diamond dust against the frothed edge of the sea. Its hills rolled, shadowed green with blurred color from wildflowers blooming.

On one such hill stood a palace, shining silver. On another a circle of stones, gray as the fog they swam in.

Small details came to life as Riley studied the painting. A gentle curve of a stream, the long spill of a waterfall, gardens lit as if with faeries in flight, a fountain where a winged dragon spewed water rather than fire.

"We have got to get there. And when we do, they have *got* to let me have a couple of samples. Some pebbles, some sand, a little dirt. There *must* be fossils. I mean —"

"Take it easy, Indiana." Sawyer gave her a poke. "Star first."

"Yeah, star first, but later." Riley looked down at the star, up at the painting. "It makes you realize why, doesn't it? They need to go back, need to be protected. It all does. The world gets screwed up regularly, routinely. But this one. It holds together. Maybe because it does, the rest of us don't go off the edge."

She held the star out to Bran. "Your turn, magick man."

As he had with the other two, Bran enclosed the star in glass. They formed the circle, performed the ritual as guardians, to send the star safely into the painting. Away from Nerezza's grasp.

"Now, gee, all we have to do is find the island, get there — with the stars — destroy the evil psycho god, and . . ." Riley shrugged. "Then the first round's on me."

"Hold you to it," Sawyer said.

Riley frowned toward the window when thunder cracked. "You're sure this is just a hissy fit?"

"I'm sure," Sasha told her.

"Then I'm going to work on the next step. I'm damn well going to find the island. It's what the hell I do."

The ugly weather continued, so holing up in the library surrounded by books near a snapping fire wasn't a hardship. Riley understood the patience required to meticulously sift through layers, but frustration tightened her shoulder blades.

They'd fought, they'd bled, they'd searched, they'd found. And none of it mattered if the island remained out of reach.

She sat back, rolled her shoulders to release the tension, scanned the walls of books. So much here, she thought, so many avenues. Any one of them might hold the answer, or at least a signpost toward the answer. But how long would it take to find that answer? How much time did they have?

She glanced toward the window as thunder cracked. And how long could six people camp inside one house — even a pretty spectacular house — without wanting to punch each other?

They'd need action, movement, progress.

She rose, wandered the shelves, reached for a book at random.

Doyle walked in.

"I got nothing," she told him. "Nothing I didn't have two hours ago. Two days ago, for that matter. If you want to dive in, be my guest. Maybe we should start a book club — and everyone takes a book each day."

She paused, frowned. "Actually, that's not a bad idea."

"We've got the stars."

"Yeah, but we don't have the island." Riley gestured toward the window with the book she held. "It's a pretty sure bet Nerezza can keep that temper tantrum going, and fighting her now, without an exit plan, doesn't make sense."

"We fight when we need to fight."

"No argument, but tactically it's going to be to our advantage to find the route to the island before we take her on. What?" Riley rubbed a hand over her face as if brushing at a smudge. "What are you staring at?"

"I don't understand you."

"You're not the first." But she understood, and set the book down. "Do you really want to get into this? Doesn't seem like your style."

"We have the stars," he repeated. "But we're not finished. We have to work together, fight together, plan together."

"Yeah, that's no problem." She arched her eyebrows. "If it's one for you, that's your damage. My feelings are my feelings. The fact that they're out there doesn't change anything. And like Bogart said, more or less, the issues of two people don't much mean dick in the big picture."

"That's wildly paraphrased."

"And true." She let out a sigh, sat on the arm of a sofa. "Not everybody gets what or who they want. That's just reality. We may be dealing with gods and magick islands and stars, but every one of us understands reality. Do I look like somebody who's going to screw up something this important — or worse, pine away — because some guy from the seventeenth century doesn't love her back?"

"No."

"Good, because I'm not. Get this, okay? I own what I am, who I am, what I feel. You do the same, and we're square. Clear enough?"

"Yeah. I've got you."

As he turned to leave, she got to her feet — slowly. "Wait a minute. Wait a minute. What did you say?"

"I said it's clear."

"No." Her heart began to thud as she

walked toward him. "You said, 'I've got you.'"

"Same thing."

"No." She took a risk, lowered her defenses long enough to look at him, really look. And saw. "You *asshole*!" Her short right jab landed hard, center chest. "You complete dick. I've got you, *ma faol.* You said that to me when I was half conscious, bleeding, broken, and you carried me out of the forest. I've got you — my wolf. *Your* wolf?" She punched him again, added a shove.

"You were hurt," he began.

"That's right, that's right." Now she jabbed a finger in his chest, drilled. "And when Bran worked on me, you held me." God, it flooded back now, over and through the memory of pain. "You told me to be strong, to come back. Come back to you. In Irish. *Teacht ar ais chugam, ma faol.* You coward."

The word dripped with derision.

"You said those things to me when you thought I was out of it, but you can't say them to my face?"

He caught her fist in his hand before it connected. "Hit me again, and we'll see who's the coward."

"Emotional midget work better for you?

You're in love with me, and you can't say it when I'm conscious because you're afraid. That's pathetic. You're pathetic."

Temper hot and visible, he hauled her to her toes. "Watch yourself."

"Screw that. I say what I feel, remember? You're the one who lies about it."

"I haven't lied to you."

"Let's just test that. Are you in love with me?"

He dropped her to her feet. "I'm not getting into this any deeper."

"Yes or no. That's simple. If you've got the balls."

"It doesn't matter what —"

"Yes or goddamn no. Pick one."

"Yes!" And the word bellowed like the thunder. "But it doesn't —"

"Yes works," she cut him off. "So good." She opened the door for him, gestured to show him hc was free to leave.

"It can't go anywhere."

"Oh, for God's sake, it already has. And if you're going to fall back on the immortal's lament, it doesn't fly. Yeah, I'm going to die. Could be today." She flicked a hand toward the storm outside the window. "Could be fifty years from now. Could be next week or I could live to be a hundred and four. Five of the six of us have that to face, and it sure as hell isn't stopping Bran and Sasha or Sawyer and Annika from grabbing what they have for as long as they can have it."

"None of them have stood by and watched the other die."

"But they will."

"It's not the same, not remotely."

"Grief is grief, but you hold on to that if you need it. I'm not asking or expecting you to hang around should I hit a hundred and four. I just wanted the truth. However long it works, it works."

"Marriage is —"

"Who said anything about marriage?" she demanded. "I don't need pledges and rings and white dresses. I just need the respect of the truth. Now I've got it, and we're back on even ground. That's enough."

She sighed, and this time laid her palm on his heart. "That's enough, Doyle, for me. Give me the truth, and stick with me as long as it works, and that's enough."

He closed his hand over hers. "I swore I'd never love again."

"That was before you tangled with me."

"It was. There's no other like you. Your eyes lured me, your mind fascinates me, your body . . . didn't hurt a thing."

She let out a half laugh. "You forgot my sparkling personality."

"It doesn't sparkle. I'd rather the edge than the shine."

"Lucky for you."

She moved into him, rose to her toes, felt his hands grip her hips. And heard someone running down the swirl of stairs.

"You need to come!" Annika clasped her hands together. "To the top. I have to get Sawyer. You need to come."

With no questions asked, they raced up.

Bran stood beside Sasha, a hand on her shoulder as she stared through the wet glass of the terrace doors.

"A vision?" Riley asked.

Even as Bran shook his head, Sasha spoke. "Not exactly. It's . . . Something's out there, but I can't see it or hear it. I just know it."

"Nerezza?" Riley walked up to stand at Sasha's other side.

"She's close — too close, but that's not it. In the sea, through the storm or beyond it. I can't tell."

"There's more." Bran turned to where the three paintings stood on the mantel.

They pulsed with light. A deep strong red through the painting of the path through Bran's forest, a pure rich blue through the painting of the house, a clear brilliant white from the Island of Glass.

"It's — I think it's their hearts," Sasha

said. "The heart of the stars beating. And there's something out there we can't see. In the heart of the storm."

"Wait." Riley pressed her fingers to her temples as Sawyer and Annika hurried in. "In my notes . . . Let me think. I've got references. The heart of the stars, heart of the sea, heart of the storm."

"I'll get your notes."

"Just —" She held up a hand to hold Doyle off. "References to the stars' resurrection — the fall and the rise. Silent breath, blah, blah, beating hearts. They pulsed when we found them, so I put it down to that, but there's references to the heart calling to heart, leading them home. And . . . ah . . . when the stars wake full, the storm breaks, land and sea. Ride the storm to its heart, and there the heart of the sea, the heart of the worlds waits."

"The Island of Glass?" Sawyer moved closer to a window, peered out.

"It's a theory. And Sasha talked about the storm, riding it. We sure as hell have the storm."

"Ride it to where?" Sawyer wondered. "Visibility is complete crap out there."

"We wouldn't be the first to follow a star. And we have three." Bran scanned the faces of his clan. "Do we trust in the fates, in the stars?"

"If I'm going to ride into that, it would be with the five of you, and with them." Doyle looked at the paintings. "The fates are bastards, but I'm in."

"I would be in, too." Annika reached for Sawyer's hand. "If it's with all of you."

"I say go for it," Sawyer agreed.

"Yes." Sasha turned from the window. "Yes. Riley?"

"Let's make us a plan, and do it."

In the deep twilight, while the storm screamed, Sasha and Annika walked outside toward the seawall. They might have been patrolling, and the black slickers turned them to little more than moving shadows.

Sasha took Annika's hand, squeezed hard. Then, wrenching her bow off her back, shot a bolt high. It exploded with light, illuminating the swarm streaming silently across the blackened sky.

From both towers gunfire erupted. On the parapet Bran hurled lightning.

Agile and quick, Annika ran to place the vials of light where Bran instructed, leaping to avoid keen wings and vicious beaks. Doyle charged to clear her path, sword lashing.

419

And the ground began to quake.

From her position on the battlement, Riley reloaded, fired, fired. She hissed when black lightning struck a tree at the verge of the forest, exploded it. As shrapnel rained, the ground burst open to swallow it.

Damned if Nerezza would destroy this place. Damned if she would. Eyes fierce, she took out a swath of flying black death.

She caught the blur of movement to her left, swung around. What had been Malmon grinned at her even as she shot him.

Thick green liquid trickled down his chest.

"She made me stronger. She gave you to me."

Her next shot missed as he seemed to vanish from one spot, appear in another. Before she could shoot again, he closed a hand around her throat, choked off her voice, her air.

"She is Nerezza. She is my queen. She is all. Give me the stars for my queen, and you may live."

Riley managed to choke out, "Fuck you," when he eased his grip.

Now he squeezed harder, lifting her off the ground so her heels drummed the air. "She gave me my pick. I chose you." Those reptilian eyes barely blinked when she plunged her knife into his belly. "I can take you back, feed off you. I have hunger."

His tongue snaked out, slid horribly over her cheek.

"The others die here, and the immortal —"

"Hey, asshole."

Malmon's head swiveled, front to back. As he blinked, as his clawed fingers loosened fractionally, Riley sucked in air.

Sawyer shot him between the eyes.

"That's for Morocco." Dead center of the forehead.

Choking, Riley lifted her gun again, saw there was no need.

"And for Riley." As Malmon stumbled back, eyes clouding, claws clicking, Sawyer took aim once again. "And that, you son of a bitch, is for Annika." The last shot simply blew away the face of what the man had become.

Sawyer gripped Riley's shoulder as she wheezed air in and out. His face was stone, his gray eyes hard as flint. But his voice soothed. "Works for zombies, so you had to figure."

"Yeah, thanks."

Malmon didn't go to ash, but seemed to dissolve, scale, blood, bone, to simply melt into a stain on stone.

Riley swallowed, winced. "I gotta say ick."

"I'll go ditto. Okay?"

On a long breath, Riley nodded. Then looked up. "Shit, shit, here come the big guns."

Nerezza rode the sky on her three-headed beast. Her hair, streaked with gray, flew in the roaring wind. Armed with sword and shield, she sliced the air with black lightning that turned to a rain of fire. Bran hurled his own as Riley and Sawyer ran down to the others.

The ground sizzled, gardens burst into flame. Beneath them, the quaking ground cracked, opening with fissures where fire spewed.

"Come on, Bran, come on," Riley urged as she dodged tongues of flame, fired her sidearm. "We've got to get her away from here. Sash!" She leaped, grabbing Sasha's arm and propelling them both aside as the ground split.

Above their heads, like a shield, the coat of arms burst. Blue, white, red in flames to mimic the stars. Fiery rain struck against it, sputtered out.

"That's our cue. We gotta go."

Sasha shook her head at Sawyer, watching as Bran stood atop the parapet, drawing Nerezza's wrath. "Bran."

"He'll make it. Trust him." Riley gripped

Sasha's hand, nodded to Sawyer. "Go."

Riley kept her hand gripped on Sasha's during the shift. She knew love now, and knew the fear that came with it. When they dropped into the boat, Doyle moved fast to take the wheel. All around them the wind and rain lashed. The roar of the storm masked the roar of the motor as he aimed from shore to sea.

"He'll make it," Riley repeated. "He's just keeping her off us until we can —"

Bran landed lightly on the boat, his arms filled with glass-shielded stars. Sasha threw her arms around him.

"Are you hurt? Bran."

"Just a bit singed here and there. Take the stars, *fáidh*. If they're to guide us, it would be in your hands."

The boat reared up on a wicked wave, crashed down. Wind and water whipped and churned.

"I can swim if I need to," Annika shouted. "But —"

"Hold on." Sawyer held on to her as the next wave threatened to swamp the boat.

Riley fought her way to the wheelhouse where Doyle stood, feet planted, muscles straining. "Get back with the others, and hold the hell on."

"I'm with you."

He glanced at her, saw the raw marks on her throat. "What the hell —"

"Later." She braced herself as the sea tossed them like rags.

"She's coming!" Sasha shouted. "And the stars . . ."

Not pulsing now, Riley realized as the next wave drenched her. Beating faster and faster, and beams of light shot from them like beacons.

To show them the way. And showing them would show Nerezza exactly where they were.

"Ten degrees starboard," she told Doyle.

"Christ. Do you see what's out there?"

A waterspout, swirling up, black against black. And the rain again turned to flames. Arrows of it sparked in the air, hissed like snakes in the sea.

As Bran lifted his arms to form the shield, Nerezza dived out of the sky.

Her lightning crashed against Bran's, and power screamed through the storm.

"Take the wheel," Doyle ordered as Sawyer's shot went wide when the boat tipped. He yanked Sasha and the stars into the wheelhouse. "Take us where we need to go. They need help." He kissed Riley, hard and brief. "Don't lose it," he added, then fought his way back to stand with his friends.

"Heart to heart, light to light." Sasha struggled not to fall as the vision flowed through her. "This moment in all the moments in all the worlds. Risk the storm, ride the storm, and open the curtain."

"Doing my best here." Teeth gritted, Riley wrenched the wheel, doing what she could to ride the mad curl of the next wave. And with her heart, and her faith, in her throat, set course for the waterspout.

Madness. Like an uncontrolled shift, a dive off a cliff. The whirling water caught them, spun them. She lost her grip on the wheel, nearly went flying before she managed to curl the fingers of one hand on the wheel again.

She glanced at Sasha, back braced, arms cradling stars like babies, and her face luminous with their light. "The guardians ride the storm, guided by the stars. The curtain opens, the storm dies. The sword strikes. And it is done."

"Your mouth to all the gods' ears," Riley screamed. "Because I can't hold it much longer."

"Look, Daughter of Glass, and see."

Dizzy, half sick, Riley squinted through the wall of water, the sheering wind.

It gleamed. Clear, shining, still in a beam of moonlight. The door to another world.

When the bow pitched up, she clung to the wheel, looked back.

Doyle stood in water nearly to his knees. Sawyer all but sat in it as he braced his feet against a bench and fired at the Cerberus.

"I can't get a shot at her," he shouted as Bran struck lightning against her shield and Annika attacked the beast.

"I can." Doyle leaped onto the bench even as the sea rocked. He struck the Cerberus, all but cleaving the center head.

And his sword met Nerezza's with a clang that shook the air.

Shook the worlds.

One of the heads snapped out toward him, and met Bran's lightning. Doyle thought nothing of it, nothing of the mad sea, the gunfire, the slash of power.

His eyes, his thoughts, his all centered on Nerezza, and the need that had lived in him for centuries to end her.

He feinted, saw the triumph in her eyes as her blade slid past his guard, gashed his shoulder.

And on that triumph, he thrust his sword into her heart.

Those mad eyes wheeled with shock. Her shriek joined the third head's howl as Sawyer's next bullet hit home.

She fought to fly up, escape, but with the

beast, she tumbled into the black, boiling sea, and was swallowed.

With her fall, the storm died. Stunned and breathless, Riley guided the boat through the door where the Island of Glass floated like a quiet dream.

Then she collapsed.

"Riley!"

At Sasha's call, Doyle whirled, bloodied sword raised.

"No, no, it's the moon. It's changed. And so am I. Damn it, damn it."

"I've got her. Somebody start bailing or we'll sink before we make shore." Doyle dropped down, helped Riley pull off the slicker, her sweater.

"I've got you." He pressed his lips to her temple as she began to change. "I've got you, *ma faol.*"

She let it take her, let him lift her above the swamped deck. And when they glided to shore as if over a quiet lake, she let him carry her to the beach where she took her first steps on the island as a wolf.

CHAPTER NINETEEN

In all her life, Riley had never regretted her lycan blood. She'd never cursed the moon or resented the change. But finding herself standing on the Island of Glass, a place of mystery and magicks, of age beyond the knowing, and not being able to speak had her cursing the damn timing.

She smelled flowers and citrus, sea and sand, the cool green of grasses, smoke from torches flanking a path winding up a high hill where a castle stood, shining silver, beaming with light. Felt the warm, soft breeze — a balm over the chilly wet.

And the desperate need to run as the feral energy of the change churned inside her. She quivered with it even as Doyle crouched beside her, a hand light on her neck.

"Don't run, not yet."

Instinct, intellect crashed and clashed inside her, yet another battle. But his eyes, strong and green, held her still. Then she braced, muscles coiled, prepared to attack and defend and she scented something . . . other.

Beside her Doyle reached for his sword.

They flowed from dark to light, the moon goddesses of Sasha's vision and art. Still gripping his sword, Doyle straightened. Bran laid a hand on his arm.

"Sheath your sword, *mo chara.* They're of the light. Can't you feel it?"

"Just how do you say hi to a god?" Sawyer wondered. "I mean one who's not trying to kill you."

Annika solved the puzzle by running forward, wet braid flying. "Hello! We're so happy! You're so beautiful. You look like my mother, and like Móraí. Like the pictures Sasha drew. We're very wet, and, oh, I have some blood." As if brushing lint from a lapel, Annika rubbed at the blood on her arm. "I'm sorry we're so messy."

"That's one way," Sawyer murmured.

Luna smiled. "You are very welcome here, Sons and Daughters of Glass." And she laid a hand on Annika's arm, healed the gash as she kissed her cheek.

"Oh, thank you. We brought the stars for you. Sasha has them. She has some blood, too. And Sawyer — he's my mate. And Bran has blood and burns. The moon is full here, so Riley had to change very fast to her wolf. And this is Doyle. He stabbed Nerezza with his sword and she fell into the sea. Now the fighting is done, and we're here. I have such happy."

"You are joy," Luna told her. "And you are loved," she said to all.

"You are courage." Arianrhod stepped forward. "And you are valued. We will talk," she said to Riley, "but you must run. Be free." Then she looked at Doyle. "On my honor, she will be safe, and she will come back to you."

The wolf turned her head, looked at Doyle. Then bounded across the sand and into the dark.

"She will always find her way to you, and you to her."

"You are strength and valor." Celene stepped to Bran, kissed his cheek. "Power and light. You are respected, and have all our gratitude."

"We are your children."

"Blood of our blood, bone of our bone. Heart," Celene added, laying a hand on Bran's, "of our hearts. Daughter." She turned to Sasha. "Will you give us the stars?"

"Yes."

Each goddess held out a hand. As the glass

around the stars shimmered away, each star floated to the hand that created it.

Pulsed, pulsed, stilled. Vanished.

"Are they back in the sky?" Annika looked up.

"Not yet," Luna told her. "But safe."

"Don't mean to tell you your business," Sawyer began, "but wasn't the whole deal about putting them back up there?"

"We're not done," Sasha said. "It's not finished."

"I didn't end her," Doyle said as he studied Sasha's face. "She's still out there."

"Your sword struck true." With one hand on the hilt of her own, Arianrhod faced Doyle, warrior to warrior. "As you are true. But your steel was not the sword that brings her end. Until her end, the stars wait."

"She cannot reach them now," Luna assured them.

"But she can reach us, even here," Sasha said as truth pumped through her. "Now the rage heals her wounds, and once healed, her madness will be complete. She will crave our deaths like wine."

"But not tonight." Celene raised her arms high. "See what I see, know what I know. This night is pure, and the Children of Glass are welcomed home."

"To take another journey." Sasha's eyes

darkened as she saw, and she knew. "Beyond the circle of power where the Tree of All Life shelters the stone, and the stone shelters the sword. One hand to draw it, one to wield it, all to end what would swallow worlds."

"But not tonight," Celene said again. "Tonight you will have food and drink and rest. Come. We will tend to you."

"She is safe." Arianrhod laid a hand on Doyle's arm when he hesitated. "And will be guided to you."

As he glanced toward the hills, shadows under a star-dazed sky, he heard the wolf howl. The sound of joy and triumph echoed after him as he took the winding, torch-lit path with the others.

The palace, rising high into the night sky, was as Sasha had foreseen. Gardens of color and scent, musical fountains, rooms with a fairy-tale gleam that glowed with light and glinted with sparkle.

No one approached them as they followed three goddesses up a sweep of silver stairs strewn with flowers and white candles as tall as a man. Jeweled ropes dripped from the ceiling, raining light as they traveled along a wide corridor into a large chamber.

An elaborate sitting room, Doyle supposed, decked out with curved sofas and chairs in the same jewel colors as the ropes of light. Tables held food — platters of meats and fruit and bread, cheeses and olives and dates. Desserts all but bursting with cream. Wine and crystal goblets.

He thought of Riley's fast. Her hard luck.

He didn't question that his clothes, his hair and body, so thoroughly drenched by the storm and the sea, were now dry and comfortably warm.

They didn't walk in a world of logic now.

A fire crackled invitingly, and though light seemed to emanate from the walls, candles flickered.

From somewhere, soft as a whisper, came harp song.

"You have questions. But the body, mind, and spirit must be fed." Celene poured wine into goblets. "And rested. Your chambers are prepared for you, when you're ready."

"There is beer." Arianrhod poured from an amber bottle, offered it to Doyle. "There will be food for her in the chamber you share when she wakes."

"And if I go out to look for her?"

"You are free to go as you please, as she is. As all are. Might I see your sword? And you mine," she added when his eyes narrowed. She drew hers, held it out to him. "I forged it when I was very young, tempered it with lightning and cooled it in the sea. I named it Ceartas."

"Justice?"

She smiled. "I was very young."

He accepted her sword, gave her his own.

"It has good balance and weight," Arianrhod decided. "It still carries her blood."

"Apparently not enough of it."

"My sword, despite its name, was not meant to bear her blood. I envy you that. I would like to spar with you."

Doyle arched an eyebrow. "Now?"

He saw a warrior's gleam in her eye before she glanced back where the others filled plates, tended wounds. "My sisters would object, but perhaps tomorrow."

"You'd have an advantage."

She exchanged swords with him, sheathed her own. "Warrior to warrior, not god to immortal."

"No. You look like my mother."

That warrior gleam shifted to a compassion he hadn't expected. "I hope a time comes when you find comfort there instead of grief. Eat, soldier, the food is good."

Now she turned to Sawyer. "The demon, the human she turned, is dead."

"Yeah."

Doyle's head whipped around as the others stopped to look at Sawyer. "Malmon's finished?"

"We've been a little too busy for the recount." Sawyer rubbed the back of his neck. "He went at Riley."

"The marks on her throat," Doyle added.

"She shot him, knifed him — body hits. I went for the head shot." He gulped some wine, struggling a little. Malmon had been human once. "It took three. Magick number."

"He is no more?" Annika asked softly.

"Melted into a pile of goo." Sawyer sent Bran a wan smile. "You're probably going to have to clean that up."

"We are sworn not to do such evil." Luna lowered her head, then lifted it. "But she has broken all oaths. And he became her evil. She turned him because she saw what he was. What was human, she destroyed. Not you, Sawyer King. You ended a demon."

"To save a friend, a sister." Now Arianrhod turned back to Doyle and from her pocket she took a key. "This will guide you to your bedchamber when you retire."

"How will she find me?"

Surprise, and perhaps a little disappointment, moved over Arianrhod's face. "You should trust, son of Cleary, Son of Glass. As long as your heart beats, she will find you."

"Now you have food and drink and comfort," Luna began, "we will give you privacy. If you have a need for anything, you have only to ask. Eat and rest well, and we will be with you on the morrow."

"No harm will come tonight," Celene vowed. "And nothing will disturb you. Be welcome here."

When they were alone, Doyle picked up the beer, sampled it, decided he sure as hell couldn't complain about that.

Sawyer lifted a hand. "Can I just say, holy shit? I'm not sure my brain's caught up with the rest of me, but we're sitting at our own personal banquet in a castle on the freaking Island of Glass. A castle, in case you didn't notice, that's made of glass."

"Bollocks," Doyle said.

"Back at you, dude. I had a good look, a good — if sneaky — feel. Plus I tapped on it. Glass. Magick glass, I bet, but wow. Plus, a god just poured me a drink."

"They're very nice. We made them happy, too." Annika bit into a little cream cake. "I like this food."

"She's right about the food," Sawyer told Doyle.

"Yeah, I could eat." But he walked to the glass doors, opened them to look out on the hills.

"She's fine. I can feel her." Sasha leaned against Bran, sipped wine. "She's more than fine. She's thrilled. This is a world few have seen, much less explored, and there's still an archaeologist inside the wolf." Rising, Sasha filled a plate, walked over to Doyle. "Eat."

"Eat, drink, and be merry?"

"Tomorrow's coming either way."

She went back to Bran.

He stroked her hair. "We found the stars, we found the island and returned them. And we should have known, I suppose, such things come in threes. So we've one more leg to go."

"I must have missed the heart." Disgusted, Doyle sat, brooded over the food.

"I don't think so." Now Bran brushed his lips at Sasha's temple.

"It's the sword," she said. "Yours could hurt her, and enchanted, make her bleed, but can't end her. We have to free the one that can, and will, from the stone."

"Somebody'll play King Arthur," Sawyer supposed. "Hope it's you, man, as you're the best here with a sword."

"We will have one more battle."

"Don't say one more," Sawyer said to Annika. "It's bad luck. Let's just say, we're taking a hike tomorrow."

"I like to hike."

"We'll make our own fun."

They talked late into the night, or what felt late, and still Riley didn't come back. Doyle let the key guide him — it simply drew him along the corridor to a wide, arched door that opened when he stepped up to it.

He hoped to find her there, waiting for him. But there was no wolf curled by the fire or stretched out over the enormous bed.

Once again he went to the doors, flung them open to a balmy, almost tropical breeze perfumed with night-blooming jasmine and citrus. The room held a curved love seat in a nook, two wing chairs in front of the fire, a sturdy writing desk — she'd like that — under a window. And the massive bed with a soaring headboard carved with symbols. He recognized some — Irish, Greek, Latin, Aramaic, Mandarin.

If his translation could be trusted, all symbolized peace.

He wouldn't have minded some damn peace.

He took off his sword, leaned it on the side of a chair. Poured himself a couple fingers of what he discovered was whiskey in a slender bottle, and settled down by the fire to wait for her.

He should've been annoyed, and couldn't figure out why he wasn't — or not particularly. She'd have run off that energy by now, and should have come back. But she was still out there, sniffing around, he supposed — literally — exploring her brave new world.

So he sipped his whiskey, brooded into the fire, and with a soldier's mind went over every step of the battle looking for mistakes.

He didn't hear her so much as feel her, and turning his head saw her standing just inside the terrace doors, scanning the room with those amazing eyes.

"About bloody time."

He rose, walked to the bed, tossed the bedding aside. He stripped to the skin, and rolled in. A moment later he felt her leap up, land beside him. Curl against him.

And finding his peace, he put an arm around her and slept.

The change came at dawn with the sun breaking the night with soft pinks, strong reds, rich golds. It moved through her, pain and beauty, helplessness and power. She shuddered with it, gave in, gave all as one became another.

And on a sigh opened her eyes to find Doyle's on her.

"What?"

"Beautiful. You're beautiful."

Still half dazed, she blinked. "Huh?"

He rolled onto her, covered her, and his mouth was hot, indescribably tender on hers. Her system, her spirit, her body, barely through the glory of the change, trembled anew at the fresh assault on her senses.

She could barely breathe and his hands stroked over her skin, molded her breasts, skimmed down to her hips. His mouth followed.

She flew up, clung, clung, clung to that edge of impossible pleasure, then let it go to take the fall.

Helplessness and power, pain and beauty.

All she was responded, gave back. Here, too, was change, a merging of two into one. They rolled over the bed, grasping, finding, taking.

He could still smell the wild on her, all but feel it beat inside her. When her mouth met his again, strong and fierce, he surrendered to all she was.

And all she was, was his.

Lust burned. Love shattered. Need beyond the physical overwhelmed.

When she straddled him, those eyes like melted gold, her body taut and glowing in those streaks of morning, he was lost.

So she took him, slow, slow, glorious torture. Then stronger, deeper, until her breath caught on moans and her heart thundered under his hands. And driving, driving, fast, wild, and straight into the heart of the storm.

She slid bonelessly down on him, rested her head on his chest. Her lips curved when his arms came around her, as they had around the wolf before they'd slept.

She'd have slept again, warm and content, if not for the sudden and desperate hunger. She hoped to God there was food of some sort close by.

"You watched me change," she told him.

"It's not the first time." He stroked her hair. "It's magnificent. Oddly arousing."

She snickered at that, then her head shot up as she sniffed the air. "Food."

"There's a kind of sitting room where —"

"No, here." She rolled off him, leaped up.

On a table were platters — that hadn't been there — eggs, grilled meats, bread, glossy pastries.

He pushed up to his elbows. "Tell me that's coffee."

She sniffed a pot as she stuffed bacon in her mouth. "Tea, but it's strong. I'm starving."

He watched her eat, still naked, still

441

flushed from sex, her hair tousled and shaggy, her hands grabbing greedily.

"I'm in love with you."

She glanced back. "Hey, you said it right out loud."

"I'm in love with you. Damn it."

"Sounds more like you. Better get your ass up if you want any of this."

"I've been married. Twice."

Riley paused, deliberately poured tea. "That's not surprising in three centuries."

"The first was about forty years after . . . after. She was young and sweet-natured. I shouldn't have touched her, but I did, and more than once, and with that she — She got pregnant. I couldn't ruin her. I had ruined her."

"So you married her. Did you tell her?"

"No, I didn't tell her. And I didn't need to, as it turned out, as both she and the baby died in the birthing."

"I'm sorry." In that moment, she felt his grief as her own. Dull and deep. "I'm so sorry."

"Not uncommon in those days. I swore I'd never touch an innocent again, such as she had been. And didn't. More than a hundred years and I married again. She was a bit older, not innocent. A widow. Barren. We enjoyed each other. Her I did tell, though I doubt she believed me. Until she grew older, and I didn't. And she grew bitter with it. I had soldier's work to do, but I always came back to her. And one day I came back to her too late. She'd hanged herself, and left a letter for me. Cursing me."

Riley nodded, sipped some tea. "I'm sorry. It sucks. For the first, if I got pregnant, it's now the twenty-first century. I'm strong and healthy. For the second, I'm not vain, and I'm not stupid. And over all that, I don't need marriage."

"I do. With you."

She choked on the tea. "What?"

"It's stupid. It's a mistake. We'll both regret it."

And looking at her, just looking at her, he didn't give a damn.

"I want the pledge. For a day, a week, for fifty years or if you live to a hundred and four."

"You're serious? You're asking me to marry you?"

"That's what I said, isn't it?" He rolled out of bed, stalked over. "Give me the damn tea."

"But I'm all aflutter."

He shot her a viciously dark look. "I didn't love them. I cared for them, both, and I pledged to them. I honored the pledge, without love, as I thought love wasn't necessary. Or possible. I love you, and I'll damn well have the pledge and make it."

"I could say no."

"You won't." He slammed the tea down. Then closed his eyes a moment. Opened them with his heart in them. "Don't. Don't say no. Give me this one thing."

She reached up to frame his face. "Do you understand I don't need this to stay with you, to love you, to accept you'll go on after I stop?"

"Yes. I don't need it to stay with you or to love you. I need it because I will and I do. I need it because in three and a half centuries, you're the only woman I've loved."

"Okay."

"Okay? Just . . . okay? That's your answer?"

"Yeah, okay. I'm in."

He shook his head, then lowered his brow to hers. "What a pair we are."

"It works."

"It works," he agreed. "I guess you'll want a ring."

"*Treweth* — the Anglo-Saxon root of betrothed. Means truth. The ring's a symbol of the promise. I appreciate symbols."

"I'll find something." He drew her in.

He'd found her, hadn't he?

"It'd be nice to stay here." Skin to skin, heart to heart. "But." With reluctance she drew back. "I've got some questions, and the first is, where are the damn stars?"

"Safe, we're told. I'll fill you in. We should get dressed, find the others."

"Great. Where are my clothes?"

"Couldn't say."

Her brows knitted. "Didn't you get them?"

"Considering the situation, I didn't think to pick up after you."

"Well crap." At a loss, she looked around the room, then walked to a delicately carved wardrobe. Stared at the contents. "You've got to be kidding me."

Doyle studied in turn, smiled. Inside hung a pair of leather breeches the color of cowhide, a simple shirt, a leather jerkin, and his own coat and boots.

And a dress the color of old gold with silver laces and piping along with kid boots.

"Seriously? You get the cool leather pants and I get a Maid Marian dress?"

"It's that or naked."

"Let me think about it a minute."

She wore the dress — and scowled at herself in the mirror. "Where am I supposed to put my gun, my knife? Where *are* my gun and knife?"

"We'll sort it out." Doyle strapped on his sword. "You look beautiful."

"I look like I'm going to a Renaissance fair." She tugged uselessly at the bodice. "That's a lot of landscape. Why are breasts such a thing?"

"I'll show you later," he said and went to answer the knock on the door.

"Good morning! Oh, Riley!" Annika swirled in. "You're *beautiful*! Oh, how pretty. Do you like my dress? Isn't it wonderful?"

She did a spin, sending the skirts flying out, all sea green and silky. "Sawyer said it's like my eyes, and yours is like yours. Sasha's is so pretty and blue. Everyone is in our sitting room. We're to wait until they come for us. We're going to meet the queen." She took a breath, focused on Doyle's face. "You're happy! I can see your happy. You're with Riley!" She threw her arms around him. "You must get Riley a ring now."

"I'll work on that."

"Will I do the stand-up at your wedding?" she asked Riley.

On a laugh, Riley stopped feeling awkward in the dress. "You bet your ass."

"Come, come. There's more food. And coffee."

"Coffee? How'd you get coffee?"

"Sasha asked." Grabbing Riley's hands,

Annika tugged. "We have only to ask."

"I missed that memo."

In the sitting room the others stood, Sasha in flowing blue velvet, Bran in the dignified black of the sorcerer, Sawyer in brown tanned pants and a hip-length jerkin over a cream-colored shirt.

"Nice threads," he said to Riley.

"Middle Ages prom dress." She studied him as she beelined for the coffee. "You got a Han Solo deal going."

"I know, right? I'm digging it."

"So, sorry I had to change and run last night, but Doyle's caught me up. Nerezza's like a bitch cat with nine lives, and the stars don't go up until we finish her off." She gulped coffee. "And so a pilgrimage to the sword stone, an Arthur the Young twist. Then we freaking end this thing."

"That sums it up," Bran agreed. "May it be so simple."

"I need my weapons," she began, then turned when a young man in trews and doublet stepped to the door.

"My ladies, my lords. Queen Aegle requests the honor of your presence."

It wasn't every day you met a queen, Riley thought as they followed the page up the wide stairs. It wasn't every lifetime you met the queen of a magick island who'd ruled for more than a millennium.

She'd expected the huge double doors, but had assumed to find them guarded. Instead they were flanked by glass urns of flowers.

She'd expected a kind of throne room, and the size met that description, along with what seemed like acres of clear glass floor. But the decor struck as simple — flowers, candles, colorful fabrics — and a throne, clear as the floor — more like an elegant chair than royal.

Then again, a chair of gold and jewels might have seemed simple compared to the woman who graced it.

She was radiant.

Topped by a diadem of jeweled glass, Titian hair spilled luxuriously over the shoulders of a white gown. The tiny clear stones scattered over it sparkled like diamonds. Perhaps they were. Her beauty stole the breath. Luminous perfection in a sculpted mouth, in vividly green eyes, and high, keen cheekbones.

When she smiled, Riley would have sworn the light shimmered.

The three goddesses stood at her right side. On her left sat a massive white wolf with eyes of bright gold.

Annika swept into a fluid curtsy. "Mother

of magicks, queen of the worlds, Aegle who is radiance, we are your servants."

"You are welcome, Children of Glass. You are welcome, Guardians of the Lights."

She rose, glided down the three steps from the throne, crossed to them with her hands outstretched. She took Annika's, kissed Annika's cheeks.

"Wonder of the sea, you have our love, our thanks. Traveler of time and place." She kissed Sawyer. "You have our love, our thanks. Child of the moon." And Riley's. "You have our love, our thanks. "Warrior of forever, you have our love, our thanks."

She moved from Doyle to Bran. "Son of power, you have our love, our thanks." And last to Sasha. "Daughter of visions, you have our love, our thanks. I would give you more than this, but your journey is not yet complete. Will you finish it?"

Sasha answered as Aegle's hands still held hers and the words rose up in her. "We will travel the path of the gods to the circle of power, and beyond to the Tree of All Life and the stone and sword. We will fight the last battle, light against dark.

"I can't see who wields the sword, or if the sword strikes true. I can't see the end of Nerezza, or our end."

"You cannot see, but you will take the

journey?"

"We've pledged to it," Bran answered.

"It's an oath," Annika added, then looked at Sawyer.

"All in." He kissed her temple. "Ah, Your Majesty."

"We could stay here." Riley drew Aegle's attention. "The guardians are on Glass, and the stars, and it's within your power to move the island to another place, even another dimension. We could stay, potentially without interference from Nerezza for a couple of centuries. Or so I've read in several records."

"You are a scholar and a seeker, and what you say is truth. Is this what you would wish?"

"No, I just wanted verification. No disrespect."

"I would give you time. You would enjoy learning more of us, more of this world. Digging."

"Very much. But there isn't time, not here and now."

"Not here and now."

"Then we finish the journey." Riley looked at Doyle. "So say we all?"

"We finish. My woman needs her weapons."

Riley's eyebrows shot up — not just at the

my woman, but because he spoke in Irish.

"In the chamber you share when you return, and garb suitable for what is to come." Aegle laid a hand on Doyle's arm. "You have only to ask. Such is our love, our gratitude. Only ask."

The queen stepped back. "It is our greatest hope that you will return here, victorious, and together with all of Glass, we will watch the stars shine."

CHAPTER TWENTY

As they started back, they passed servants, ladies-in-waiting, courtiers — as best Riley could figure. Each would stop, bow, or curtsy. It struck her as awkward as the dress.

"So that was our royal pep talk."

"Wasn't she beautiful?"

"I'll give her that." Riley nodded at Annika. "She lives up to her name. And she looked about what — sixteen? Had about two miles of red hair."

"But it was like Sasha's," Annika said. "Like sunlight, in many braids."

"Black." Sawyer twirled his fingers. "Curls."

Riley stopped on the stairs. "Red — Titian red, long and loose. Emerald green eyes. Sasha?"

"Black, but swept up. Her eyes were more like yours, Riley, but a few shades deeper."

"All things to all people." Riley nodded as they continued. "We saw her as we imagined her — or somewhat. You spoke to her in Irish," she said to Doyle.

"She was speaking in Irish."

"English and Russian," Sawyer said.

"She spoke to me in my mind once, in the language of the merpeople."

"Of all the strange, I guess it's not the strangest," Riley considered.

"And it wasn't just a pep talk. She gave us something." Sasha looked down at her own hand. "She gave us light. Didn't you feel it?"

"I felt something," Riley admitted. "Let's hope it works."

"We make it work. We're ending it, and Nerezza, today."

Riley turned to Doyle. "Sir Pessimism's taking a turn on the Optimistic Highway."

"She looked like you," he said shortly.

"She what?"

"I saw you. That's who she was, the form, for me. Whatever the hell it means, we make it work. We're not losing this. I'm not losing you. So we end it. Gear up. Let's get moving."

He stalked off.

"Doyle's happy," Annika said. "He loves Riley. He's going to get her a ring."

"We'll worry about the last part after we end the bitch. And I'm damned if I'm doing it in a dress."

She peeled off, followed Doyle.

He stood studying the new items in the wardrobe. "You'll be happier with this."

"She looked like me?"

He took out Riley's gunbelt, set in on a table. "I didn't know you when you were sixteen, but yes. Your face, your hair, your eyes. Those are eyes I trust, and that's what I felt. We're not going to lose this."

"All right then." Riley put her hands on her hips, scanned her wardrobe choices. "This is more like it."

In sturdy trousers and a leather vest with pockets for extra clips, she went back to the sitting room with Doyle. She picked up a hide canteen, sniffed the contents. "Water." And strapped it on cross body. "Couldn't hurt."

Sasha and Bran joined them. Bran patted a leather satchel. "Salvaged from the boat. A few light bombs."

"Water." Riley offered Sasha a skin. "Any idea how long a hike?"

"I don't know." She turned when Annika and Sawyer came in. "I guess this is it. I thought — it seemed — as if we came together to find the stars, get them here. But this is it. We're guardians, and it's always been leading here."

"We will guide you to the path."

The three goddesses stood in the doorway of the terrace, backed by the warm light of the sun.

They walked together, two by two, down to a courtyard where a fountain spewed rainbows, where flowers soared and spilled and fruit dripped from trees like glossy jewels.

People stood in silent respect. Children raced and waved.

They moved through a gate, past a grove, then a green field where a man and the boy working with him stopped, doffed their caps.

Riley heard the cluck of chickens, the coo of doves, the throaty hum of bees. A woman with a little girl on her hip smiled at Riley, dropped a quick curtsy. The little girl blew kisses. Others stood outside of cottages, tidy as postcards, hats in hands or hands on hearts.

In a small bay, fishermen stopped casting their nets and saluted.

"The people of Glass are with you." Luna gestured as they crossed a stretch of white sand toward the path. Flowers and baskets of fruit, glinting stones, pearly shells heaped at the verge. "Offerings to the guardians, and wishes for a good journey."

"On this day, at this time, the path is only

for you." With her sisters, Celene stopped. "Only you can walk it. What waits at its end is only for you."

"Brave hearts," Luna said. "Walk in light."

Arianrhod set her hand on the hilt of her sword. "And fight the dark."

And they were gone.

"I'd say that's god-talk for you're on your own." So saying Riley stepped onto the path, started up.

The first quarter mile was paved with stone, lined with trees, a gentle rise. It turned to hard-packed earth as the trees thinned and the rise steepened.

How many miles had they walked together since they'd started? she wondered. She should've kept a log.

In places the path narrowed so they went singly. In places it roughened so they navigated ruts, climbed over rock. On one outcropping Riley stopped, turned to look back.

The island went absolutely still below her, like something caught in a ball of glass. All color and shape without movement. A painting spread over sea and sky.

A bird caught in midflight, a wave frozen above the shore.

When the worlds still, she remembered. And so it had.

Then a deer leaped over the path, a bird took wing. The standard on the palace waved in the breeze.

At the end of the path, she thought, lay the end of the journey.

She leaped down, continued the climb.

The path wound, and a little stream bubbled beside it. Water spilled over rock, tumbled into a small pool where the deer drank.

"I ran this far last night," she told the others. "Part of me wanted to keep going up, but something just told me not yet. I stopped by that pool, the water so clear I could see my reflection, and the moon's."

"Let's hope we get up there, get this done before you see the moon again and go furry."

Riley shook her head at Sawyer. "Last night was the third night here. But I'd sure as hell like to get it done before dark."

She fell companionably into step with him. "I was thinking about Malmon."

"Gone and no regrets."

"That's something I was thinking about. She chose him, lured him, seduced him, and turned him into a demon. One who worshipped her. He didn't just kill for her, he very likely saved her life, at the very least nursed her until she got herself back."

"And?"

"She did nothing to save him. Because he meant nothing to her. Look, he was a bastard when he was human, as evil and twisted as they come, but she ended that human life. As somebody who knows about change, I'm telling you *that* change had to be agony."

"Hard to wring out any sympathy there."

"With you," Riley agreed. "The thing is, she didn't have to change him to get what she wanted out of him."

Sawyer stopped, narrowed his eyes. "I hadn't thought of that, but you're right. One hundred percent."

"She did it for fun. And when he failed, even after he saved her miserable existence, he was just a kind of diversion. Yeah, he tried to kill me, but she sent him in to pave the way for her. And after all that, bang, you're dead. Thanks to you. Odds are she could've given him what Doyle has, instead it's over like a fingersnap for him. And she doesn't care."

"You thought she would?"

"I'm saying if she didn't give him a thought — someone — something that fed her, nursed her, did her bidding, worshipped her, fucking died for her, she sure as hell

458

doesn't care about any living thing. Dark or light."

"I could've killed him if he'd still been human, but not the way I did. I couldn't have just . . . not if he'd been human."

"I know." Riley gave him an elbow jab. "That's why we're the good guys."

A few paces ahead on the rugged path, Annika began to sing.

"And that," Sawyer said.

"And that."

They climbed while the sun wheeled past noon with the stream rising with the path. Quick, frothy waterfalls poured over ledges of rock, but nothing came to drink. No bird soared overhead or darted through the trees.

Riley scented nothing but the water, the earth, the trees, her companions.

When the worlds still — she thought again.

Then there was . . . something. Something old, potent, alive. But not human, not beast, not fowl, not of the earth.

"There's something —"

But Sasha had already stopped, was reaching for Bran's hand as he reached for hers.

"Do you feel it?" Sasha's words were barely a whisper over the music of the water.

"Power," Bran said. "Waiting." Bran glanced back at the others. "Let me have a look first."

But Sawyer shook his head. "All for one, man. That's how it is."

Doyle's sword slithered out of its sheath. "Together."

And together they crested the high hill.

There the path ended, and there stood the stones, a perfect circle, graduated in size from one on each side no higher than Riley's waist to the king stone, taller than two men.

They stood, quiet gray, under the strong afternoon sun, swimming in a shallow sea of mist.

"Not as massive as Stonehenge, but more symmetrical," Riley observed. "I bet when I measure them, each set is precisely the same in height and width, and an exact ratio."

The archaeologist led the way, moved straight up, laid a hand on a stone. Pulled it back. "Did you hear that?"

"It . . . grumbled," Sawyer said.

"No, it sang!"

"Annika's closer. More a hum, right?" Riley asked. "And it gave me a little jolt. Not painful, more like: Think about it."

"Here stand the guardians, placed here by the first." Sasha held her hands out to the circle. "The circle, the dance, the source. Light and dark, as one must have the other.

Morning sun and dark of moon. Joy and sorrow, life and death. Here is truth. And from it springs the tree, and beneath the tree the sword. Walk through, and wake the sword."

She lifted her face. "Oh, I can barely breathe. It's so strong, so beautiful. Walk through!"

Bran walked between the stones. They hummed, soft and quiet, the sound building when each of the others walked in, stood with him.

Light lanced out of the sky, struck the two smallest stones. Like a chain of fire, light streamed around the circle, struck the king stone. Voices rose like the wind in one strong, soaring note. The stones pulsed with it, shined silver with it. The mist burned away, revealed the ground of glass.

As the stones quieted, the sun showered over the hundreds of bare branches of a great tree that stood alone. Beneath it sheltered a gray spear of stone with a naked sword carved on its surface.

"Looks like step two." Because her skin still quivered, Riley cleared her throat, sucked in a breath, then started across the circle to once again walk between the stones.

"Of the stone." Riley walked around it, crouched in front of it. "Any idea how to get it out?"

"Reach in. Wake it. Free it. It's all I know," Sasha told her.

Riley straightened, stepped back. "Doyle makes the most sense. Agreed?"

That got nods all around.

Doyle studied the carving. A bit smaller, slimmer than his own, but a fine-looking blade with a simple, unadorned hilt. He gathered his faith, his trust, his hope, reached for it. Hit solid stone.

"I feel nothing. Should I? Only that it's not for me to take it."

"Then Bran. I'm sorry," Annika said quickly.

"No need." Doyle stepped back. "Your go, brother."

Bran laid his hand on top of the stone, used what he was to try to *feel* through it. Shook his head. "Like a locked door," he murmured, skimmed his hand down, laid it over the carved hilt. "Or a power sleeping."

"Well, it needs to wake the hell up. Maybe there's a code or a pattern. Maybe some sort of incantation. We just need to figure it out. Give me a minute to . . ."

Riley ran her hand down, fingers tracing the carving for a clue.

The stone trembled, sang in a sound like rising joy. When shocked, she pulled back her hand, she held the sword.

"Oh, shit."

Immediately she swung to Doyle, held it out.

"It's not mine." He wondered if she felt the light beating around her. "It's yours."

"What am I supposed to —"

It all but leaped in her hand. Against her closed fist the rough stone hilt began to change, to smooth. Light streaked up the blade so she instinctively lifted it up to protect the others.

The sun struck it, searing. Before her stunned eyes the stone became clear polished glass.

"Did everybody see that?" Her heart thudded, her ears rang as she lowered the sword. And still its power raced up her arm, through her body. "It's glass."

"Like the palace." Sawyer reached out, ran a finger over the flat of the blade. "You've got a magickal glass sword, Riley."

"It sparkles," Annika murmured. "And makes rainbows."

"And holds power. Can you feel it?" Bran asked her.

"Oh, damn skippy. It's like the stars. There's a pulse in it. And it . . . it feels like mine, but let's be practical. I'm no swordsman. I know the basics, but that's it. I'd love to nail Nerezza with it, but I'm going to need a lot of training."

Sasha gripped Riley's shoulder. "She's coming."

Doyle ranged himself beside Riley. "Learn fast," he told her, and drew his sword.

She came with a swarm, turned day to night.

Riley shifted the sword to her left hand — she'd need to get a lot closer for it to do any good — and pulled her gun.

They spilled out of the sky, slithered and shambled out of the trees, dark, twisted things with snapping fangs, swiping claws.

Bolts and beams and bullets struck against the dark. Shrieks tore the air as light exploded.

On the beast mangled by Doyle's sword, Nerezza rode with them, pure madness now, her beauty gone, her hair a tangle, wild gray snakes, her eyes sunken, burning black.

Her lightning crashed with Bran's, and the aftershocks knocked Riley off her feet. Something crawled burning over her boot. Even as she jerked back, Annika turned it to ash. Firing, firing, Riley flipped to her feet. Almost without thought, she slashed with the sword. The thing she cleaved screamed, vanished in a flare of light.

She felt the pump of power now, the thrill

of it, and slashed, struck, jabbed, hacking her way through a swarm.

"I need to get closer. I can do it, I can take her. Can you get me up there, behind her?"

Sawyer shook his head. "Trying to bring her ride down, but these things block it. They keep coming."

He slapped in another clip, and Riley saw blood dripping down his hand.

"We need cover. We need to —"

"Die here!" Nerezza screamed. "Die here, and I feed on your power. All that you are is mine. This world, and all die with you."

She shot down flame. Annika deflected the first, but the second ball exploded in front of her, sent her flying back. Sawyer rushed to her as one of Sasha's bolts killed the creature before its sharp wing scored Annika's face.

"Into the circle. Lure her into the circle," Sasha shouted. "I think — Bran!"

"Yes, yes. The power. I'll draw her in."

"Leave that to me. What's she going to do?" Doyle demanded. "Kill me? Keep her off Riley." He fought his way closer to the circle, managed to turn to meet Riley's eye. "This isn't Malmon. Aim for the heart. Drive her to me, push her to me. Some magick wouldn't hurt."

"You'll have it." Bran hurtled lightning at Nerezza's flank. "Keep the pressure on her."

"She'll go for Doyle." Teeth gritted, Riley fired. "Once she sees he's alone."

"But he's not alone," Sasha reminded her.

Bran leaped on one of the stones, hurled a vial of light. As it exploded, the Cerberus screamed in pain. The slash of its tail missed Bran by inches as he jumped clear. But the maneuver turned Nerezza toward Doyle in the heart of the stone circle.

"Immortal. Burn and bleed."

He rolled away from the fire, jumped clear of that lashing tail. Closer, he thought. Just a little closer.

"Bitch," he called back. "This time I'll cut out your heart. Sword to sword. God to god!"

"You are no god." When she swooped, he struck, but her quick turn had him slicing the side of her beast. The sword he'd carried for centuries snapped in two like a toy. "And that is no sword."

Bran threw lightning to draw her off as Doyle pulled his knife. As he pivoted, the Cerberus clawed his back, struck him down.

The others rushed toward the circle. As the blood of an immortal, a guardian stained the glass, light burst like a bomb. It sent Riley sprawling, had her ears thundering, her breath lost. Through the haze she saw Bran struggling to his knees, heard Sawyer cursing. And saw Doyle unarmed, alone.

Overhead Nerezza laughed. "Can you grow your head back, immortal?"

She dived, a sword raised over her head.

Like Bran, Riley struggled to her knees, knew she'd never make it. "Doyle!"

When he turned his head, she saw the pain in his eyes, the regret. "Bullshit on that. Catch!"

She threw the sword, and all her faith.

He lifted his hand, closed his fist around the hilt. With a warrior's cry, he sprang up, whirled away from Nerezza's sword. He drove the Sword of Glass through her heart.

She didn't scream. The beast beneath her, all those that flew or crawled sizzled away like water in the sun or melted like ugly chalk drawings in the rain.

Day burst back to life.

She fell into the circle, the mother of lies, eyes glazed with fear and madness.

"I am a god." She croaked it out as her hair thinned, as her flesh shriveled.

Doyle gripped the sword in both hands. "You're nothing." And plunged it into her heart again.

The blood bubbled black. Her fingers became bones that clacked together. "I want. I want." Black eyes wheeled as the flesh of the face flaked away.

Doyle gripped Riley's hand when she limped to him. Looked around once as the others, bruised, burned, bloody, came with her. "We ended you."

She withered to bone without a sound, and the bone went to ash.

"She can't come back?" Annika hugged close to Sawyer. "She's gone?"

"Look." Bran gestured.

The hundreds of branches of the tree leafed out green, bloomed with fruit and flowers. The air, so full of the sounds of battle only moments before, now sang with birds and breezes. A doe wandered out of the woods to crop at the grass.

The stones stood silver and shining on the hill of Glass. The king stone bore the guardians' coat of arms.

"Good answer." Then Sawyer dropped to his knees. "Sorry. Ow."

"Let's have a look. We'll do what we can here," Bran added, "then —"

"We've only to ask," Sasha remembered. "I'm asking for us to be brought back. If we've done what we were meant to do."

"You really think they're just going to — Oh," Riley said as she found herself, and the others, standing at the start of the path.

"Excellent."

They began to limp and wince their way toward the palace.

"We couldn't just wish to be healed?" Annika wondered.

"People should see their warriors. They should see what it costs to stand for the light," Doyle told her, and put an arm around her to support her. "To do what's needed."

They wept, and they cheered as the six passed by. And wept and cheered all the way to the doors of the palace where the goddesses waited.

"We will tend you now." Celene stepped forward, raised her voice. "Tonight, there will be celebration. Tonight is for music and dancing, for wine, for joy. Tonight is now and forevermore, the Night of the Guardians."

"I'm going to bleed all over the floor," Sawyer began.

Luna stroked his wounded arm. "You will not. Come now to be tended and fed and bathed and rested. We are your servants today."

It wasn't so bad having a goddess as a servant. At least not when, Riley decided, it included luxuriating in a sunken tub full of hot water that a pretty young maid scented with jasmine. Or having every ache in your tired body rubbed out with oil.

She didn't even mind — too much — putting the dress on again. Not when she had permission to explore, take samples. Some stones, some scrapings, a little dirt, some sand. A couple of flowers she'd never seen before.

When she rushed into the sitting room to find the others, she was all but flying. "You won't *believe* what I've seen. They have chickens that lay colored eggs. I saw a baby dragon — the adults prefer caves. A freaking baby dragon."

She grabbed a bottle, poured a glass not caring what it might be.

"And the library in this place? It makes yours look like the book turnstile at a gas station, Bran. Every book ever written, in every language. I mean freaking Hogwarts doesn't have what they have."

She gulped down what proved to be wine. "And their society? No war, not since that whole uprising with the Bay of Sighs — which, by the way, is back. People like their work, whatever they choose. Farmers farm, weavers weave, bakers bake. If they need to cut a tree, they plant another. Always. And — What?"

"We got around some, too," Sawyer told

her. "Annika got to swim with some mer-people in the Bay of Sighs. Sasha's done half a million sketches. Bran, he's been holed up with other magic types."

"We went up," Bran told her, "consecrated the ground within the circle."

"Doyle's been busy, too." Sasha continued to sketch.

"Yeah? With what?"

"Nothing much."

Sasha lifted her head, stared holes through him.

"Fine. All right." He stood up, pulled something out of his pocket. "I got this."

Riley stared, dumbfounded, at the ring. The pure white stone sat in a simple band. Its brilliance needed no adornment.

"You don't like fuss," he said.

"No, I don't. But how did you . . ."

"Just ask, right? I just asked if there were any jewelers, and I had about a hundred rings pushed at me."

"Sasha and I helped from there," Annika told her. "Because it was confusing."

"I don't happen to have any money on me that works around here anyway. And they didn't want any. But . . ."

"He had in his pocket a pipe — a musical pipe — he made as a boy," Annika said helpfully. "He traded."

"That's . . . Jeez, that's sweet."

"It gets sweeter," Sasha told Riley. "He asked Bran to engrave it."

"Engraved." Riley snatched the ring from Doyle's hand, turned it to look inside the band. *"Ma Faol."* Her throat simply closed as her heart leaped into it. All she could do was look at him.

He took the ring back. "Are you going to give me your hand?"

"Damn right I am."

"It's called the Stone of Glass. I don't know what the hell it actually is."

"I'll be finding out." It astonished her that her eyes stung, that she had to fight back tears. "And I can tell everybody you're a cheap bastard, and it's glass."

"Bet you would." He slid it on her finger. "You're stuck now."

Annika applauded. "Kiss her, Doyle! You need to kiss her now."

"Yeah, kiss me, Doyle." Despite the dress, Riley boosted up, wrapped her legs around his waist. "And make it good."

He made it very good.

EPILOGUE

A royal celebration required fancy, Riley discovered. She also discovered Annika was a force of nature when the mermaid's mind was set.

She banished the men, decreeing the women would dress together.

"It's special," Annika insisted as she patiently fastened what seemed like half a million buttons on the back of Riley's gown. "When we have a special celebration, my sisters and I prepare together. You're my sisters." She rested her cheek on the back of Riley's head. "I'll miss you so."

"Don't cry." Alarmed, Riley turned. "We won. We saved the worlds."

"We're still going to see each other." Sasha moved in for a hard group hug. "We're a clan, remember? We'll come to your island, and Bran will make your pool so you can come to us. And we'll all go to wherever Riley and Doyle are."

"It's an oath."

"Pinky swear." Riley held up her pinky. "A very serious oath." She took Annika's, hooked it, and Sasha added hers. "Done. I love you guys, sincerely. And I'm going to need regular Sawyer and Bran fixes."

"Could I have a favor?" Annika asked.

Sasha kissed her cheek. "You have only to ask."

"I'm very excited for the celebration here, but . . . Could we have one of our own? Just us, when we go back to Bran's? A night for the six of us, without worry and weapons, before I go back to the sea?"

"That is a most excellent idea." Riley looked at Sasha. "You up for that?"

"Absolutely. Biggest and best celebration ever."

"And done again. Okay, Anni, how about the big reveal?" Riley gestured to the mirror Annika had covered with a tapestry.

"Oh, yes." But first she gave her friends a long study, and a nod of approval. Then swept the tapestry aside with a flourish. "We are beautiful!"

"Whoa." Riley blinked.

She'd seen her companions, of course, Annika in a gown of blues and greens as iridescent as her mermaid's tail with her hair a glory of sleek braids streaming down her back. And Sasha, hair in long, soft waves over a fluid gown of silvery blue. But she barely recognized herself in the fitted gown the color of crushed rose petals with a glimmering gold underskirt.

She touched a hand to her hair — Annika had managed to fluff and curl and add some style.

"We're rocking it." She slid an arm around Sasha's waist as Annika did the same. Joining them. "We're badasses who clean up really well."

"Badasses," Annika repeated and laughed. "Beautiful badasses."

"That's who we are." Riley shot a finger at their reflection. "Let's go party."

She figured the endless primping time worth the effort when she saw Doyle's face. And more when he took her hand, bowed over it, kissed it. "Warrior queen. Mine."

"You look pretty good yourself." She brushed her fingers over his doublet of dull silver. "Ready to do this thing?"

He offered his arm, and though she laughed, she laid hers on it so they walked, all six, up the wide stairs.

People in their finery crowded the ballroom where tables groaned with food on platters of silver and gold. Lights sparkled from the ceiling, massive candles glowed, and jeweled trees shined in air scented with the perfume of masses of white flowers.

Doors and windows stood open wide to bring the sound of music and celebration from outside in.

As the six entered, conversation stopped. At some signal, the happy din from outside stilled. Men dropped to one knee; women swept into deep curtsies. And the queen rose from her chair, walked to them.

"Tonight we honor heroes." She curtsied before them, head bowed. "Your names, your deeds will be remembered for all time, and celebrated on this night through the ages. You, and all who come from you, will be welcome here, always."

She rose, took Bran's hand, took Sasha's. "Bran Killian, Sasha Riggs. You have only to ask."

"I've been given more than I ever dared to wish. I found myself," Sasha told her. "And love. And family."

"I have my heart." Bran brought Sasha's other hand to his heart. "Brothers, sisters. What I am, what I have, is stronger for it."

"You are well matched. When it comes my time for a life mate, I hope to find such harmony. Our blessings on you."

She turned to Sawyer and Annika, took their hands. "Sawyer King, Annika of the waters, you have only to ask."

"Everything I could want is right here with me," Sawyer said. "I don't travel alone anymore."

"I wished for Sawyer, with all my heart, and my wish was granted. I kept my oath, and my people can have pride. I have a new family, and we have promised to come together."

"Child of the sea, your heart is so kind. Would you not ask for the one thing still held inside it?"

Now Annika bowed her head. "The moon must turn, my lady, for the worlds to be. I can't ask."

"The moon will turn, and you may ask."

"But I . . ." She lifted her head, eyes wide and full of hope. "The legs? I could keep them, walk with Sawyer?"

"If this is your wish. Daughter of the sea, and of the land. Would you wish to be of both worlds?"

"Oh, yes! Sawyer."

"Wait. She wouldn't have to give up her parents, her sisters, her people?"

"She has, as you have, given all. She gives up nothing. Yes," Aegle said, smiling back at Annika. "There can be children."

Tears sprang to Annika's eyes as she laughed, flung her arms around the queen.

Riley braced, waiting for lightning to strike at the breach in protocol. But the queen only laughed in turn.

"You are joy, and deserve to have it."

"Thank you, thank you. Sawyer!" Annika whirled, threw her arms around him. "I can walk and dance with you. We can make children."

When she whispered in his ear, he cleared his throat. "Yeah, we can do that, right after the party." Heart in his eyes, he looked over Annika's head to the queen. "Thank you."

"You would not ask it for yourself. You are well matched. Our blessings on you."

She turned to Doyle and Riley. "Doyle McCleary, Riley Gwin, you have only to ask."

"I have a million questions," Riley began, and made Aegle smile.

"This is not a wish, but study. You may stay or come back as you will, and learn. The Island of Glass is forever open to you. If you stay, time is different here. You would have more."

"No. No," Doyle said, firm. "You have work, you have your pack. We're fine," he said to Riley.

"It is for her to ask or not. Would you give up the moon, Riley Gwin, the change and the wolf?"

"I —" Everything inside her knotted. "It's who I am. Doyle —"

"It's who I love." To cut her off, he gripped her hands. "You thought I meant to strike you down that night, the first change, after the battle. But I *was* struck. And began to change. Those eyes, *ma faol.* No, you give up nothing."

"It's who I am." Content, Riley turned back to the queen. "Having the door open here, that's a great gift to me. Thank you for it."

"I would have been sorry if you'd chosen differently."

As Aegle spoke, Riley saw the deer leaping over the path, the doe who came out of the woods, the woman holding a little girl on her hip, the rosy-cheeked maid who'd filled her bath.

"You're a shapeshifter."

"I am in all, of all. I was always with you. And you," she said to Doyle. "Will you ask?"

"I have family again, and with them succeeded where I'd failed for three centuries. I have my wolf."

"The dark marked you, giving you what some men seek, knowing it would bring you grief. Light can lift it. Would you cast away immortality?"

"It can't be done. Even Bran —" Doyle

caught the look in Bran's eye. "It can?"

"I asked, and was shown. It can be done."

"Hold on. Not for me," Riley insisted. "And not on impulse. Dying's no picnic, and —"

"Three centuries doesn't qualify as impulse." Hope, real hope brought a kind of pain.

Bittersweet.

"A life with you? A real one? Really living, knowing a day is precious and finite? It's what I want. It's more than I ever thought to have."

"Then you must accept." Aegle held out her hand. A servant rushed forward, gave her a glass goblet. "From your brother."

Bran took the goblet, and a vial of clear liquid from his pocket. "This is the water of life, conjured of light. Its purity defeats the dark, breaks the curse." He poured the water into the goblet. "If you choose to be mortal, drink."

Doyle studied the water, thought of his life, the deaths, the battles, the long roads traveled alone.

He lifted the goblet to Bran, then to Sasha, to Annika and Sawyer in turn. And last to Riley.

To the love of his true life.

"I want a pack of kids," he said, and drank.

"Wh—What?"

"You heard me." He waited a beat. "I don't feel any different."

"Be glad you didn't do a Nerezza and age three centuries. Define pack."

"We'll talk about it." He turned to the queen. "The first girl of our pack will have your name. However many days I have from this night, I'll be grateful."

"Well matched. I see an adventurous life ahead. Blessings on all of you. A queen may reign with kindness and care, with wisdom and justice, people may prosper, but without those who will risk all to stand against evil, no world can flourish."

There was music and feasting, wine and joy. The color of sweeping skirts, the sparkle of light. Late in the night, amid the celebration, the queen and her goddesses led the way to the beach.

Arianrhod held out the sword cased in a simple leather sheath. "This is yours."

"Seriously?" Riley stared at it. "I'm allowed to take it?"

"It is yours."

"She was our sister," Luna said. "We will mourn what she might have been."

"And grieve for what she chose to be," Celene added. "And cherish what has come home. For Aegle, the radiant, the Fire Star."

"For Aegle, the radiant, the Water Star." Luna turned with her sister.

"For Aegle, the radiant, the Ice Star." Arianrhod lifted her hand with the other goddesses. In them the stars whirled and pulsed.

And flew, streaking into the sky, leaving their trail of light on their journey to the moon. The people of Glass roared as the stars settled, a perfect curve, to shine.

"And there they will ever be, for all the worlds to see, to wonder, to hope." Once more Aegle held out her hands. "Safe journeys, Guardians of Glass. The door will always be open for you."

"Go in joy." Celene crossed her hands over her heart.

"In love." Luna laid a hand on hers.

"In peace." Arianrhod tapped a fist on hers.

And Riley found herself standing with the others by the seawall of Bran's home.

"Wow," Sawyer managed. "That just happened."

Laughing, still wearing the ball gown, Annika turned cartwheels over the lawn.

"Home again." Bran drew Sasha close.

"And all's well."

"I have a magick sword."

Doyle glanced down at Riley. "You're going to need training."

"Yeah, yeah, but I've got a magick sword." She drew it, lifted it toward the sky. "And look."

The sword glinted as it pointed to the three stars under the moon. "There they are. We did that. And what do you think astronomers are going to have to say about it?"

"Only you," Doyle said with a shake of his head. Then he cupped her face, looked into the eyes he loved. "Only you."

"I call for a moment. Gather up, team." Sawyer managed to grab Annika.

"A major moment." Riley clasped Doyle's hand, slid an arm around Sasha's waist. Waited while the others moved in close, joined.

So the guardians could stand, above the sea, under the Stars of Fortune.

United.

ABOUT THE AUTHOR

Nora Roberts is the #1 *New York Times* bestselling author of more than 200 novels. She is also the author of the bestselling futuristic suspense series written under the pen name J. D. Robb. There are more than 500 million copies of her books in print.